THE FAE OF THE FJORD

THE FAE OF THE FJORD

Elle Thrasher

To the readers who want to explore the world without leaving their comfy reading chair. This one's for you.
Let's go to Norway.

CONTENT NOTICE

For a full list of content notes, please visit the <u>author's website.</u>

PRONUNCIATION GUIDE

Espen -- Ess-pen

Øyvin -- Oy-vihn

Balder -- Bahl-derr

Bente -- Ben-teh

Dagny -- Dahg-nee

Fjell -- Fyell

Freija -- Frey-ah

Halvar -- Hal-vahr

Jorunn -- Yoo-runn

Kjetil -- Sheh-till

Leif -- Layf

Oddvar -- Odd-vahr

Skolvik -- Skoll-veek

Solveig -- Sool-vay

Stavanger -- Stah-vang-err

Torsten -- Torr-sten

Trygve -- Tryg-veh

Ylva -- Yll-vah

1

LENNIE

Aiming the lens at the forest across the fjord, I lined up the shot, tightened the focus, and clicked. I pulled the camera away from my face and frowned as I peeked at the screen. Tall pines shot into the sky, blanketing the base of the cliffs that rose up on either side of the Norwegian fjord—the deep, watery inlet that stretched inland from the North Atlantic. Glancing up at the scenery I'd tried to capture, my heart stuttered as I took in the breathtaking blues and greens I'd traveled across the world to experience. While the photo was adequate, it didn't even begin to come close to the real thing. I could do better.

I readjusted the aperture and took a deep breath. Lining up the trees around a tiny clearing, I found what I wanted, and clicked.

It was a much better shot than the first—the composition was more balanced, and the foreground was less blurry—but there was a speck of silvery light in the clearing I hadn't noticed earlier.

A horn blared from the valley below. Startled, I dropped the lens cap and glanced toward the noise. A white ship shifted away from the dock in the village below, pointing its bow out of the harbor.

"Fuck," I muttered under my breath and started running down the mountainside I'd hiked up this morning toward the little village of Skolvik on the water.

The crew on the cruise-ship had warned me before—okay, maybe *several* times—that if I missed the designated check-in time, they would leave me behind. No exceptions. Those assholes waited for no one, and now I realized how true that was.

I'd zoned out during most of the lecture this morning as we debarked the cruise ship for our daily excursion, but now they came back to me as I hurried down the rocky path. Consequences like having to find my way back to the port where the cruise had started, Stavanger, collect my luggage from said dock, and deal with Customs and Immigration when they asked why I'd missed the boat. The latter were manageable, but the worst part would be figuring out a way back to Stavanger, which was over five hundred miles south of my current location.

Yeah, I was well and truly fucked this time, but I ran like hell anyway.

The crew's parting words rang through my head as I bolted down the hillside. "Do not be late, Ms. Martin. This is your final warning. The ship sets sail promptly at 5:00 pm local time, Lennie."

My legs pistoned and feet pounded against the rocky path as the chilled air buffeted against my face. The bag on my back smacked against me and my water bottle started leaking, spraying liquid across the arm of my rain-jacket. I did my best to keep my balance, grabbing onto tree-limbs a few times to save my ass and head. Was I fast and physically fit? Yes, decently so. Was I graceful? Nope, never a day in my twenty-eight years had I been labeled that.

When the terrain finally leveled out, I sprinted toward the dock. Rounding several small buildings, and dodging some of the locals—who scowled as my blonde-ish ponytail may have whacked them in the face—I reached the gangplank at the tiny harbor. Or at least, where it should have been...

The boarding ramps had been pulled back, the water quietly lapped against the dock, and the ship... the small, white cruise-ship that was supposed to take me further north on a sightseeing tour of the Norwegian Fjords, was gone.

Well, not gone, but far enough along the watery passage that there was no way in hell I was getting on-board. Unless I found a dingy with an outboard motor strong enough to pull up alongside it, like a pirate. Breathing heavy, I quirked a smile at the thought of commandeering a vessel to take on a boat ten times the size. That kind of thinking had got me into trouble in the past, and no doubt would in the future too.

I scanned the little marina for something small and floaty, but all I could see were white pleasure boats and a derelict trawler that had probably been moored due to overfishing along the coastline.

A deep chuckle sounded behind me and I spun.

"Du kommer ikke til å finne noe brukbart der," a man muttered looking between me and the harbor, the wind playing with the wisps of gray hair that stuck out the sides of his wool-knit hat. The old man continued walking past me, shaking his head, his hands clasped behind his back.

"I don't speak Norwegian," I said, a bit too sassily considering my current predicament. I knew a few words, but they may have been: hello, thank you, yes, no, and two beers. Which, according to my app, were: *hallo, tusen takk, ja, nei,* and *to øl.*

The man laughed again and came to a stop, his shoulders rising and falling underneath his big rain-jacket. "You Americans never do." He had a thick accent, but I understood an insult when I heard it. You didn't live in South Boston for three years without hearing smack-talk and brutal honesty on the daily.

I sighed and glanced back at the cruise-ship that was now a blip between the mountains.

"*Følg meg*," the man mumbled, his voice a grumbly tone that sounded more at home in a troll than a little old man. "Follow me," he said sternly.

"Why should I do that?" I asked, rubbing my hand across my forehead as panic crept in. "There has to be a cab or a bus around here that can take me to the closest city."

I spun around, searching the harbor for any signs, scanning my surroundings. To my left was the path to the village where the man had started walking, in front of me was the main road into town and the mountain side that rose up beside it, and to my right was the tourist center... and a sign for a bus-stop. The blue-and-white logo for mass transit was a beacon of hope, and my lips tugged into a gentle smile.

"That will not be here for a while," the man said, following my gaze with a raised brow.

"That's fine. I'll just wait out here," I replied, pointing toward the wooden bench next to the small building with posters covering the windows—one of which advertised the cruise I had just missed.

"You will be waiting a long time."

I bit my lip and rolled my eyes. I was troubleshooting this mess and did not need his negativity. "When does the next bus arrive?"

He grinned, the scruff around his mouth and jaw twitching. "Three months."

I started. Three *months?!* That was ludicrous! These were modern times; there was no way buses ran that infrequently.

"No way," I countered, my stomach starting to churn with annoyance and a hint of anxiety. "It's 2023, you need buses for the tourists." I waved at myself as an example.

He shook his head again in frustration, and unclasped his hands, sticking them into his jacket pockets with force. "You are correct."

I smiled at my own little slice of victory.

"But," he continued, "when Autumn arrives and the last ship of the season leaves"—he pointed down the fjord behind me—"there is no need for the bus anymore. It only comes back one time or two times in the winter if we have little snow."

My smile faltered as the weight of my mistake set in.

"You might be able to convince someone to drive you down the fjord to Heimsund—a bigger town that has buses—but most of us will laugh at you." He grinned again, like he was quietly relishing in my misfortune.

My shoulders sank and I shuffled my feet. I just needed to regroup and figure out another plan. I could totally convince someone to give me a ride to wherever I needed to go... Admittedly, I knew almost nothing about Norway and had no idea where to go, other than this Heimsund that he'd mentioned, but I'd figure it out. I *always* figured it out in the end. Whether it was a problem with my camera or the boring documents at work, I could triage the shit out of a situation.

"Like I said," the man piped up again, and I dragged my attention back to him. "Follow me."

I took a deep breath and nodded, out of ideas for the moment. The man spun on his heel and started walking toward the village center. For only the eighth time in my life, I did as I was told, and followed.

2

LENNIE

The village of Skolvik was quaint and cute, sitting at the very end of the deep fjord. Bright, natural-toned buildings and homes dotted the water's edge as boats bobbed in the soft waves. Buttressed on all sides by steep hills that curved into sharp mountains covered in pines and birch trees, it was a picture perfect scene and exactly what I expected of Norway. Which is why I'd gone on the damn cruise in the first place.

I loved landscape photography. Ever since my parents gave me my first camera when I was nine, I'd spent my free-time perfecting my craft and exploring. That first camera was nothing special—a basic digital point-and-shoot camera, but I was obsessed. Then, when I graduated from high school, my grandmother had gifted me a DSLR camera—my first manual camera. I'd used that thing for years before saving up to buy my current baby, a state-of-the-art device with a lens that cost me almost as much as the camera itself. What started in the fields and gullies of Ohio, had continued after college in Boston, and then stayed my passion when I reluctantly moved back to Columbus, Ohio due to the insane cost-of-living in the city. Now, whenever I could, I saved up to go on trips around the world.

My latest trip-turned-current-disaster had been a spontaneous adventure. A well-placed ad on my phone had me sold instantly, especially since the tickets were deeply discounted for the last sailing of the season. If I hadn't captured some spectacular shots over the past week, I'd have said the whole trip was a damn mistake.

Now, I needed to rectify the error my tardiness had created.

"What's your name?" I asked, jogging to catch up to the old man as he walked down the street. He moved fast for the age his gray hair and curved stature portrayed.

"Oddvar," he said, his accent throwing the vowels and rolling the Rs into tones I could never hope to replicate.

"Okay, Oddvar," I said, overextending the A and, based on the rise in my new friend's wispy, gray-brows, absolutely butchering the name. *Oh well, points for trying.* "I'm Lennie. Where are we going?"

"My coffee shop. There you can figure out what you want to do next." He never slowed as we wove between the small wood-buildings with tiled rooftops, and I walked quickly to keep up. "And we will talk to my friend, Solveig. She can help you, too."

Cool. Great. Progress, I guess. His tone seemed put-out—either because I was an American or an annoyance, to be determined—but at least he was helpful. I could ignore the way he'd taken great pleasure in seeing me miss the boat. Hell, I could only imagine the faces I'd made as I watched the ship sail away without me. I would have been amused, too.

Rounding another corner and traipsing down a tiny road devoid of vehicles, I kept up with the Norwegian and his silence. A few minutes later, he stopped in front of a storefront on the corner and stepped up to the wood-and-glass door. The small shop had wooden walls with peeling white paint, a few windows on either side of the door in the center, and a simple sign that read: Kafé. A tiny road ran between the buildings, too narrow for cars, and appeared to be for pedestrians only.

A bell chimed as Oddvar opened the door and stepped inside. I followed closely behind him, taking in the café as Oddvar shucked off his jacket and hung it up on a stand by the door. The interior of the building was tiny, but the space was used effectively. Light wood tables and chairs lined the walls beside the windows, and at the back of the room, centered slightly to the right, was a counter and cashier-machine. Aside from the two of us, the shop was empty, seemingly closed for the day.

"You like coffee?" he asked as he busied himself behind the counter, pouring water and setting up a large coffee pot.

Does a bear shit in the woods? It was a little late in the day for the dark stuff, but I never turned down coffee. "Yes," I replied, taking a seat at the closest table and setting down my camera. Pulling off my backpack, I set it on the chair beside me, making sure the contents—including my laptop—didn't fall off.

Oddvar continued his silent treatment, and it didn't take long before the smell of a nutty, bitter caramel roast permeated the space. I shrugged out of my rain jacket, resting it over the back of my chair and grabbed my camera.

Shit.

The lens cap was missing. I thought back to my run down the mountain, and then further back to taking photos at the top, trying to figure out when I'd last had it. I tilted my head back with a sigh, remembering I'd dropped the damned lens cap when the ship's horn blared. I added re-hiking the mountain to my mental to-do list, but that was a problem for tomorrow-Lennie.

The sun had started to set while I sat in the shop. It was getting late, and I needed a place to stay tonight, then transportation tomorrow to a bigger city further down the fjord to get me toward Stavanger, and probably something from the American Embassy so I didn't get myself into trouble considering my passport was still in my luggage on a cruise ship without me.

With a groan, I grabbed my cell-phone out of my jacket and called the Norwegian Fjord Tour that had abandoned me.

After talking to the cruise company customer service—who not so graciously told me to figure my shit out and get my stuff before the end of the year or they'd donate it all—I called the person that would be the most likely to help me out of my current situation. The first call went to voicemail, so I tried again. The second call was picked up on the fourth ring.

"I need your help," I mumbled into the phone pressed to my ear.

A low grumble sounded across the line. "Do you know what fucking time it is?"

I glanced at the clock above the shop-counter and did the mental math. Six in the afternoon, minus seven hours, was eleven in the morning.

"It's eleven a.m."

"On a Sunday!" my brother exclaimed, his voice hoarse.

I bit my lip, but couldn't keep the sneaky smile at bay. The fucker was hungover. If I didn't need his help, I would have rubbed it in his face or played heavy metal music down the line. But as it was...

"I missed the boat."

Howls of laughter battered my ear-drum, and I pulled the device away from my head until he caught his breath.

"Your tardiness was always going to come back to bite you in the ass, sis," Ryan laughed down the phone. I growled like a toddler at his words and their truth. "I'm surprised Mom and Dad didn't take away that camera of yours in high school with the number of detentions you racked up for being late to math class."

"How do you know it was the camera's fault?" I asked, trying to play it cool, but my voice betrayed me by rising several octaves.

"When is it not?" I could hear my brother's signature smirk, and I didn't like it. Not one bit.

Ryan was the younger of my three older brothers, and currently gallivanted around Chicago. He was 32 and did something in public relations, and had the personality to be good at it. He was always the charismatic one, and when my high school teachers found out I was his little sister, I saw heart-emojis bursting out of their eyes. That same feeling did not transfer to me once they saw how many shits I gave about being in class—except art, that one I aced every year. Oh, and, some of my science classes I'd done okay in, but only when they focused on environment and earth sciences. The rest were boring, like my eldest brothers.

My two other siblings, Andrew and Jared, had both settled down after marrying their college sweethearts. It was kind of creepy how alike they were. Andrew was two years older than Jared, both now well into their thirties. Both had been good students, won football scholarships to The Ohio State University, and set the gold standard for all the Martin kids to follow. Which Ryan, at least, did.

Me, on the other hand, I'd always been the rebel. Ever since my mom and dad found out they were having a happy-surprise-accident-baby, I'd been the odd one out. But I was still their only girl, and I lorded that shit over my brothers to this day. The stuff I got away with was spectacular—

"Are you listening to me?" Ryan's voice dragged my attention back to the phone call.

"Partially," I admitted with a sigh, lazily brushing my fingers across the table.

"Well, get your partial shit together because this call is going to cost you a fuck-ton of money."

I shuddered at the thought of the cell-phone bill I'd find when I eventually got home. I wasn't even connected to wifi right now, so my data usage wasn't going to be pretty either.

"So, you missed the boat because the scenery was too beautiful and it had to be captured," Ryan said, mimicking my usual excuse for being late to just about everything.

"Pretty much," I replied. "And my luggage is on-board, along with my phone charger, and passport."

"How many times have I told you to always carry your passport on you when you're in a foreign country," he said with an exasperated sigh.

"I know, I know, I know." I waved away the lecture. I'd been an idiot. Wasn't the first time, and wouldn't be the last either. "Can you help me or not?"

Ryan groaned and debated it for a second. No doubt wondering how he could use this against me at future Thanksgiving dinners or the annual Martin family reunion next spring.

"Just don't tell Mom, please," I added, trying not to sound like I was begging. I was going to fix this mess, but if I could have my annoying brother working in my favor back in the US and making some calls for me, I might be able to solve this without too much damage to my already measly bank account.

"Fine," he conceded, and I sent down a quiet thank you to hell, which must have frozen over for my brother to so easily agree. "I'll call the embassy for you and see what we can figure out."

"Thank you," I said, my shoulders sagging in relief.

"Don't thank me yet," he scoffed. "This shit's gonna cost you, sis."

"I know."

"Good," he said, and then hung up.

I lobbed my phone onto the table and leaned back in the chair.

One problem down, three to go.

3

LENNIE

"Drink up," Oddvar said, his voice gruff, as he set a small cup of coffee on the table in front of me. Steam drifted up and the smell of straight black bean-nectar was an assault to my nostrils. *Had he heard of creamer?* By the lack of any around, and the man's firm gaze, I was going to guess it wasn't standard in Norway and would not be offered this evening.

"Thank you, Oddvar," I said, wrapping my hands around the beverage, feeling the comforting heat beneath my palms. He winced at my pronunciation, but I was too tired to try the throaty tongue-roll thingy like he did when he'd told me his name. It was time to tackle another part of my to do list. "Do you know of somewhere I can stay that isn't too expensive?"

I may have been able to afford the trip out here, but I'd used almost all of my money on the cruise. My emergency funds didn't plan for hotel stays. So, hopefully the local hotel was cheap, or there were other options, like a tent or a park bench out of the wind.

"Yes, as I said earlier. I will take you to Solveig," Oddvar replied, returning behind the counter and wiping it down with a rag.

I stared at him blankly, waiting for him to elaborate. Was Solveig a person? Or a place? This meant nothing to me.

His dark brown eyes assessed me before he continued. "She runs a guest house. A... what do you Americans call it? An inn, at her house." He rambled like he was trying to find the right word to describe the place. Fortunately for him, I'd take anything that didn't bankrupt me.

"A bed-and-breakfast?" I supplied as he waved his hand through the air, then pointed at me.

"Yes."

"Okay, thank you." I bobbed my head, hoping this Solveig had reasonable rates.

Oddvar nodded at the cup in my hands. "Drink, then we go."

"Yes, sir," I muttered and took a sip, then let out a wheezy gasp. Fuck, it was hot... and strong. I'd be wired for hours after this, I was sure of it.

Setting down the mug to cool, I grabbed my camera and started flicking through the pictures I'd taken today before things had gone to shit. They were gorgeous, part skill and part natural beauty that remained untouched by humans. Pointy pine trees in all shades of deep green swept across the terrain, and the fjord almost glittered in the gray sunlight. I clicked through some more and stopped when I reached the last photo.

It was similar to the one prior, but with one glaring difference. In the middle of the shot, peeking through the trees, was a flash of silvery light—as if a lens flare had appeared in the forest... a very unnatural beam of light. I'd never seen anything like it, and it most definitely did not come from the sun, which had been hiding behind the clouds.

The door chimed and someone entered the café, but I didn't bother to look up, too busy zooming in on the silvery-something on my camera.

"*Litt sent å være åpen?*" A thick and gravelly voice said.

"*Hun rakk ikke skipet i tide,*" Oddvar muttered from somewhere across the room.

I didn't pay attention considering I couldn't understand them, so I focused on the picture. It looked like there were two figures beneath the silvery light. I tried enlarging it, and the camera beeped at me, letting me know I'd reached maximum zoom. With a grumble, I continued staring at the human-shaped figures. *What the fuck was that? Were they wearing something to throw the light like that?* I'd heard of scarves and jackets that refracted light in weird ways, distorting images, so maybe that's what was happening.

Someone plopped down opposite me at my table and coughed.

I started at the sound and looked up.

The man across from me was big in every sense of the word. From his broad shoulders, to the sharpness of his jaw, to the sizable hands resting on the table between us. He had choppy dirty-blond hair, deep-blue eyes the color of the fjord, and pale skin. His full lips curved into an unwelcoming smile as I continued scanning him. Before I could ogle him further—and try to visualize what was hiding underneath his thick navy-sweater—I set down my camera and clicked it off.

"Har du ekstra kaffe?" the man said, not averting his eyes from me as I crossed my arms over my chest. Maybe the aggressive staring was a Norwegian thing, but sitting at my table while he continued to speak in a language I didn't understand was grating on my nerves. Sure, I understood that I was the foreigner here, but leering like this wasn't polite in any country.

"Ja, men dette er alt jeg har i kveld," Oddvar said, not that I had a clue what that meant, but he uttered words the stranger in front of me understood. Then Oddvar brought over a little to-go cup of steaming coffee for the man, who thanked him with a nod, before Oddvar quickly disappeared behind the counter again.

The newcomer didn't move to grab the cup, but his eyes creased as he continued to stare. Whatever it was he found so interesting, I wasn't amused. I mean, who sits down at someone's table and starts glaring at them?

"You gonna keep staring, buddy?" I challenged, leaning back in my chair with the bravado of a woman who didn't have any more fucks to give.

He scoffed. "Any good photos?"

I glanced at the camera between us, before meeting his gaze again.

"Just mountains and trees," I said. Which wasn't a lie. The thing was full of photos of the fjords, mountains, and forests.

He flicked his brows and said, "Ah, American."

"What do you mean by that?" I narrowed my eyes at him.

"Nothing," he replied with a smarmy smile that had me clamping my palms together. "But here's what you need to do."

I leaned back and crossed my arms, biting my lower lip as I prepared for whatever this asshole was about to say. If there was one thing in the world that annoyed me the most, it was a man telling me what to do.

"Tourists are only needed here in Skolvik during the summer and early autumn season. Thereafter, we no longer require your *dollars*." He said the currency like it was filth and tilted his head to one side. "Any continued influx of visitors, even just one, is a threat to the region's wellbeing, especially the fjord."

"Tell me how you really feel," I deadpanned, giving him a swift upward nod to continue while the blood in my veins started to boil.

He took a sip of his coffee, then leaned in, resting his forearms on the table. "The amount of pollution you alone can create is a problem. Even if you draw in extra financial benefit, ultimately, you're not wanted here. You're not needed here, so leave."

"Not even a please?" I seethed, reaching the end of my tether. I took a deep breath and then added, "I can't be the first tourist who's been stuck or decided to stick around a little longer."

He grabbed his coffee cup and scooted his chair away from the table, the scraping sound loud in the near-empty café. "Every season there is always someone who gets left behind or who decides they want to stay. They usually leave when the first storm arrives. It used to be people visiting from Germany, but lately it's always a dumb American." He finally stood from his chair, and I took in the full height of the beast, his arms filling out every inch of his sweater. *Why were the hot ones always dicks?*

I straightened up and ignored the insult as I realized the tidbit of information he just dropped. *Wait a second... Leave?*

"How do they get out of here?"

He sauntered over to the front door before turning back. I spun in my seat, keeping my eyes locked on him, waiting for his answer... a little glimmer of hope sparking in my chest at the thought of being able to get home.

"Boat," he replied curtly.

"Like, they ask someone with a boat or there is a ferry that takes them down the fjord?"

He shook his head and took a sip of his drink. "None of those."

"Then what?" I asked with an exasperated sigh that only seemed to amuse the guy even more. The tiniest hint of a smirk tipped his lips up, and I wanted to smack the look from his arrogant face.

"They go on the little ship with the town's deliveries."

"You mean, a boat delivers your groceries and stuff?"

He nodded. "Exactly. Cheapest and easiest way down the fjord."

"When does the next one arrive?" I asked quickly, almost stumbling over my own words as I tried to eke out more information from the man.

"In one week."

Fuck me sideways. I grumbled, and the man smiled at my misfortune. "You don't happen to know of anyone else that might have a boat or a car and be willing to help out a poor tourist?"

"No."

I groaned in frustration and brushed my hand across my forehead.

Meanwhile, the asshole nodded to Oddvar and said, *"God kveld."*

"Ja, god kveld," Oddvar replied while sorting something behind the counter.

The man left, and I said nothing else. My brain was already flying through plans to get myself on that goddamn ship.

My new to-do list now consisted of: locating lodging, finding my lens cap, buying extra clothes for the week, and getting my ass on that boat.

"You finished?" Oddvar asked, pulling his coat back on and nodding at my coffee cup.

I grabbed the cup and downed the black liquid. It warmed my throat and felt like jet fuel in my stomach. Nodding at the now empty mug, I stood up and crossed the room, placing it in the metal sink behind the counter, before grabbing my stuff and pulling my own jacket on. I wasn't sure how Oddvar felt about the exchange that had transpired between me and the blond guy, but if he had thoughts on the matter, he remained mum.

"To Solveig?" I asked, zipping up my jacket and hoisting my bag onto my back.

Oddvar nodded and we made our way through town to his friend's house.

4

LENNIE

Oddvar walked me through town, past small boutiques and businesses that were closing for the day, and around to the north side of the harbor. A five-minute walk down an asphalt path on this side of the fjord led us to three larger houses, one white, one red, and one blue with white trim. Oddvar—sprightly for his age—kept a brisk pace and aimed for the blue house that faced the fjord. As we got closer, I questioned how on earth you entered the thing, because at the front wasn't what appeared to be a main entrance. Upfront was a fenced-in deck that backed onto the small path, which, in turn, sat above the rocky drop into the fjord itself.

At the last minute, Oddvar pivoted and headed toward the rear of the house. I quickened my steps to keep up with the man, and found what he'd been aiming for. The front door was at the back of the house, which was fucking bizarre in my book. But, alas, on my travels I'd learned that not everything was as straightforward as a cookie-cutter suburban house with a white picket-fence or a three-story brownstone.

Reaching the door, Oddvar knocked twice and then we waited, him with his hands behind his back and me with my palms in my jacket pockets.

A ray of sunshine opened the front door with a smile and short white hair. "*God kveld, Oddvar,*" she said, which sounded like a greeting, but also a bunch of gibberish to my non-Norwegian ears.

"*Ja, ja,* good evening," my older companion replied before waving at me. "This is the young lady I mentioned in the text."

The woman nodded, her eyes crinkling at the corners. "Yes, the American who missed the boat." She stepped aside and waved us both inside.

I politely obliged, but quickly added, "I'm Lennie." I really didn't want to be known as 'the American who missed the boat.'

"I'm Solveig," the woman replied as she closed the door behind us, shutting out the cold. "You are welcome to stay with me until arrangements can be made for your trip home."

"Thank you. I really appreciate it. How much do you charge?"

Her soft and gentle smile grew. "How about fifty American dollars per night? I will include breakfast."

That sounded like a freaking bargain. I could practically hear my bank account begging me to take the deal. "That works," I replied, trying not to sound *too* relieved. "Thank you."

"Wonderful. How about I show you around?"

I nodded, and Oddvar mumbled something in Norwegian that I could barely hear. Thankfully, Solveig understood the sounds that came out of his mouth, and a moment later Oddvar left.

After his departure, Solveig showed me the living room, kitchen, then upstairs to the guest room and bathroom across the hallway. The entire house was constructed of light-colored wood with bright walls. Even with the sun gone for the day, the interior glowed and looked like something out of a minimalist architecture magazine—everything had its place, and there wasn't an ounce of clutter in sight. It was the polar opposite of my tiny apartment back home.

The guest bedroom was minimally appointed, but somehow still cozy. The small double bed was covered in a blue-striped duvet—oddly folded in half instead of draped across the width of the bed—and a wooden dresser sat beside a tiny closet built into the wall.

"Will this be all right?" Solveig asked, her voice heavily accented, but her English was impeccable.

"This is perfect. Thank you so much," I replied, setting down my bag and resting my hands on my hips.

"Well, I'm making dinner. If you want some stew, you are welcome to join me in an hour."

"That sounds amazing."

"Wonderful. I shall let you get settled," she said, and left the room, closing the door behind her.

I took a deep breath and stretched my neck from one side and then the other. *What a day.*

While I waited for dinner to be ready, I unpacked what few belongings I had in my backpack, and took a five minute power-nap before heading downstairs.

Our meal was delicious, and my conversation with Solveig was cordial and lighthearted. Apparently, she'd lived here her entire life and couldn't imagine living anywhere else. However, she asked me loads of questions about the places I'd visited around the world, with northern Italy being the one she wanted to know the most about. I politely indulged her, happy to share the tales from my travels—at least the ones socially acceptable to discuss at the dinner table. I may have been a bit of a rebel and had a few rowdy adventures along the way, but Mom had taught me proper table manners.

After dinner, I crawled into bed. With exhaustion weighing heavily on my limbs, and a full stomach warming me through, it wasn't long before I fell asleep.

The sound of my phone beeping and buzzing woke me up. I leaned over and grabbed it off the nightstand, blinking the sleep out of my eyes. It was a bit fuzzy, but the name of the person video-calling me was legible in my bleary state.

With a grumble, I accepted the call.

"Andrew, I'm trying to sleep."

My oldest brother smiled back at me, with his big toothy grin, short dusty blond hair in perfect position, and the dark brown eyes we'd both inherited from our mother filled with warmth and care.

"I didn't mean to wake you," he said, "but, I wanted to make sure you're okay."

"Ryan texted you didn't he?" I pushed my hair back and pulled the covers up higher, frustrated at their antics.

Andrew nodded. "As soon as he hung up on you, he texted me and Jared. But I thought I would give you some time to cool down after your chat with him. You two always get feisty after interacting for more than five minutes."

He wasn't wrong about my relationship with Ryan, but I wasn't going to tell Andrew he was right. His ego was boosted enough by Midwest society and the picture-perfect suburban neighborhood he called home.

"I'm fine, Andrew."

"Okay, good. Trust your gut and get your butt home," he said, a hint of parenthood seeping into his voice. "We'll keep this from Mom and Dad, for now, but if she starts asking questions, I will tell her."

"Could you be more of a first-born child?" I narrowed my eyes at him, annoyance lacing my tone.

Andrew chuckled. "Don't do anything stupid... and don't anger any Vikings."

"I'm going back to sleep now," I grumbled.

"All right. Love you, sis."

"Yeah, yeah. Love you too, Andrew."

I hung up, and flicked my phone to its home-screen. Sure enough, sitting there waiting for me was a text message from Jared, the last of my brothers. I was surprised he bothered, what with the demands of his new veterinarian practice. After a knee-injury in his sophomore year of college, Jared's dreams of playing pro-football had been shattered. So, he pivoted and ended up continuing his education, becoming a vet. His job took up much of his time, and he rarely checked in with me. When he did, it was in the form of a quick text.

I opened the one he'd sent while I was sleeping.

Jared: Ryan told me what happened. You good, sis?

I typed out a quick response:

Lennie: Fine. Be back soon. Don't tell Mom.

Surprisingly, he texted back immediately.

Jared: K

I snorted. Typical Jared. It was shocking how he'd managed to find a wife with those communication skills. I opened another text that had come in while I was sleeping, this one from Ryan.

Ryan: Embassy says you're fine to stay without any repercussions for ninety days post initial arrival.

I sent him a thumbs-up emoji in reply and shut off my phone, throwing it back onto the nightstand. It was at 22% and fading. I would need to find a charger at the store tomorrow. Right now though, sleep took priority. I buried my head in the soft pillow and heaved the covers over my head, blocking any remaining light from my comfy cocoon.

5

LENNIE

Solveig was, honest to hell, one of the sweetest ladies I'd met on my travels. She was up early, already had coffee made for me—with milk to go in it—and had even prepared breakfast to-go. It wasn't my usual breakfast of oatmeal with random stuff on top, but it was delicious. A fresh bread roll, butter slathered over it, with smoked salmon and three thin slices of cucumber on top. I downed my coffee, and after thanking Solveig for the food and drink, wandered into the village, munching on the last of my yummy breakfast.

I'd worn my spare clothes today, which I always included in my backpack for emergencies. It wasn't the cutest outfit, but it was convenient, and fit nicely into a packing-cube, stuffed into my bag. The black long-sleeve shirt had some stretch to it, and worked with the jeans I'd worn yesterday and thrown on again today. Pair that combo with my hiking boots and my navy rain-jacket, and I almost looked like a local. At least, a very sporty local who had thrown her long blonde hair into a ponytail again for ease.

It wasn't a particularly warm morning, but the sun was starting to peek through the gray clouds, and the dew that hung over the little town made the entire place smell fresh and clean. There were no major pollutants here, except the cruise-ship that had abandoned me like a moldy husk of corn.

The town was barely waking, the curtains still drawn over many of the neighbors' windows, and no activity around the little white houses. It was quiet as I strolled toward the harbor, and realizing it was too early for any clothes stores to be open, I decided to knock something else off my to-do list instead: find my lens cap up the mountain.

Tightening the camera strap around my neck, I aimed for the trail beside the harbor, and started climbing like I'd done the day before.

The trail was completely empty compared to yesterday when fellow hikers had been out and about. The trek wasn't too long, but my thighs got a workout as I ambled up the rocky path, traipsing over moss-laden logs as I snapped another twenty photos of the flora and fauna. When I reached the clearing at the top where I'd been yesterday, I took a deep breath and started searching for my missing camera lens cap. It was black and shouldn't blend too much with the rocky ground. I scoured the terrain, and trod as lightly as possible in case I accidentally stepped on it. Which, admittedly, wouldn't be the first time, but would be seriously inconvenient considering current circumstances. Unlike a phone charger, I highly doubted I'd be able to replace a lens cap here in this little town.

"Looking for something?"

I jolted at the male voice and straightened before spinning around to face the owner.

Leaning against a large, mossy boulder was a man with a mop of dark hair, pale skin, a short beard, and a cocky smirk that said he knew exactly what I was looking for. He was wearing a black jacket and what looked like black rain-pants with a checkered reflective-stripe around the calf of each leg.

I gave him a winning smile and said, "It's probably the piece of plastic in your hand, Sunshine."

The man chuckled, and his amber eyes shimmered in a way I'd find attractive if he weren't pinching my lens cap between his fingers.

"Littering is heavily frowned upon in Norway. Some might even fine you for it," he said, his English perfect with barely a hint of an accent.

I stepped forward and plucked the lens cap from his grasp, careful not to look too closely at him. "Thank you. I'll be sure to remember that." And I wouldn't intentionally litter—I valued the nature around me too much to even consider it. What had happened yesterday was an accident.

"Get any good photos?" The man asked, still perched against the boulder. That was the second time in two days a hot stranger had bombarded me with this question.

Rubbing the black disk on my shirt and then blowing some air across it for good measure, I made sure it didn't have any debris on it before I clicked it onto the end of my camera—where it belonged. "Yes, mostly trees and waterfalls. You have a lot of them here."

"We do," he chuckled again. The noise was kinda sexy—husky and warm—it did things to my insides that shouldn't be allowed around a stranger. I shook my shoulders and took a deep breath through my nose. "They really are majestic, some might even say *magical*."

"Sure." I scoffed and glanced toward the area I'd photographed yesterday. The spot where I'd seen the silver flare was back to its regular gray-and-green coloring. Not a flicker of weirdness in sight.

"Haven't you heard of the legends and tales about the magical creatures that call this fjord home?" he asked, as I turned my back on him, fully entranced by the view.

But even facing away from the man, I couldn't hide my snort. Yes, they'd told us the stories on the cruise ship about monsters akin to the Loch Ness Monster that lived beneath the surface, but... "They're bullshit," I replied and turned my focus to the rocky ground and the moss trying to creep between the individual stones. "But, you might want to check out the clearing across the way, saw some weird silver shit over there yesterday. Caught it on camera, too. Could have been someone littering more than a misplaced lens cap."

"What exactly did it look like?" he said over my shoulder, suddenly right behind me.

Spooked, I spun on instinct and landed a swift punch in his ribs. He let out a grunt. Before I could retract my fist, his hand wrapped around my wrist and we both stilled—shock in our eyes. Or, at least, that's what he could likely see on my face, because I'd spotted the word printed across the top left of his jacket in a silvery font that matched the reflective material on his pants. It was only six letters:

Politi.

Fuck me sideways. I was 99% certain I'd just punched a cop.

I bit my lip and held my breath, unsure how I was going to get myself out of this one. Panicked flashes of Norwegian prison cells ran through my mind. Were they as bad as the ones in the US, with metal bars, a bucket for my shit, and crappy little beds? Or dungeons hidden in the middle of nowhere with ship-planks to sleep on? Maybe they had fancy wooden doors and flat-pack furniture like an IKEA display? I was about to find out, and then probably get shanked by a Viking when I inevitably opened my goddamn mouth and said something stupid.

The man breathed steadily, but said nothing, his amber eyes boring into mine with a ferocity that made my skin tingle.

I'd never punched a cop before—drunk dude at a bar that was getting too handsy? Sure. With three older brothers, I learned to swing hard and fast. But even I wasn't dumb enough to punch law enforcement. Now, looking at the man before me, I realized I'd gone too far, even in self-defense. A Viking's shank was in my future, and I'd never be heard from again. My mother would be beside herself.

"Ummm, so, how much trouble am I in right now?" I finally asked, my voice wavering slightly.

He dropped my wrist and took a step back, the rocks crunching under the weight of his black boots. "None," he said. "If you show me what's on your camera from yesterday."

Was he for real?

I blinked at him, confusion racing through my mind as the thought of meatball-only prison meals subsided. "I'm sorry for hitting you... but you really shouldn't sneak up on people like that."

He shrugged and bobbed his head from one side to the other, as if actually considering my suggestion. Which was lunacy, because my mouth got me into more trouble than out of it, so I highly doubted it would get me out of accidentally hitting a cop.

"Maybe," he said, then bit his lower lip and continued thinking, narrowing his eyes at me.

"Okay..." I waved my hand requesting his name in the international signal for *insert info here.*

"Espen."

"Okay, Espen. How about I show you my photo with the silver litterers, and we forget about this whole punchy situation?" This was a long-shot, but I'd give it a try if it meant I didn't get in trouble.

At the mention of the silver light, Espen straightened and nodded. *Thank fuck.*

I sighed and grabbed my camera, clicking through to the weird photo and passed it to the cop.

He stepped closer again, holding my camera. I could feel the heat radiating off him, and see the specks of dark-brown in his amber-colored eyes as he inspected the image. He smelled like moss and leather. Up close, I could make out his short lashes and the muscles in his jaw jumping. I was starting to feel tingly around the man—almost attracted. I mean, he was good-looking. Hell, I'd even go so far as to classify him as hot-as-fuck.

His jacket brushed against mine as he said, "Your name?"

"Lennie Martin," I said, discreetly splaying my fingers to rid myself of the ache in my knuckles.

"And you took this yesterday?"

"Yes."

"Anyone else seen it?"

"No," I replied, then shifted my weight away from him slightly. No one had seen the photo... except, maybe that guy at the café last night. He could've easily looked over my shoulder when he walked in. But why would that matter?

"Are you sure?" Espen asked, probably sensing my hesitation. He side-eyed me, waiting for a response.

I sighed and rested my hands on my hips. "There may have been one guy last night at the café. But, I can't be sure he saw anything. My back was to him when he entered."

Espen handed back my camera and I draped it back over my neck while he let out a low hum. "What did he look like?" he asked, invading my personal space with his odd authority and messy hairstyle.

I turned off the camera and let it rest against my chest, the strap around my neck taking the weight. Having him this close had my throat tightening, and goosebumps skittering across my arms.

"Well?" he said, drawing my attention back to his question and stopping my thoughts from considering the size of his hands as he crossed his arms.

I shook my head, refocusing. "Tall, blond hair, minor scruff, broad shoulders, grumpy with an attitude of asshole, and a hell of a staring problem."

Espen grumbled. "I know the man."

Why the annoyed tone, though? Was it such a problem if someone else saw the photo? Deciding not to be argumentative, and considering I'd just punched Espen, I asked, "I take it he might be problematic?"

"No." Espen rubbed his hand across his face and through his hair, messing it up even more. "But he's a pain in the ass."

"Ha! Glad I'm not the only one who thinks so. Don't put him on the town's welcoming committee. Seriously, bad for tourism." If given the chance, I wouldn't have been surprised if the Asshole had tried to drop-kick me out of town.

Espen let out a bubble of laughter that made something in my stomach flutter. "He hasn't been for decades."

I chuckled, and stopped. *Decades?* The man I'd met had been forty, at most.

"Wait, what?"

Espen stilled. "What?" He raised his thick brows.

"I could've sworn you just said—"

"Nevermind," he quipped and stepped back, resting his hands on his hips. "Thank you for showing me the photo. Do you like yoga?"

Give me whiplash or what bro?

"Yeah. Sure." I shook my head at the sudden pivot, but decided to roll with it considering I was miraculously off the hook for punching him. So, I circled back to our original topic. I was still curious about it. "You know what that silver thing is?"

"Ye—," he started, before quickly switching to, "no."

I blinked, giving him a deadpan stare. Here I was thinking men were pretty straightforward creatures. Turns out they made them a little differently in Norway. Must be all the fresh air or something.

"You really gonna lie to me?"

He sighed. "You wouldn't believe me."

I tilted my head, eyes squinted in challenge. "Try me."

He smirked, and the fire in his eyes gave me the feeling he wanted to *try me* in more ways than one. I squirmed a little, standing straighter, but wasn't wholly opposed to the idea, either.

"You've already said you don't believe in magic."

"Yeah, because it's animated crap that only happens in movies." I snorted.

He widened his gaze, leaning in closer to me as he whispered, "Are you sure?" Standing this close, it was impossible not to notice the way the dark flecks in his eyes flickered, like a silvery light briefly replaced them. It happened so fast, I almost didn't catch it, but... what the fuck *was* that? I took a step back and sucked in a gulp of air. It was a trick of the light, nothing more than the sun playing with colors.

"Magic is bullshit," I reiterated, shaking my head as I took another deep breath. "What's in the photo?"

Espen backed away and settled on the big boulder again. Resting one of his boots against it, he recrossed his arms and sighed. "I may as well tell you." He shrugged. "You've seen too much already, and I can't have you telling people about it around the village... or elsewhere, for that matter."

"Clearly," I said with a pound of venom and sass in my tone that had always landed me in trouble as a kid. Kinda like punching a cop in a foreign country. Some things apparently never changed.

He took a deep breath and locked his gaze with mine. "What you photographed was likely the illegal transfer of magic from one fae to another."

I stilled.

My knees buckled.

And then I laughed. Full on, hunched over, belly-meet-thighs, laughed. Because, oh man, did they need to take this guy off the roster down at the station.

"They won't fire me," Espen said.

I steadied myself by placing my hands on my knees. Apparently I said that last bit out loud. Oops.

Espen laughed, too. But it didn't sound as warm as it had earlier. This chuckle was more jovial and slick. He lifted his hand and placed it on his shoulder. I watched as his police jacket and black pants flickered and were replaced with a dark-green military-style coat with tubular collar, a short cape over one shoulder, and brown leather straps criss-crossing the front. Beneath that was a pair of gray pants and tall brown boots. He looked like some medieval warrior with ancient camouflage.

It was as if he'd...

It was like...

It was... magic.

I passed out.

6

LENNIE

Blinking open my eyes, I strained to see through the brightness invading my senses. Minimalist decor and light-wood tones glowed in the light as my brain caught up with the rest of my body and woke up. I was on my back, on what appeared to be the sofa in Solveig's living room.

"Oh good," a voice trilled, and I shifted to see Solveig walk into the room from the adjacent kitchen. She set a jug of water and a glass on the coffee table and poured me a drink. "Glad you're awake. We were a little worried."

"We?" I asked, sitting up and taking the glass from her outstretched hand.

"*Ja*. Me and Espen. He brought you back here. Said you were light-headed after hiking up the mountain where he found you."

Espen.

The cop.

The man who'd mysteriously changed outfits like some mirage had washed over him. The same man who said magic was real.

I stared at the water in my hand, and promptly put it back on the table. My mouth was dry, but after what I'd witnessed this morning, I wasn't entirely sure the local water was safe to drink. Hallucinogens were the only answer to whatever had happened, right? Solveig, thankfully, didn't remark on my actions.

"What time is it?" I asked, adjusting my disheveled ponytail and glancing toward the window. The sun had come out, and the fjord shimmered in the rays of light.

"Just after lunch," Solveig replied. She pulled the sleeves up on her cream sweater and smiled. "Would you like something to eat?"

The answer to that question was always yes. But, I did feel a little queasy. I twitched my nose. "How about just a light snack?"

"Of course," she said, and made for the kitchen.

I nodded and thanked her before she left the room. I'd hit the jackpot staying with her—I should be paying triple for this kind of care and service from my gracious host. Not that I could afford to do so, though.

My crazy morning aside—which I didn't want to think too hard about—I had a long list of things to do today. First and foremost, hit up the local boutiques for some clothes and toiletries. I could live without makeup, but underwear and a few more outfits would be needed if I was staying here until that supply-ship showed up on Sunday. That was my ticket out of here, and I just needed to get by until it took me up the fjord to the bigger city where I could get some form of transit south to Stavanger where my cruise-ship would finally dock.

Solveig gave me a sweet roll with icing drizzled on top. I'd drooled a little while I watched her make the topping—powdered sugar and water—simple as hell, and delicious, too. It was the perfect mini-meal while I walked to the clothing store she'd suggested in town.

The village was now awake, with people milling about the streets. I stared in fascination, especially at the man zipping through town with long roller-blade looking things on his feet and ski poles in his hands, while wearing an all-in-one skin-tight suit that was *not* family friendly. I was so caught up in what the man was doing that I missed the arrival of another "thing" and startled at their greeting.

"He's summer skiing," Espen said, appearing beside me.

With a shrug and acceptance of what was apparently normal around here, I turned to the dark-haired cop. His eyes shone with something like glee, and I spun on my heels, avoiding him as I headed toward the store Solveig had mentioned.

"Thank you so much, Espen, for bringing me down the mountain when I fainted," he said with a high pitched tone, keeping pace beside me. "Thank you for saving me. The wolves would've eaten me whole—"

I scoffed. "Are there seriously wolves up there?"

Espen grinned. "It's rare, but yes."

"Are you one of them? A werewolf perhaps?" I asked, even though I didn't believe he was a wolf. Or that magic was real. Or that whatever happened this morning had actually happened. Because... no, it most definitely wasn't worth thinking about anymore. Magic was bullshit, illusions for kid's birthday parties, and traveling fairs. Total bullshit.

"I'm not," Espen replied and clasped his hands behind his back in a move I'd seen Oddvar do yesterday. "And, by the way, you missed the turn for the clothing store two streets ago."

I pulled to a stop with a grunt and finally looked at him fully. He was still in his black uniform, the large jacket shielding him from the light breeze off the fjord. A head and a half taller than me, Espen was a lithe but sturdy build, with a friendly smile and mischief in his eyes. The latter were amber in color and so much brighter than my plain brown ones.

"And you weren't going to mention this sooner?" I asked, my usual snarky sass bubbling to the surface.

He beamed. "I thought I would see how far you would go before you realized, but I also feel a little guilty after the way we left things this morning."

"Really?"

"Yes and no." He pointed back the way I'd come, and I pivoted, heading in the new direction. Espen stayed by my side, guiding me toward the store whether I wanted his company or not. Passersby waved and nodded, greeting him happily as we walked. Clearly, everyone in this town knew him.

A few minutes later, we arrived at a storefront with mannequins and a tent in the window. When Solveig had said this was the perfect place, I hadn't expected all-terrain gear and boots, but I wasn't in a position to complain.

Espen was a gentleman and opened the door for me to enter. An electronic bell chimed, and a woman with short, bottle-blonde hair smiled as we crossed the room toward the women's clothing section.

"Do you not need camping gear?" Espen asked with a chuckle.

"No." My reply wasn't harsh, but certainly efficient, as I started perusing the racks of shirts. The stock was varied from athletic materials to knitwear and I pulled aside a dusty-pink t-shirt made out of stretchy material, a basic black cotton-shirt, and a dark-blue quarter-zip sweater that was big and cozy-looking.

Espen continued to trail me as I moved on to pants. "Are you going to follow me for the rest of the day?" I asked, slightly bothered by his proximity.

The man brushed his fingers over a pair of shorts before facing me. "Maybe. Thought you might need a friend, especially if you keep fainting."

My shoulders slumped, and I took a deep breath through my nose. "You know why I passed out," I whispered, hoping the woman up front couldn't hear us.

"No," he said, meeting my gaze. "I don't." A smirk grew on his lips, and he stepped up in front of me. With only a few paces between us, he reached out and touched my shoulder. "All I did was this."

A wave of warmth washed over my skin, and he removed his hand. I glanced down. My outfit from this morning was missing, replaced by a copy of the dusty-pink t-shirt I held and a pair of black yoga pants that had a slight flare at the bottom. I sucked in a breath, my heart pounding, and felt my eyes widen.

Looking up, I found Espen smiling and a sneaky gleam in his gaze. I did my best not to hyperventilate. Or move. Hell knew I didn't need to accidentally smack a cop again... like ever. But the rational, logical part of my brain couldn't keep up with what I was seeing.

"How are you doing this?" I mumbled, staring down at my body again. It didn't feel any different from what I had been wearing, but it appeared as if I had put on an entirely new outfit.

"Magic," Espen replied quietly.

"Is bullshit," I said, finishing his sentence on a whisper, even though what was happening could only be described by the word he'd just uttered. Which was madness. "Make it stop."

"Okay," he said, and placed his hand on my shoulder again. The wave of warmth returned, and I watched as my appearance shifted back to what I'd been wearing two minutes ago.

"Do you still think it's bullshit?" he asked, taking a step back and leaning against the display table of pants.

"Yes."

"Are you sure?"

"No," I replied honestly, scrunching the clothes in my hands. Either someone had slipped me drugs when I wasn't paying attention, or magic was real. I couldn't quite believe my eyes, but I'd also felt the shift, the... *magic*... fall over my skin when Espen changed my clothes. "Explain."

He grinned like he'd caught a fish in his net. "How about you find some clothes for the week, and I'll tell you over dinner."

Hesitating, I took a deep breath. "Hypothetically, if magic is real, why are you telling me about it?"

His smile faltered and he cleared his throat before replying, "Because in this situation, I believe it is wiser to have you in the know and on my side, than a loose cannon creating larger-than-life fabricated stories about what you saw and share that photo with the world. America has Area 51, England has Stonehenge... Skolvik will not become the Norwegian equivalent."

Okay, he had me. That was a decent explanation for the hypothetical. I narrowed my eyes at him and his frustratingly handsome floppy hair. "How do you know I need clothes... and how did you know I was staying with Solveig, by the way?" I didn't recall telling him where I was staying, or how long I'd be here for.

"Small town," he shrugged. "And I'm a police officer. It's my job to know what's going on, including when a mysterious American tourist missed their boat."

I drew my lips into a firm line and glared at him.

"So, dinner tonight?"

"And why should I trust you?" I waved my hand at him. "Whatever you are?"

"I'm a fae," he whispered with a gentle smile that had the corners of his eyes crinkling.

"Okay," I said, sounding very much not okay. "You're like a magical troll?"

"I prefer *sexy* troll." He smiled, and I stifled a laugh.

Rolling my eyes and picking up a pair of yoga pants like the ones he'd *magicked* onto my body from the display table beside us, I said, "Fine. I'll go to dinner with you, but I want more information about this magic nonsense."

"Deal."

He looked way too happy with himself. "Tonight, dinner, tomorrow... who knows... perhaps you'll join me for yoga in the woods."

I squinted, trying to see if there was some sort of innuendo or if this dude was really serious. Were we talking about yoga or *yoga*? "Don't get your hopes up."

"I already have." He winked. "You looked good in those tight yoga pants."

I scowled at him, but couldn't help the smile that grew on my face. This guy was slick and friendly as hell. Randomly grabbing another pair of pants, I spun toward the dressing room. "Where should I meet you for dinner?"

"Fisken," he replied instantly. "The restaurant by the public docks."

I threw my items into the dressing room and spun around, holding the long curtain in my hand. "I'll meet you there at seven."

Espen beamed, and a warmth settled in my chest at the sight. "It's a date."

I slammed the curtain shut and set about trying on the clothes I'd selected, heat radiating from my chest and an anxious energy coursing through my veins. Because, apparently, fae and magic were real.

7

LENNIE

Espen left while I was in the changing room, which finally gave me the peace I needed to find underwear, another tee, a couple extra sports bras, and socks. Solveig had graciously offered her laundry machines to clean my current outfits, but it was still wise to grab some more stuff so I wasn't constantly having to clean my clothes.

I grabbed a five-pack of long socks and mulled over the magic nonsense that Espen had shown me as I looked for some comfy sports bras, the rest of my future purchases slung over my arm—yoga pants included. In the woods, Espen had mysteriously changed his outfit from his police uniform into attire that looked like it belonged in *ye olde times*. I mean, who wore a cape outside of attending a Renaissance fair?

That shift was ludicrous, but then, this afternoon, in this very store, he'd changed my clothes without so much as yanking my pants off me.

I snatched a bra in my size off the hanging rack and shoved it between my arms and chest where I was stashing the rest of my purchases.

The whole concept of magic being real and not in movies was overwhelming, and too much to take in. So, it was bullshit. Complete and utter bullshit. It was probably all in my head, right? I'd been eating a lot less processed sugar during my trip so far, and getting a lot more fresh air than I'd get on a normal day in Ohio. Maybe that was the reason why I was seeing things? Because, if it wasn't, and magic was in fact real, that would be fucking absurd.

Confused and determined to get some answers out of Espen that evening, I wandered over to the checkout, paid for my new stuff, and headed back to Solveig's house.

I arrived at the restaurant and bar called "Fisken" at seven for dinner with Espen. The drizzle outside made my hair frizz, but the soft warmth inside the building would certainly dry it out quickly, even if I did look a bit frazzled now.

A low hum of chatter rose from the few occupied tables, but it wasn't too busy. Taking a moment to gather my bearings, I looked around the space. The walls were made of dark wood with photos of fishing boats and mountains hanging on them, exactly what you'd expect in a little town on the water. To my left was the bar, and to the right were tables facing the bank of windows that looked out over the public harbor, boats bobbing up and down on the water.

I spotted Espen sitting at one of the old wooden tables near the back of the room and shucked off my rain-jacket as I approached him. He smiled as I rolled up the sleeves on my black shirt, slung my jacket over the back of a chair, and joined him.

"Glad you made it," he said, his eyes flickering with glee again. He'd replaced his uniform with a long-sleeved black sweater, dark green pants, and a pair of dark boots that might have been the same ones he'd been wearing this morning. The more casual look suited him, with his dark-brown hair a mess on top, but cut shorter on the sides, and I couldn't help but realize how attractive he was. It was sorely tempting to reach out and run my fingers through... I shook my head away from the thoughts that were bubbling up and refocused on the table between us.

"I'm looking forward to some explanations." I picked up a menu from the middle of the table and ignored Espen's quiet chuckle when I realized the entire thing was in Norwegian. Any trace of a smile faltered when I looked over the unfamiliar words. My app of basic Norwegian phrases hadn't prepared me for this, and all the other places I'd been to on my trip so far had their menus in English, or at least photos of the dishes so I knew what I was ordering. Plus, I'd forgotten to buy a fucking phone charger, again, and it was deader than dead. My app couldn't save me, nor could a quick internet search.

"Would you like me to translate?" Espen offered kindly after I'd stared at the menu for entirely too long, hoping magic *was* real, and it would translate itself for me.

I sighed and, because it was the easier and quicker option and I was starving after my shopping adventure, I decided to do the unthinkable. "Can you just order for me?"

Espen nodded politely, his smile not concealing any sort of victory. When the waiter came by for our order a few moments later, Espen muttered something about "*pølselapskaus* and *øl.*" The former sounded completely garbled, the latter I knew exactly what I was getting—beer.

When the waiter left, I dared to ask, "What exactly did you just order other than beer?"

"A potato-based stew of sorts with vegetables and sausage. It's served with a snappy flat-bread," he said, before quickly adding, "very tasty. Loved by kids, locals, and tourists."

I snorted and placed my napkin across my thighs. "Thank you for not ordering me something outlandish. The cruise-ship staff already tricked me into trying some gelatinous icky *loo-tee-fisk* that tasted disgusting."

Espen chuckled as the waiter returned with our beers, setting them down and wandering off again. "You mean *lutefisk*. Yes, that is an acquired taste for some, but certainly a lot more palatable when served with bacon."

Now there was something we could agree on. Give me bacon any day of the week, for any meal, and I was a happy camper. I took a sip of my beer and relished in the taste, leaning back in my chair. More chit chat followed, mostly about the village and the weather, and then our food arrived, smelling damn delicious.

"Tell me about yourself," Espen said as he dove into his meal. He really was treating this as a date of sorts, which made me slightly skeptical... but only slightly. I had been the one to ask for more info, and if this was what I needed to do to get it out of him, then so be it.

"What do you wanna know?" I replied, taking a bite of the stew. The hot potatoes, carrots, and what I thought tasted a bit like rutabaga, were perfection and super hearty after a long day. The snappy flat bread—that looked like a large cracker—was also a fantastic vessel for pieces of sausage.

"The usual. Family, friends, hobbies." He gave me a friendly grin between bites of stew, and I couldn't help feeling relaxed around the guy. Maybe he was onto something with that forest yoga he'd mentioned earlier if it made him chill like this.

After swallowing my own mouthful of hot stew and a piece of the cracker-bread, I gave him a quick rundown of my life: Lennie Martin in 5-minutes or less.

"Mom, Dad, three older brothers. Born and raised in the state of Ohio. Twenty-eight years old. I enjoy hiking, photography, and exploring the world. Lived in Boston for three years after college, until it bankrupted me and I moved back to Ohio—Columbus, specifically. Now, I have a desk job that puts food on the table and money in my account for trips like this one." I took another bite of my dinner before adding, "Small group of friends from high school and college who I still hang out with on a regular basis, but most of them are married or have kids. How about you?"

Espen leaned back in his chair, his bowl empty as he'd practically inhaled his meal. He took a sip of his golden beer and said, "Parents died a while ago—old age. Two sisters, both older and live quite a bit further north of here, where we grew up. I see them and their kids a few times a year when I can get away from work. My job, as you know"—I bit my lip at the smirk and teasing look he gave me—"is a police officer. I help the town, but my primary duties lie in the forest. We are a small unit, so I serve as our forest ranger, too."

"Like a yoga-loving park ranger?" I said, and took a final bite of my delicious and filling dinner.

"Yes, I guess you could say that," Espen replied. "I like hiking, foraging for mushrooms, exercise, and yes, yoga." He finished with a wink.

I smiled back at him, still not entirely sure if he was serious about the yoga part or if it was a dirty innuendo, but I was at ease with the conversation. Plus, still curious about the magic stuff and... "How old are you?" He'd failed to mention that so far.

He stared at his drink and shifted minutely in his seat, eyes locked on the tiny bubbles floating up through the liquid. "Thirty-ish."

I leaned back in my chair and took him in. "Oh really?"

He nodded and without looking at me directly, he whispered, "A fae never reveals his age."

I wasn't entirely buying it. He certainly looked like he might be in his thirties, but I had a sneaking suspicion that was far from the truth. Weren't mythical beings supposed to be ancient or something? "Why do I think you're lying to me, Espen?"

A hint of a smile graced his lips, but a feminine voice said, "He's 225."

I turned and found a short woman chuckling as she circled us and pulled up a chair. Espen let out a long sigh as she sat down, resting her forearms on the table.

Mentally, I was trying to process Espen's old age and attempting to match that with the man—creature—who most definitely looked like he was in his mid-thirties, at most. Physically, I was openly staring at the woman who'd joined us. She had a round face, brown hair cut into a bob, rosy cheeks, and eyes the color of a mountain—somehow gray and brown at the same time. If this woman knew Espen's age, then what were the odds she was one of these fae thingies, too?

"Hey, I'm Nora," she said in perfect English.

"Lennie," I replied, giving her a gentle nod.

"Nice to meet you," she added with a small smile before turning to Espen, who was still intently studying his beer. "Why is she not laughing at your age, Espen?"

Espen glanced up, but didn't reply. His dark lashes brushed across his pale cheeks.

"What happened, Espen?" Nora asked, half-stern, half-playful.

The police officer shook his head, and I thoroughly enjoyed watching him squirm a bit. Apparently, I was a problem—which most definitely wasn't a first for me. This magic stuff though, that was new.

"We ran into an incident," Espen said. "And Lennie captured it on camera."

"What?" Nora paled slightly, her eyes widening, but Espen continued, blatantly ignoring her look of panic.

"Looks like another illegal transfer. I'm already looking into it."

She took a deep breath, her chest rising sharply before her eyes darted to me briefly. "We can't have that happening again. You know what happened last time. You know what could happen—"

"I'm well aware of the consequences," Espen practically growled, and Nora's nostrils flared at his sharp words and shift in tone.

"*Og hvorfor har du fortalt et menneske om oss? Er du gal?*" She continued with what sounded like a scathing whisper through her clenched teeth.

"I'm not crazy, Nora. I've had enough of a scolding from my Council, I don't need to hear it from you too."

"*Hvorfor gjorde du det?*" She muttered, leaning back and crossing her arms over her chest.

"I had to make a decision on the spot. She'd seen enough already. The Council may not fully support my actions, and I may have lost some trust with them because of it, but they agreed that the image could not get out into the world."

Nora shook her head and muttered something that sounded vaguely like "Men."

I looked between the two of them, feeling restless. Espen still hadn't explained anything about his magic, and I didn't like being left out of the loop. "Would you two care to explain what's happening? Kinda rude to talk around me like this, don't you think?"

Espen turned to me and bit his bottom lip as he playfully flicked his thick brows upward once. It was a move that screamed challenge accepted. He opened his mouth, but Nora jumped in.

"Not in here," she said rather formally, cutting him off. "Too many humans."

So, she *was* one of them. Clearly there were more of them than just Espen. He'd mentioned a council, so there must be quite a few more than just these two. But why was it okay for them to tell me about the fae and this illegal magic stuff and not the others in here? Was it really only because I'd taken the photo? If that were the case, Espen should've just stolen my damn camera, or even just the memory card. I mean, I'd have hunted him down for it, but if he asked nicely, I probably would've just deleted the picture. He must've had some alternate reason to tell me about them, which, admittedly, made me feel even more curious.

I glanced around the restaurant, noticing it had indeed filled up. Almost all the tables were full; the only vacant seats were the big booths at the very back of the space.

I turned back to the two fae. "When *can* you tell me?" That had been the whole point of this dinner-date, after all. Espen was supposed to explain his magic voodoo stuff. Instead, it had felt like a real-ish date with him trying to get to know me.

"Tomorrow," Espen replied.

Nora shrugged like it was a satisfactory answer.

I still wasn't entirely sure I could trust the guy, or whatever he was planning in that head of his. "When, where, why?"

"That's what I would like to know, too?" A strong voice said, and I glanced up into a pair of blue eyes that raged with the power of a midnight storm.

8

LENNIE

The tall, blond behemoth strode across the room, aiming for our table. Espen straightened in his seat, while I leaned back and took a sip of my beer. It was the rude man from Oddvar's café, wearing a navy jacket, black jeans, and a holier than thou attitude.

He nodded slowly to Nora, almost like a bow, then turned to Espen.

"Espen," he said in greeting, his tone flatter than a pancake.

"Øyvin."

The man gave me the up-down. "American."

"Asshole," I replied with a smarmy smile.

"No, thank you."

"You'd enjoy it." I winked, taking his salacious pivot and rolling with it. I wasn't lying either—I'd had nothing but rave reviews. Øyvin grimaced like he'd never entertain the idea.

Espen spluttered into his beer glass and drew my attention from the beast. "Before you two start a brawl, maybe you could tell me why you're here?" he said to Øyvin.

Nora had remained silent during the entire interaction, but her smirk was visible from the corner of my eye. She reached out her hand and lightly tapped my wrist, sending a sharp sting across the skin there, like

I'd swatted a bug zapper. I retracted my arm and brushed my palm across the spot that she'd touched. The prick wasn't painful, but was strong enough to notice. Before I could ask her what the fuck she was playing at, Asshole started talking.

"Balder sent me to speak with you. One of our scouts found markings in the woods—"

"They wouldn't happen to be in the forest on the north side of the fjord?" I asked, interrupting him.

His eyes widened, and Espen turned with a matching look of surprise on his face.

"What?" I quirked a brow in confusion at their expressions.

"He said that in Norwegian," Espen replied, and I suddenly understood their reaction. He spun toward Nora with a glare. "What did you do, Nora?" Nora chuckled once.

I glanced down at my wrist, checking it for any marks. Where she'd shocked me was blank, no scarring, no discoloration, nothing. "You mess with my hearing?" I asked her, blunt but curious as to how I could suddenly understand every word of a language I knew next to nothing of ten minutes ago.

She bit her lip, then said, "Might flicker on and off, but I thought it could be useful."

"Thank you." Now, *this* was magic I could get behind. My Norwegian wasn't even rudimentary, and now I understood everything that was said around me... without anyone else knowing either.

I smirked at the thought. *This'll be fun.*

I'd just have to watch people's lips closely when they spoke so I could discern when someone was actually talking Norwegian and it was being translated by whatever magic tomfoolery this was, or English. Wouldn't do me any good to be responding to people in English when they were speaking to me in Norwegian, especially strangers.

"Oh, and he's 237," Nora whispered with a cheeky grin, subtly pointing toward Øyvin. "We age slowly once we hit eighteen."

My eyes widened, and I tilted my head in manner that said, *thank you for that tidbit.* She nodded back like we were now compatriots, in league against the two males. And I didn't mind that one bit.

Espen slowly shook his head, his dark locks shifting with the movement, and turned back to the broody Asshole. "You were saying?"

Øyvin sighed and restarted his monologue. "Balder's scouts found markings in the forest on the north side of the fjord." He shot a glare at me, and with a quick glance over his shoulder, continued. "It looks like another transfer was made. As it was in your territory, I thought it best to inform you. I wasn't aware you already knew."

"Have you told Halvar?" Espen asked.

"No."

Espen sighed, his shoulders slumping. "You're going to ask me to do it, aren't you?"

Øyvin tilted his head slightly in agreement, a deep frown taking over his face. "Halvar's not a fan."

I scoffed. "I wonder why?"

I got an eye-roll for that quip, but I took another sip of my beer. From the sound of this conversation and Nora's information about his age, it seemed a safe bet to assume Asshole was another one of these fae things. How many of them were around here? We were now up to these three plus a council, scouts, and whatever Nordic names had just been uttered.

Espen turned to Nora, a pleading look in his eyes. "Can you tell Halvar?"

"No, you know I don't get involved in my sister's business," she replied with a shake of her head. "Especially not her Head Guard."

Espen let out a long sigh and rubbed his hands across his short beard. "Fine. I'll head up there tonight," he conceded, settling back into his chair. He turned to Øyvin and added, "You can tell Balder that I'm looking into it and will report it to the Fjell."

Øyvin gave him a brief nod of acceptance, then fell back into his broody asshole-ish state by glaring at me. I gave as good as I got, and glared right back.

"Tomorrow we'll take a closer look, and I'll tell you about our people," Espen said to me. I was about to thank him and ask why on earth I would be needed, when I was interrupted.

"You cannot be serious," Øyvin grumbled.

Espen and I glanced up at the man, while, out of the corner of my eye, I spotted Nora swipe Espen's beer and take a long sip.

"She's seen too much already, and I could do with the help keeping things... classified." Espen's usually friendly demeanor took on a new tone—darker, firmer, like that of a leader who was done messing around.

"Fine," Øyvin said, sounding anything but fine. "Let me know if there are any problems." And, with that, he bowed his head to Nora, again, and left in a huff. I decided, there and then, that Øyvin was a douche-ca-noe-extraordinaire that needed to chill the fuck out. Or, at least, pull the stick out of his ass.

I turned to Espen, who had just noticed his missing beer and was glaring at Nora as she finished the drink. "So, you need me tomorrow? And will explain everything then?"

He shook his head at the short-haired woman—who grinned at him—and focused on me. "Yes, I will need to photograph the area, and could use your help to..." his voice dropped to a whisper, "keep this out of the office." He gave me the universal look for *wink-wink, nudge-nudge.*

"On one condition," I said, taking some control of the situation and working it to my favor. "If I help you, you need to make sure I get on that boat to get down the fjord and back to Stavanger."

"Deal," Espen said, extending his hand across the table.

I took his palm in mine, the heat of which was comforting, and shook it. I would be his camera-woman and help him keep the investigation away from prying eyes—which likely meant the humans at the police station—and he would help me get the fuck out of here on Sunday.

"Good," I replied before quickly adding, "I still don't understand why someone in town can't just give me a ride down the coast where I might find other transit options."

Espen bit his bottom lip, and Nora let out a loud laugh. "That's because everyone thinks your misfortune is funny," she said. "And no one wants to drive over six hours along the zig-zag roads to help you."

9

ESPEN

The American was a problem and a delight. The former, because she'd somehow photographed fae magic, which in itself should've been impossible. And the latter, because her wily mouth and luscious curves captivated me, and I couldn't tear my eyes away. Fortunately, she was warming to me after our altercation in the woods this morning, and had accepted my dinner invite. Unfortunately, Nora and Øyvin barged in and ruined what was turning into a nice evening.

The tall Fjord Fae did have a point though. The fae in our area were broken into three sections—Fjord Fae who dwelled in the water, Fjell Fae under the mountain, and my own people, the Forest Fae—and, while independent, we watched out for each other when it concerned the potential exposure of our world. All day I'd avoided heading up the mountain to inform the Fjell Fae of the magic transfer, but I couldn't put it off any longer. Queen Freija, her Head Guard Halvar, and their people, needed to know. I owed it to them as part of the Forest Fae's alliance with the Fjell Fae, too.

So, after saying good night to Lennie downtown, I walked up the mountain road and swept into the forest with Nora. Between the light rain and the dark night sky, the trails were free of humans, making it easy for us to stay hidden as we took one of the hundreds of trails that led into the cliffside itself.

"I like her," Nora said, her voice breaking the silence between us and the birch trees standing sentry in this part of the woods.

I agreed. There was a lot to like about our lost tourist. Lennie was fiery, spoke her mind, and could throw a hell of a punch. That hit she got in this morning had taken me by surprise and knocked the wind right out of me. "I like her, too."

"Just make sure she understands the secrecy she needs to keep about everything she sees," Nora said sternly. "You know what will happen if word got out that could harm my sister."

I nodded, fully aware of the subject she was referencing. Halvar, Freija's Head Guard and my counterpart for the Fjell Fae, would likely rip any threat to shreds before burying them in a stony grave. He was old and powerful, and would do anything to protect his Queen. Something I wish I could do, but would never have the chance to after what happened twenty years ago.

Our steps slowed as we reached the hidden cave entrance that led into this part of the mountain. The opening was shielded by a magical veil that appeared as moss and rock, no different than the scenery around it. Magic discouraged humans from approaching it, but if a human happened to try walking through it without the approval of the Fjell Queen, they would be rebuffed—like walking into a wall.

Nora and I slipped inside. The drizzle ended, but the temperature within the cave-like hallway dropped, sending a chill across my cheeks where my beard couldn't protect me.

"This is where I leave you," Nora said, turning left down another hallway. "Good luck," she added over her shoulder as she sauntered deeper into the mountain.

"Thanks," I muttered, knowing full well I'd need all the luck I could get.

The maze of hallways within the mountain was vast and lit by magical lanterns. Torsten, a friend of mine and the partner of Leif, one of my own Forest Fae, was in charge of the lighting within the mountain. Lanterns were mounted on the rocky walls every few meters, casting a warm glow throughout the tunnels. I took a deep breath and admired Torsten's work, the immense effort that went into keeping the lights on in here. He had a sunny disposition, which was probably what had drawn Leif to him in the first place. Both were rays of sunshine, but with one belonging to the Fjell and the other the Forest, it had taken a few decades—and the new alliance—for them to be comfortable living between the two places. Previously, intermingling had been frowned upon, but not outright banned. Yet, it still had made many uneasy in declaring their true feelings for a member of another faction.

I put a hand to my shoulder and transformed my human attire into my formal uniform as I'd done in the forest to show Lennie my magic. The transformation was quick, and my trousers and sweater disappeared, replaced by my gray wool jacket, a short green cape over one shoulder, gray pants, and brown boots that matched the pieces of leather on the ensemble. While I was more comfortable in my more human attire, there was a possibility I'd be seeing the Queen tonight, and I should pay her the respect she deserved by wearing the pesky thing.

Taking a deep breath, I squared my shoulders just as a voice came down the hallway.

"Making a late-night report?" Torsten said, his tawny hair, tied into a bun on his head, and stout form coming into view as he lifted his hand. Within his grasp was a tiny ball of silver light—the magic he used to keep these tunnels' lanterns lit for the Fjell residents. He was in his uniform, on duty, the dark gray-and-black outfit similar to my own.

"Yes. Is Halvar in the throne room?" I asked, following Torsten down the hallway to my right.

"Last I saw him," he nodded beside me.

"And the Queen?" I asked, wondering if Freija was still awake. It wasn't late by any means, but the woman was older than she looked and tended to retire early.

Torsten shrugged, his own cape jostling with the movement. "You'll see for yourself." He veered down another smaller tunnel that was dark. "Good night!"

"Say hello to Leif for me."

Torsten beamed, his eyes crinkling at the corner. "Will do."

I strode deeper into the behemoth mountain that housed over seven-hundred fae and stretched for miles in all directions. A few minutes later, I turned down a crystal lined hallway with silver markings dancing across the dark walls. The heart of the mountain glowed, matching the majesty of the woman who reigned here.

Stepping past two guards and into the throne room, I was greeted by a silver-haired brute. Halvar wore a uniform similar to Torsten's, with an empty sword belt at his hip, and stood before the throne—protecting it, even though it was empty. He was a big fae, a son of the mountain, and had seen more life and death than I ever wanted. With sky-blue eyes and a silvery beard, he looked fit but wisened. No one knew exactly how old he was, but he was a lot older than my 225 years.

"Espen." His voice rumbled across the space as I stopped before him.

"Halvar," I replied with a slight tip of my head. We'd been in an alliance ever since my own Queen of the Forest died, but I always showed this man respect. One, because he deserved it as Head Guard of the Fjell Fae, and, two, because I never wanted to be on the receiving end of his wrath. Rumor had it he fought alongside the Vikings, and that they'd held him in such reverence that stories were told of his might on distant shores for centuries.

"I came to share a report. A situation has occurred that I thought you and Queen Freija should be aware of."

Halvar nodded. "Proceed, and I shall inform the Queen."

I took a deep breath and shared what had happened. From Lennie's unfortunate photograph, to the report from Øyvin, I left nothing out.

"You are running an investigation, too?"

"Off the books," I replied. "I will have Lennie assist with photography so we aren't using anything that belongs to the government or the station." Halvar nodded, and I quickly added. "I'll make sure she doesn't share our existence with anyone else."

"How will you ensure that?" he asked, crossing his arms over his broad chest, signs of the beast beneath peeping through his guarded veneer.

"She wants to leave here. I'll make sure she gets on the next cargo ship on the promise that she never speaks of us or this area ever again. I already plan on talking to Oddvar tomorrow to help coordinate her passage."

Halvar didn't move, his face still in its usual stoic state. "Make sure she does, or the threat to our secret will be removed."

I gaped in surprise, but should have seen this coming. "You've taken up killing humans now?"

His stern gaze didn't waver. "I will do whatever is necessary to secure the safety and wellbeing of the Fjell and its inhabitants," he said, crossing his arms and giving me the sinking feeling that he would, indeed, follow through on his threat.

Unwilling to stay another minute longer, or anger the old-man, I gave him a curt nod and retreated. "Give my regards to the Queen," I said as

I exited under the white-and-blue crystalline archway that matched the style of the throne.

Halvar replied with a low grumble.

I left the mountain, changed back into my human attire, and walked home to my little cabin. The whole journey home, I mulled through the investigation and thoughts of the American woman that had landed herself in the middle of it all.

10

LENNIE

The sky was overcast when I woke up the next morning. I frowned at the cloud cover through the window, thinking through the plans for a hike with a fae to take photos of magic something or other. While I loved hiking and photography, I couldn't say this was my usual itinerary. Given the lack of transportation out of this little town, I didn't have much choice but to take Espen up on his exchange. I needed to get back south so I could get my stuff from the cruise ship—including my passport—and fly home to the US before I lost my job and drained my bank account. I just had to survive the next five days investigating fae magic with a local cop until the cargo ship could hopefully take me back down the fjord.

If my brother's caught wind of this shit, they'd think I was high. Good thing my phone was still dead and they couldn't reach me. Honestly, that thing needed to stay off as much as possible so I didn't rack up an obscene phone bill.

Once I pulled on some of my new clothes, I grabbed my backpack, camera, and reusable water bottle, and made my way downstairs. My bright and kind hostess was at the kitchen-table, drinking her morning coffee when I walked in.

"Good morning, Lennie," Solveig trilled with a warm smile on her face.

"Good morning, Solveig," I replied, finally nailing the pronunciation of her name. Fourteenth time's the charm. She beamed, recognizing the little win.

"Where are you off to today?"

"I'm going on a quick hike with Espen," I said, filling up my water bottle at the sink.

"Ah, he is a good man," she said, and I bit my lip as I tightened the lid on my drink. From the little I gathered last night at dinner, the fae were secretive amongst the humans here. Solveig likely wasn't aware that Espen wasn't a "man"—at least not by her definition. And it wasn't my place to reveal their secret. "He's so nice," she added. "A good tour guide for you."

"Yeah, I hope so." I threw my bottle into my bag and slung it over my shoulders.

"There is a bread-roll with ham and cheese in the fridge if you would like that for breakfast, or I can recommend some options in town?"

Honest to hell, this woman deserved the world for how well she took care of her guests. I mean, feeding me would always win you favor, but Solveig seemed to go above and beyond.

"I'd love the bread-roll to go, thank you."

She pointed to the fridge, and I helped myself.

With a nod and a thank you, I sauntered out of the kitchen to the front door. Slipping my feet into my hiking boots—and holding my breakfast between my teeth while I tied the obnoxious laces—I prepared for departure. I grabbed my coat, secured the camera strap around my neck, and headed out the door to find a magic-wielding police officer that liked to do yoga in his free time.

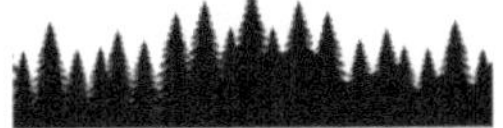

I finished my breakfast as I walked to our meeting point. The trail-head was a little further down the paved path that Solveig's house backed onto. With the fjord to my left and rounded shrubs to my right, I breathed in the fresh morning air during my pleasant five minute stroll. I'd left the house with what I thought was plenty of time, but knowing my habits, there was a good chance I was already late.

As if to prove my point, I reached the trailhead to find Espen leaning against a large sign in the shape of a log cabin with a moss-covered roof. He was back in his black uniform, the reflective word "Politi" emblazoned on his left breast, pretty damn visible even in the dull light of the day. So visible, you'd think someone might notice it before they decided to punch the wearer. Maybe I needed glasses? Or self-control?

I stepped up beside him. Espen smelled like moss, leather, and pine, blending in with the forest around him. I'd bet he could stand in close proximity to a doe and it wouldn't even know he was there.

"Morning," he said, slowly taking me in from boot, to head, to tip of my ponytail. "You'll be pleased to know that I've spoken to Oddvar, and he has secured your passage on the supply boat on Sunday."

"Thank you," I said, giving him a grateful smile, but immediately thought about my bank account that was turning into nothing but mothballs. "Do I owe him anything?"

Espen shook his head, and I relaxed my shoulders. "Oddvar's son is the captain of the boat. You don't owe him anything."

I breathed a sigh of relief. "Thank you." I didn't know what I'd done to deserve such luck, but I most definitely appreciated it. Shaking my hands toward the device hanging around my neck, I pivoted to today's task. "Well, I've got my camera. You ready?"

"Let's go then," he smiled.

We traipsed into the woods along the rocky dirt path, tall trees rising on all sides, and dewy ferns tapping at our ankles. The smell of moss and pine drifted around me, and the crunching of our footfalls was the only sound aside from the light chirping of birds somewhere in the distance. The landscape was so different from that in Ohio, steeper for one, but also teeming with luscious greenery that I couldn't help but fall in love with.

The trail zig-zagged upward and narrowed the higher we hiked. We were on the north side of the fjord, the deep inlet just visible between the trees and foliage, its waters glistening in the soft morning light. Espen kept pace beside me, stepping back to let me go in front of him when the path got too small for us to walk side-by-side.

After about ten minutes of peaceful silence, I decided it was time for Espen to start filling me in on the details he was supposed to share at dinner last night.

"So, start explaining what you are and this whole magic business."

"Only if you promise to never speak of it to any human... ever," he said with a stern look in his eyes. "Because if you do, I myself won't kill you, but others likely will."

A shudder ran through me and I nodded. "Deal." Then I waved my hand at Espen, requesting that he answer my initial request, doing my best to ignore the second-hand death threat I'd just received.

"First of all, we've already established that magic is not bullshit."

"Debatable," I scoffed, as he settled in beside me, slowing his pace so we could chat more easily.

He bit his lip playfully before he said, "Second of all, there is a bit of history to unpack."

"I like history." I shrugged. Sure, I'd almost failed my American History class in high school, but I wouldn't mind a story. As long as it detailed what the hell this guy was. "Go on."

Espen took in a big breath, hesitating, and I wondered how much trouble he'd get in for disclosing information about the fae. But he began his tale about them and their magic as we trudged deeper into the verdant forest.

"The fae have lived in Norway for centuries. We are wardens of the natural resources, protecting them from harm, and, in turn, receiving power from them."

"Like a magical ecosystem?"

"Exactly. Our magic is given to us from earth, and we use it to help life flourish."

"So, you're like an elf?" I looked over at him, taking in his rakish hair, thick brows, and solid physique that screamed I-like-the-outdoors. "Do you have pointy ears?" I asked unabashedly. Which was probably rude, but to hell with it. I wanted to know and right now I was picturing—

Espen placed his hand to his left earlobe and a short point appeared. The tips of his ears were indeed sharper than those of humans.

My eyes felt like they were going to pop out of my head and roll down the hill into the fjord as I blatantly stared. "How does that work?"

"Think of it as layers. Most fae have the ability to shift their attire by manipulating a layer of magic over their clothes. The same applies to our ears, but only our ears—like magical evolution to keep our species hidden from threats. This base-level ability is drawn from the air, and can be used by all of us. Some of us, however, are a little stronger and can manipulate more layers. Nora is one such fae. She can manipulate the layer of not only appearance, but some sounds and light."

That would explain how she altered my hearing so I could understand snippets of Norwegian.

"But her sister, Queen Freija, is much stronger in that regard. Each fae faction has their own abilities, too. Forest Fae, like myself, can use magic to help the trees and animals thrive." He stopped walking and I pulled to a halt. Crouching down, he placed his palm against the mossy soil beside the trail. A minuscule flicker of silver light glowed from beneath his hand and he lifted it away. A few seconds later, a tiny speck of green breached the surface—the start of a new plant. My breath caught in my throat, and Espen watched my face closely. I glanced into his eyes, the amber warmth calming and caring. "It will become a skinny birch tree one day."

"That's... amazing," I admitted, in awe of what I'd just witnessed. This wasn't bullshit. Not at all. "What about the others—Øyvin and Nora? Can they do that, too?" I asked, still watching the tiny sapling as it shook off the remaining soil holding it captive.

"Not really," Espen said as he started walking once more. "Each faction has a specialty. Fjell Fae—like Nora—have magic that is rooted in the ground and mountain. Fjell means mountain in Norwegian. And then there are the Fjord Fae, like Øyvin. Their element is water. They can manipulate the element, move it around, breathe underwater, but their primary objective is to keep the fjord clean for the wildlife here."

I took it all in. Shocked and amazed at the magical world that existed beside the one I knew and loved. Plus, their ability to protect nature spoke to a part of my soul that loved every iota of the environment—my photography muse. "What about the stuff I caught on camera?"

"The silver flare you saw is our magic made visible. You can see flickers of it from time to time, but during a transfer there is no way to hide the power."

"Why would someone transfer their power to another?" I asked, stepping over a mossy log that had fallen across the path.

"It's a good question," he replied, pressing on through the dense woods. "One we asked ourselves twenty years ago when it first happened. But the best theories are to harm the Queen of the Fjell or the King of the Fjord. The royals' magic is intertwined with the wellbeing of the entity and fae they protect, so by attacking said entity, it would be slightly easier to overthrow a monarch.

"Last time," He paused, his head down. "Last time things didn't end well. Forest Queen Ragnhild was weakened by illegal transfers and then killed in battle by a southern faction of the Forest Fae—relatives of ours from the southern coast of Norway. The uprising was unusual, but not unheard of, in our history. What *was* alarming was the speed with which they attacked and how easily she was killed. It was as if someone had drained her and her forces before the war began. Both Queen Ragnhild and my mentor, Mads, died in the battle that also took out two hundred Forest Fae."

Espen's shoulders had slumped, his steps faltering slightly, as he spoke. The weight of what happened had clearly taken a toll on him. Inhaling a gulp of damp air, I said, "I'm sorry for your loss."

He nodded, his eyes somewhat distant as he waved his hand, dismissing my words.

"Did the Forest Fae catch whoever was behind the uprising?" I asked gently, curious but cautious of the subject matter. War was never a palatable subject, but the information might be helpful to this investigation.

Espen stepped out into a tiny clearing off the side of the trail and I followed, brushing aside some pine tree limbs.

"We didn't." He traipsed across the open space covered in mossy boulders and clusters of tall grass then paused. The sun seeped into this slanted spot, giving us a slight view of the fjord and the mountain on the other side—where I'd taken the troublesome photo.

"What happened afterward?" I rested my butt on a rock and watched him gaze into the treeline behind us.

"I brought the living back home, and, with the guidance of some Forest Fae elders—the Council—our faction formed an alliance with Queen Freija and the Fjell Fae."

I swallowed the lump in my throat at his insinuation, and my chest tightened. He'd been there. He'd witnessed the slaughter of 200 of his people, the death of his Queen and mentor. Fucking hell.

"Is she the Queen of the Forest now, then?"

He shook his head. "We aligned with the Fjell for greater protection from this happening again, and as thanks for the assistance they provided after the battle. You could say we have a close friendship instead of assimilating our two factions. We coexist harmoniously."

"What about leadership? Was your Queen... Ragnhild... replaced?" This had to be the most attentive I'd ever been during a history lesson, but I couldn't stop—I wanted to know more. I was intrigued by their powers, leadership system, and how they'd resided within human society without being exposed.

"No," he said firmly, turning his warm gaze to me. "There is no ruler. We have the Council and my people placed their trust in me to be a representative and protector for them. Mads, the previous Head Guard of the Forest Fae, was training me as his successor. The role was handed to me upon his death," Espen explained, a hint of melancholy in his tone.

He shook his head, then his arms, as if shaking away the weight on his shoulders alongside the heavy memories. "Enough of that. What is your favorite yoga pose?"

The whiplash again. But Espen smiled like it was his usual tactic to throw people off or pivot the subject to a happier one. He kept bringing up yoga though, so maybe he was serious about doing it in his free time... or perhaps he was obsessed with a different kind of *yoga*. Either way, I chuckled and thought through the poses I knew from watching videos online. I wasn't overly flexible, but there was always one position that I enjoyed more than the others. "Corpse."

Espen snickered and licked his bottom lip.

"What about you?" I asked, tearing my eyes from his mouth.

He took a step back and lifted one foot, resting it against his other thigh. Then he brought his hands to his chest in a perfect prayer position. "Tree pose." He beamed.

I let out another bubble of laughter, the mood around us officially lifted. "Should have guessed. You're a tree hugger aren't you?"

"I am," he admitted with a smile, still holding his balance, not even swaying slightly. "You should try it. Really good for the complexion."

"Tree pose or hugging trees?"

"Both."

"How is hugging a plant good for my skin?" I stood from the boulder.

He pointed to a thick pine tree and raised his brows.

I sighed and conceded to his madness. Rolling my eyes, I wandered over to the large tree and wrapped my arms around its trunk. The bark was rough beneath my cheek and it smelled earthy and damp.

"See? Doesn't that make you feel good?" he said, not moving an inch.

"Sure, but what the fuck is it supposed to do for my wrinkles and adult acne?" It should be illegal to have *both* acne and wrinkles simultaneously.

If hugging this thing would rid me of those suckers, I'd sleep out here. I pulled away from the tree, glanced at its rough outer layer, and stopped breathing for a second.

Silver.

Silver marks, like knife slashes, were etched into the thick brown bark.

"Espen, this is the spot I photographed, isn't it?"

"Should be, yes."

"Look at this."

He appeared behind me. Reaching over my shoulder, he ran his hand over the markings. "Shit."

11

LENNIE

Espen's warm breath tickled against my ear as he pulled his hand away from the tree. Waves of tension rolled off him, and the change in his easy-going personality was jarring. I didn't dare move. Standing at my back, he scanned the tree trunk's silver scars. The marks were thin—practically invisible at a distance—but deep. At this vantage point you could easily see them criss-crossing the thick bark.

I glanced over my shoulder, lifting my eyes to Espen's face. Gone was the playful yogi I'd come to know. That bubbly man had been replaced with the warrior from today's history lesson—one who had seen far more death than I could comprehend. His thick eyebrows were drawn into a firm line, jaw clenched.

"How bad is it?" I whispered into the few inches between our bodies, the warmth from his chest shielding me slightly from the damp air around us.

His darkened eyes met mine. "As bad as it was twenty years ago."

My stomach muscles tightened and I swallowed the lump that had formed in my throat.

"Can you take a photo of this, please?" Espen asked softly, taking a step back into the clearing.

With a nod, I removed the lens cap from my camera, slipping it into my jacket pocket so I wouldn't lose it again. I started snapping away, making sure I got some wide shots, and turned on the macro function for more detailed close-ups.

While I documented the evidence on the tree, Espen scanned the other flora in the clearing—checking for more scars.

"Over here," he said, crouched down beside a boulder and a tree on the other side of the open space. Beside the gray rock was a bolt of ferns he held to one side to reveal his findings. Across the base of this withering tree were more tiny silver scratches. I took some more photos, making sure to get a couple from different angles, in hopes that it might help Espen's investigation.

"Can you heal them?" I asked, nodding at the marks.

Espen tilted his head from one side and then the other, like he was uncertain. He brushed his palm over one of the lines. My heart rate sped up, hopeful to see his magic work wonders again. I watched closely as a faint glow emitted from his hand, then petered out. Espen pulled away and rose to his feet with a sigh, and my shoulders fell as air whooshed out of me. The sliver he tried to heal had puckered, like it wanted to close up, but couldn't quite do it.

He shook his head lightly as he stared at the marks. "If it needs more energy than that, then I'm afraid the marks are permanent... again."

I stilled, my breaths an even tempo as I took in what he was saying. History was repeating itself, and someone—or some*thing*—was out there in the woods harming the land and attempting to harm the fae. Just the thought had my veins humming with anger.

"These scars are a result of the immense amount of magic that was illegally transferred from one fae to another," Espen explained, wiping his hand across his short beard. "That flare in your photo was basically an explosion of magic that left marks on things around it." He pointed back to the injured tree.

"What can you do?"

"Catch them before—" He spun, amber eyes darkening as his gaze swept over the clearing.

A bush rustled to my left, and a flurry of nervous energy took over my body as I turned toward the sound. I dropped my camera, letting it hang around my neck, so I could free my hands.

Espen stepped toward the noise.

Another rustle sounded from behind me, and I spun, putting my feet into a ready-position like I was about to tackle one of my brothers in a full-blown wrestling match in the living room. As the only girl in a family of football players, I had my fair share of practice.

"You found them, then," a low voice rumbled as someone stepped out from the shadows in front of me.

The someone was the shape of a behemoth Asshole.

"What the fuck are you playing at?" I grumbled at Øyvin as I dropped my fisted hands back down to my side, adrenaline still pumping into my veins. He gave me a minute smile that most certainly wasn't friendly. Nah, that shit was definitely an "I don't care" half-grin I'd seen my brothers' ex-girlfriends give me when I was a kid and trying to get the boys' attention. It was belittling and dismissive, and I despised it. Those feelings were pretty damn accurate for this guy, too.

He wore his large navy rain jacket, cargo pants, and big hiking boots that looked like they could cause severe damage to the terrain.

Espen leaned against the large boulder again as Øyvin stepped into the light of the clearing, leaving me near the shadows. "You're brave for sneaking up on her like that."

Øyvin scoffed. "Why?"

"Lennie punches first, asks questions later. And she can throw a hell of a punch."

Øyvin leered at me. I gave him my best "fuck you" smile—the same one I'd given the ladies at church before my Mom decided I should stay at home on Sunday mornings. "Espen learned first hand."

He glanced over at Espen, who was beaming from ear to ear.

"She hit you?" Øyvin raised a brow before returning his icy glare to me. "You should lock her up for that."

"I considered it," Espen replied. "But I couldn't have her spouting about silver shiny things in the woods, now could I? Figured I'd keep an eye on her myself, have her help with the investigation."

And for that I was grateful as I wasn't excited to see the inside of a Norwegian prison.

"What are you doing up here anyway?" I asked Øyvin, my sass level as high as a fucking eagle on the hunt. I pulled the lens cap out of my pocket and clicked it back into place on the camera.

"I came to see the marks for myself," Øyvin said matter-of-factly. "I wanted to see if our scouts' report was true."

"It was," Espen said with a hint of gloom. I kind of missed the happy-go-lucky version of him. Not that there was anything wrong with this Espen, but, for some reason, I liked his smile and bubbly attitude.

Espen nodded at the tree behind me and then to the one I'd hugged on the other side of the clearing. "Someone stood there and the other stood there," he said. "There are some other marks, but the largest clusters are at those two points."

"Do you have any idea who would do something like this?" I asked, aiming my question at the blond-haired jerk.

Øyvin's blue eyes snapped to mine, and I felt an onslaught of animosity and annoyance from his gaze. The feeling was mutual.

He raised his large hands and said, "It wasn't me or my men."

My men? Was this dick the King of the Fjord?

"Does King Balder know how bad it is?" Espen asked, and I was relieved that this Øyvin-schmuck wasn't fae royalty.

Øyvin shook his head, his short sandy hair barely shifting with the movement. "Balder sent me to confirm the findings from our scouts. I'll make my official report today. He knows I'm here to have a look." He strode across to the tree I'd hugged and grazed his large knuckles across the lacerated bark.

Espen and I watched him closely as he surveyed the damage there, poking and prodding at the scars. Øyvin then backtracked to where I was standing, passing me as if I didn't exist, and scanned the other marks. He said nothing while conducting his own research of the evidence. After five minutes of pure silence, Øyvin let out a low grumble and ran his hand through his hair.

"I thought the same," Espen said, as Øyvin moved to stand between us, his back toward me.

"Care to enlighten the human?" I said, feeling slightly weirded out by using the word "human." Sure, it was accurate, but it still felt odd talking to these creatures that also looked human, but were very much *not*.

I couldn't see Øyvin's response to my snarkiness, but knowing what little I did about the asshole, it was probably an eye roll or a grunt.

Espen, on the other hand, gave me a brief smile, as if he were happy to have me there, but not so happy about the information he was about to share. "The amount of fae magic that was transferred was enough to cause lasting damage to the surroundings and the perpetrators," he said, reminding me of the fact that he couldn't heal these scars. "It was a big transfer that is likely trying to weaken one or both of the remaining fae royalty—or my own people, again—by taking magic that is meant for healing our environment. Think of it as a break in the ecosystem."

I nodded, recalling the magic process he'd mentioned earlier—how the fae were wardens of the natural resources.

"The illegal transfer is one or more fae cycling power *away* from where it is supposed to go—the forest, mountain, or fjord—and funneling their magic elsewhere instead, thus weakening its intended environment."

"Can you tell who did it from these marks, or maybe from the photos?" I pointed at my camera.

"Maybe." Espen shrugged. "I can't be certain until I see the photos and can zoom in."

Øyvin straightened and strode to the trail at the south end of the little clearing. "Our source of magic is the same. It's our abilities and how we use the magic that makes us different."

Espen nodded, confirming Øyvin's statement. "We should go see if there is anything else on those photos. It might tell us more about the culprit."

"Okay," I agreed, equally curious as to what we would find when I uploaded the images to my computer.

"Perhaps we can grab your laptop or cables and head to my house to look at them. That way we can keep Solveig out of this. I can make us lunch, too." Espen stood from the boulder and motioned toward the trail head.

I nodded, never one to turn down a free meal.

"I'm heading back to the fjord," Øyvin grumbled, already striding back into the woods.

"Give my regards to the King," Espen said, as the Fjord Fae trudged off through the trees, leaving us to our work.

12

ØYVIN

The American was a problem and infuriating. The former, because she'd been exposed to our world, even before Espen had dragged her into it head-first. And the latter, because of her fucking attitude. I didn't like it.

Irritation fueled me as I walked away from where I'd left her with Espen, reaching the edge of the fjord at a point where it bent out of sight of the town. The thick brush here along the shore hid me from any onlookers and was an ideal entrance point to the Fjord Fae domain beneath the surface. I stepped into the cold, my boots sloshing into the slate-blue waters. Once I was waist-deep, I pushed off from the bank and dove under. The fjord enveloped me in her chilly embrace, the cool temperature having no effect on me thanks to my being a Fjord Fae, and my muscles finally relaxed after my run-in with Espen and Lennie.

Instantly, my senses changed. Gone were the sights, smells, and sounds of the human world above. Instead, the fjord sang her song to me—a quiet melody of swishes and movement from the creatures that called it home. The area closest to the surface was clear, tiny fish the size of sardines scuttling behind rocks as I passed, but the deeper I went, the darker and murkier the water became.

I pushed the water around me with a gentle nudge of my power, having already created a thin layer of air that would keep me dry. Descending deeper into the profound abyss, the sun no-longer reaching these dark depths, I swept my hands forward and then back, helping me reach my destination quicker than merely propelling myself with power. While I could swim like humans did, using my Fjord Fae powers in tandem with the usual swimming motions tripled my speed—pushing me on faster than any land-dwelling creature.

After a few minutes, a litany of cave entrances came into view. Wholly invisible to the human eye or any fishing sonar—thanks to a layer of magic from King Balder—the subterranean pockets were the entrances of homes and the royal household. Not all of the Fjord Fae lived underwater here—some made homes out in the open under bubbles of air made to look like rocks on the fjord bed and some lived above the surface, like me—but most lived in the rocks along the jagged edges of the deep water, where the mountain above met the watery valley below.

Silvery lights flickered near the entrances to the caves, and I aimed for the largest one which had rugged carvings of aquatic figures and animals above the archway. A carving of a scaled serpent curled around the entry with fish of all shapes and sizes dancing around it, desperately avoiding its sharp maw. The entire artistic display was a show of power fit for royalty. Balder and his ancestors had lived here for centuries. It always left me in awe of how this home—a veritable palace—could survive not only the pressure of the fjord, but the weight of the mountain above it.

I brushed my hands across the top of the entry and swung my legs into the pocket of air as I'd done so many times before. The motion sent me flying inward, and I landed on my feet, thumping onto the dry ground within the hall. The soldiers guarding the entrance nodded to me in greeting, standing straighter in their gray and navy-blue uniforms, their short capes draped from one shoulder. I was their boss's boss, and had been for the past century. I expected the utmost respect from my men, and always got it. In turn, I respected and would always thank them for their willingness to serve their King and fellow Fjord Fae. We rarely saw battle anymore, but the threat of instability always lingered.

I shook off the droplets of water that seeped into my pants when I first submerged, and strode into the King's home, completely dried off.

People bustled past, each one busy with their work for the day as I wove deeper into Balder's domain. The hallways down here were similar to the tunnels in the mountains above in Fjell Fae territory, but where they had rocky walls, ours were polished smooth. Specks of white quartz shimmered within the mottled stone walls, and rugged wooden artwork, from eels hiding in reeds to salmon jumping, decorated the space. A minute later, I reached my destination—the king's chambers. I strode into the wing that housed the throne room, Balder's offices, a meeting room, and my own office when I wanted to get some work done down here. I'd decided long ago that I preferred living above the water. It wasn't so much that I didn't like living beneath the surface—I did, it was homey—but I liked having the separation between where I lived and worked.

I found Balder in his study sitting behind his large wooden desk that looked like something he'd plundered from an old ship, like a lot of the furniture did here in our underwater world. The king leaned forward in his chair, reviewing some charts and had an antique atlas open on his desk, not bothering to look up when I entered.

I stood just inside the doorway, waiting for his cue to speak. Balder was one of the oldest fae of the entire fjord region, but you'd never know it from the way he looked or moved. With a thick scraggly blond-and-silver beard, eyes the color of algae, sharp features, and the countenance and build of a warrior, Balder was a fae that shouldn't be crossed.

Still studying the charts in front of him, Balder said, "Did you see the marks for yourself?" His voice had a low rumbling timbre that could set off waves.

"Yes, sir," I replied as he looked up and pushed aside the papers he'd been examining. "And it is as we suspected. There was indeed an illegal transfer from one fae to another. The scars on the trees were thin, but deep. Looked like Espen or some other Forest Fae had tried to heal one of them. The line had puckered, but didn't close."

Balder twitched his nose. "That is concerning."

I nodded in agreement. If the Forest Fae couldn't heal the trees, then no one could. "I haven't received any reports from my men of weakened shields or power failures in our territory."

"That's good," Balder sighed, leaning back in his chair with his hands steepled in front of him. "We can't let the pollution wall down. We can't allow the humans to find us down here. Let them think any blips on their radar are their beloved creatures from folktales and myth."

I nodded again. Humans had a tendency to explain the unexplainable with tales of beings that would haunt their dreams. From the creepy Nøkken that would lure you into bodies of fresh-water, to the trolls that dwelled within the dense woods that would eat wayward children who couldn't answer a complicated riddle. While slightly inaccurate, these stories helped us stay hidden.

Taking a deep breath, I steadied my resolve to ask my next question. I doubted it would see my head severed, but Balder had moods, and my predecessor had found an unsavory one the day I was appointed Head Guard. "Have you felt any weakening of your powers?"

Balder sucked on his teeth and glanced around the room full of bookcases and trinkets, even a chessboard abandoned mid-game. "No, I haven't noticed anything. But, I'm forever battling the tainted sources in the waterways to our west. Those humans and their oil," he grumbled.

At the far entrance to the fjord, kilometers upon kilometers away from Skolvik, where the ocean met the country, the humans had shredded the shoreline, replacing the pristine land with equipment, refineries, and factories for their oil. Much of the inky-liquid was brought in from the oil rigs in the North Atlantic, but there were often little spills and the human element caused immense damage to the waterways. It was a never ending fight for us to keep the waters running clean, and stop the pollution from flowing further down the fjord. We'd even erected a magical wall beneath the surface to buffet any pollutants and keep the inner fjord untainted.

"Glad to hear that you are okay, but please let me know if you want me to increase our efforts on the wall to keep the pollution at bay. While none of us are as strong as you, we can pair some of our soldiers up. I will not have you weakened with this transfer business happening."

Balder nodded, his eyes slightly distant, as he considered my suggestion. As the most powerful of the Fjord Fae, he used layers of his magic every day in an effort to keep the pollution out of our waters. Paired with the power from the Fjord soldiers stationed along the western front, and we were almost insurmountable to pollutants, but if we could ease some of the load on our monarch, then I'd gladly move some soldiers around.

"Do it," he said eventually. "If this transfer nonsense escalates, I don't want to find myself unable to protect my people."

"Yes, sir." I gave him a curt nod and made for the exit but stopped as he spoke again.

"And Øyvin." He stood from his chair, his large form towering over the furniture. The fact that he fit into dwellings down here was astonishing—the humans wouldn't be wrong for thinking he was one of their myths if they ever saw him wandering the streets. He rarely left the fjord though. "Let me know about any new developments with the transfer business."

"Of course," I replied and strode from the room, ready to inform my soldiers of their new positions.

13

LENNIE

On our way back to the village, Espen and I stopped at Solveig's house to pick up my laptop and camera cable so we could go over the photos I'd taken of the magical scars on the trees. Then, with the promise of lunch hanging over my head, we wandered back through town toward Espen's house. We passed Oddvar's café, which was bustling with customers, a boutique with silver nordic jewelry in the window, and started to climb a trail that meandered up the hill on the southern side of the fjord.

"There's no road to your house?" I asked, half-jokingly while taking in our surroundings—a copse of pines, curling ferns, and not a hint of gravel or asphalt.

"No," Espen replied from beside me. "I live in a cabin. No roads in or out up here. Just me, nature, and the local wildlife."

I was about to ask him more about the type of animals that lived around here, when we cleared the treeline and our destination came into view. I couldn't contain the gasp that escaped me.

Nestled beside three slim birch trees in a small meadow was a modest log cabin made of dark timber. Its roof was covered in grass, a little chimney jutted up at the back, and tiny square windows looked out over the area. The entire scene was straight out of a fairy tale.

"Yeah, okay, I get the no roads thing," I said as we wandered up the well-trodden path to the front door. I could feel Espen's sense of peace beside me, and that, or the fresh air, had my shoulders and muscles relaxing, too. I wouldn't want anyone to find me up here either.

As he unlocked the door, I turned toward the fjord and gawked at the view from up here. It hadn't felt like we'd climbed that high as we'd hiked away from town, but what I saw took my breath away.

Espen's home offered a clear view of the village and fjord, the water glittering in the dull gray light. You could almost see the entire valley from up here. Even though I'd seen views from my hikes, every time I took in the beauty of my surroundings here I could hardly breathe.

"I know," Espen whispered behind me. "It's beautiful."

I nodded, at a complete loss for words, my fingers itching to photograph the stunning vista. Pictures could never do this view justice, though. It was stunning.

"You hungry?"

I nodded again, drawn by the lure of lunch, and followed him inside.

Espen's home smelled like the forest had taken up roots indoors, and I kind of liked it. Inside the cabin was a small sofa with knitted throw pillows, a tiny wooden dining table with two chairs, and a compact kitchen with shelves full of mugs, plates, and spices. Beside the kitchen was a short hallway that looked like it led back to a bedroom and bathroom.

We both unlaced our boots by the front door and pulled them off, setting them on a floor tray to avoid tracking in too much dirt. I shucked off my jacket and hung it beside Espen's on a hook on the wall.

Espen made for the kitchen as I flung my backpack off and set it on the sofa. I retrieved my laptop and cable to the sound of clattering noises. Glancing over to the kitchen, I watched with curiosity as Espen pulled out a pot while holding a can of something. I shook my head and set my gear up at the table, putting aside a small potted fern to make room for my stuff.

"Tomato soup?" Espen asked, holding the red-labeled can in one hand and a ladle in the other.

"Yes, please," I grinned.

"Great," he said, setting to work. "Do you like egg in your soup?"

I leaned back in the dining chair and blinked a few times. "Can't say I've ever had egg in my soup." Pho? Sure. Tomato soup? No.

"It's hardboiled," Espen said, dumping the can contents into the pot on the stove. He opened the short refrigerator beneath the counter and retrieved a bowl of brown and white eggs. "I make them ahead of time. Easy snack or I have them in my breakfast sandwiches." He held one up and cast an inquisitive look at me, one brow cocked.

"Ummm, yes, thank you." A sexy man was cooking for me. So, yeah, I'd try whatever he wanted to feed me.

While Espen prepared our lunch, I tightened my ponytail and started transferring today's photos off my camera. As they loaded, I decided to grab the silver flare photo, too, just in case he wanted that for evidence as well.

Espen brought over our meal and included some whole-wheat bread beside the bowl of soup. The hardboiled egg had been sliced, and the yellow-and-white discs floated on the surface. My stomach grumbled at the sight as I pushed aside the laptop—which was still downloading the files—and we dug in.

We ate our lunch in relative silence, hunger getting the best of both of us. While the sight of the egg bobbing in the soup was strange, I couldn't deny the egg-in-soup thing was delicious and perfect after a morning hike.

Once finished, Espen grabbed our bowls, plonked them into the sink, and returned to the table. He pulled his chair around and sat beside me, our knees touching ever so slightly. My breathing hitched at the small contact, and a teasing warmth rose from my chest up my neck, likely tinting my cheeks rosy.

"So, what do we have?" he asked with a slight twinkle in his eyes.

"Not a lot." I shrugged, shaking off the tingling sensation in my hands as I pulled up one of the macro-shots of the silver scars we'd found on the trees today. This zoomed in, the thin, but deep, lines etched across the bark were painful to look at.

One image after another revealed the detailed view of the damage. If I hadn't known about the fae and their magic, I would've thought some animal had come through and marked their territory, but after inspecting the photos, I could tell this was much more sinister. The scar that Espen had tried to heal had puckered, and the bark around it—as well as the other scars—was a withered gray. This tree was dying. The surrounding landscape seemed unharmed though—the ferns and brush were lush and green in comparison.

Any lightness that had exuded from Espen before now faded away as we reviewed each image. My eyes danced back and forth between the images on the screen and Espen sitting at my side, seemingly making mental notes based on his narrowed eyes and the fact he kept biting his bottom lip.

"This is not the norm," he said absentmindedly, his gaze never wavering from the screen.

I reached the last one and was about to ask him if he had any ideas on who might be behind the illegal magic transfer, when a pop sounded behind me and my ponytail fell, my blonde hair brushing across my shoulders. *For fuck's sake.*

Letting out a slow sigh, I reached down and found the broken hair-tie. The elastic had given up completely, and even if I tried tying it in a knot, there was no chance this thing would ever hold my thick-ass locks again.

"Here, let me take that," Espen said, plucking the detritus from between my fingertips. He stood and sauntered into the kitchen, tossing the broken elastic into the garbage. Opening a drawer, he retrieved a ball of cooking rope and a pair of scissors. With a quick glance over his shoulders, he measured out a few lengths of the string, cut it, and returned to the table. "May I?" he asked, standing behind me.

"Sure." Fuck yeah he could play with my hair. That shit was bliss on steroids. I always accepted whenever my nieces wanted to play hair stylist, even after they'd tried to give me bangs a couple of years ago.

Espen gathered my strands into his palms, lightly brushing his fingers across the base of my neck. I held it together and refrained from quivering at his touch, but it was difficult. The way he swept his hands across my hair, gently tugging it all into a bundle, sent little feverish sparks across my skin and I curled my toes.

"I don't think it's someone within the Forest Fae faction," Espen said, drawing me out of my slight arousal.

"Because?"

He fastened the rope around the low ponytail he'd created, the material pulling softly as he looped it into a small bow. Sitting back down, he added, "We wouldn't voluntarily harm the forest like this. I suppose a Forest Fae could've been forced to do so against their will, but... I don't know. There's also a chance that someone, an outsider, an old rival from the Southern or Northern factions may be trying to infiltrate. They'd be foolish to do so, but...." He let out a long sigh, resting his elbow on the table, looking at me with a half-distant gaze.

"Well, at least we've narrowed it down somewhat."

He chuckled, the sound warm and inviting. "Are you always this positive?"

I let out a single laugh. "Fuck no. But it seemed like your usual rays of sunshine had dimmed, so I thought I'd be kind for a moment. Don't expect this to be my norm." I gave him my best smile, and got one in return.

"We don't always have a lot of sunshine around here—it's gray for a large portion of the year—but when we do, it's spectacular." He smiled, but the look didn't reach his eyes, and I wanted to reach across the small space between us to hug him, but I held back. "I try my best to be positive, for myself, for the Forest Fae, for the fjord." He glanced toward the window, and a heaviness settled over his features.

In that moment I saw the leader side of Espen. The one who watched over everything like an eagle in flight, as if he alone was the one to bear the burden. And I guess, in a way, he was. From what he'd told me, I knew he'd been elected defacto leader in his Head Guard role for the Forest Fae after his queen and mentor were both killed in the last war they fought—the last time an illegal transfer like this had gone down.

"You'll figure it out," I said reassuringly. "Do you need these photos transferred to your laptop?"

He shook his head, defeat sagging his shoulders. "Please take care of them for now. I'll let you know if I need to look at them again. Thank you for your help."

I nodded and closed my laptop. "Thank you for telling me about the fae and for helping me catch that ship out of here in five days."

He smiled again and dipped his head, his luscious brown locks falling across his forehead before he swept them back. I twisted my fingers in my lap at the sight.

"You like hiking, yes?" he said, randomly pivoting the subject—which seemed to be a habit of his.

"Yes," I replied, dragging out the vowel.

"Do you want to go hiking with me tomorrow? It's my day off," Espen said as he brushed his fingers across the wood table, removing some invisible lint.

"Sure." It wasn't like I had anything else going on while I waited for the supply boat, and hiking for photography had been the initial plan for this trip all along. "Where should I meet you?"

14

LENNIE

"Coffee? Right before a hike?" I asked Espen as I met up with him outside Oddvar's café, pulling my jacket tighter to shield from the morning chill.

"There's *always* time for coffee," Espen replied with a grin, and my heart skipped a beat, because that was *the* answer—the only statement one should ever mention in regards to a cup o' joe. He handed me a reusable mug, and I took it, welcoming the warmth on my hands in the chill of the morning.

I was glad I'd bought a few new outfits as I looked down at my new pants and dark-blue quarter-zip sweater, plus my rain jacket. Espen wore a pair of dark cargo pants and a dark green jacket that made his eyes pop.

"Is this black?" I asked, recalling the way Oddvar had served it to me before I dared to take a sip of the hot beverage. It also gave me an excuse to look away from the comforting heat in Espen's gaze.

He chuckled. "No, I added a bit of milk and sugar."

"Thank you," I replied, and tested a sip. It was perfect—just the right amount of sweet and roasted caffeinated nectar. "Where are we off to then?"

"I thought we'd head up behind the village into the woods. There are some nice spots that would be perfect for photos." He nodded at my camera hanging around my neck.

I smiled, waving him forward as I took another sip, thankful for the coffee and the company.

We traipsed through the village, headed past little white houses made of wood with slate tile roofs I hadn't seen before, and followed a road with no markings save for a speed limit sign with the number 40 on it. A few minutes outside town, a trail entrance appeared between some bushes, and Espen pointed to it. I wandered toward the path, lost in my thoughts about the Forest Fae.

Espen was a conundrum. Fae, yogi, and magic stuff aside, he always made a point of walking beside me or fell behind, never in front.

He *never* led.

I'd never experienced anything like it with any other guy I'd hung out with before. It was as if he always wanted to be at my side, watching my reaction to the countryside from the corner of his eye. Honest to hell, I didn't mind it. It made me feel like an equal, even if I didn't have magical powers like him.

The trail was wide enough for two, but significantly rocky and gave my thighs a good work out as we climbed higher into the Norwegian forest. The smell of pine, earth, and morning dew wrapped me into a state of awe and comfort. The trees in this part of the forest were covered in a thick layer of moss, but only on one side—the bark on the other side strained to reach the few rays of sunlight that poked through the clouds ever so often.

As the terrain got steeper, I drained the last of my coffee, wanting my hands free in case I fell. Espen took my cup and placed it inside his own before stuffing them into the pouch on the side of his backpack that was vacant.

"You like it here?" Espen asked, filling the serene silence that had fallen between us.

I laughed softly. "I mean... it's not the worst place to get stuck." I waved my hand at the thick forest around us, mesmerized by the majesty of this part of the world. "And I seem to have made friends... kind of."

Espen grinned. "Am *I* the friend? Please say I'm your friend," he added, batting his eyelashes innocently.

I took a moment, pretending to think about it, before saying, "Sure, but let's just say I wasn't expecting to make any friends on this trip. Especially not one with," I waved in his general direction, *"abilities."*

The look on Espen's face was pure glee as he beamed at me. The mischievous expression made me think he probably thought the abilities I mentioned weren't the magical ones he'd already shown me. Typical guy. I eyed him, wondering what it would be like for him to kiss me, for this tension that was building between us to pull me under.

"You were not what I was expecting when I heard a tourist missed the boat."

"What were you expecting?" I asked, stepping onto a rocky outcrop near a wood-and-rope bridge. I glanced down into the deep ravine below, the sound of crashing water drifting upward with the mist.

"I was expecting a cheerleader," he said, drawing my attention away from the sharp drop. "The typical American stereotype."

I scoffed and took a few steps back to where Espen stood beside the bridge. "Well, I was a cheerleader for a little while. My Mom desperately wanted me in a skirt with pom poms at my brothers' football games. They all played at one point, and adding a cheerleader would complete her perfect little sporty family."

"A little while?" He arched a brow in question.

"I got kicked off the team for unsportsman-like conduct." I shrugged. It wasn't my finest moment, but you know, whatever. Shit happens.

Espen chuckled, shaking his head. "What did you do?"

I scrunched my nose as the memory came back to me. "The head cheerleader, Melissa, used a nasty word for me and my friend, saying we belonged at the bottom of the pyramid because of our size."

"That's mean," Espen replied, but narrowed his eyes at me. "What did you do, Lennie?"

I let out a long sigh. "I cut off her ponytail." Even in my memories, I could hear the screaming voices of both Melissa and her mother as I did it, see my mother's appalled expression as she apologized profusely, dragging my smug ass off the field. But really, Melissa had looked better with a bob and I doubt she ever called anyone fat again. I did that bitch a favor.

"Wait, how old were you?" Espen asked, pulling out his water bottle and taking a sip.

I crossed my arms. "Eight."

Espen coughed, choking on his drink. "Remind me to never let you near sharp objects," he said, waving his index finger at me.

"You're fine. Just don't ask me to be the base of the pyramid."

"I would never do such a thing. You always deserve to be on top." He winked, and something fluttered in my stomach. I grabbed my own water bottle and occupied my mouth by drinking and avoiding saying anything else that might get me into trouble... or into his bed.

We were just friends.

I didn't have the hots for a sexy-troll-magic-fae-thing.

After our quick stop for a drink, we continued over the bridge and eventually reached a clearing. The forest thinned, parting to reveal a farm and field, right there on the slopes of the damn mountain. I'd grown up in farm country, but the flat fields in Ohio did not look like this.

I grabbed my camera off my chest and prepared to take some photos. Espen stepped up to the old wooden gate nestled between the rocky wall-turned-fence that contained a flock of sheep. I took a quick photo of him before angling the camera at the fluffy livestock that grazed peacefully in the lush green grass.

"You coming?" Espen asked and I glanced over to where he was now standing on the other side of the rock-wall!

"What the fuck are you doing?" I yelled, frantically looking around for anyone that could claim he was trespassing.

"Hiking." He shrugged. "Why the panic?"

"Because you're trespassing on farmland," I whisper shouted as my heart raced. One didn't grow up in rural America without a healthy fear of being shot in the ass for trespassing.

He furrowed his brow, narrowing his eyes at me, before nodding in realization. "Doesn't work the same way here."

"What the fuck are you talking about?" I asked, stepping up in front of him, staying on the correct side of the barrier. This trip had gone off the rails already, and I didn't need any other problems—like a bullet to the butt.

He crossed his arms and tilted his head. "Here in Norway we have a rule called *allemannsretten.*"

"The what now?" I raised my brows, blinking rapidly. Nora's magical layer of translation didn't work on that last bit I guessed, because all I heard were garbled letters and noises.

"*Allemannsretten* gives people the right to roam or, in more legal terms, the right of access to nature. Essentially, the land belongs to all the people of Norway, and everyone has a right to use it without harming it. We are all taught to respect property, especially farmland. Usually, agricultural fields are not part of the law, but lucky for us, part of my job with the local police includes acting as the Ranger for this area. I also know the owner." He beamed, shifting his head toward a small wooden building across the meadow. "As long as we respect his land, do not disturb the animals, and close the gate, we may walk through."

That was a concept that did not exist at all in the US, and definitely not in Ohio.

"So, you can walk and hike anywhere you want?" I asked, still somewhat skeptical of the idea and wary of the odds that I could get in trouble... even if I was hiking with a magical-yogi-cop.

"Within reason, yes." Espen nodded. "You must pick up after yourself, do no harm to nature, and do not camp within five hundred feet of a residence or building." He rattled off the facts like he'd memorized the law, which he probably had considering his line of work as both cop and ranger.

"That simple?"

"That simple." He set his hands on his hips, and a slow smirk spread across his face. "Now, are you going to join me, or do you not have enough stamina to continue to our destination?"

I turned off my camera and let it hang against my chest before replying with a smug grin of my own. "Oh, honey. I've got stamina for days."

Espen quirked a brow, his amber eyes gleaming. "Let's go then."

The rest of our walk to Espen's secret destination was pleasant, but sneakily uphill in a lot of places. One second I thought the terrain had leveled out, the next my thighs were burning. We wandered—carefully—through a few more tiny fields, remembering to close the gates we used, and narrowly avoiding piles of sheep shit. The entire time, Espen pointed out little hidden gems for me to photograph or showed me berries that were safe to pick, and which were best left for the animals.

It wasn't long after his lecture about the tart but tasty cowberries that I heard a rumbling noise—like a boulder continuously tumbling down a rocky facade. Curiosity drove me forward until we turned past a thick copse of trees and found the source of the noise.

A massive waterfall.

Gallons of water crested over the cliff high above us, crashing down into a rocky ravine. Espen pointed to a little outcrop beside us that was slightly sheltered from the mist that now coated me from head to boot, and I aimed in that direction.

Retreating away from the edge, I plonked down on the mossy soil, removed my backpack, and grabbed my raincover for my camera. It had taken years of saving to buy this camera—the love of my life—to replace the old one that my grandmother had given me, and I treated it like the precious piece of equipment that it was. My baby could handle some moisture, but the amount of water in the air here wasn't safe. I buttoned it up to protect it from the elements and grabbed a few shots from this vantage point before putting the camera away again as my stomach grumbled. It had been several hours since we set-off, and the uphill hike had left me starving.

Following my same train of thought, Espen pulled out the picnic spread that he'd prepared for us. The two granola bars I still had in my backpack were measly in comparison, so I shoved them back into my bag. I grinned as Espen handed me a sandwich with butter, ham, and cucumber. It was surprisingly delicious, and, once devoured, Espen pulled out a small chocolate bar for each of us.

"Chocolate? On a hike?" I said, taking the sugary goodness with gratitude. Chocolate was right up there with coffee for me in the "never turn it down" category.

"It's a tradition in Norway." Espen tore into his own bar. "Plus we need the sugar high for the hike back down."

The bar was only three small squares, but I wasn't complaining as the dark chocolate melted in my mouth.

After our lunch and some more water, I snapped some photos of the waterfall, capturing how the dim light reflected off the mist casting rainbow effects through the haze. Espen watched me from his spot on the ground, and, while I'd normally find it annoying to have someone monitoring me that closely while I photographed, for some reason I liked his attention.

Once we'd packed up, we headed back to the trail and started our descent.

"How'd you get into yoga?" I asked, breaching the comfortable silence between us.

Espen kept pace beside me, matching my smaller strides even though he had long legs and was a good five inches taller than my five foot six stature. "My sisters always liked yoga, so that's where it initially started. But, once I joined Ragnhild's guard, I started doing it more regularly as part of my training regimen. It keeps me calm and grounded, helps me focus too," Espen explained. "I always enjoy a good workout. How about you?"

My brows flew skyward. "Do I like working out?"

He nodded, motioning me to answer the question.

"Yeah, I'm not a regular at the gym, but I couldn't grow up around my brothers and not be into sports and athleticism in some form." I let out a low chuckle. Growing up with Andrew, Jared, and Ryan had most definitely shaped me into an athlete... but I rebelled a bit there, too. I never stuck to a sport very long. "I tried soccer for a year, swimming for a week, and softball for a couple of years. My Mom refused to let me try gymnastics after the cheer debacle."

Espen shook his head and laughed. "Your childhood sounds a lot different than mine."

"I mean, you're old, and magic, so I'd imagine it was."

He flicked his brows at the mention of his age. "Yes, my 'childhood' was a couple hundred years ago during an era that was vastly different than the one we live in now."

"Horse drawn carriages and shit?" I asked, half teasing, half curious.

"Try horse drawn sleighs and dinner by candlelight," he replied, tilting his head as if recalling the memories from long ago. "But you're not wrong about the differences. As children, we are raised with growing responsibilities. Everyone contributes to the Forest, learning from it as we both grow and change. Children are given more freedom, but we don't do sports the way you do. Sure, some kids these days join the humans for games of *soccer*," he said, intonating the word we Americans used for the sport known as football in the rest of the world. I rolled my eyes at him, before he laughed and continued his story. "But it isn't as common. We still spend a lot of time outdoors until we are of age to take on fae jobs or further integrate into the human world."

"What kind of jobs do your people have?" I asked, stepping around a slick boulder.

"It varies based on abilities and level of power." He shrugged. "Some are healers, some plant new specimens, others become guards or farmers or wildlife rangers."

"Did you have a job before you became a guard?"

Espen nodded. "I was originally a healer as the forest responded well to my magic. Then, when I enlisted in the guard, word got out regarding my skills." He waggled his brows at me, and I chuckled. "Queen Ragnhild personally requested that I be mentored by her Head Guard." Espen stepped behind me as the bridge we'd returned to was too narrow to cross side-by-side.

"So, Mads became your mentor and you trained with him to one day take on the role?" I said as I walked onto the bridge.

"Exactly," Espend replied. "Well done for remembering his name."

Honestly, I was just as shocked as he was that I'd remembered his mentor's name. I'd never been good with names—usually, they went in one ear and out the other, never getting caught by memory cells within my brain. Why this one stuck, I had no idea.

"Well, don't expect miracles. What's your name aga—"

My words cut off as I dropped, falling between two wood boards that snapped beneath my feet.

Air was sucked from my lungs, and I couldn't even scream as some-thing caught my wrist before I fell into the misty ravine below.

Gasping, I looked up. Espen lay panting on his stomach, his head and shoulders peeking through the broken board I'd just fallen through. He tightened his grip around my wrist, knuckles white, eyes wide.

"Don't wriggle," he said through gritted teeth.

I didn't dare nod or move, but my heart beat so hard I was surprised my whole body didn't jerk with each beat. I just hoped he could see my agreement in my eyes, because they felt as wide as the chasm I now dangled above.

Slowly and steadily, Espen began to peel himself off the wood-planks on the bridge, carefully lifting me with one arm—which was wholly impressive, no matter my size—but I didn't dare say a word. He reached his other hand down. "Grab on, gently."

I lifted my right arm and grasped his hand, wrapping my fingers around his wrist. He continued pulling me up in movements so slow, they felt like a lifetime. Surely my ribs were bruised from the slamming of my heart. As my head reached the hole I'd fallen through, Espen grunted and pulled quickly. I was hoisted up, lightly scraping my ass across the boards that remained before he set me on my feet. Not waiting a second longer, I was suddenly enveloped in Espen's arms. I clung to him, hitching my legs around his torso, as he leaped across the hole and sprinted across the rest of the bridge.

We reached the other side, both of us panting and holding on to each other for dear life. He didn't stop until we stood with my back against a tall pine. Seconds ticked by as we caught our breath, Espen with his legs spread into a triangle, one hand braced against the tree, while his other hand held my thigh. My calves were still firmly crossed behind his back, as I sucked in lungfuls of air, and my camera was safely nestled between us.

"Are you okay?" he asked, his warm gaze meeting mine.

"I will be... but I might have pissed my pants." I couldn't feel anything warm and wet down there, but the adrenaline coursing through my veins was numbing me to all sensations, except Espen's hand that was seriously close to cupping my butt.

"I don't smell anything," he said, his lips curving into a cheeky smile.

"Fae have heightened smell, too?" I panted.

"In some cases."

I bit my lip and hoped I didn't reek of sweat.

Espen flicked his gaze to my lips, then let out a throaty grunt and set me down on my feet. He took two steps back and ran his hand through his dark hair. "Ummm... I need to secure the site."

I nodded, swallowing the tight lump in my throat and shaking off the tingly sensation in my limbs.

Espen straightened up and pulled off his backpack. He retrieved a knot of neon-pink rope and began to untie it. Creating a loop in one end, he slid the circle of rope over one of the bridge posts before crossing down to the base of the other post, letting the bright fiber block the entrance to the passage. By the time he was done, the entrance was cordoned with a big neon-pink X that would hopefully stop anyone from using the bridge.

"That should be okay until we can send a crew up to fix it," he said, returning to me and hoisting his bag onto his back again.

I agreed. "Let's get back to town before it gets dark or I get eaten by a bear."

Espen nodded. "Or a wolf."

The hike back down was considerably quicker and we made good time. The setting sun's rays bounced off slate rooftops and windows as we left the trail and entered the far end of the village. Sweat beaded at my neck and I unzipped my jacket to let in the light breeze. I was hyper-aware of how desperately I needed to shower and wash my armpits after almost dying. I pulled my hair into a ponytail to stop it from sticking to my cheeks.

As we traipsed through town toward the harbor where we'd part ways, the sound of sirens met my ears. I glanced over at Espen in question. His brow was furrowed and he picked up his pace, striding ahead of me—for the first time today—toward the noise. I followed, staying right on his heels, until we found the reason for the siren.

On the edge of town, near the tourist center by the harbor, was a massive rock slide.

15

ESPEN

Boulders the size of small cars were strewn across the southern road, blocking it entirely as they piled against the steep incline of the mountain. The swath of material was as tall as a building at its highest point, with trees and debris scattered all around.

I ran up to the scene, Lennie right behind me, and found my colleagues securing the area.

"Stay here," I said firmly to Lennie. She did as requested, which was rather miraculous considering her obstinate personality. But, then again, the place was teeming with police officers, and she'd already made it clear how often she landed in trouble.

I strode over to the chief of police, Bente, a stoic no-nonsense woman with a shock of white hair and a dark sense of humor that was only on display during night-shifts or at the bar when she had the day off. She was always a joy to spend time with, and a great boss. "Any injuries?" I asked.

"Espen." She nodded in greeting. "No, thankfully not."

"When did it happen?"

"About twenty minutes ago," she said, her eyes landing on me briefly before she continued surveying the area and the other officers corralling bystanders. They were using one of the police cars, white with neon-yellow stripes, as a makeshift barrier until better barricades could be put up.

"What can I do?"

"It's your day off, but I need everyone's help." She gave me a tight smile that was more of an apology than anything else.

"That's okay. This is bad," I said, because it really was. This was the main road in and out of town. With this blocked, and the hillside insecure, we had a serious safety issue on our hands. Plus, the size of the rockslide would take a week or more to clear.

Bente gave me a quick nod. "Thank you. Help the boys move the people further back, and block any entry to the tourist center. I cannot have anyone going in there in case there are more landslides into the fjord."

"Yes, boss." I spun on my heel and headed back to Lennie, who was tinkering with her camera and completely oblivious to the other man walking up behind her. I should've probably warned her, but I also wouldn't mind watching her punch Øyvin in the stomach if he caught her off-guard.

"Lennie," the Fjord Fae said, unfortunately announcing his presence before the American could take a swing.

She turned and glared at him.

"Øyvin," I said in greeting as I joined them. "Any damage below?" From what I'd seen, the landslide had washed slightly into the fjord.

"Not too bad," Øyvin replied, his straw-like hair fluttering slightly in the light breeze. "Some fish habitat was damaged, but the material seems to have settled near the water line with minimal damage further beneath the surface." He spoke firmly, but not too loud. Most of the humans recognized him as a quasi-harbor master, but he didn't have an official job in the human world. King Balder kept him on a tight leash, and his work to secure and protect the fjord waters was a daily challenge with the number of pollutants further down the passage.

"Good," Lennie and I said at the same time. A small smile graced her lips briefly, before it turned back into a snarl as she watched Øyvin.

"Well, looks like you definitely won't be leaving town by car," Øyvin said, aiming his comment at Lennie.

She rolled her eyes at him, but he was right. With the road blocked, her only option really would be the supply ship that arrived in four days.

"I need to stay here and help," I said, turning to Lennie. "Thank you for joining me on a hike today. I'm sorry our day ended like this."

She smiled softly. "More like thank *you*."

"Of course." I grinned, glad that I'd been able to save her from falling to her death when the bridge broke. The entire incident had left me on edge. Thankfully the panic had subsided from the sheer terror I'd felt when I saw her drop in front of me. I couldn't remember another time I'd been so glad I had fast reflexes.

Lennie stepped back and straightened up, almost like she was shaking free of something. The memory of us pressed together against the tree perhaps? Because that vision had been playing on repeat in my mind the entire trek back to town. "I'm gonna head home and shower," she announced. "Good luck."

She spun, sneered at Øyvin, and walked away, blonde ponytail swishing behind her.

"You think this is related?" Øyvin asked, referencing the magic investigation and drawing my focus away from Lennie's backside.

"Maybe," I said, running my hand through my hair. "But it's not like it's unheard of around here either."

He huffed and crossed his arms. We surveyed the scene for a moment in pure silence before he said, "I don't like it."

Admittedly, neither did I. Either it was sheer coincidence that the timing of the rockslide had happened so close to the illegal transfer that had damaged the woods, or something else was going on. "Whatever it was, I need to get to work. I'll let you know if I find anything... interesting."

Øyvin grunted—never one for many words or lengthy goodbyes—and wandered back into the village.

The next few hours were spent herding humans away from the debris, erecting blockades and fencing to stop people entering the area, and calling the various agencies that needed to be notified and brought in to assist with the clean-up.

By the time I was able to stand still for more than two minutes, the sun had set and I was exhausted. The hike we did this morning wasn't easy, and I'd now been on my feet almost all day. While fae didn't tire as quickly as humans, I was still drained from the events of the day—almost losing Lennie when the bridge gave way beneath her feet, and then the fear for my people and the humans had set in as soon as I heard the sirens.

I glanced over the scene. Thankfully the rockslide had settled completely. The local police force had done an excellent job at blocking off the site, and the public had been pushed back a safe distance. There weren't many onlookers left—most had probably gone home for supper, but a few remained with their phones out trying to take a photo. I recognized every single one of them, including Halvar...

Halvar?

Shit.

The broody, giant Fjell Fae was standing off to the side in the dark, the blue lights from the patrol car bouncing ominously off his stoic face.

He never left the mountain. *Ever.*

This couldn't be good.

Steeling myself, I walked over to him and braced for the worst.

"Queen Freija has requested a meeting with you, the young lady, and Øyvin," Halvar said in his natural gruff tone. His body was relaxed beneath his thick brown waxed-cotton jacket, and I was pretty sure this was the first time I'd ever seen him in jeans instead of his usual uniform or black attire.

"Has something happened?" I asked.

He stared at the tumble of rocks and debris behind me, and quirked a single brow.

"Aside from this?" I added with a wave of my hand.

"We can discuss tomorrow morning at her office." Since Queen Freija didn't *have* an office—at least not one that I'd ever seen—that meant we were being summoned to the throne room. "There are... concerns."

My brow drew down at his word choice. There were gaping holes between the lines, and any assumption that could be slotted between wasn't good. "Is the Queen all right?"

Halvar stared into my eyes. "No."

16

LENNIE

"Ah, good. You left your camera at home," Espen said, striding toward me in his police uniform the next morning. I was heading to Oddvar's café for coffee before I went to the store to buy a phone charger I still hadn't grabbed. After the life-threatening events yesterday, I needed a calm day to recover.

I didn't stop walking, but I looked his way. "Why does that matter?"

"We have a meeting to go to," he said just as Øyvin stepped around the corner and ruined my morning with his presence. "Perfect timing," Espen greeted the brute. I scowled at Øyvin's thick gray sweater and blue jeans, which, unfortunately, almost matched my own. I'd picked out my dark gray fleece jacket and navy jeans—which Solveig had graciously thrown in the laundry for me last night so I had some clothes to wear today. Mistakes were clearly made, though, as the Asshole and I looked ready for a family portrait session.

I huffed and crossed my arms. "What are you talking about, Espen?"

"We've been ordered to meet with"—he glanced around and gently touched my elbow, pulling me aside, away from passersby—"Queen Freija. All three of us."

"She wants to talk to me? A human?" I asked as a tingly and not unpleasant sensation ran up my arm where Espen's fingers still pressed against me.

"Apparently. And, before you ask, no, I don't know why."

My mind reeled, coming up blank as to any reason why the queen of *anything* would be interested in me. "Is it the investigation? Is the rock slide related?"

Espen shrugged and removed his hand. "Maybe."

"Did Nora come find you or call you?" Øyvin asked, stepping up on Espen's other side, both of them now towering over me.

Espen shook his head and said, "Halvar."

"He left the mountain?" Øyvin's blond brows hit his hairline. I glanced between the two men, but didn't have time to question who this Halvar was. "Shit. Let's go."

We strode out of town and up into the woods, Øyvin leading the way as we followed yet another trail—how many trails could one little town have?—between pines, ferns, and birch trees. It wasn't an unpleasant morning; the sun had even deigned to show its face between the clouds. But today I was sans coffee, and it was a damn shame. Jet fuel was needed if I was going to get through the day, especially if I had to spend it around the Asshole.

No one spoke as we steadily climbed up the mountain-side, listening to the sounds of the woods and its inhabitants. Far too quickly, my thighs began a minor protest. Yesterday's hike with Espen wasn't excessive, but it had done a number on my muscles.

At one point, the trail widened, and we were able to walk all three side-by-side. Unfortunately for Øyvin, this put me right beside him, and I took the opportunity to poke the bear a bit.

"So, what does a big brute like yourself do for fun? Steal candy from children? Throw barrels of ale like a shot put? Crochet? Fishing? Crochet *while* fishing?"

A flicker of something happened at the corner of Øyvin's lips, and I honed in on it, ignoring Espen's snickering.

"Come on big guy, what's your poison?"

"Sometimes reading, sometimes music," he said firmly, his lips falling back into a solid line again. "No fishing."

I blinked but tried to hide my surprise at the rather tame list of hobbies. He didn't need to know he shocked me with his admission. "Next you're going to tell me you don't eat fish because they're your friends."

He said nothing and kept looking forward.

"Seriously?" My brows shot skyward at having nailed the guy's eating habit. Then I gasped. "Are you one of the sharks from *Finding Nemo*? You're Bruce, aren't you? A reverse pescatarian?"

Øyvin rolled his eyes. "No, I don't eat fish. I protect them and the fjord from idiots like you who think going on a cruise is a good way to spend your free time, never thinking about the damage it does to the planet and waters."

"Would you prefer I drive all around the coastline instead?" I snapped, matching my strides to his obnoxiously large ones.

"I'd prefer it if you weren't here at all."

I scoffed, but his harsh words egged me on. "You know, not everyone can live in such a beautiful place. If I can capture that beauty in my photos for others to enjoy, then I'm happy."

He glared at me, walking faster, but I picked up my pace to meet his. No way was I backing down now. "Your happiness and frivolity will only lead *more* people to this region, causing more damage."

I couldn't entirely disagree with him, but travel in Norway was wildly expensive. If I hadn't got the cruise tickets on sale, I wouldn't have come. "Well, you don't need to fucking blame me for the behavior of others. I'm not wholly responsible for the polar ice-caps melting, you dick!"

"Bitch."

"Asshole."

Espen slid between us, his back to me as he met Øyvin's glare. "Perhaps we should lower the volume and put on smiles for our meeting?" His upbeat tone and the way he shimmied his shoulders barely hid the warning beneath his words. Our chat with Queen Freija was important enough for him to revert to police-officer-Espen, not his usual carefree-and-jovial-Espen.

I breathed through my nostrils, trying to calm my temper and the rage coursing through my muscles.

Øyvin quirked his brow and strode ahead of us, heading straight through the rocky mountain wall up ahead without another word.

My eyes bulged at the sight of him nonchalantly—but also with his signature fuck-the-world swagger—strolling straight through the stone facade. He didn't even flinch or go splat. He just disappeared.

"Please tell me there's a train to a wizarding school on the other side of that wall."

Espen chuckled. "Let me explain."

I nodded, keeping my eyes on the mountain, my mouth hanging open. I couldn't look away from where Øyvin had just disappeared. Sure, I'd seen Espen use his magic in the woods and change outfits, but this... this was another thing entirely. "Yeah, that would be great."

He huffed and if I'd been capable of looking at anything other than the spot where Øyvin had been, I'd probably find Espen's usual cheeky grin plastered across his handsome face. "The Fjell Fae live in the mountain," he started. "There are maybe a hundred entrances around the area that are hidden from the humans using layers of magic. This is one of the main entrances."

He waved his hand against the rocky disguise and it rippled slightly, like wind brushing against the surface of a pond. "It won't hurt. You won't feel a thing."

I eyed him and the magic warily.

"Do you trust me?" He asked, holding out his hand to me.

Now that was a good question. If he'd asked that forty-eight hours ago, I probably would have said no. But, after yesterday, when he'd saved my life and carried me to safety, I guess I could trust that he didn't want me dead.

"Yes." I nodded. "I trust you."

He smiled as I placed my hand in his and we walked into the mountain. We stepped through the mirage—which felt like walking through a puff of air from a heating vent—and entered a well-lit cave. The inside of the mountain looked like someone had chiseled their way through the stone with gargantuan picks and hammers, the jagged edges catching the light from nearby lanterns. It wasn't cold in here, but there was a slight damp chill now that we were out of the sunlight and surrounded by rocky walls.

"We should change clothes to meet the Queen," Espen said, turning me to face him before dropping my grasp. "May I?" He held his hand above my shoulder, close but not touching.

"Knock yourself out." I shrugged. He scrunched his brow, then shook his head—probably confused by the American phrase—before touching my shoulder. As soon as he did, a warm shift settled over my skin like a heated blanket. It wasn't painful by any means, but definitely noticeable.

Feeling a little like Cinderella after the fairy godmother transforms her, I looked down at the dress that had appeared on my body. The skirt and bodice were made of a thick dark-green wool with silver embroidery—almost like celtic markings—woven into the hem and the fabric that rested across my breast. A white undershirt covered the tops of my boobs, and was clasped shut by a silver broach at my neck. It was a gorgeous outfit and matched the one I'd seen him magically change into the first day I met him.

"Is this okay?" he asked, scanning me from top to toe, before flicking his gaze back to mine.

"Yeah, it's hefty, but mobile," I said, sinking into a squat. "I can move in it. Could probably even tackle a guy." I crouched forward into a perfect ready position, the same one my older brothers had taught me decades ago when Mom finally let me play football with them.

Espen chuckled and tilted his head, watching me closely as if trying to understand the way my brain worked. Good fucking luck—I was a mystery even to myself.

He pressed his hand to his own shoulder and his police uniform disappeared, replaced with the jacket with dark green cape combo he'd previously spooked me with. This time though, his ears shifted too, slight points appearing at the top of each. My traitorous body warmed at the sight of his cheeky grin, something fluttering in my stomach.

Shaking myself free from his knowing gaze, I asked, "So, where exactly are we going?"

Espen opened his mouth to reply—

"Throne room," Nora said, strolling up behind him in a long dress like my own. Her's was a dark gray, though, with the same silver embroidery. "Best not to leave my sister waiting."

"She's not wrong," Espen said, pointing down the hall.

Nora, walking backward like a tour guide, led us through a winding maze of tunnels, all lit by little orbs of light in lanterns at carefully marked intervals, roughly every six feet. It certainly brightened the space and distracted me from the fact that I was walking within a fucking mountain.

"How many Fjell Fae live in here?" I asked, doing my best not to butcher the Norwegian name for *mountain* in front of a royal fae who called one home.

Nora gave me a proud smile. "Over seven hundred fae, with more in other mountains around the country. This mountain stretches far down the side of the fjord and is almost 30 kilometers wide at its broadest point. We have everything we need in here—light, water, food, clean air—all thanks to our own people and their abilities."

"Nora here can tell you everything you need to know about the Fjell," Espen interjected. "She's both their historian and a painter."

Nora winked and continued her monologue. "The Fjell Fae have lived here for centuries under my family's reign. My sister, Queen Freija, has been on the throne for over two hundred years. Any questions?" Nora asked as we turned another corner, slowly descending into the mountain, the chill non-existent in my magic dress.

I mulled through some ideas while we continued our walk, and landed on one that might prove helpful to ask now rather than later. "Is there anything I should be aware of before meeting with the Queen?" Like how to stay out of trouble.

A wide grin spread on Nora's face. "Let her speak first and do not disrespect the Fjell. Do those two things and she will like you."

"Okay," I said. That should be easy.

"Anything else?" Nora asked Espen as we came to a stop before a shimmering blue stone archway. The rocks in the walls here were almost clear, but glowed and cast a pale blue light across all three of us.

"Don't anger Halvar," he said, and Nora chuckled before she left us, waltzing through the archway and into a room made of the glowing stones.

"How do I know which one is Halvar?" I asked as Espen extended his arm, motioning me through with him.

A low chuckle rumbled from his chest. "You said you trust me. You'll know."

17

LENNIE

My eyes blew wide as I looked around the throne room. It was spectacular, something out of a damn movie. Whatever rock it was made out of shone like the insides of an ice cave, glittering whites and blues dancing in the low light. At the center of the room was a throne of the same pale blue stone, its tall back blending into the mountain itself. A forty-something-year-old woman perched in it, her hands gently placed in her lap. Her dark blue dress, covering almost every inch of her, brushed the slate-colored floor.

Something shifted to her left, and I glanced at the movement. A beast of a man stepped beside the throne, his gigantic form shadowing the bronze-haired woman beside him. The fae-man-beast-thingy wearing all black stared at me, his gaze narrow and unwelcoming, and my breaths grew shallow. Espen was right; it was easy to guess this was Halvar.

The Queen's welcoming smile was the opposite of the harsh cold wafting off the man to her left. She nodded to Øyvin as he stepped up beside me, as if appearing out of thin air, wearing his own gray-and-navy uniform. Nora had taken up a seat along one of the walls in the chamber where benches were carved into the glossy rock.

Glancing between her and the Queen, it was easy to see that they were sisters. Where Nora's short brown bob haircut framed her round face, Freija had more chiseled features, as if the fullness had slowly chipped away over the centuries. Freija's hair was also more gilded than Nora's, a wave of coppery brown swept up into a bun with small tendrils brushing against her pale cheeks. But the stand-out feature that revealed their relation was their eyes. Both fae had sharp brown-and-gray eyes that shimmered almost unnaturally. It was eerie, but beautiful, and I couldn't stop staring. I'd never seen anything like them.

"Thank you for coming today," Freija said, her voice a gentle timbre. "I appreciate the reports I have received thus far, but thought it wise to meet and discuss the matter at hand."

Both Espen and Øyvin bowed their heads lightly in a reverent display of grace. I hesitated momentarily, not sure if I should do the same, but no one had said anything about needing to bow on our walk here. Instead, I stood still and kept my mouth shut.

"Øyvin, is all well with King Balder?"

"Yes, Queen Freija. He sends his regards, but, as you know, we are fighting our own battle with the pollution further down the fjord," Øyvin replied, sounding like a soldier giving a report to his superior, his hands clasped behind his back.

"Indeed. It is a challenge and I commend his efforts," Freija said with a flicker of a smile. "We appear to be facing a challenge of our own." She cast her eyes to Espen, who didn't move. His hands were relaxed by his side, and his breathing was steady. "Did you see anything unusual in the rock slide?"

"Not at first," Espen responded, and all three Fjell Fae in the room raised their eyebrows. Halvar's features quickly returned to a stoic scowl though, and Espen continued, "I went back last night when all the humans had gone to sleep and sent my colleague back to the station, taking over his duties as watchman. I pressed some magic into the debris. After a minute, there was a reverberation in the rocky-soil, and I caught a glimpse of a silvery scar on one of the largest boulders."

The room stilled, and Nora muttered something under her breath that I could only assume was an expletive based on the cutting glare she received from her sister.

Freija reset her dainty shoulders and took a deep breath. With a quick glance at Halvar, she said, "Well, it is as we feared, then. Someone is trying, once more, to bring down the monarchs."

I swallowed the lump in my throat, unsure why it was there in the first place, but certain that whatever was going on here, was bad. Both Espen and Øyvin straightened up, but didn't move an inch.

"And you, young lady," the Queen said, her unearthly gaze landing on me.

Ah shit. Here we go. I was probably about to get my mind wiped for being human and knowing too much, or locked up in a dungeon never to be heard from again.

I took a deep breath and braced for her next words.

"Thank you for capturing the evidence with your camera," she said, and I nodded, giving her a tight smile sans teeth—just in case that was offensive or Halvar thought I was a threat. I certainly hadn't missed the size of his hands, and didn't want to be on the receiving end of them. Freija continued, "Without it we might not have been able to act as quickly. So, thank you."

My shoulders slumped in relief, and I tipped my head slightly. "It was sheer fuc—"

Øyvin's hand clapped over my mouth before I could finish my sentence. I glared up at him, and thought better of punching him in the balls in front of the nice Queen. Instead, I pried his fingers from my face—ignoring the way they brushed against my lips—before finishing my answer. "You're welcome. I'm glad it was helpful." I felt rather than saw the pride emanating from my right side where Espen stood.

Freija looked between the three of us, a slow smile forming on her face and crinkling the corners of her eyes. "We will be increasing our security measures, closing some of our entrances, and securing any parts of the mountain that may be loose." Her missive was firm and clear as she stood from her throne. "I have also instructed Halvar to prepare for my birthday in two weeks time."

Nora coughed and looked up at her sister. "You can't go through with the event. Not now. It's too dangerous."

Freija took a deep breath, not turning to the other fae. "I shall use the annual celebration of my birth to draw out any suspects. It has already been agreed upon," she said with a quick nod to Halvar.

He bowed his head ever so slightly, the glow from the stones shining off his silver hair and beard.

"In that time," she continued, turning back to the three of us. "I expect you to hunt down the culprit and, should you find them, bring them to me." Her eyes darkened and, for the first time since entering the room, I actually feared the woman and whatever power lurked beneath the surface of her calm exterior.

The guys beside me nodded, gruff remarks coming from Øyvin in thanks as we were dismissed.

We spun in unison and strode out of the throne room, entering the maze of hallways once again. While we wound our way back to the entrance, Espen and Øyvin chatted, making plans for what to do next.

Thankfully, none of this was my problem, because I was leaving in three days. I'd do what I could in the meantime, if only to make sure

Espen lived up to his bargain and got me on that damn supply ship that Oddvar had secured my passage on. Other than that, my work here was done.

18

LENNIE

After finishing a nice sandwich for lunch that afternoon, I stomped out of Oddvar's café, a piping hot cup of coffee—with milk and two sugars—in my hand, and a Forest Fae at my back.

"It's just for today," Espen pleaded as I strode down the street toward the store so I could finally buy a charger for my phone. Could I borrow one from Solveig or someone else? Probably, but I wanted to troubleshoot this problem myself. Plus, the longer I left my phone off, the smaller my cell phone bill would be when I got home. I just needed to call my brothers to make sure they hadn't told Mom, and check for any messages from the cruise ship.

Espen kept up beside me, matching my strides with his longer legs. We were back in our human clothes: me in my dark gray fleece jacket and navy jeans, him in his black police uniform with reflective strips.

"I don't need a babysitter, Espen." I was a grown ass woman who could take care of herself.

"But what if you fall over or get attacked by a bear?" he asked, and I stopped, my lips pursed.

"I'll punch it in the nose."

Espen chuckled, a warm sound that sent flutters into my stomach every time I heard it. His smile wasn't bad either. Maybe it was the short beard, or the dark mop of hair that made me feel this way. Hell only knew. "I'm quite certain that only works with sharks," he said.

I shrugged and continued walking toward the grocery store, hoping they stocked chargers. "Nobody likes being punched in the nose. I bet it would work with a bear, too. I'll make sure to report back." When he didn't leave my side, I said, "Don't be an asshole, Espen. The village already has one of those; you don't need two."

As if speaking his name had summoned him, the fae in question stepped around the corner and almost plowed right into me. "I'm here," Øyvin grumbled, as displeased with today's babysitting plan as I was.

"Wonderful," Espen said, way too chipper about all of this, before turning back to me. "I figured he could take you on a sightseeing tour of the fjord or something."

Øyvin and I wore matching deadpan expressions, and damn it, I hated having anything in common with the man.

Espen rolled his eyes. "Why, what a wonderful idea, Espen," he said with a high-pitched voice, swaying as he spoke. "It will be so nice to spend the day on the water, seeing the beauty that is Norway. We'll have such fun together."

A short sigh left my chest, and I took a sip of the jet fuel in my hand. "I'm not getting out of this, am I?"

"Not at all," Espen replied, giving me a toothy grin.

"You know too much. We can't have you wandering around and getting into trouble or telling anyone," Øyvin added, giving me the straight truth, which seemed rather miraculous for the grouch. Then again, he wasn't a fan of mine and liked to annoy me with his presence. So, maybe he said it to push my buttons. Either way, I took another sip of coffee to calm my aggravated nerves.

"Yes, exactly," Espen said, backing away from us. "On that note, I'm going back to work. Try not to kill each other." He spun on his heel and sprinted down the road, turning toward what I could only assume was the police station that I most definitely did not want to visit.

A low rumble emanated from behind me, and, instead of turning toward it, I waltzed in the other direction back toward the shore and the path to Solveig's house. Plan A: join Øyvin on a tour of the fjord. Plan B: go home and try to buy a charger tomorrow, avoiding the Fjord Fae and his awful personality. The second option sounded so much more palatable.

Unfortunately, Øyvin had a broad stride and caught up to me as I reached the edge of the harbor.

"You know, you could just go home," I said, heading away from the downtown core with the last of the white-colored, wooden buildings to my right, and the fjord to my left. Boats of all shapes and sizes bobbed on the nearly smooth surface, and the breeze shifted the smell of the water and pine through the village.

"I need to make sure you don't do anything stupid," Øyvin practically growled, and tugged on my arm, spilling some of my coffee onto the asphalt.

"Asshole!" I ripped my hand out of his grip and stumbled closer to the shoreline, following the path out of town that didn't have any buildings alongside it until you reached the collection of houses where Solveig lived.

"You have quite the mouth on you," he snarled.

I chugged the rest of my drink, unwilling to let it go to waste should he decide to jostle me again. It tasted heavenly, but burned my mouth.

When I was done, I threw away the cup and recycled the lid in the garbage station that sat along the walkway.

"I'm aware. Haven't had any complaints about that either, though," I said, swaying my hips to provoke the bull.

He grumbled and muttered something under his breath that sounded like "stupid human," but I couldn't be sure.

"You know, you really should get laid. It would probably help take the edge off whatever bullshit—"

Before I could finish my sentence, Øyvin stormed toward me and pushed me into the fjord. I landed with an almighty splash, narrowly missing the rocks, and sank. My ass touched the bottom, and, thankfully, it was shallow enough that my head stayed above the cold water. Based on the grimace on the Asshole's face, submersion had been his initial plan.

"What the fuck was that for?" I yelled, water sweeping around my stomach.

He shrugged and folded his arms across his chest. "I was asked to show you the fjord." He waved his hand at me. "Done."

With a huff and an expletive that my mother's friends would balk at, I rose to my feet. Water dripped from every part of me, the cool droplets returning to the fjord where they belonged. "Manhandle me one more time, buddy," I said, climbing over the rocks, pulling myself back onto the pathway, and shifting to a standing position in front of him. "And I'll kick you in the balls."

Øyvin grumbled, his cobalt eyes turning stormy, and grabbed my shoulders, spinning me on the spot. Before I could yell at him again, he wrapped his wide arms across my front, pressed my back against his torso, and dove into the water. I was practically a mermaid bust on the prow of a pirate ship as we careened, face first, into the fjord. I held my breath as the water closed over our heads, completely submerged in the icy water.

If I survived this, I'd be *severing* his balls instead.

Øyvin held me tight against his chest as we were propelled forward by what I was assuming was his magic. Espen had mentioned something about Fjord Fae being able to manipulate the water. So, being able to push it aside and swim like a fucking torpedo kind of made sense. Surprisingly, an air bubble settled around us, keeping us dry and letting us breathe beneath the surface. Or, at least, it kept *Øyvin* dry. I was still very much soaked from my prior dip into the fjord.

I scanned my surroundings, my eyes growing wide and my heart hammering at the sight before me. The light was dim beneath the surface, but I could clearly see schools of fish hiding in the rocks near the shore, and little cave-like structures dotted into the mountain where it fell beneath the water. As we pressed on further down the fjord, I dared to glance over my shoulder. It was a mistake, though, as Øyvin's light stubble grazed against my cheek, sending a shiver down my spine. Whether he noted the touch or not, he said nothing, and we plowed on further along the fjord.

After a solid twenty minutes below the surface—which, for my human mind that needed to come up for air regularly, was fucking wild—the water grew murkier. Øyvin shifted his weight, and our bubble rose above the darker patches until we eventually broke the surface. Still wrapped tightly in his arms, Øyvin showed off by launching us out of the fjord and onto a tiny pebbled beach. He landed on his feet and set me down, before stepping away from me like I was a live-wire. Usually a wise move, but in this case, I could have used the support. My legs felt like jelly and I wobbled on the spot.

"Follow me," Øyvin grumbled, stalking up a rocky trail between some skinny trees like a mountain goat.

With a huff, I followed the Asshole, doing my best not to slip as my feet and clothes were still soaking wet. The air temperature was mild-ish, but the slight breeze at this end of the fjord had a cutting chill in it. I shivered, water squelching in my boots as I scrambled up onto an outcrop where Øyvin had stopped to take in the view. "Any chance you could magically dry my clothes?" I asked, sitting down on the cold cliff.

His stormy gaze raked over me before his eyes rolled so hard I was shocked they didn't get stuck in the back of his head. With a wave of his hand, a blanket of heat swept across my clothes and I was miraculously dry again. I gave him a brief nod in thanks, not wanting to be *too* kind to the Asshole. I didn't want him to think I'd changed my mind and started to tolerate his presence. Shaking off *that* unlikelihood, I turned my focus away from my annoying companion, and looked out over the fjord.

The water gleamed in the foreground, with a sparse layer of trees on the opposing hillside giving way to patches of gray rock jutting up behind it. A simple, but majestic display. However, perched on the other side of the fjord beneath a bluff was what looked like some sort of factory. Warehouses dotted the immense dock space and large ships were moored to its flank. Further back from the shoreline sat silos—not too different from the grain silos we had in Ohio—and miles upon miles of meandering pipes. At this distance, the people working over there were mere specks, ants compared to the size of the equipment around them.

"What is that?" I asked, nodding toward the gray-and-brown cluster of buildings and metal.

"Poison."

I glanced over my shoulder to judge if his comment was sarcastic, but seeing the stoic Fjord Fae's expression, I didn't laugh. He'd tightened his jaw and his fists were clenched at his sides, his eyes locked on the scene across the fjord.

"It's one of several oil refineries you'll find along the Norwegian coast-line," he explained. "You humans rely on oil, and the North Atlantic will gladly provide it to those brave enough to weather her storms. But, it comes at a cost." I wanted to argue with him for lumping me in with his general distaste of humans, but held myself back—then wondered if maybe the dip in the fjord had rattled my brain. His eyes darkened and his voice turned more grumbly than his normal timbre. "They've become better at avoiding oil spills, but the damage comes from the ships, the destruction of the shoreline, and past malpractice that has polluted the ground and surrounding waters."

"Well, fuck," I mumbled, glancing back at the operations.

Øyvin grunted in agreement before sitting down beside me, leaving a gap so we most definitely could not accidentally bump into each other. Which I appreciated, even as my breath caught temporarily in my throat at the movement. This close I could see the different shades of blond in Øyvin's hair, the way his stubble curved over his chin, and how extremely long his eyelashes were. *Why did men always have such enviable lashes? It wasn't fair to womankind.*

He turned toward me and flicked his gaze to mine.

I sucked in a quick breath and looked away, brushing my hands across my jeans while mumbling, "How far down the fjord are we?"

"A little over half-way."

Hold up.

I turned slowly, my eyes squinted as anger rose in me. "You mean you could've torpedoed me down the fjord this entire time?" My voice reached an exasperated crescendo as I peered over at the grumpy fae. The same guy who could've saved me from a week of waiting and a near-death experience.

He rolled his eyes and shook his head. "There's quite a bit further to go, and two very good reasons why I can't do that."

"Go on."

"Number one: I'm King Balder's Head Guard. I do not have the time to forsake my duties to help a wayward human get home. I have people I'm accountable for and a fjord to keep clean."

"And this annoying babysitting operation slash fjord tour is not a dereliction of duty?"

Øyvin grumbled, resting his hands on his knees. "Today is actually my day off, but even then, I don't stray far from the fjord."

I let out a huff but conceded that he kind of had a valid point. "What's the second reason you couldn't save my ass and help me down the fjord?"

His lips twitched into a minuscule grin, and I did a double-take wondering if my eyes were deceiving me. "I don't want to."

I scoffed in reply and let out an expletive that would've had me grounded if I still lived with my parents. "Why do you hate me so much?" I asked, brushing my fingers across the tufts of lavender that stuck up between the cracks in the rock.

"You're annoying and you clearly don't understand the impact of your actions."

I snarled at him. "Is this about saving the world from pollution again? What the fuck do you want me to do? I want to see the world and photograph it."

He stood up, brushing off his pants, his sapphire gaze boring into mine. "Take photos of the world around your home."

"I don't want to."

"And why not?"

"Because... Because I don't want to." I said, partially avoiding his question. It wasn't that Ohio was ugly—quite the opposite, the gullies and trails were gorgeous—but I was bored with my surroundings.

Travel and photography were ways for me to escape the mundane parts of life, to live a little and capture the beauty around me. From trips to Hawaii to see the beaches and volcanoes, to hikes in Peru (where I needed a special tea to stop the altitude sickness and accompanying headaches), I wanted to experience what the world had to offer and document it. I wanted to see everything mother nature had created, and I couldn't do that by staying in the fields of Ohio. My carbon footprint was probably substantial because of my frequent flights, but I alone couldn't be blamed for global warming. I could do better, find more eco-friendly ways to travel, but...

"Why are you so grouchy, anyway?" I asked, pivoting the topic away from me.

"I'm responsible for the health and safety of the Fjord Fae on a good day. Good days do not include the illegal transfer of magic."

He did have a point about the silvery-magic-stuff. Even Espen and the Fjell Fae seemed remarkably alarmed by it. Plus, the new landslide just seemed to make matters worse for the Fae... and they still didn't know who was behind it or why these attacks were happening.

"Do you have any clue who might be behind the transfer?" I asked, rising to my feet and stepping back from the cliff-edge.

Øyvin shook his head and ran his hand through his short hair. "The landslide complicated matters."

"How so?"

"I've only ever seen magic like that done by a Forest or Fjell Fae."

My eyebrows hit my hair-line and I let out a choked cough. "You mean, someone like Espen might be behind it?"

"No, not him, but I've seen Forest and Fjell Fae shift the earth in battle before," he said, reminding me that he was old enough to have fought in the war that Forest Queen Ragnhild had died in.

"What if someone was mimicking the power?" I asked.

Øyvin looked me in the eyes, his gaze darkening. "It would likely be stolen powers, if so. The Forest and Fjord Fae seem fine, but Queen Freija did not look like her usual self. I fear something may be weakening her."

I shoved my hands into my jacket pockets and shuffled from one side to the other, careful to avoid trampling the wild lavender. "What... what would happen if she died?"

Øyvin swallowed audibly and his voice dropped even lower. "If the King or Queen dies, this region will fall into ruin. Animals and plants will die, rock slides will become the norm, and the waters would be filled with filth, killing marine life."

"The forest is fine after Queen Ragnhild died, isn't it?"

"Only because Espen had the power to heal large swaths of it and protect it from further harm. He may not look it, but he is extremely powerful."

"Work together, then. Build a new alliance where all three factions work together, and fight back against whatever or whoever is doing this."

"Easier said than done when you're also fighting outsiders and their damaging actions." He nodded toward the refinery and warehouses across the water.

I grumbled and let out a long winded sigh.

Øyvin shook his head and took a step toward me. "But you're right," he said, and my eyes widened at the statement. "Life on the fjord would be a lot easier if we could all work together." Taking yet another step closer, he brought us chest to chest. Before I could throw another comment or question at him, he wrapped his thick arms around me and plunged us into the fjord below.

We breached the fjord's surface just outside the village, away from prying eyes, on a narrow rocky beach surrounded by tall pine trees. Øyvin dropped his arms from around my waist and set me down less than gently. My footing faltered on the slick rocks, and my head spun like I'd had too much tequila. Before I could topple onto my ass, a hand at my shoulder steadied me.

"Easy there," Øyvin said, retracting his hand like he'd just realized what he was doing.

"How does your torpedo swimming not give you the spins?" I asked, glancing over my shoulder at the completely dry Fjord Fae, his tawny hair shifting lightly in the chilly breeze.

"I've had over two centuries to grow accustomed to the sensation, and I was born beneath the surface, so the pressure doesn't bother me," he remarked and then strode past me.

I rolled my eyes at his back, but followed him through the grove of trees and onto a pine needle-covered trail that I assumed led back to Skolvik. The more I thought about his remark about being born underwater, the more questions popped into my head. One question in particular bothered me enough to voice it, even though I wasn't sure if the grumpy Asshole would consider answering.

I caught up and fell in beside him, making sure I didn't trip on any of the rocks that jutted up from beneath the crunchy forest floor. "Do you draw your powers from the water?" I asked.

He narrowed his eyes at me and furrowed his brow.

"What I mean is, do you need to be near the water to have your powers?"

He relaxed his features and pressed his lips together briefly before shaking his head. "You're asking if I need to be *near* the fjord to have the water powers?"

I nodded.

"No, there is water in the air." He waved his hand around us. "That's enough to assist us in doing certain things like making it rain."

I blinked twice and almost walked into a tree. *Make it rain?* Damn. That was some next level shit.

Øyvin caught my arm and steered me back onto the trail before I was taken out by a pine. He swiftly released me as we emerged from the woods and stepped onto a paved pathway with a sign noting a short distance back to the village. "I always *prefer* being close to the fjord because of my duties, but also because of my affinity for water. I like being near it—the sound, the feel, it makes me content."

My lips curved into a smile at his confession. I knew that feeling well. "The state I live in back in America—"

"Ohio," he said, sounding out the vowels like all the other people I'd met on my travels that had never heard of the state before.

I nodded, tucking my hands into the pockets of my fleece jacket. "That's the one. It doesn't have a lot of water. There is a huge lake at the top of the state, but other than that, we're landlocked."

"You don't have other lakes or rivers?" he asked, coming to a stop and turning to me. His eyes widened like the mere thought of no waterways was an unspeakable disaster.

"Oh, we do," I laughed and halted. "The rivers and gullies in Ohio are beautiful." In fact, they were my favorite thing to photograph when I couldn't afford to travel outside the state. "But there are no other large bodies of water, nor ocean. So, I've always enjoyed being near the water." I gestured to the fjord at our right as it gently lapped against the brush covered boulders along the shoreline. "It was a rarity growing up and brings me joy, too."

He gave me a lopsided grin, and my chest tightened at the sight. I gazed into his eyes and, for a split second, saw a happiness I'd never witnessed from Øyvin. My mouth and brain emptied of any words that could fill the growing silence, and heat spread over my cheeks. Øyvin lifted his hand and swept a stray piece of hair from my forehead, his fingers lightly brushing across my skin before he tucked the strand behind my ear. My eyes fluttered shut and I leaned into his touch, the warmth of—

No. No, no, no, no. Not the Asshole.

My eyes flew open and Øyvin's smile disappeared, his hand falling back to his side like he'd been burned. We both reared back from each other, looking anywhere but at the person across from us. Just because we had one thing in common didn't mean I *liked* the oaf.

"So, don't take you out to a desert then. Noted," I said with a cough, trying to pivot us back to our prior topic of conversation as my lungs fought to regain control of my breathing.

"Mm-hmm," he mumbled, brushing his hands across his pants, and moving again, increasing his pace toward the village.

I shook my arms and followed after him.

What the fuck just happened?

No, it wasn't worth thinking about.

Øyvin was an asshole. We hadn't bonded over a joint admiration for H_2O. There was no way in hell. He'd verbally thrown me on my rear when I'd missed the cruise ship, then literally thrown me in the fjord earlier today.

We despised each other.

Loathed, not liked.

Whatever had just transpired was a momentary lapse in judgment. Nothing more.

We reached Solveig's house that sat along the path by the water—the enclosed back porch facing the fjord—and I practically bolted for the front door on the other side of the building. "Okay, bye. Thanks for the tour," I yelled over my shoulder, catching him nod once and then briskly continue along the footpath.

I speed-walked to the door and unlocked it with shaky hands, the key giving me trouble that was wholly unnecessary. Stepping into Solveig's house, I slammed the door behind me and fell against it, my back pressing into the wood and glass. My chest heaved again, and I set my palms on my knees.

"Are you all right, Lennie?" Solveig asked, stepping out of the kitchen in her Nordic-patterned sweater and black pants. "Do you need a glass of water?"

Water... Fjord... Øyv—

"Nope." I straightened and waved away her offer. "No, I'm fine. Thank you."

She shrugged and retreated back into the kitchen.

I sucked in another breath and mentally reassured myself that I was fine. Totally and utterly, fine.

19

ØYVIN

I gave her a curt nod goodbye, acknowledging her swift departure before I spun on my heel and strode toward town, not daring to glance back over my shoulder. A dim glow settled over the wooden buildings of the village, the late afternoon autumn light dwindling faster as we got closer to winter. I kept my pace steady as I lost myself in my own thoughts.

What had I done? Why had I touched her? Had she really leaned into it?

I'd had a moment of madness. It likely settled in when she laughed and shared her fondness for water. Then I'd smiled. *Ancestors save me, why had I smiled?*

Perhaps she was right—which I was loathe to admit—but it had been a while since I'd seen any... action. I hadn't met a fae I'd been interested in recently, nor met any pretty little things I could enjoy for a night.

Lennie is pretty, though.

I shivered at the intrusive thought and drew my shoulders closer to my ears as I swept past Oddvar's Café on my way home.

Yes, she was attractive—with those curves, that unruly mane of hair, and brown eyes that always looked like she was calculating some sort of scheme. But therein lied the problem with her: she was trouble, and a human who knew the secret of our world, knew about the fae. Plus, there was her attitude.

I *hated* her damn attitude.

I let out a short huff. Lennie was trouble with a capital T, and she would be leaving here on Sunday.

A few minutes later, I reached for the key in my jacket pocket and unlocked the front door to my house. Wrenching the knob and pushing inside, I let out a deep breath before slamming the door shut.

Whatever had just happened between us was a momentary lapse of judgment—an inconsequential blip—and I would forget it had ever happened by tomorrow morning.

20

LENNIE

"Any threes?"

"Go fish," I replied, and Espen let out a low grumble of frustration as he drew another card from the pile between us. The collection of cards in his hand was steadily growing and his patience was dwindling. I loved to see it.

It was a quiet Friday night playing card games with a magic fae creature that looked like a handsome guy—you know, a typical way to end the work week—and I'd donned my navy quarter-zip sweater and leggings for the occasion, while Espen was in jeans and a sweater. Tomorrow was my last full day in Skolvik. The supply ship would be here on Sunday, and I'd finally be heading south to get my luggage from the cruise that had abandoned me like a sack of moldy corn husks.

Tendrils of Espen's dark hair fell across his eyes as they'd done all night, which only seemed to aggravate him more. Instead of brushing them away with his hand or a flick of his head, he'd set his lips askew and blow it out of the way. This cycle was repeated again and again and again as we continued our card game.

"Any tens?" I asked, one brow raised.

He sighed and handed one over. That card gave me a full set and I beamed at him. His hair settled back across his brow once more, and I scoffed. "Why don't you just tie that back?"

Cutting it would be stupid. His shaggy hair did, admittedly, look really good on him. But a cute little toddler-style ponytail that made him look like a unicorn wouldn't do any harm to his luscious locks.

He shook his head, but an idea crossed my mind at the same moment. "Where's that ball of string?" I asked, recalling the material he'd used to tie up my hair a few days ago when my hair-tie decided to quit while on the job.

Espen narrowed his eyes. "What are you thinking?"

I set down my cards and stalked over to the kitchen. Scanning the shelves, I found nothing but plates and crockery.

"Top drawer on the left," Espen said with an exasperated sigh.

I opened the drawer—an everything-but-the-sink one based on the array of contents—and found what I was looking for. Grabbing the small ball of twine and a pair of scissors, I returned to the sofa.

The string was soft but strong—perfect for lashing together a makeshift scrunchie. I wrapped a few loops around my fingers, and cut off the piece. Putting aside my tools, I glanced over at Espen who was sitting at the other end of the couch, watching me warily.

Sidling up next to him, I motioned for him to dip his head and lean closer. "Do you trust me?"

"Depends on where you left the kitchen scissors. I don't want to end up with a haircut, or does that only apply to cheerleaders?" he remarked with a sneaky grin.

"Fuck you." I chuckled and nudged his knee.

His smile didn't falter as he leaned forward, and I lightly brushed my fingers through his silky hair. Honestly, what conditioner did this guy use? Bringing the dark brown tresses into a soft peak, I looped the string around the bundle and pulled, tightening it before finishing up with a mini bow to hold it all together. Leaning back, I took in the sight before me: Espen biting his lower lip, looking ridiculous but with his hair well off his brow.

"It should hold," I muttered, a warm sensation curling up my leg from where our knees touched. "Now, you really *do* look like a sexy troll. Should we give you a bedazzled belly button, too?"

He squinted at me. "A bedazzled belly button? You mean to match my sparkling personality?" A slow smirk spread across his lips, and Espen wobbled his head, the little ponytail shifting but not unraveling. "Or do you just want to undress me?"

I licked my lips, pleased with my work on his hair, but all too aware of how hot my cheeks were starting to feel. Just the thought of undressing him had my fingers itching to pull off his sweater and brush across the hard planes of his abdomen. I knew he was strong—he'd saved me from falling into the ravine—but how many muscles was he hiding under there? How would they feel beneath my palms?

Shaking myself free of the intrusive thoughts and refusing to respond to his question, I slid back to my spot on the other end of the sofa before allowing another quick glance at Espen. His eyes flicked to my mouth, then returned to his cards.

He coughed softly. "Any twos?"

I shook my head, feeling slightly victorious, among other things. "Go fish."

Espen let out a frustrated grumble and picked up another card, sorting it into his ever growing collection.

"Øyvin wouldn't be caught dead doing this on a Friday night." I chuckled, trying to ease the tension in the room.

Espen snorted, a bubble of laughter escaping his chest. "No, he's probably playing his piano or cleaning his boat."

His WHAT?

I stilled and the room grew silent, the specks of dust too scared to flit about the space for fear of triggering my wrath. "What did you just say?"

"Øyvin has a piano."

"The other part," I said, my voice dropping to an icy tone.

"His boat?" Espen waved his hand toward the window. "He lives in his boathouse on the fjord. One of the red ones at the curve of the harbor. Didn't he show it to you yesterday on your tour?"

"No," I huffed. "He did not."

"What? Then how—"

"He took me on a tour *in* the fjord," I said, and Espen's eyes widened. "Not *on* it. I was a human submarine!"

I clenched my teeth, tossed my cards onto the coffee table, and stomped to the small window at the front of Espen's cabin. Pushing aside the little checkered curtain, I glared at the fjord below.

"Where?"

"What?"

"Where is his house?" I growled.

Espen appeared at my side and slid the curtain shut.

"Why do you need to know? I thought you liked visiting me?" He winked, but clearly didn't take the hint.

I didn't respond. Instead I shoved my feet into my boots, threw open the door, and traipsed outside leaving my jacket behind.

Espen muttered something behind me, but I kept walking down the rocky path toward the fjord, toward the bastard fae that had lied to me. I'd asked Øyvin in the café if he knew of anyone with a boat, and he'd said no. Had that question been phrased as 'a person with a boat'? Yes, but he'd still withheld information. I didn't have time for fucking *loopholes*.

This whole time the prick had a boat and could've helped me. Yes, he probably couldn't leave the area because of his job or whatever, but he could've let me or someone borrow the boat. Hell, I could probably have asked Oddvar to skipper the vessel and help me get down the fjord.

"He didn't mean it."

I glowered as Espen ran up beside me, keeping a steady pace. I raised my brows and pulled my hair into a ponytail—which was impressive considering the uneven terrain beneath my feet. "You knew?"

"Knew what?"

An exasperated groan left my lips, and I stomped into the forest, following the trail down the hillside. "You knew he had a boat this whole time? You knew he could've taken me down the fjord days ago."

"Ah, that," Espen said, looking only slightly guilty. "I knew he had a boat, but I honestly thought you knew and that he'd laughed in your face when you asked for help."

He basically had—and yesterday he'd even mentioned the two reasons why he hadn't swum with me down fjord—but that was beside the point. Right now, I was angry at the Asshole and a little bit annoyed at the handsome thing dodging trees like a pro as he wandered beside me downhill.

"Which one is it?" I asked when we reached the small collection of boathouses. Each one was red with white trim and a slate gray roof. All five of them sat over the water, but were built on the rocky edge of the fjord. The boulders led right up to the stilted foundations where the water lapped at the pylons.

"I—I'm not entirely sure I should tell you," Espen hesitated, running his hand across his short beard.

I set my hands on my hips and narrowed my gaze. "You have two balls, yes?"

Espen's lips quirked, amusement shining in his eyes. "Yes."

"You want to keep both?" I pincered two of my fingers like a pair of scissors.

He shook his head like I was too much to handle. "The last one," he revealed with a sigh. "Don't do anything stupid. We're all on edge. We just want to help our people."

I grumbled, unwilling to listen to reason right now.

I left a smirking Espen on the shore as I stomped across the wood dock that led to Øyvin's front door. It wasn't a small building, but it wasn't overly large either—it looked like a garage with a floor above it. There was a door that faced the street, with a window on either side and a little square window near the triangular roof. I also spotted a side door along the broadside of the red house. That was where I aimed my anger.

Twisting the handle, I threw the door open and stormed inside, then was instantly assaulted by damp air and the sound of water lapping against a hull. To my left was an open garage door letting in cool air, the fjord visible from where I stood. And right in front of me, moored and roped within the water inlet inside the building, was a perfectly sea-worthy white speedboat.

"What are you doing here?" A cold voice skittered across my skin and I spun, slipping on the wet wood beneath my feet. Øyvin grabbed my arm before I fell onto the boat and hurtled me across the room. I landed with a thud against the wall, not far from the door I'd just entered through.

Before me stood one angry Fjord Fae. His eyes were wide and his jaw was as tight as my own.

"You fucking... lying... piece of shit," I seethed.

A grumble emanated from his chest, which was only covered by a thin white shirt, the sleeves rolled up his forearms exposing thick muscles that jumped with tension. "I have never lied to you."

"Lies by omission are still lies, Asshole," I snarled, my lungs heaving for air. Glancing to my left, I grabbed the first thing I saw—a plastic buoy—and threw it at Øyvin's head. He ducked, and it landed in the boat with a dull thump. "Try being nicer to visitors."

Øyvin grumbled and lunged toward me. I shifted back into the wall behind me as he pressed his hands on either side of my head, caging me in. "You break into my house and expect me to be *nice* to you?" The lines on his forehead deepened, and his chest lightly brushed mine. The air between us warmed and swelled, ready to explode.

"You could've gotten rid of me days ago," I hissed. "Found someone to float me down the fjord in your boat and been done with me once and for all. I wouldn't have had to wait until Sunday. You wouldn't have had to babysit me yesterday."

He grimaced, his nostrils flaring, breaths sawing in and out of both of us. "Like I said, you aren't—"

"Wanted here, *needed* here," I interjected on a whisper, using the words he'd told me the day we'd first met at Oddvar's café when he'd so rudely pointed out that I was unwanted. "I'm a problem and a threat to the fjord and faes' wellbeing, aren't I?"

He let out a low grumble, letting me know exactly how he felt with the anger raging within his eyes. "You're trouble. Thankfully, the supply boat arrives in less than 48 hours."

"You know what we do with troublesome problems in the US?" I asked, not leaving him time to answer. "We handle them. We remove them as quickly as possible. You could've done so when you had the chance. You could've helped yourself."

He growled—straight-up *growled* like an animal. I returned the sentiment with a grunt of my own, and then, without thinking it through, I kicked him in the shin. He stumbled back, removing his arms, and freeing me from my temporary confines.

"Bitch!"

"Asshole!"

"Why don't you just fucking walk away from the fjord then?" he yelled, sweeping his arms wide. "Go climb some mountains to get back to your cruise ship in Stavanger?"

"With that kind of logic, I may as well fucking swim!"

"Fine!" he replied, and before I had a chance to catch my breath, I was flying into the water behind his boat, through the open garage archway, landing outside the building entirely.

The freezing cold fjord closed above my head for the second day in a row, and my lungs contracted from the blow. Keeping my eyes shut tight, I righted myself and kicked upward through the water, using my hands to carve through my frigid captor.

I broke the surface only a few seconds after being submerged, and dragged in a deep breath. The air above the water was almost as cold as the fjord. Sucking down more oxygen, I blinked away the droplets on my eyelashes and spun around.

Øyvin leaned against the side of the boathouse, a wicked grin on his face, his blond hair rippling lightly in the evening breeze.

I swam toward the ladder by his feet, muttering a new expletive with every stroke.

Øyvin didn't move, and he most definitely didn't offer a hand to help me out of the water. I grabbed onto the top rung and hauled myself up and over the edge of the dock. My chest heaved as I caught my breath, and I raised my arm, giving Øyvin the middle finger.

"Stupid." He scoffed.

"Y-you threw m-me in the d-damn fjord!" I stuttered, unable to stop the shaking from entering my voice. My clothes were soaked through, plastered to my body, and chilling me to the bone. *"Again."*

"You said you wanted to swim. Seemed appropriate since I needed to throw a human out of my house for breaking and entering."

I put up my other middle finger in response.

A flicker of a smile twisted Øyvin's lips as he added, "Like you Americans say, I had to take out the trash."

I shouldn't have gone for his shin; I should've aimed higher when I had the chance.

I rolled onto my stomach and pushed off the now wet dock that wrapped around the side of the building. Stepping up in front of him, I lifted the end of my ponytail and twisted it. A stream of water fell from my soaking tresses and landed on his feet. He bit his lip and hissed, now the proud owner of wet socks.

"Fuck. You," I growled and stomped off, back down the road to Solveig's house. The entire trek I mulled over ideas to get revenge on the Asshole. I had one day to do it, and wringing my hair out over his feet was not enough—I had to think bigger. Perhaps I could sneak lutefisk—the slimy, fishy *delicacy*—into his house and stink up the place. Or maybe I could throw neon pink glitter all over his boat. A smile crept across my face as I strode through the village, the white-colored buildings of the downtown core standing sentry against the inky waters of the fjord that lapped against the hulls of the boats in the marina.

His boat.

21

LENNIE

I devoured my early lunch, the ham-and-cheese sandwich and hot coffee from Oddvar's a treat as I watched locals wander past the café window. After bundling up in jeans and a fleece sweater this morning, I'd thrown my hair into a ponytail and had traipsed back up to Espen's to retrieve my rain-jacket, before strolling through the village to hatch my afternoon plan. Was this idea going to be somewhat stupid? Yes, which was why I'd gone to Oddvar's first to consume some courage and calories.

I was going to commandeer Øyvin's boat, drive it out a little ways, and set it adrift down the fjord. I already had it on good authority—also known as Espen—that Øyvin was working today. So, sneaking in undetected shouldn't be too difficult. Espen had rolled his eyes at me when I mentioned that I'd be paying a visit to Øyvin's house. I hadn't even revealed what I was going to do, but he'd still said, "Don't end up at the police station."

Clearly, the male didn't know me very well at all. I had no intention of getting caught.

I'd had all night to ruminate on my idea, picking my course of action, and then spent my lunch hour building myself up to pull it off. Fully aware that I was going for a swim, I'd left my camera at Solveig's. There was no need to cause severe damage to my baby while completing this prank, however much I wanted photo evidence to look back on.

After finishing up my lunch, I paid Oddvar and gave him a quick nod as I strolled out the front door of the café. Outside, the clouds had come out, blanketing the entire region in a gray cloak. I pulled my zipper up, stepped out of the way of the "summer skier" as he glided past in his skin-tight suit that highlighted *everything*, and headed toward Øyvin's boathouse.

I arrived to perfect silence. Not a single noise emanated from the red building on the shoreline. It was just me, the fjord, and the sleek white boat inside. *Perfect.* I checked the front and side door, jiggling the handles, both locked. Taking a deep breath and steadying my pulsing heart rate, I crept along the little dock to the back of the building that faced the fjord. The garage door was half-closed, but there was enough of a gap that I could potentially squeeze around and under.

Where was the *Mission: Impossible* theme song when I needed it?

Sidling up against the wall, I squatted and gripped the white trim that lined the entire portal to the garage. With a prayer to the guy downstairs, I swung my left leg down and around, hitching it onto the wooden-platform on the other side of the wall. My muscles spasmed and my fingers got a workout for the ages as I quickly shifted underneath the metal door, using my momentum to crash, butt first, onto the interior planks with a thud.

Letting out a small chuckle of victory, I quickly surveyed my dark surroundings. Water lapped against the boat's white hull, buoys and rope hung on the far wall, and a tiny lamp was on above the side door casting a glow across the space. Without waiting a second longer, I untied the thick ropes from the cleats and stepped onto the boat. It wasn't large by any means but had a bench at the back, two seats in the middle including the captain's chair and steering mechanisms, plus two small seats up front. Luckily, the key was in the ignition, and with a few sputtered starts, the engine roared to life.

Now to open the damn garage door.

I searched around the control console and found a clicker that looked a lot like the garage door opener my parents had. Since it wasn't a red button with warning labels around or an image of a skull and crossbones, I clicked it. A motor high above me started whirring and the large white door lifted upward, letting in a cold breeze and the smell of pine and water.

My lips twitched into a wicked smile, and my heart thrummed in my chest, victory another step closer. I successfully reversed out of the boathouse, thankful for the summers on a little boat with my family on the Great Lakes and the bumpers that helped me avoid a disastrous collision or scraping the patina. I didn't have a death wish: I was fairly confident Øyvin would murder me if his boat came back damaged. I just wanted to yo-ho-ahoy it down the fjord a little ways, for the sake of making his life difficult.

Once I'd cleared the building and was safely out into the fjord, I shifted the throttle into drive and coaxed the boat in a westward direction. Wind whipped at my ponytail as I stood in front of the captain's chair, hands on the wheel. Nobody else was out on the water, which was exactly why I'd opted to do this in the afternoon. Most people were at work or school, and as the lone tourist in town, I had zero responsibilities to tie up my day.

It was just me, the fjord, and the boat.

With towering evergreens and slivers of silver birch trees climbing up the mountainside, I wished I'd brought a camera. The fjord was gorgeous from this vantage point on the water. The clouds hung close to the tops of the hills, and the town grew smaller as the boat continued humming along slowly, barely a trace of a wake behind it. The water was a beautiful mottled blue, green, and gray as it reflected its surroundings like a choppy mirror or mosaic of stained glass. The majestic—

Thud.

I gripped the steering wheel and slowed the engine to idle, my knuckles turning white, my breaths coming hard and fast. "What the fuck?"

Thud.

The noise was definitely coming from the left side of the boat. I glanced over but saw nothing untoward. *Had I hit something underneath the surface?* There was nothing on the little monitor thingies on the dash, but I also hadn't paid any attention to them. This wasn't a fishing trip.

Thud.

A pale hand reached out of the water and slapped against the boat's railing. I jumped, letting out a strangled scream as the Asshole hoisted himself onto the boat. His denim button-down shirt and black pants were soaked and clung to him, little droplets of water filling the boat—he'd clearly been too angry to create that bubble thing he used the other day. The boat rocked from side to side as he narrowed his eyes, a low rumble emitting from his chest.

I took a step back, and eyed the odds of me making it into the water before the Fjord Fae killed me. He was one big motherfucker, and had just swam upside the boat like a humanoid submarine—I didn't have a chance. So, I settled on deflecting. "Fancy seeing you here," I said with a toothy grin.

His scowl somehow turned down further. "What the fuck are you doing with my boat?"

My smile faltered, and I pushed my ponytail off my shoulder. "Joy ride?"

He took two steps toward me, bringing us chest to chest, his grimace unyielding.

"What are you, a shark?" I scowled at his annoyed face, his blue eyes conveying how badly he'd love to kill me. "Should I punch you on the nose to make you go away?"

"Sharks don't live in this fjord."

"Just assholes, then. You'd think the water would be a lot browner." I crossed my arms, and he nudged me out of the way of the captain's console. Wrapping one hand around the steering wheel and the other over the throttle, Øyvin took control of the boat and pointed it home. I let out a long vexed sigh at my own failure, slumping into the chair next to him.

"What were you hoping to achieve?" he grumbled as the boat glided toward his house.

"A damn sight more than *this* shambles," I huffed, disappointed in myself.

"Why don't you just go home?"

"That's kinda what I've been *trying* to do. I could've left a lot quicker if you weren't such a selfish prick." Both of us increased our volume with every sentence, the blood in my veins pumping harder and harder. "The supply ship arrives tomorrow, though, so I'll be gone soon."

"Good." He didn't look at me, just scowled and steered the boat back to his house.

I let out a harrumph and averted my gaze, focusing instead on the calm waters ahead of us and the reflection of the trees across them. My plan had gone to shit. I'd barely made it out of eyesight from the village, and already I'd been busted. Young Lennie would be appalled by my inability to pull this off.

Maybe I should've gone with the lutefisk idea. My hands would've smelled for days, but at least it would have been more successful.

We cruised to the outer-edges of the village and into the boathouse.

"Stay there," Øyvin said and jumped out of the boat, landing smoothly on the internal dock like he'd done this a thousand times.

I watched for a few seconds as he tied up the boat to the cleats before hoisting myself off the vessel. Øyvin turned to me, groaned and muttered something rude under his breath, then continued his work.

Conceding to my own failure, I shrugged and headed for the door. It wasn't the first time one of my pranks had been foiled, and I highly doubted it would be the last. Turning the knob and then yanking the side door open, I made to step out of the boathouse—

Øyvin slammed the door shut, his hand plastered against it above my head. "What were you thinking?"

I turned on the spot, my face level with his chest, and glanced up into his darkened gaze. "That payback's a bitch."

He scoffed.

"How did you find out anyway?" I asked, narrowing my eyes at him before glancing at his lips.

"A friend below"—he tilted his head toward the water—"noticed my boat out on the fjord and informed me."

Fuck. I hadn't even considered the Fjord Fae beneath the surface. Rookie mistake.

"I can either report you to the chief of police," he said, making a point of *not* mentioning the yogi-fae-cop that'd probably let me off the hook... again. "Or you can wash down my boat."

"How about neither?"

"One or the other."

"No."

"Yes."

"Bite me."

With a frustrated growl, he surged forward and pressed his lips against mine. My heart slammed in my chest at the sudden move, but within seconds I was grasping his shirt in my hands, clutching him to me as he crowded me against the door. My back rubbed against the weathered wood and he lifted my leg, running his palm down the underside of my thigh. Wrapping my calf behind him, I pulled him in closer, chest to chest, and moaned as he deepened the kiss with a vicious fervor.

Damn it, why is he so good at this?

The thought flitted through my head as we used our mouths to devour each other in an anger-infused haze. I was too caught up in the sparks of pleasure that sang through my veins and the throbbing in my core to care about hating the fae right now. The way his length hardened against my stomach, his large hands palmed my ass, his teeth tugged on my bottom lip—he blissfully overwhelmed my senses.

I pushed against his chest, fingers fumbling as I started unbuttoning his shirt. I got three unfastened before he pulled back and ripped it open, sending the little buttons skittering across the floorboards. I skimmed my hands down the muscled planes of his torso before flicking my eyes up to his. Unadulterated lust and hunger shone through, his pupils blown wide. With how my core spasmed and begged to be touched, I didn't doubt that my own gaze looked very much the same.

I rolled my lower lip between my teeth, and he growled. Lifting me up, I hooked my legs around his waist and my arms around his neck as he grasped my ass and walked to the other door. He kicked his boot against it, and the door flew open, crashing against the wall inside.

I didn't get a chance to survey my surroundings before I was thrown onto a brown leather couch. Lying on my back, Øyvin hovered above me with one hand on the sofa-top, the other on the armrest, and his knee between my thighs.

"Tell me to stop."

"Not a fucking chance," I groaned, desperate for the hate-sex that was about to go down.

He mercifully obliged, unfastening and removing my boots in record time before yanking down my pants, pulling my underwear with them.

A groan escaped from low in his throat and I unzipped my jacket, pulling it and my sweater off and dropping them onto the floor. His eyes flicked up to my chest before returning to the apex of my thighs. Tantalizingly slow, he swept his fingers up the inside of my legs, and a deep shudder ran through me. My synapses fired and my core pulsed as he trailed two fingers across my soaking center. I moaned, and, without further warning, he plunged those digits into me. I swore at the sensation, arching my back for more.

"Greedy," Øyvin muttered, his eyes bright with approval.

"You fucker."

He chuckled and curled his fingers inside me, sending a fiery jolt of pleasure up my spine. A whimper left my lips, and the corner of his mouth curved into a spiteful smile. After swiftly removing his fingers and popping them in his mouth, he disappeared for a few seconds before returning and ripping open a condom wrapper—the zipper on his pants undone. He freed his cock and rolled on the condom, watching me closely the entire time.

In that moment, I didn't care how I felt or who he was. I wanted and needed release—to rid my body of the pent up tension that had been riding me for the past twenty-four hours and stoked into a frenzy in the past ten minutes.

Returning his hands to my legs, Øyvin shifted and settled between my thighs. Without further fanfare, he lined up and plunged into me. I let out a guttural sound and clung to his shoulders, loving the stretch of his invasion. He roughly pressed his lips to mine, devouring me yet again. I opened my mouth, taking as much of him as I was giving of myself. With a groan from both of us, he increased the aggressive pace of his thrusts, pounding me into the cushions. Raking my nails across his back, I bucked against the cresting waves of pleasure. Electricity hummed through my veins, overpowering my senses, as the ache in my core grew and grew and grew. A wave of pleasure finally washed over me, bathing me in euphoric bliss. I dug my heels into Øyvin as he stilled and shuddered, finding his own release.

We lay there for a minute, wrapped up in each other, panting and spent. He pressed his forehead against mine, letting our breaths intermingle, before swiftly pulling back and out of me. Another spasm rocked through me at the removal, and I swallowed a whimper.

Øyvin scrambled off the sofa and left, heading through a small door by the kitchen. As the sound of water met my ears, I sat up fully and a sinking feeling settled over me.

I just hate-fucked a creature several hundred years older than me.

I shook my head, swallowed the conflicting emotions, and frantically searched for my discarded clothes. Locating them on the other side of the wooden coffee-table, I straightened up and took the moment to take in his home. A small kitchen sat in the back corner to my left, then there was the little bathroom Øyvin had disappeared to, the sofa in front of me and a small tv hanging above a fireplace at my back. I pulled on my clothes as my eyes bugged out at the final piece of furniture in the room. To my right, beside the door to the boat, was a gorgeous, old upright piano. Before I could run my fingers over the keys, Øyvin sauntered back into the room, all tidied up—save for his now broken shirt that hung open, revealing the abdominal muscles of a fae-creature-asshole-thingy that would definitely *never* feature in any of my daydreams. Ever.

"Don't think this means I like you," I said, pointing a finger at him before sliding on my boots.

He leaned against the small kitchen counter, messing up his blond hair with his hand. "Wouldn't dream of it, even in my nightmares."

"Good." I nodded, not uttering another word. Crossing to the front door, I unlocked it and wandered back toward Solveig's house, feeling aftershocks from my nerve-shattering orgasm the whole way home.

22

ESPEN

I awoke in the middle of the night to a muffled rumbling sound and the earth shaking minutely beneath my bed. Ever since Lennie arrived in the village, I'd had vivid dreams—most featured her in all her sassy glory, and in a few she was even doing yoga with me. Whatever the thundering noise was, it must've been a dream, too, because Norway didn't get earthquakes.

Rolling over and burying my head into the pillows, I began to drift off again to the thoughts of Lennie joining me on the mat until—

A heavy-metal tune—the ringtone I'd assigned to my boss, Bente—sounded from my bedside table and I bolted upright, scrambling to reach across the bed to answer. "What happened?"

"Another landslide," Bente said, her no-nonsense tone traced with a hint of sadness that had my stomach flipping upside down. "There are injuries."

I launched out of bed, nestled the phone between my shoulder and ear, and started pulling on my uniform that hung on a hook beside my closet. "Where was it?"

"The East Road, near the trail."

Shit. That was where I'd hiked with Lennie the other day. If that road was blocked, too, then the entire town would be trapped—no entry, no exit, except by boat. "Did it block the entire road?"

"Yes."

Shit. Shit. Shit.

"Report to the site in fifteen minutes."

"I'll be there in five," I replied and hung up.

Earth and boulders were strewn across the road, the land having given way and shifted like a collapsed sandcastle. It wasn't unlike the last land-slide, but, as Bente had mentioned, this one apparently had injuries. A police car was parked and pointing its headlights at the debris as another officer set up the floodlights. But even in the dark and drizzle, it wasn't hard to miss the shattered taillights of a car poking out beneath the rocks.

The firemen arrived a moment later, three of which ran directly to the car, seemingly unafraid of the potential risks of more movement from the earth. While they did their job, attempting to find signs of life and extract the vehicle from the chaos, I assisted my fellow officers with securing the area by setting up more barricades. The entire time, I focused on my work, my duty as a "human," and avoided using my fae powers to lift or remove the boulders from atop the car. While I could have eased the weight of the soil above the stranded humans, I couldn't shift the whole thing without outing myself as *other*. It was the worst kind of torture—being unable to help when help was needed the most.

But it wouldn't have made a difference. One of the firemen turned back to us and shook his head, and my stomach turned over at the gut-wrenching reality of what had occurred.

For hours I assisted other officers and the firemen at clearing the debris enough to fully access the crushed car. By the time the sun rose, casting an eerie glow on the scene, we'd removed enough material to safely extract the deceased occupants from the car.

It was Mr. and Mrs. Anderson—a local older couple, both in their late fifties, who enjoyed a late dinner at Fisken every Saturday night. I'd known them both for almost a decade and was heartbroken at the loss.

My stomach turned at the gory sight, the likes of which I hadn't seen since the war in the south. I stepped away, letting the firemen finish retrieving the bodies and turned to where Bente stood beside the police car, overseeing the scene and keeping back the few people from the village that had woken early to see what all the commotion was.

"It's the Anderson's," I said quietly, making sure no one else heard the name until we'd notified their next of kin—their daughter who lived in the capitol city, Oslo.

Bente sighed and shook her head, her white hair damp from the dreary rain. "I'll call Emma Anderson. Can you monitor the people while I head back to the station to notify her?"

I nodded, and she departed, striding back into town toward the police station.

"I heard what happened," a female voice I immediately recognized said from the gathered crowd. Lennie squeezed her way between two villagers that had been practically camped here for the past three hours. They grumbled at her, but she just rolled her eyes at them. Their responding snort fell short of gaining her attention as her forlorn gaze met mine. "Are you okay?"

I nodded. The shock of what happened had worn off, that telltale tingling sensation in my bones easing away slowly as the morning dragged on. Seeing her here also soothed something in me. Like everyone else in the crowd, she was wearing her rain jacket and a pair of jeans. Her blonde hair hung down, brushing the top of her chest and framing her face perfectly. "Your boat is today. Are you ready to leave?"

A beat of silence went by as we stared at each other before she answered, "Yeah, I've packed my stuff. It's at Solveig's waiting to go this evening."

"Good," I said and shuffled on the spot. "Umm, the supply ship should've arrived an hour ago. Oddvar let them know earlier this week to expect you. All you need to do is meet them at the docks at 8 p.m. tonight."

She scrunched her brow and crossed her arms. "That's kind of late."

I couldn't hold back the tiny chuckle that escaped me, amused by her reaction to such a common-place thing in my world. "The crew like to grab dinner at Fisken before they head out. The captain is Oddvar's son, remember?"

She tilted her head and nodded gently. "Yeah, that makes sense, then." She matched my stance and shuffled her feet a bit, before adding, "You gonna see me off or should I say my goodbyes now?"

"Do you want me at the docks?" I asked, sincerely hoping I'd get another chance to see her.

She shrugged. "I wouldn't mind it. If you can get away, that is." She nodded at the chaos behind me.

I glanced over my shoulder, before turning back to her. "I'm sure I can step away for a bit."

She smiled, her cheeks flushing a tad pinker than usual, before she shook her arms and straightened up. "Okay then. I'll see you later. Gotta go say goodbye to Oddvar and get one last cup of coffee."

I returned her grin, and nodded. "I'll see you later, Lennie."

She spun and sauntered back through the thinning crowd, dodging past the two grumbly guys again. With each step she took away from me, something inside my chest spasmed.

23

ØYVIN

Espen was rubbing the top of his chest with his fist when I emerged from the crowd, narrowly avoiding bumping into the American that plagued my dreams. Her moans had left a mark, as had her fingers where they'd scratched up my back yesterday.

Shaking off the memory, I stepped in front of the Forest Fae.

He jolted at my sudden appearance, and I smiled at the impact I had on him, the inner thoughts I'd clearly just disturbed. Based on where he'd been looking, I could easily guess who they'd been about.

He cleared his throat. "Good morning. Everything okay?" He didn't mince his words, keeping them brief and to the point with humans within hearing range, and I appreciated that about him.

"All fine this time, but I had a visitor this morning."

"If you want to invite me to join your escapades, you need only call," Espen said with a quick grin.

I rolled my eyes and shook my head. "Not that kind of visitor. Halvar stopped by."

Espen's gaze widened, and his eyebrows hit his floppy hair that was in need of a comb.

"Freija has requested another meeting—"

"Should we grab, Len—"

I waved my hand. "Just us. Halvar was very adamant that it was just you and I meeting with her this time."

"When?" Espen asked, glancing around, likely reassuring himself that the onlookers were staying behind the police barriers.

"Her office. After lunch. Can you attend?"

He nodded. "I'll have someone take over."

"Good." I spun on my heel and walked back to my boathouse.

Several hours later I traipsed up the hillside and into the mountain. As soon as I crossed the threshold, I placed my palm against my left shoulder and shifted my appearance, my ears elongating slightly and my Fjord Fae Guard uniform materializing—formal attire was always favored when meeting with one of the royals, especially when said meeting was happening in the throne room. It wasn't my preferred choice of clothing—I liked more casual knit sweaters and jeans—but at least I could use my fae powers to mimic my uniform over my body like a mirage. Clothes shifting was one of the powers I used the least, but it was always helpful when you needed to avoid any humans spotting your unusual attire or ears.

I strolled into the mountain, nodding to the guards I passed along the way. As I reached the entrance to the throne room, I found Espen already inside, conversing with Queen Freija.

The noble and her Head Guard, Halvar, lifted their heads at my arrival. Espen, wearing his green Forest Fae uniform, glanced over his shoulder giving me his signature beaming smile, albeit more sluggish than usual. I'd never understood that fae's unrelenting joy, and probably never would.

With a bow of my head, I approached the trio. Halvar was in gray-and-black attire, his uniform looking ready for battle, while the Queen wore a long emerald dress of thick material that swallowed her delicate frame. Her hair hung down neatly on either side of her face, the dark brown tresses brushing across her chest.

"Øyvin, glad you could join us," Freija said respectfully, as we both knew I was exactly on time. Espen had just been early, which wasn't surprising. "We were just discussing last night's landslide."

"Any news?" I quirked a brow as I stepped up beside Espen.

He shook his head. "I haven't been able to search the scene. With the death of the Andersons, there are too many people around."

I shrugged. He had a fair point.

"I think it's safe to assume this was a repeat of what happened the other day," Halvar said, his burly timbre echoing off the sky-blue quartz of the glistening throne room.

"Agreed," I replied, my tone echoing the displeasure I felt within.

"Have you seen any other impacts internally?" Espen asked, not shifting when Halvar narrowed his eyes at the Forest Fae.

Halvar glanced to his left, looking at the Queen for a quick second, before turning his light-blue eyes back on us. Crossing his arms over his chest, he said, "There is nothing that you need concern—"

"Halvar, please," Freija interjected, lifting her hand, and her Head Guard stopped and clenched his jaw. "What he *meant* to say is that I have felt weaker; the magic of the mountain seems to be weakening with every one of these natural events. Whomever is behind this is targeting me as they did my dear friend, Queen Ragnhild, two decades ago."

Espen and I froze to the spot, our chests barely moving as the Queen uttered words I'd been dreading. Words I knew would hit hard for the fae beside me. Words that stirred an unwelcome emotion inside my own chest.

Freija continued, "But I shall not be drawn asunder. Øyvin, I know we have no formal alliance with the Fjord Fae, but has Balder informed you of any weakening of his magic, any pollution increase in the waters?"

I shook my head. "None, your Majesty. King Balder's magic does not appear weakened at this time, but he is constantly challenged by the humans and their pollution of the fjord."

She took a deep breath and tilted her head slightly. "I understand. If Balder should see fit to do so, please inform me if anything changes. As you both know, it is the monarch's duty to worry for our people, and my concerns are great at present." I nodded, and she continued, "With that said, we are proceeding with my birthday celebrations in two weeks' time."

Halvar grunted, not saying anything to disagree with his monarch, but it was evident he very much did not agree with this decision. Sensing the tension in the room, Espen and I stayed silent, unmoving.

"All Forest Fae and Fjord Fae are welcome to attend the event in the great hall. The festivities will commence at dusk." Freija turned to me before adding, "Please extend the invitation to King Balder."

Halvar grunted again.

I bowed my head. "I shall."

Freija smiled and rose from her seat before tilting her head in thanks, then left the room. Halvar followed closely behind her, exiting through a side entrance, but not before he cast a glare over his shoulder. I refrained from reacting, even though that look sent a brief pang of fear into my chest as he departed.

"Well, could've gone worse," Espen piped up, bouncing on the balls of his feet, seemingly unaffected by the death-glare we'd just received.

Rolling my eyes, I turned for the entrance to the throne room, making my own exit. I needed to get back to work and check in with my scouts for updates on the oil that was supposed to be delivered to the refinery tonight.

Espen caught up with me, and we walked in relative silence until he almost crashed into a rushing Nora.

"Gentlemen," she sputtered, her breaths labored as if she'd been running from a troll.

"Nora," Espen said by way of greeting, while I just stared at the short Fjell Fae with rosy cheeks.

"Here to see Freija, I presume?" she asked.

We both nodded, but she barely paid us any attention, her hands full of books and what looked like a quill, the likes of which I hadn't seen in decades.

"I have to get to work. Another fae needs their story documented. Dinner tonight, though? Fisken?" Nora asked as she whirled around the corner, ducking into the opening of another tunnel.

"How about tomorrow?" Espen said. "I already have plans."

"Ah... saying goodbye to someone?" A knowing glint shone from her eyes, and she flicked her eyebrows once.

Espen nodded, and I swallowed hard.

"I'm on duty at the western coast, another time perhaps," I replied, my voice frustratingly strained.

"I'll see you at Fisken tomorrow at seven, then," Nora said and disappeared down the glowing passage, heading deeper into the mountain.

Espen and I walked toward the main exit in silence, both mulling over the words of the Queen and the events of the past week.

"Are you sure there aren't any scars or problems in the fjord?" Espen asked on a sigh, breaking the peace.

I took a deep breath, steadying my annoyance at the invisible finger being pointed at the Fjord Fae. "If there was, my scouts would have informed me."

Espen held his hands up as his fae uniform slowly faded until he stood before me in his black-and-silver police uniform. "It was just a question. We still don't know who is behind all of this, but—"

"There is evidence it could be someone from any of the three factions."

"Yes, I agree. But the worst damage appears to have been above the waterline. And I don't believe a Forest Fae would do this sort of harm without being coerced."

I lifted my hand to my shoulder and slowly removed the magic mirage of my Fjord Fae uniform, the gray-and-navy material vanishing into thin air, leaving me once again in my cream-knit sweater and dark jeans. "You clearly haven't been down the fjord in a while."

"You know I've been busy," Espen sighed. "Getting out west isn't easy when I have responsibilities here among the humans."

I refrained from scowling but whatever look crossed my face had Espen shaking his head.

"I know it's bad; the pollution will never get better unless humans rely less on fuel and its byproducts."

With a grunt I sauntered out of the mountain, Espen following closely behind.

"You going to the docks to say goodbye?" he asked, not making eye contact or even stopping for that matter.

"Already did."

Espen let out a humm that sounded very much like he didn't believe me. He was right though, I hadn't.

I didn't want to say goodbye.

We may have slept together, but it hadn't meant anything. Lennie was leaving, heading home to America, where she would go on with her human life, taking her precious photos, and never returning to our little village at the end of the fjord.

"You okay there?" Espen pried as we traipsed through the woods, the breeze keeping us company, and the afternoon sky barely visible through the canopy.

I grunted a reply, which had Espen chuckling.

"I know she got under your skin—"

"I'm going home," I grumbled, cutting him off as we reached the edge of the village. I didn't want to talk about her any more. She was leaving. End of story, end of trouble, end of whatever this ache was in my chest.

24

LENNIE

A light breeze flitted around me and the stars had begun to twinkle in the clear night sky. I waited on the pier with my over-stuffed backpack by my feet, watching the large supply ship bob on the inky water. The ship's hull was a menacing black—ready to carve through the waters—and aboard lay short stacks of pallets where crates had sat earlier in the day.

"So... this is goodbye," someone said behind me.

Turning slowly, I took in the Forest Fae ambling down the dock. Espen was still in his police uniform, eyes a little darker than usual, heavier—probably from what had happened last night. I couldn't blame him.

"This is it," I said, my voice a little chipper in hopes of seeing him smile again.

He came to a stop in front of me before rocking on the balls of his feet and looking me over like he was memorizing the image. My skin tingled in response as if he could see beneath my layers of clothing, *truly* see me. It was heartwarming, and something I wasn't accustomed to feeling, something I couldn't quite name, washed through me.

"It was nice to meet you, Lennie," he said, stepping closer and wrapping his arms around me.

After a second of hesitation, I melted into his hold and let out a deep breath. "It was nice to meet you too, Espen. Good luck with everything." I leaned backward and looked up into his amber-colored eyes. "I hope you find the culprit of all this chaos."

He sighed and stepped back, releasing me from his arms and letting his hands fall to his sides. "Thank you for your help."

"No problem," I replied, pushing a wayward hair behind my ear as my chest tightened with each word. "Thanks for not shoving me in jail when I punched you."

He scoffed a laugh, his lips quirking into that cute smile of his as he ran his fingers through his dark hair. "You're welcome. Try not to do that anymore."

"I'll do my best."

For a moment we just stared at each other, the gentle lapping of water against the nearby boats the only thing keeping us company. I was at a loss for words, which was unusual for me. But there I stood, unable to utter a single syllable because none of them felt good enough to encapsulate this departure.

With a drawn out exhale and a gentle smile, Espen said, "Goodbye, Lennie."

I returned the grin with one of my own, though it didn't fill my face. "Bye, Espen."

He sauntered backward, his hands still firmly in his pockets until he reached the start of the pier. There he turned and disappeared into the village without another glance in my direction.

Watching, waiting, as if expecting him to return, I stood there for a while, the wind sending errant strands of hair brushing across my cheeks as my heart beat harder than it had five minutes ago. Why had saying goodbye to Espen felt so difficult? I'd only known him a week, yet now

I rubbed my fist across the top of my chest, trying to soothe the pang there.

"Are you ready?" a gruff voice said, startling me.

I spun and looked at the man behind me, his wool hat sitting slightly askew atop his head. He had weather-worn features and was a younger version of Oddvar with thick brows and a gravelly tone.

"Almost," I said with a sigh. Turning around again, I took one last glance across the village that I'd called home for the past week, mentally photographing the scenery. From the little lights in the windows of the white houses, to the tall pine trees that blanketed the mountainsides. Skolvik was a beautiful little oasis. A magical sanctuary for both humans and those creatures that I'd somehow befriended.

"Are you waiting for someone else?"

Was I? Øyvin had made it quite clear that he didn't like me when I first arrived, but over the past few days things had taken a turn between us. From the moment he showed me what lay within the fjord, to the way he gently tucked my hair behind my ear like he couldn't stop himself, I could feel him warming to me. Then there was the explosive hate-sex—which had been stellar. But, what stuck in my mind now, wasn't how good it felt to have him inside me; it was the way he'd pressed his forehead against mine afterward. When our throes of passion had waned, our climaxes reached and diffused, he'd rested his forehead against mine and breathed us in, that moment filled with more emotion than I'd been prepared for.

"Miss?" A voice seeped through my thoughts, dragging me back to the present.

I shook my head, freeing myself of the memories with the Fjord Fae, and shoved my hands into my jacket pockets. My right hand brushed against something soft, and I pulled the material out gently. Lifting it up, I held the piece of string in front of my face, and then chuckled at the sight of my makeshift hair tie. The one Espen had used to hold my hair back. I studied the small rope and the way it danced in the wind. My mind whirled and my chest spasmed as I chewed on my bottom lip.

Of course there was also the Forest Fae that had clearly gotten under my skin. Falling for one's hero seemed so cliché, but with Espen, how could anyone blame me for developing a soft spot for the ray of sunshine? Not only had he saved my life, but he'd been warm, welcoming. Hell, he'd even put his neck on the line with his own people by telling me about their secret world. No guy I'd ever previously met, let alone dated, had ever done so much for me in such a short space of time.

"Are you all right?"

I scoffed, not looking in the man's direction. "Depends on who you ask."

The Norwegian captain behind me snorted. "Well, are you coming or not?"

I returned the string to my pocket and glanced around again, taking a steadying breath.

I should leave. I'd wanted to for the past week. It'd been almost all I could think about, the goal I'd been chasing when I wasn't helping the local fae solve a mystery. But... something felt off. In me, in the air, who the fuck knew. Something seared in my chest and it wasn't heartburn. Maybe there was something in the water I'd been drinking for the past week, because I didn't feel right. It was like standing on the edge of a cliff—a stupid idea—just to get a photo of a major attraction. Adrenaline flooded my system and I shook my head.

"Pull yourself together, Lennie," I muttered to myself, ignoring my audience.

I looked toward the cabin on the hill, invisible from this angle, but I knew it was there. Espen was probably there by now, worried for his people, for the fate of the fjord... What would happen to them after I left?

After everything I'd experienced here, would I be able to return home to my day-to-day routine?

Did I want to?

My life at home was good: I had my family who loved and supported me, and a small group of friends I hung out with ever so often. They would certainly miss me if I stayed a little while longer.

My job would definitely miss me—probably fire me. But, that didn't bother me nearly as much as it probably should. I'd taken the boring desk job to put food on the table and enough money in my account to afford my photography excursions around the world. What harm would there be if I pushed out my departure date?

I could cancel my flight and hopefully recoup the cost or reschedule my flight back to the US. And, if I stayed, I could potentially see even more of the country. Hell, now that I thought about it, I'd even be willing to put down my camera and stop constantly photographing the environment around me and actually help it thrive instead. Maybe, just maybe, I could stay and help the fae solve the illegal magic mystery?

"Miss, last chance. Are you coming aboard?"

I shook my head, and the captain let out a frustrated sigh. Looking around once more, I took in the majesty of the scenery even as it was cloaked in darkness. The breeze shifted, sending my hair into my eyes, and I brushed it back, thinking of the rope in my pocket, but not reaching for it.

Then...

"Fuck it," I mumbled, grabbed my backpack, and walked off the dock toward the village.

25

LENNIE

My breaths came out in steady puffs as I reached the front door of Espen's cabin. The lights were on inside, and my heart hammered at the thought of what I was doing, what I had done... again. But damn it, leaving on that boat just didn't seem like the right thing to do. These people, this land, needed help. And, if I was being introspective, maybe I did, too. So, I set down my backpack and knocked on the door.

A few stomps sounded before the door swung open and a bleary-eyed Espen answered. He'd changed out of his uniform and into a plain green sweater and jeans but looked just as handsome as he always did. His watery gaze landed on me and widened, his jaw slackening slowly.

"What are you—"

I lifted the string from my pocket and brought it into the light streaming out of the house.

Espen flicked his eyes from my face to the little rope and back to me again. He braced one palm against the door frame and ran his other hand across his jaw, disturbing his short beard.

I quirked a brow after several beats of silence went by. "Are you breathing?"

"I—I'm not sure."

I tilted my head and returned the string to my pocket, securing it shut with the zipper.

Espen licked his lips and shifted, turning to look back into his cabin then back at me. "I'm not dreaming am I? I was lying on the sofa and there was a knock—"

I poked his chest, the pectoral muscle firm beneath my touch. "I'm here."

He shook his head again, then cupped my face and pressed his lips to mine.

My heart hammered and a fluttering sensation coursed through my veins as he stole my breath. Just before I melted on his doorstep, he pulled back. His eyes were dilated and his lips split into a big smile.

"I couldn't get on the boat," I whispered as he removed his palms from my cheeks. A slight chill crossed them in the absence of his warmth.

His chest heaved and he pressed his thumb against my bottom lip, as if reassuring himself that I was real, that he'd just kissed me to the point where air decided to permanently vacate my lungs. Without thinking, at least not with my head, I flicked my tongue out across the tip of his thumb.

He let out a low rumble from the back of his throat, and I smirked.

"Wait here," he said and disappeared into the cabin. I picked up my bag and stepped inside, setting it down next to some of Espen's shoes by the front door. Before I had time to wonder where he'd gone, Espen came hurtling around the corner with a dark green yoga mat in one hand then shoved his feet into a pair of boots.

My forehead scrunched in confusion. "Where are you going? This sounds presumptuous when I say it out loud, but I was thinking more along the lines of taking clothes *off*, not putting shoes on when I came to see you." He stepped in closer, our faces mere inches apart, and his eyes shimmered with happiness.

"Do you trust me?"

I let out a deep breath and tried to stifle a smile, but something about Espen made that damn near impossible. "Yes."

With a spark of victory in his gaze, he grabbed my hand and dragged me outside, shutting the door behind us with his yoga mat under his arm. We wandered into the field beside his cabin, the wild grass short in some spots and longer in others. I tried to tamp down my disappointment that Espen was more interested in *literal* forest yoga than bedroom *yoga,* but I couldn't help but be happy in his presence. Once we reached a clearing between the woods and the house, Espen stopped and let go of my hand. With a flick of his wrists he unfurled the yoga mat.

"Please tell me that's for the good kind of forest yoga," I said, pointing at the green mat.

He turned to me with a mischievous smirk and I rolled my bottom lip between my teeth. Stepping into my personal space, he invaded my senses with his strong form and the sumptuous smell of moss and leather with a dash of evergreen in there, too. Our breaths came in steady waves, our chests rising and falling in tandem as he brushed an errant hair off my cheek.

"I'm so glad you stayed," he whispered, cradling my head with one hand while sliding his other around my waist.

At that exact moment, I couldn't help it. I was glad I'd walked away from the harbor, too. "Make it worth my while," I said, my voice huskier than I'd ever heard it.

A low, satisfied rumble emitted from Espen's chest in answer. "Oh, I definitely will."

He pressed his lips to mine in a soft but firm kiss that sent a wave of heat crashing through my body, promising a helluva lot more. I sank into his hold and wrapped my arms around his neck, needing to be closer. He swept his tongue across my mouth, requesting entrance, and I happily relented, falling further under this magical feeling that was brewing inside my chest.

After a few minutes of the best kiss of my life, I pulled back, desperate for air.

Espen gave me a rakish grin, like he knew exactly what he was doing. And, honest to hell, he really did. "Lie down," he said, nodding to the mat at our feet.

I sure as fuck wasn't going to say no. For only the tenth time in my life, I did as I was told, and laid down on the yoga mat.

Looking up, my breath left my lungs again. Not just at the sight of Espen pulling off his sweater, but at the starry sky above us, a hint of green light dancing above the mountain across the fjord. Espen, now completely shirtless, glanced up at the northern lights and smiled.

As our eyes met again, he crouched down on his knees by my feet. Achingly slow, he started untangling my laces and pulled off my boots, gently placing them in the grass beside us. Next up went my socks, which he carefully slipped off my feet. Cold air brushed across my toes as he wrapped his fingers around my ankle.

I slowly unzipped my jacket, fully aware of his eyes locked on my every movement, the heat of his gaze visible thanks to the light of the stars and the aurora borealis shifting above us.

His hands slid along my rib cage, pushing up my shirt and then my sports bra. Fingers traced over my nipples and I sucked in a breath at the feel of the cold air mixed with his hot touch.

"Perfect," he said, and I almost combusted at the sound of his voice, every nerve alight. He leaned above me, resting on his forearm, as he unfastened the button on my jeans.

"We're gonna freeze," I murmured.

"I promise to keep you warm," he said before his hot mouth latched over my nipple, sucking lightly, drawing a moan from deep in my throat.

Pulling my jeans and panties down my legs, Espen marked every inch with a kiss, and the spot where I desperately wanted his mouth grew needier by the second. Pull, kiss. Sweep, kiss... until he reached my feet and expertly tugged my pants over my toes, setting the clothes aside.

With a sly grin and a shimmer in his gaze, Espen undid his pants revealing no boxers or briefs. His dick was hard, and looked exactly the same as any human dick I'd had the fortune of meeting, which shouldn't have been surprising after my encounter with Øyvin. But, in Espen's case, he was significantly more endowed than any of my priors. I rolled my lip between my teeth again and flicked my eyes up to his. His smile widened and he leaned over me where I squirmed, wanton and needy.

"Are you on birth-control?" he asked, hovering above me, bracing his palms on either side of my head.

I nodded, my breath sawing in and out of my lungs, desperate to take things further. He hadn't even touched me, but my core was already dripping. "Yes. Are you clean?"

"Yes."

"And things don't work differently because—"

He smirked, notching his dick at my entrance. "Same equipment, same process. I'm just magical."

"Well, that's yet to be—"

He thrust inside me and cut off the end of my sentence as my mouth fell open. I wrapped my legs around him, groaning at the fullness as he pushed in deeper, waiting for my body to adjust before he started moving. I grabbed his hair as he traced kisses down my neck, holding him to me until I couldn't take it any longer. "Move, damn it."

Needing no further instruction, Espen pulled back, then slammed back in, drawing noises from my mouth I'd never heard before. Encouraged by the sound, he kept up an unrelenting pace, surging inside me, again and again and again, hitting all the right spots. His fingers tangled in my hair as our lips found each other and continued kissing, claiming, devouring.

With each move, my core fluttered around him, desperate for more. He must have sensed my need, because two seconds later his fingers found my clit and he started caressing the bundle of nerves. I shuddered in response, the sensation building and building until I detonated, moaning into his mouth.

He was still hard, and smiled against my lips as I came down from my high.

"Do you know the move, downward dog?"

I nodded and let out a satisfied sigh, because I'd happily take more of that, thank you very much.

He winked, and I chuckled, pulling my jacket from my arms and yanking my shirt and bra over my head before I rolled onto my stomach and pushed my ass toward the starry sky. Grabbing onto my hips, Espen kicked my legs wider, stretching my trembling muscles.

"Where's your hair tie?" he asked, his voice heavy and husky.

I braced my weight on one shaky hand, and quickly reached into my jacket pocket next to me, pulling out the makeshift one he'd created for me. Holding it up, he quickly took it and I placed my hand back down, redistributing my weight across the mat. Cool air drifted across my rear as he stepped beside me. He pulled my hair back and fastened it with the loose bit of rope. It sure as hell wouldn't hold it in a ponytail, but it would keep the strands out of my face.

I stretched deeper into the position as he returned to his spot behind me. Wiggling my ass in his direction, I heard a throaty chuckle before he slapped his hand across my ass cheek. My core clenched at the sharp sting, and I moaned, my knees buckling slightly.

"Oh no you don't," Espen said, gripping my hips and returning my legs into the spread out yoga position. In this stance I was completely at his mercy, angled slightly by the gentle slope beneath us, but still vulnerable to whatever he wanted to do with me. "Don't move."

"Wasn't planning on it," I mouthed, sure as hell not going anywhere.

"Good," he replied, before leaning over, pressing his slick cock against me, and grabbing my hair. With a gentle tug, he pulled my head back and wrapped my hair around his fist so I stared up the grassy hill. I groaned as he rubbed himself between my entrance and clit, then back again. Wiggling once more, hoping for another slap, I got what I asked for and then he thrust inside me. The sting on my scalp and ass sent shivers down my spine, the sounds of our bodies slapping against each other filling the otherwise quiet night.

At this angle, Espen hit all the right—and deep—spots to have my nerves sparking. He dropped my hair, and his hands gripped my hips, holding me in position as he pounded into me, keeping an even tempo that left me breathless, yet aching for more. My legs quivered, arms burned, knees wobbled—if I didn't explode in the next five seconds, I was going to my knees. Espen must've sensed that I couldn't hold the position much longer as he slowly lowered us to the mat without removing himself.

"Press your chest down," he said, sliding his palm down my spine and gently applying pressure between my shoulder blades.

With my knees on the mat, I sank deeper into the modified pose, feeling the stretch in my upper back, the fullness between my thighs, and let out a satisfied groan. Espen took that as his cue and started pounding into me again, only this time, much harder and faster.

My breaths sawed in and out of my mouth, the euphoric precipice closing in. The stretch, the fullness, it was all too much, and I shattered. I moaned through my release as Espen chased his own. He shifted both hands back to my hips, tightening his grip, the bite of it so much more in my current state of bliss. With a few more deep surges, he exploded inside of me.

My legs shook as I slowly lowered to my stomach, removing his dick from my swollen core in the process. I collapsed onto the yoga mat, spent, happy, and definitely interested in more once I could feel my thighs and arms again.

Espen curled up beside me, our noses nearly touching. I caught his satisfied grin before he shifted, nuzzling against my neck. "Told you I'd keep you warm."

"You certainly are a man of your word."

He chuckled, pulling me onto my side and into his arms.

Staring at the sky, watching the green-and-teal lights dance above us, I relaxed into his hold. While I certainly had been mad that I'd missed the cruise ship, I most definitely was happy I'd chosen to not get on the supply boat. And, not that I'd tell him to his face, but that might have been some of the best sex of my life.

26

LENNIE

I awoke in a tangle of sheets by myself, the sound of a shower shutting off greeting me in my sleepy haze. The scent of my second round of *yoga* antics last night lingered in the air and the satisfied ache between my legs was a welcome sensation as I stretched my limbs.

Espen wandered into the bedroom, a white towel slung low around his hips, beads of water slowly descending his torso. He caught my gaze and gave me a cheeky smile. "Good morning, Lennie."

"Morning."

"How are you feeling?" he asked, his gaze raking over me and the sheet I'd pulled up over my chest.

I took a mental inventory, assessing every limb and extremity, plus the state of my blissed out mind. "Fine."

Espen's eyes widened in panic. "When women say 'fine' it usually means the opposite. Are you sure you're all right? I didn't hurt you, did I?"

His concern was adorable, so I let him sweat it for a moment as I pretended to think it over. When he looked ready to combust, I said, "I'm feeling really good, Espen. Don't worry."

He let out a long breath, his shoulders sagging as relief washed over his features.

"Where are you staying?" he asked, pivoting the topic with a shake of his head.

I rolled my shoulders and the joints popped before I sat upright. I doubted I could stay with Solveig again—that seemed too imposing, especially considering my departure date was very much unknown. "Hadn't thought that far ahead."

With his back to me, Espen dropped his towel and tossed it to the side. "You could stay with me."

I vaguely caught the smile he threw over his shoulder considering my attention was drawn down to his perfectly toned ass. "Are you sure?"

"Of course." He nodded, slowly pulling on a pair of boxers.

"I don't want you to think that what we did last night suddenly means something," I remarked, pointing between us.

He shook his head and crossed the room. Pressing his fists on either side of my hips on the bed, he brought his face to mine. "I don't expect it to. But I like you and if you need a place to stay, you're welcome here. This can be whatever you want it to be." He tilted his lips into a smile. "And if you want to *go* again, you need only ask."

My core spasmed at the look in his eyes and the words on his tongue. Before I dragged him back into bed, I swallowed hard and asked, "How angry will your boss be if you're late for work?"

"Very," he replied before planting a kiss on my lips and pushing off the bed. He crossed the room and started pulling on his uniform. "There's coffee in the cupboard above the kitchen sink, and eggs in the fridge. Make yourself at home."

Later that morning, I sauntered down to the village and stopped by Oddvar's for another cup of coffee. The bell chimed as I stepped inside, and Oddvar's wispy eyebrows hit his hairline. I gave him a quick smile which he vaguely returned with a twitch of his lips before spinning around and filling a mug with coffee.

"Morning, Oddvar."

"I see you don't know how to climb aboard boats," he said, turning back and proffering the steaming cup of nectar with my desired milk and sugar already added.

"Apparently not." I accepted the drink with a chuckle and thanked him.

"So, you are staying then?" Oddvar asked as I took my usual seat by the window.

I sighed and nodded. "For a little while."

"Okay." And that was that.

The old man went back to his work—fetching beverages and sandwiches for other patrons—and said nothing more than a clipped goodbye when I paid and left for the convenience store in hopes of finding a charger for my phone.

I returned to Espen's house with my successful shopping trip completed. After letting my phone charge for ten minutes, I started it and connected to the wi-fi using the password that Espen had given me before he left for work. Messages started pinging like crazy, and I opened my texts. Majority of which were from my dear brothers.

Ryan: Answer your fucking phone, Len.

Andrew: You okay? We're starting to get worried over here.

Jared: Andrew asked to check in. Text Y if alive.

Having an overprotective older brother to look out for you was nice sometimes, but three was overkill. They were cute when they were worried but also seriously annoying. They'd been like this when I was in high school too—not trusting any of the boys, especially the ones on the football team. Which was fair, but damn did it prove problematic when I wanted some D after a Friday night game. None of the players would go near Andrew and Jared Martin's little sister. Fucking ridiculous is what it really was.

Andrew: Evelyn, this is serious. Please call us or I'll have to tell Mom and Dad.

Ah shit. The full name from Andrew was never a good sign.

*Jared: *skull emoji**

Ryan: Brace yourself.

Andrew: I told Mom and Dad. They're really worried. We all are. If you don't call us back, I'm calling the embassy.

I grumbled. Opening my chat-app, I clicked Andrew's smiling face, and video called him. Hoping this would be cheaper than an actual phone call, I prepared for the polite tirade I was about to receive from my eldest brother.

"Thank God, you're alive," Andrew said, his face popping up on my screen. He was the male older version of me, with dark blond hair and ochre eyes. Wearing a collared shirt, he looked ready for work, and I could hear his two daughters giggling in the background.

"My phone died. Sorry."

"For *days*? We were starting to think you'd done the same. For Christ's sake, Evelyn."

I sighed and started groveling. "Andrew, I'm sorry. I'm fine. I just got caught up in some stuff and didn't get a new charger until today. I called you as soon as I could."

His brows knit together and he pinched the bridge of his nose. It was a move I'd seen my Dad do countless times too—mostly in response to something I'd done. "At least you're on your way home."

My stomach dropped and I grimaced.

"You *are* on your way home, right?"

"About that...."

"Lennie, please tell me you're in Stavanger about to get on a flight back to Ohio."

"No."

Andrew let out an audible sigh through his nose and ran his free hand across his jaw. "Do I want to know?"

"Probably not."

He shook his head. "You know Mom worries about you when you travel alone." Ugh, now he *sounded* like Dad too.

"I'm well aware, but things didn't go according to plan."

"They never do with you."

He had me there. My adventures had a tendency to go off the rails, but this one had seriously veered off track.

"Look, Lennie," Andrew continued. "I'm glad you're okay, but I need to get to work and you need to call Mom immediately."

"I will. I promise."

"Good. All right, love you, Sis."

"Love you too," I said and then he hung up, leaving me to my next task. Calling Mom.

I set my phone back down on the kitchen table, letting it charge while I mentally prepared myself for the reprimand I was about to endure. Mom definitely had a right to be angry with me. I had gone too far this time, but I'd still followed her rule: always inform her and Dad when I was traveling somewhere. They'd put it in place after I went to the Grand Canyon with my brother Ryan one spring break. We hadn't bothered to tell them, and Mom lost her cool when she found out afterward, claiming that so many hiking accidents happened there—true—and that it was always best to tell someone when venturing on hikes or entering certain terrain—fair enough, also true. So, I'd followed the rule ever since. However, my communication skills once I was on the road had never been the best, and this instance was clearly not helping matters.

Taking a deep breath, I picked up my phone again and video called my Mom. It was early back in the US, but she'd have been awake since six anyway.

It rang three times and then... "Oh thank the heavens, you're all right."

"Hi Mom."

"I'm very disappointed with you for not having your phone on and missing your cruise ship."

"I know, and I'm sorry."

"As you should be. Your Dad and I have been extremely worried. When your brother told me you'd missed your ship, I thought I'd misheard him. Then I find out that all three of your brothers knew before me...." She shook her head, her dark brown locks shifting across her shoulders as she patted her palm against the top of her chest.

"Again, I'm sorry. I'll do better." I mean, I was a grown-ass woman, but I did appreciate their love and care for me.

"You certainly will. Now, when does your flight land? Are you flying through Chicago to Columbus or Cincinnati? Do you need Dad to come pick you up at the airport?"

"Soooo, about that."

Her eyes widened slowly and her lips pinched together. "Evelyn."

"I'm staying in Norway for a little while longer."

"Why? How long? With what money? When—"

"I'm not sure how long, but probably another few weeks. I made some friends here and they are letting me stay with them."

"But *why*?" she asked, her tone escalating toward panic.

Now there was a good question. Because I felt some sort of need to stay and help. Because this town was adorable, and I met two guys and a whole host of other characters that I liked (but also didn't like). Because the fjord needed to be saved from whatever chaos was bearing down on it. Because the thought of going home now to my boring life in Ohio after knowing that so much else existed out there sounded absolutely fucking miserable.

I still wasn't sure about the *why*. Maybe it was all of the above. Whatever the real answer, I'd made my decision and I was going to stick with it.

"Because I had the opportunity to stay and help out a local community with some photography stuff," I replied. It wasn't exactly a lie, but it most definitely wasn't the entire truth. The latter was something I couldn't exactly share with anyone or I'd get in serious trouble with the fae.

"Is this because of a man?"

"Really, Mom?" I deadpanned.

"Did you meet someone?"

It dawned on me what she was struggling to say. "I've met several guys, Mom. But I'm not staying because of one of them." The words felt odd coming out of my mouth for some reason I didn't want to analyze too closely. "You won't be getting a wedding out of me any time soon."

"A mother can dream," she said with a sigh.

I shook my head. "I'll let you know when I've booked my flights home," I said, pivoting from one of her favorite discussion topics.

"Good, and please check in with me more often, at least every Sunday."

"Will do."

"I love you, Evelyn. Please stay safe."

"Love you too. And I'm always safe."

She scoffed. "We both know that's a lie."

I laughed as I ended the call and set the phone back down on the table. Stretching my arms above my head, I eased the tension out of my muscles and decided I'd call the airline company next and try to get a refund for my flight before heading out for dinner this evening.

But, I had one other task to complete first. As I launched myself onto Espen's sofa, I typed out a quick message to my brothers.

Lennie: I'm alive. Staying in Norway for a few more weeks.

*Andrew: *heart emoji**

Ryan: Don't have too much fun. You owe me for waking me up early last week.

Jared: K.

27

LENNIE

Monday night Espen and I wandered into town for dinner, then bolted into Fisken to avoid the rain that had started hammering the village. I shivered as we both pulled off our jackets and hung them on the old-fashioned coat rack by the door, water dripping onto the wood floor beneath them. Rubbing my arms, I took in my surroundings, noticing how crowded it was as Espen waved to a woman at a table across the restaurant. A waiter spotted us and motioned us forward, and I followed Espen toward his friend. We wandered over to the table, its inhabitant giving me a welcoming smile as I took a seat.

"This is Ylva," Espen said, motioning toward the woman as he sat down in one of the vacant chairs. My head tilted to the side as I studied her, noticing her dirty blonde hair that fell below her shoulders and sharp features. She was slim in stature and wore a wool sweater with Nordic patterns across the chest. "A good friend of mine," he added with a knowing look, which led me to believe she was a Forest Fae like him, "and my second in command."

I nodded to her. "It's nice to meet you."

"Espen has told me about you," Ylva said with a tip of her beer glass.

Part of me was surprised Espen had mentioned me, but I had been working with him lately, so it wasn't shocking. "Has he now?"

"Mm-hmm," she murmured, her eyes glittering with mischief.

"Only nice things," Espen said, leaning toward me. "I promise."

Considering my usual behavior, and the fact that I'd punched him—a knee-jerk self-defense reaction—when we'd first met, I highly doubted his sentiments had been solely good. I glanced back at Ylva and saw her barely contained grin. Yeah, she most definitely knew about the first time I'd met Espen.

"Anything to report this evening?" Espen asked, looking at Ylva, whose amused gaze broke away from mine.

She let out a long exhale and surveyed the room. Seemingly satisfied with whatever she saw, she said, "There was an issue with wolves north of the Langholm farm."

Espen stilled, his jaw tightening.

"Myself and a few others sent them away without any harm to livestock or farmland—"

"But?" Espen interjected.

"—but, the locals are now a bit spooked." She narrowed her eyes at him. "I'm surprised you weren't notified at the station."

"If they did call it in, I wasn't informed." Espen wiped his palm across his jaw before settling back in his seat.

"Care to explain why these big bad puppies are a problem?" I asked, looking between the two of them before turning to Espen.

He sighed and clasped his hands together, resting his wrists on the table edge. "They're only a problem if they start picking off the sheep or any other animals, which always causes a ruckus with the *locals*," he said, that last word sounding more like a codeword for *humans*.

"Can't you just monitor the fields or have them moved to a safer location, like a sanctuary?" I asked, waving my hand toward the windows.

Espen and Ylva looked at each other, a silent conversation briefly passing between them. "It can be a bit more of a complex situation than that," Espen replied, choosing his words carefully.

"I'll go get us some drinks then," I said, sensing this conversation would include a lot more information that I wouldn't understand. I rose from my chair and turned toward the lightly packed bar, chatter rising from the high stools that were occupied. As I crossed the room, I was intercepted by Nora with two full glasses in her hands, wearing a brightly patterned sweater and black pants.

"Beer?" she asked, pulling up alongside me and proffering a tall glass of amber liquid.

"Thank you." I accepted the drink and swallowed a large gulp while watching Espen laugh with his second in command. Something warmed my chest at the sight, but I tried to shake it off.

I wasn't one for emotions or attachments—I'd always been a *wham, bam, thanks man*, kinda gal—and hadn't ever really pictured myself settling down. And, even though Espen was single and older than me—honestly too old for *any* human—he seemed like the kind of yogi-fae-cop thingy that *would* settle down and have a family. I wasn't sure how I felt about the spark between us, if it could even be called that...

I took another large swig of my drink as Espen looked over and gave me a gentle smile and a nod to Nora. I smiled back, the corners of my eyes crinkling.

Nora looked at me, then Espen, then back to me, letting out a low humm before gasping. "You didn't?"

I turned to her, catching her widened gaze with my own. "Didn't what?"

She looked between me and Espen again, her mouth dropping open and an excited look washing across her features. "Oh, you *totally* fucked Espen. Is that why you stayed? Which, I'm glad you did, by the way, but—"

I clamped my free hand across her mouth. "Shut up, right now."

Her lips shifted into a grin beneath my palm, eyes alight with laughter at my reaction.

Just then, the door opened, and Øyvin walked in, his gaze lingering on me for a second too long before he rolled his eyes, brushing past me. "Trouble."

"Øyvin," I replied, dropping my hand from Nora's face. The tension in the room rose swiftly, and I swallowed down the lump that was forming in my throat at the sight of the Fjord Fae. The way that damn cream-colored sweater of his hugged his shoulders and arms had my skin flushing, and memories of what lay beneath clouded my thoughts.

Like he could hear me thinking, he glanced over his shoulder and the corner of his lips twitched as he reached Espen's table. Nora inhaled loudly.

"Nooooooo," she gasped, her eyes darting to the big blond fae and back to me, a wide grin taking up her face. "You didn't."

"I don't know what you're talking about." I busied my mouth with my drink and made an attempt to escape the deteriorating situation. Nora's hand shot out and grabbed my upper arm, not letting me leave. For such a small thing, she was strong as fuck—her grip like an iron shackle as she pulled my attention solely onto her.

"Part of me wants every gory, smutty detail, and the other part of me wants to shove my fingers in my ears. I've known them both for over a century."

I quirked a brow at her comment and remained silent.

She didn't back down though. A second later she was in front of me. "Please tell me you're staying in town for quite a while. We haven't had this much excitement since—well. Not a good kind of excitement, anyway." With a shake of her head, she dismissed the somber thought and went back to the topic at hand, unfortunately. "So, who did you do first? Or was it a dueling swords situation? Now that I say that, I could see—"

"Nora!" I hissed, leaning toward her as my eyes bugged.

The others looked over at us, but Nora waved them away and pulled me into an empty booth. Unable to shake her hold on me, I sidled onto the leather seat and she plopped down beside me, blocking my exit, but keeping an eye on the other fae in the room. And, more specifically, the two fae that I had indeed fucked.

"Your cheeks are bright red and your hand trembled minutely after my first accusation, so don't bother lying." She propped her head into her palms, resting her elbows on the table. "Now, please, tell me the story."

I stared at my half empty glass, trying to decide what to say, if anything. While I wasn't embarrassed about my actions, I also wasn't sure what the future held with either of the males.

Did I want a repeat performance? Abso-fucking-lutely. But was there more to my magnetism to them than just sexual chemistry? I wasn't sure I was ready to think too hard on that.

Nora's eyes were wide in anticipation and her lips were spread into a tiny smile. "Espen does yoga. I'd imagine that helped you get into all kinds of *positions*," she said, not holding back at all as she leaned into my space. Even as I pulled away from her, my mind shifted to the angles he'd hit last night and heat washed over my skin at the thought. Nora grinned like she'd caught a massive fish. "There it is."

"Fine." I stalled by taking another sip of my beer, shaking my head as I set it back down. It had been a while since I had a girlfriend to chat with, and I was coming to like Nora. "Yes, yes, and *hell yes*."

Nora clapped her hands excitedly, bouncing in the booth. "I'm going to need more details than that."

"Why?"

She glanced over her shoulders before lowering her voice. "I'm a three-hundred-and-fifty-two year old fae historian that doesn't get out of the mountain enough. Give an old lady some good gossip. Also, we're friends. Friends share."

I shook my head, but her words meant something to me. While I didn't know her well yet, she'd been welcoming and hadn't completely shunned me when she found out I was a human that knew about her world. It was like we were in a secret club together, and slowly getting to know one another, on our way to becoming friends for real. And, clearly, Nora liked to hear about cock.

"Lennie..." she said, tapping her fingers on the table as she eyed me hopefully.

"Nora...."

"I'll live for at least a few more centuries." She crossed her arms with a wicked look on her face. "I have time to wait."

"Fine," I relented, and she sat upright like a puppy getting a treat. "I hate-fucked Øyvin at his boathouse after trying to steal his boat."

She snort-laughed and almost fell out of the booth. "H-his boat? You didn't?"

"I did," I said, taking another sip of my beer. "Failed because someone ratted me out."

Her eyebrows shot up, a broad grin taking over her face. "And then he thanked you by fucking you?"

I pursed my lips, glancing over at the male in question. "Not exactly. Heated words were exchanged and then sex happened."

"I love it." She downed the rest of her drink before grabbing mine and chugging that too. "Now, what about Espen?"

"What about me?" the fae said, sliding into the booth across from us, and I started at his sudden appearance.

"We were just discussing how nice you are for letting me stay at your house," I said with a forced smile, hoping Nora understood my unspoken words to keep her damn mouth shut. Friends could chat about cock, but not tell the cock that they did so. It was girl-code or some shit.

"I *am* a gentleman." Espen placed his hand over his heart and grinned.

"Yes, well," Nora said, tapping her fingers on the table, her eyes darting sideways at me briefly, "always nice to have it both ways."

I practically growled at Nora for the innuendo and for stealing my beer—I needed that safety blanket to avoid this conversation. Just then, the others joined us—Øyvin taking a seat at the end of the table, while Ylva set down a tray of ten shot glasses filled with light, amber liquid and then sidled into the booth beside Espen. I squirmed in my spot, considering sitting on my hands, and choosing to shove them under my thighs when Espen gave me a pointed look like he understood exactly what kind of conversation we'd been having.

"Aquavit?" Ylva asked, breaking the tension and pointing at the arrangement of shots.

Without saying a word, I lunged forward and grabbed one, then downed it. Liquid fire sluiced down my throat, and my eyes widened in panic. *What the fuck was that?* I sat back and placed my fist in front of my mouth, coughing and sputtering, trying to catch a breath that didn't make me feel like a dragon about to set the building ablaze.

Nora took the glass from my hand as the rest of the group grinned at me—except Øyvin, but he bit his lip which was just as much of a similar reaction.

"It's a sipping liquor," Ylva piped up, giving me a tentative smile. "Sorry."

I waved away her apology, but couldn't voice anything other than an "mm-hmm."

The others picked up a small glass each and took a genteel sip.

"It's made from potatoes and caraway," Espen said, passing me another shot glass of the stuff. "A bit like vodka."

I winced and leaned away, wrinkling my nose at the beverage.

"It's not as bad if you sip. I promise," he added, nudging the drink in my direction.

Deciding I could trust him—and would pace myself this time—I pulled the little glass closer but waited a few minutes before taking a dainty-ass sip. Thankfully, Espen was right, it wasn't as bad. It most definitely still burned, but I could taste the nutty and earthy notes of caraway this time around.

"What were we talking about anyway?" Ylva asked, glancing around the table.

"Nora's job," I said, finally feeling able to speak without spewing fire. "That was my next question." And a much better subject than my sex-scapades when both parties sat at the table with me.

"I record stories for *my mountain people*. From major events to the last tales from the dying," Nora said, taking a sip of the liquor and lowering her voice so no one but those at our table could hear.

"That seems like a very important job... and kind of sad," I said.

She smiled briefly, pushing some of her short brown locks behind her ear, all of her excitement from our previous conversation gone. "Yes, on both counts. But, I'm glad I can capture the dying *individual's* memories and record them for posterity."

"They have a wall," Øyvin butted in, and Nora nodded.

"What do you mean?" I asked, taking a tiny sip of aquavit like the lady I was. I could practically hear my mother's derisive snort at the thought.

"Most stories, like those I write down from a dying *mountain people*, are recorded in large tomes that we keep in the library. But major events, battles, births of royals, those are all recorded the old fashioned way. Those tales are magically carved into the mountain by me." She downed the remnants of her shot before saying, "Would you like to see some of them?"

I choked on my own shot of aquavit, the burning sensation coating the back of my throat unpleasantly again even as excitement raced through my veins. "Y-you can let me see that? It's not forbidden or some shit?"

She shifted her head from one side and then the other, her lips set in a firm line. "Well, you've already been inside and met my sister—"

"And Halvar," I added, a wary shiver running up my spine at the memory of the beast of a fae.

"—and him. So, I don't see a problem with it. Just don't take any pictures or tell anyone about it."

My mouth gaped slightly, glancing at the table full of fae around me. "And just like that, I get to see this stuff?"

Nora shrugged, a small smile playing across her face. "I *am* the Fjell historian and sister to the Queen. It comes with some benefits."

I bet it fucking did. "Okay, deal."

"Great," she said, standing from the booth and dragging me with her. "Let's go."

28

LENNIE

Nora and I traipsed up the hillside, heading straight for the main entrance of the mountain—the same one I'd entered through with Espen and Øyvin when we'd visited the Queen. The rain had let up to a light drizzle, the clouds blocking the light of the moon, putting me and my very human eyesight at a severe disadvantage. I moved as swiftly as I could under the cover of darkness, tripping over logs and rocks every fifth step. Nora, on the other hand, didn't seem to have any trouble navigating the terrain, moving with the ease of a cat.

Like last time, we stepped through the magical entry that looked like a sheer rock face. A ripple of warm air washed over me and my skin tingled more than it already was thanks to the alcohol I'd consumed. The world wasn't quite spinning, but aquavit was no fucking joke and I could feel the buzz.

Even though I'd seen the tunnels before, I couldn't help but gawk at the lanterns hanging every few feet, casting a sparkling glow over the rough-cut rock walls. Before I could reach out and touch the walls, exploring it like I hadn't been able to the first time, Nora started walking and I was forced to follow as we wound through tunnels, descending deeper into the belly of the mountain.

"Nora, you're great and all, but you need to slow down or you're gonna lose me. And, I don't ever like to admit weakness, but seriously cardio after shots is a bad idea at any age," I said between heaving breaths, gripping my side. Damn, that alcohol had done a number on me. Or perhaps I was exhausted after last night's exercise with Espen? I shook off the thought. "This one time in college I thought drunk baseball sounded like a fun idea, but seeing double while balls flew at my face wasn't nearly as exciting as it originally sounded. At least not like that, anyway."

Nora laughed, the happy sound bouncing off the walls around us, then thankfully slowed and hooked her arm through mine. "No more shots for the human."

I shook my head. "Not after beer, and not before hiking up that hill."

She chuckled, and we continued walking for another several minutes, winding deeper into the mountain. Eventually we turned a corner and wandered through a low archway into a cavernous space with blank rock walls.

A chill swept over my face, the air in here slightly colder than that of the tunnels as I looked up. Pair that with the darkness—only dismal rays from the entryway enlightened the space—and this was the perfect recipe for eeriness. At least, that would explain the creepy sensation that skittered up my spine until Nora unlooped our arms and placed her hand against the wall.

A moment later, silver swirls started to appear on the cave walls, casting an ethereal glow as they grew and morphed into images. I wasn't sure what I was expecting—maybe primitive cave paintings like from ancient times, which some definitely were—but most were far more detailed. The pictures were indiscernible at this distance, but looking at the ones closest to the entry, they almost looked like ancient runes and engravings.

My mouth hung open as I sauntered deeper into the space, taking it all in. One image was of a boat with little stick figures in it, large fish swimming beneath them. Another drawing had figures wielding hatchets, swords, and shields—Vikings. One after the next, each told a story, even if I didn't understand the context. Nora remained silent as I surveyed the shining marks, each revealing another layer of the Fjell Fae history.

"How long have the fae existed?" I whispered, any other volume feeling too loud for what appeared to be hallowed space.

Nora pushed off the wall and stepped closer, her gaze tracing over the images. "No one knows exact numbers, but at least several millennia."

I checked my face to make sure my eyes were still where they were supposed to be, feeling my brain implode at this new information. "Are you serious?"

She nodded. "Ages and lifetimes vary wildly. Some Fjell Fae live to be five-hundred-years-old, others double that. Many start to lose track though."

"Do you know who's the oldest?"

She shook her head. "But I'd wager that Halvar has been around for a long time. He served in my father's army, and may have even fought for my grandfather, but I'm not sure. Every time I ask, he just grunts and walks away."

I snickered, fully able to picture the hulking fae of few words. I cast my eyes back to the carvings, inspecting them more closely—the intricate marks glowing like the lanterns that dotted the tunnels.

"How do you draw these?"

Nora stepped forward, eyes roving over the wall as she moved. "The Royal line has some light magic from our ancestors. I'm able to use that to carve the scenes into the rock."

"So, you're also the one who lights all the tunnels?" I asked, looking around the room, taking it all in, trying to understand how they could create light in such a dark place, so far underground.

Nora let out a gentle laugh, turning back toward me. "No, I don't. There's one particular Fjell Fae that has similar magic to mine and Freija's. He is in charge of all the lighting within the fjell."

Overwhelmed by the sight of so much history before me, something so few humans had ever seen, I stood in silence—rare for me.

"The power I use to make these drawings is just like his magic, although mine is much more diluted," Nora continued, stroking her palm across the cave wall, seeming lost in her thoughts. "My sister and I have a blend of all the powers of the Fjell Fae. From creating and lifting boulders, to healing cracks, and even shifting appearance and sounds. Our power stems from the mountain, and we, in turn, take care of it and our people. We do what we need to do to make sure the Fjell Fae live long and prosperous lives."

"Like the Forest and Fjord Fae do for their realms?" I asked.

"Yes, exactly." She shoved her hands into her back pockets, offering me a small smile. "All our powers have an elemental skew. It's our responsibility to use those abilities to protect the natural resources around us."

"And as royals you inherit more power than others?"

Nora let out a breathy sigh and wrung her fingers. "In a way. The history books are inconclusive on where the royal line started, but Freija and I inherited more power than normal fae upon our birth. Fae power is a gift from earth, and in return we use it to help our domain. When we were born, we got a little extra, like the magic I used to rewire your hearing, making you understand Norwegian." She nodded to my ears, and I brushed my fingers across them. That party trick sure had been useful.

"For the Fjell Fae, when the first born of the first born ascends to the throne upon the monarch's passing," she continued, staring at the shimmering stories on the wall, "they are gifted the deceased's power so they may continue to lead the Fjell Fae."

I followed her gaze, trying to make sense of what she was telling me. "So, basically, the mountain—earth—recycles the monarch's power to the new monarch?"

Nora nodded. "Exactly. There's a whole private ceremony after the coronation," she added with a wave of her hand.

A sudden chill went up my spine and I hugged myself, running my hands up and down my arms. While I was still wearing my jacket, the chill within the cave still seemed to seep into my skin, my bones. Or perhaps it was the room and the history around me. I yawned and then quickly snapped my mouth shut as Nora laughed, her full cheeks growing wider with her smile.

"Looks like it is well past someone's bedtime," she remarked, placing her hand against the wall by the entrance, shutting off the carvings like that particular spot served as an on/off switch for the room.

I nodded and moved over to her, using the light from the tunnel to guide me. "Alcohol hits a little harder after twenty-five."

"I wish I could relate, but seeing as I was under 25 over 300 years ago, it all seems a bit foggy," she replied, grabbing my arm and looping it through her own. "Let me walk you back to the entrance. You think you can make it back to Espen's by yourself?"

I nodded. "Just keep talking to me until we get to the entrance." I'd need the extra motivation to stay alert until the night air outside could smack me in the face.

Thankfully, Nora obliged, regaling me with stories of her drunken escapades as a much younger fae—the ones she could remember at least.

A lot of the stories had taken place within the confines of the mountain, but the funniest ones, by far, were when she'd had to dunk her head into the fjord to wash away the severe buzz only to then walk back to the mountain and have her hair start to freeze.

Giving me a quick once over by the entrance to the mountain, Nora patted me on the shoulder and sent me on my way. I thanked her, and stepped out into the night.

29

LENNIE

I stumbled off the path from the mountain, wandered onto the street, and headed across the village toward Espen's house. My breath fogged the air in front of me as I walked under the sporadic street lights through the sleepy town. The cold air had settled across the buildings, leaving a layer of frost on the windows of the houses I passed. All the stores and most residents had turned off their lights for the night already, but some homes still cast a warm glow across the narrow streets. I shoved my hands into my jacket pockets, wishing I'd brought gloves and a hat.

"You stayed," a voice said, startling me as I rounded the corner by Oddvar's Café. Øyvin stepped out into the soft beam of a street-lamp, his hands firmly planted in the pockets of his rain jacket and his eyes brimming with a warmth I could barely look away from.

Why'd he have to be so stubbornly handsome? And, dammit, why am I calling him handsome? I blame the alcohol.

"What a keen observation," I replied and kept walking as my throat tightened. It was oddly nice to see him again, and I was annoyed with the flush I felt creeping across my cheeks.

A low grumble emanated from his chest as I sauntered past him.

"Why?"

"Because I wanted to," I said as he caught up and matched his pace with mine. In all honesty, I still wasn't entirely sure of the answer to that question. Why *had* I stayed? In the moment I'd wanted to stay and help, but now it was starting to feel like I'd stayed because I had unfinished business here. What was happening out here was so much more exciting than my life back home. Norway was rife with color and opportunity, whereas Ohio just didn't seem as important right now. Either way, when it came time to leave, I couldn't find it in me to climb aboard that damn supply ship I'd spent a week waiting for. I couldn't go home... at least, not yet.

Silence brewed between us before he spoke again. "We should talk."

My brows rose, but I didn't bother turning toward him. "Since when are you talkative?"

That question was met with another growly noise that sounded like an expletive, and I smiled to myself, stopping to turn toward where he'd paused in the road. "Fine, you want to talk? Let's go back to your house and we can discuss the investigation. *That* is why I stayed."

I don't know why the words came out of my mouth, why I'd suggested going to his house. Nothing good could come of it. We'd either end up at each other's throats again or...

I swept my tongue across my bottom lip and shook the intrusive thought away.

Øyvin ran his fingers through his hair and sighed, looking up at the dark sky.

"Well, if you don't want to hear about my list of suspects—" I added, making to move on with my journey.

The Fjord Fae encroached on my space, bursting my happy bubble by bringing us chest to chest. "Don't talk about it out here," he seethed.

"So, you *do* actually want to talk about the investigation?" I peered up at him, daring him to suggest something else. *Go on then, tell me what you really want?*

He took a deep breath, his shoulders shifting with the effort. "Yes. That is what we should talk about."

Honest to hell, that aquavit had gone to my head because I couldn't control myself around him. The need to touch him seared through me, pushing me on. "You sure? There isn't something *else* you want to get off your chest?" I poked the beast, his pecs rock hard beneath my finger.

He glared at the offending appendage, looking ready to bite it... or suck it.

"Come on then, Sharky," I said, stepping back and sauntering past him toward his house on the fjord, "we've got things to discuss."

I didn't look back, but I knew he was watching. My spine tingled as if I was in the presence of a predator, and I exaggerated the sway of my hips in response.

We entered Øyvin's boathouse and shucked off our jackets and shoes. This time I took a second to appraise the space, which had been the furthest thought from my mind the last time I was here. His main living space was sparsely decorated, but featured blond hardwood floors and white cabinetry in the tiny corner kitchen, giving it a *Scandinavian coastal* style. A small circular dining table sat to the left, with four wooden chairs dotted around it—all of which had been pushed in to allow walking space. To my right was the living room area, with that leather sofa we'd previously *enjoyed*, a bookcase beside the small fireplace, and a piano against the far wall.

"I'll text Espen," I said, because he should be here if we were indeed going to discuss the investigation. I reached into my jeans for my phone... and found nothing. I tapped each pocket and my backside, coming up empty. I'd left it at Espen's to charge.

"Problem?"

"Damn it." I crossed my arms as I sat down on the piano bench. "Can I borrow your phone? You have Espen's number, right?"

He rolled his eyes and pulled his cellphone from his pocket, tossing it into my outstretched palm without a word.

"Brave," I said with a flick of my eyebrows.

He tilted his lips into a tiny smirk, his blue eyes darkening into bottomless oceans. "You try anything stupid and I'll throw you into the fjord again."

I guffawed at his insinuation and threat. "Your phone would get wet if you did."

He shrugged and sat down beside me. "Yes, but I can dive in and create an air pocket around it so I don't have to put it in rice for a week."

"And you'd let me sink to the bottom and get soaked?"

"Yes."

I shoved his shoulder, but he didn't move, didn't even budge from his spot beside me on the piano bench. Finding Espen's name in the contacts, I typed out a quick message that would get him over here pronto.

Øyvin: Been kidnapped by the beast from below. Send help to his house. — Lennie

Before I gave it back, I took a quick selfie, giving the camera the middle finger and a mischievous grin. Lennie Martin at her fucking finest—my Mom would be so ashamed.

Øyvin snatched the phone from me before I could do any other damage—like set the image as his background—and stashed it away.

"What do you want to do while we wait?" I asked.

His jaw twitched and he ran his palms across his jean-clad thighs. Without saying a word, he spun around and faced the piano, settling his thick fingers above the ivory keys. As he started to play, I turned around too, watching him move with a grace and fluidity that was shocking considering his size.

The melody was somewhat sombre, a tune filled with swells and valleys that conveyed more than any lyrics could. It kind of reminded me of landscape photographs—pictures that said a thousand words without anyone ever having to open their mouth to impart them. The tune drew me into a mesmerizing trance, where the only things around me were the trilling notes, the smell of clean linen, and the warmth of Øyvin's arm and thigh brushing against mine. My breaths grew more ragged, and I crossed my ankles to avoid my toes curling. Øyvin spotted the movement out of the corner of his sight and a minuscule smirk quivered upon his lips. That alone drew me out of my haze and I tapped a random key, ruining his perfect melody.

Øyvin tightened his jaw at the invading *dummm*, but didn't stop.

"I wanted to..." he started, drawing my attention away from the ivories even as he continued to play. "I wanted to apologize for the way I spoke to you last week."

I stilled, my breath catching in my throat and my eyes going as wide as satellite dishes. When I said nothing, he continued, "I was being overprotective and my choice of words was unkind. I also appreciate you staying to help with the investigation."

I pressed my lips together, unsure what was happening or how to respond, because the last thing I ever expected to hear out of the stoic Asshole's mouth was an apology. *Is this really happening, or have I passed out in a ditch thanks to the late night and aquavit?* Øyvin continued to play the beautiful tune, turning every so often to check on my facial features—which probably resembled the shock I was feeling—and eventually I conceded an, "Okay."

The acceptance earned me one of his lopsided grins that made him look like he'd won some sort of prize, and that just didn't sit well with me. So, being the respectful lady that I was, I pressed one of the keys again... and then once more for good measure, ruining his beautiful song.

Before I could make an additional attempt, Øyvin grabbed my wrist and lifted it above my head. I wobbled on the bench and he steadied me, stopping me from falling off. My breath caught in my throat, and his chest shuddered.

"You really are trouble."

"You have no idea." I grinned.

He surged forward and pressed his lips against mine, guiding my hand and letting it settle on his shoulder. I looped my other arm around his neck, dragging him as close as I could. Running his palms down my arms, sides, and stopping at my hips, he squeezed my curves and a low hum escaped from his lips.

With an animalistic grumble, he shifted me so I sat astride the bench, and then rose while dragging my ass to the edge of the seat. My heart hammered within my chest and my breathing turned ragged and needy, matching the pulsing between my thighs.

He pressed me down over the length of the bench, the soft cushion taking my weight. Spreading my legs, he knelt before me, then swept his hands up my thighs. My breaths quickened as, with deft fingers, he slid the top of my pants down. I lifted my hips to ease his endeavor, and he slowly pulled them over the curve of my ass. Øyvin continued shifting the fabric down my legs, taking my underwear with it. His eyes met mine, deep pools filled with lust.

Exposed and wanting, a shiver ran through my spine and heat welled at my core. A hint of a smile graced Øyvin's face, like he was soaking in every second of my need.

Leaning over me, and not wasting another second, he swept his tongue across my center. My toes curled, and I grabbed his hair, keeping him where I so desperately needed him. Caressing my calves, he continued worshiping my core—sucking, licking, giving me everything and then some.

"Øyvin, fuck," I groaned as sparks shot up and down my spine.

A grumble was all I got in return as he detached himself and rose to his feet. With one hand, he pulled his sweater off, keeping his eyes locked on me the entire time. The move was probably the hottest thing I'd ever seen, and the view afterward wasn't bad either.

Before I could request his return to my swollen clit, he lifted me off the bench, kicked it out of the way, and laid me down on the floor. I followed his lead, ripping my shirt and bra over my head, desperate to be rid of any barriers between us. The wooden boards were cold beneath my back and in stark contrast to the burning fae who settled above me. Not wanting to wait a moment longer, I unzipped his pants, pulled him out, and lined him up, rubbing the tip of his dick against my entrance, both of which were slick with desire. He pressed his forehead against mine and then pushed inside.

Fucking hell.

I swallowed thickly, heat pooling at my core and a desperate need zipping down my limbs. My head lolled to the side and I moaned as he picked up the pace, rocking against all the right spots, bringing me closer to that pleasure-filled precipice. As my back arched involuntarily, I grasped at his shoulder blade and the piano keys above us, sending a low note reverberating through the room. The resonance matched the chaos unfurling between my thighs.

Øyvin pressed on, pushing me over the edge and groaning through his own release with shuddered bursts and shallow breaths.

Both of us fully sated, he relaxed above me, keeping us in an entangled embrace. My lungs heaved, and the smell of our actions permeated the air around us. With wavering hands, I ran my fingers down Øyvin's spine and he shuddered, his dick twitching inside me as his head dropped to my neck.

"Don't stop on my account," Espen's voice sounded from the doorway to the boathouse, and I stilled. I grabbed Øyvin's hair and tilted his head out of the way so I could see our surprise guest.

"How long have you been there?" I asked.

Espen grinned slowly, his gaze on fire. "Yeah, Øyvin, how long have I been here?"

I took a deep breath, then pulled Øyvin's head away from my neck so I could look him in the eyes. He peered up from beneath his golden brows, a salacious sparkle in his gaze. My heart hammered in my chest, the waves of pleasure slowly subsiding in my limbs and between my thighs where his cock remained buried. I must have missed Espen's arrival, I certainly hadn't heard him over the noise of Øyvin's thrusts, my moans, and my hands grabbing across the piano keys.

"Let's just say, I caught most of the show." Espen leaned against the doorframe, his arms crossed, the material of his shirt tight across his shoulders and chest.

I tilted my head back, staring up at the wooden beams on the ceiling. My veins were humming, my thoughts spinning so much that I didn't have any comeback. I was swimming in bliss and had nothing to say.

Slowly, painfully so, Øyvin pulled out of me, rising to his full height. His jeans hung loosely off his hips, his cock still exposed. He extended his hand to me and I took it, only to be hauled off the floor and into his arms. Shocked by the sudden shift, I wrapped my legs around him, and he grabbed my ass in his broad palms while Espen watched us, saying nothing.

"How about we take this upstairs?" Øyvin asked.

I let out a shaky breath and surveyed Espen, who tilted his head and gave me a look that said he was game if I was.

Biting my lip and sliding my arms around Øyvin's neck, I nodded. "Fuck yes." A threesome, with these two? I was definitely in a ditch having some sort of fever dream, or my body was about to be rocked into blissful oblivion.

A low rumble of approval rolled from Øyvin's chest, and he strode out of the room, heading for the loft above us.

Øyvin dropped me unceremoniously onto his large bed, and I was immediately hit by the smell of clean linen and rain. His room was minimally decorated, as if only the essentials were necessary, plus an exceptionally comfortable duvet and sheets.

Øyvin stood beside the bed, while Espen shucked off his jacket and pants, his eyes locked on my body the entire time. My skin pebbled under their attention and my nipples were rock hard. Being naked in front of either of them set my senses on fire, but being bare with both of them in the room was like a fucking inferno raging beneath my skin. Hot and bothered didn't even come close to describing how I felt.

I laid down to watch the two specimens, both of whom were eying me like ravenous wolves. "So, you two are okay with sharing?" I asked, hoping to hell they'd say yes.

They both smirked and glanced at each other.

"Is... is this something you two have done before?"

Espen chuckled and Øyvin rolled his eyes. Grabbing my arm, he spun me on the bed so I was lying across it at an angle where my ass sat close to one edge and my head lolled across the end near him. The position brought me face to face with his cock, and I wasn't entirely mad about it. Not one bit. "No," he replied. "But when you've lived as long as we have, pleasure is pleasure."

Espen clamped his hands around my ankles before slowly letting his fingers drift up toward my thighs, leaving gentle caresses as he went. My core throbbed at the sensation, and I closed my eyes, basking in the pleasure until a low grunt sounded behind me.

I opened my eyes to find Øyvin, now in all his naked glory. *Fuck me sideways.*

"Open wide," he said with the faintest smirk, his eyes shimmering with the lust I'd seen downstairs.

I quirked a brow in challenge. *How was he hard again already?*

Øyvin narrowed his eyes, then nodded to Espen.

A sharp pinch on my thigh and then the slide of a finger against my clit had my mouth falling open in a moan, and next thing I knew I was groaning around Øyvin's girth. I could taste myself on him, and beads of pre-cum slid down my throat. I wanted more.

Espen slid his fingers across my center, before plunging two inside me. I arched my back at the sensation while Øyvin took the opportunity to push deeper into my mouth.

I couldn't see what was happening at the other end. I could only feel what Espen was doing to my body, and somehow, that heightened everything. My senses were all on high alert. The sound of our breaths, the smell of our actions, the feel of every nerve-ending between my thighs sparking like the fucking Fourth of July.

Espen pressed the tip of his cock against my entrance, teasing, then slowly pushed inside. I groaned around Øyvin, who started slowly pumping in and out of my mouth. Grabbing onto him, my hands dug into his thick, muscular thighs, and I took control of his motion and tempo, setting a slow but steady pace.

It was all overwhelming, but fucking spectacular. The in-and-out on both ends had me aching for more, the stimulation of both my core and mouth almost unbearable. Espen's thrusts increased in pace, and before I could stop to catch my breath, Øyvin clamped his hands over my arms, keeping me in place. The sensation spiraled and my skin felt like it was burning. My core spasmed, and the telltale sign of impending euphoria built and built and built until I exploded around both of them.

Øyvin popped himself out of my mouth, ferociously fisting himself as Espen continued pumping deeper and deeper, my body quivering around him as he worked me through my orgasm. Both males were breathing hard and the sight of them both working toward their undoing was almost enough to have me orgasm again, but my body merely continued tingling with aftershocks. With a groan from both of them I watched as Espen finished inside me, then witnessed Øyvin cumming all over my chest—the white ribbons of cum trailing between my breasts.

Espen pulled out and flopped down on the bed next to me before he began tracing patterns across my hip. Øyvin backed away and settled on a wooden stool beside his dresser. He tilted his head back against the wall, but kept his darkened gaze on me. Holding his stare, I licked my lips and then swept my fingers through the mess he'd left on my body. Not a single muscle on his relaxed form moved, except a minute twitch in his jaw, as I curled my tongue around my fingers, tasting him.

"We should do that again some time," I said, bringing my hand back down to the rumpled sheets while I tangled my other hand into Espen's hair. "You two interested?"

Espen let out a throaty groan. "Fuck yes."

I chuckled as he leaned over and kissed my cheek. Shifting slightly onto my side, I glanced over at Øyvin—this time looking at him right way up. "And will you be joining us?"

Øyvin took a deep breath, watching his mess slide down my chest, then rose from his little chair. He opened the dresser beside him and pulled out a plain white t-shirt, then strode across the room in a few short steps. As he reached out, grabbed me, and pulled me to my knees, I wet my lips with my tongue. The sheets tangled around my feet, my breathing stuttering as he stared down at me and began to wipe up his cum, starting near my belly button and making his way across my breasts. Before I could say anything, he pressed his lips to mine and stole my breath. Pulling away sharply, he brushed my hair behind my ear, threw the dirty t-shirt across the room, then nodded—accepting the offer for a part two to this escapade. My lips curved into a satisfied smile as thoughts of what else we could do together drifted through my mind.

"Good," Espen said, shifting across the bed and leaning against the headboard with his eyes closed, "give me twenty minutes."

30

LENNIE

The next morning, I awoke between two fae—one snoring lightly in his sleep, the other sleeping like a rock—both shockingly virile for their age. Honestly, if you'd told me how old they were I'd laugh in your face. Both Espen and Øyvin looked like they belonged in the Roman statue section of a museum. Although... their combined ages would actually put them... *Don't do math, Lennie. Just, don't do it.*

I shook the thought free and turned onto my side, facing Øyvin.

"Good morning, Trouble," he muttered, his voice husky with sleep as he cracked his eyes open.

"Morning, Asshole."

He grinned. "We can try that next time."

"You mean, you want me to find a strap-on?"

He scoffed, and an arm yanked me backward into something very similar to such a device.

"I think he means you," Espen whispered into my hair, and I shivered in response.

"Well, I'm game if you two are," I said, looking between the two of them. A serene warmth settled over me, and I felt the sudden need to say something else—juuuust in case their subtle smiles were signals of thoughts progressing too far ahead. "While I enjoy both of you, I'm not interested in any definitions at this time," I said as diplomatically as possible considering my state of undress. "But, I also wouldn't mind continuing *this*."

Øyvin gave me a lopsided grin, and Espen chuckled before saying. "We can let *this* be whatever you want it to be. Right, Øyvin?"

The Fjord Fae nodded, his eyes locked on mine, and a sense of peace eased through my limbs. I valued my freedom and independence, and wasn't ready for any *settling down.* "Good," I said. "Wouldn't want you two to think I was suddenly your—"

A knock sounded from the front door, and all three of us stilled.

Øyvin creased his brow and shook his head, clearly not expecting visitors. Letting out a deep breath, Øyvin got up, yanked on his jeans, and grabbed a clean sweater from his dresser, throwing that on too as he left the loft. Since the loft was walled in we couldn't see him, but we could just about hear him as he crossed the room downstairs and greeted the visitor with a low grunt.

Espen removed the bit of sheet between us and pulled me flush against his chest, my ass firmly planted against his cock.

"Who is it?" I asked, unable to hear exactly what was being said downstairs.

Instead of grinding against me, Espen wrapped his palm across my mouth, silencing me. "Shhhh," he whispered into my ear, his breath tickling my neck.

I wriggled, but he just tightened his hold—his arms constricting my movement like a damn anaconda. After a few more hopeless squirms, I relented, mumbling against his hand instead. "What are they saying?"

Espen's heart was beating fast against my back as he quietly replied, "The investigation."

I stilled completely, my chest shuddering as I swallowed the shock that invaded my system.

"I don't know who it is, but it sounds like one of the Fjord Fae councilmen—the king's council."

I digested the information by refraining from moving. I didn't need to land myself in more trouble with fae of the fjord, especially not a representative of the king. Nor did I really want Øyvin to get busted for having us up here... however appealing that thought might also be.

Espen continued, "The councilman is asking about the wall down the fjord... and the wildlife... something about concerns with the fish upstream."

I was amazed Espen could actually hear anything. All I could make out were low grumbles, probably from Øyvin, and the sound of my own pulse. It wasn't like this was the first compromising position I'd almost been caught in—I was famous for terrible ideas—but this, for some reason, felt different. The consequences of getting caught were bigger—more was at stake. Perhaps it was the investigation and my knowledge of the fae... or perhaps it was the two fae I'd fucked last night. Either way, it was a helluva way to start my morning. Fuck, I hadn't even had coffee yet and my heart was already racing.

The mumbling downstairs concluded and the front door clicked shut. A moment later, Øyvin leaped back upstairs and appeared in the doorway. Espen slowly removed his hand from my face, and I took the chance to talk.

"Who was that?" I asked.

"The King's Chief Advisor," Øyvin replied, his jaw tight and his arms crossed as he leaned against the door frame.

Espen flopped onto his back and let out a long sigh.

"And he has concerns about the wall and the fish upstream?" I questioned, not bothering to cover up when Espen pulled at the sheets. So be it if I was naked. It might be a bit distracting for the grumpy Fjord Fae, but it might also get him to vocalize more than his usual grumbles.

Øyvin quickly glanced at my tits before flicking his eyes back up to mine. "The King and the Council have some concerns about the fish upstream in light of the recent landslides. They want me and some soldiers to check on them today."

"And the wall?" Espen asked, rolling out of bed and pulling on his pants.

"Just the usual concerns, but I'm going to do a full inspection as I do every week."

"Perfect," Espen said. "Shall we have breakfast?"

My stomach rumbled in answer, and Espen smiled, tugging me from the bed to my feet.

"So, let's discuss our leads," I said, plopping onto the couch with my morning coffee that Øyvin had made—it was sans creamer and sugar, and definitely an inferior roast compared to whatever Oddvar brewed, but after last night's shenanigans, I needed the liquid energy. Breakfast had been good, the bread rolls with salami filling up my starving belly, but coffee was what I ultimately required to get on with my day.

"I think we can safely say Queen Freija is not to blame for this," Espen said, sitting down beside me.

"Are you *sure*?" I asked, not entirely certain of the history or politics of the three factions, and not ready to dismiss anything yet.

"Positive," Øyvin replied, taking a seat on his piano bench but facing us, firmly grasping his coffee mug. The object seemed so small and fragile in his large hands.

"I'm just playing devil's advocate." I raised my empty palm and shrugged. I didn't necessarily disagree with them, but I felt like it needed to be said. Just in case. "I guess that means Halvar is out of the running for culprit, too?"

Both fae nodded, and I agreed. Based on the behavior I'd seen in the throne room, I doubted Halvar would ever do anything to jeopardize the health and wellbeing of his Queen and her people. No, that man would protect his flock at all costs.

"Do either of your factions have enemies?"

The Fjord and Forest Fae looked at each other for a while as if silently communicating or, at the very least, having a staring competition. I poked Espen in his side when no one responded after a while.

Espen sighed. "There are always threats from different regions, fae who are angry and decide to take it out on others."

"And they regularly choose to attack Skolvik?"

Espen tilted his head from one shoulder then to the other, as if saying 'sometimes.'

"Why?"

"Stories claim this fjord as the birthplace of our kind," he replied, taking a sip of his own coffee. "Fae have allegedly lived here for millennia, and there are claims that this area is as close as one can get to the ancestral power as possible, where we may be our strongest."

"It's nonsense," Øyvin chimed in with zero exuberance.

"Okay, so there are threats to both the Fjell, Fjord, and Forest Fae from other factions. Like there was twenty years ago? When this happened last time to the Forest Fae?"

Both nodded.

"But no one ever found out who it was that killed the Forest Queen, right?"

"Correct," Espen said solemnly and took another sip of his drink, staring toward the window by the front door.

I placed my mug on the tiny coffee table and pulled my legs onto the sofa, curling them under my ass and facing the two fae.

"It could very easily be someone from the south again, trying to pull power from us," Øyvin said, downing his drink and setting the empty mug beside mine.

"Then we mark them as our main suspect for now. Any particular individual?" I asked.

Øyvin glanced over at Espen who took another very large gulp of his drink, like he was avoiding the question.

I raised my brow at Øyvin, hoping he could fill me in on whatever tension just rocked up next to me. But, as per usual, he remained mum.

"Espen, is there anyone in particular—"

"It would have to be their descendants," he muttered, wholly lost in a trance.

"What?"

"It would have to be the descendants of the people who fought for the southern factions twenty years ago."

"Why?"

"Because they were obliterated on the battle field," Øyvin finally chimed in, an ounce of something I couldn't quite place—sadness perhaps—lacing his words.

"Do I want to know how?"

I glanced at Øyvin who looked at Espen again. I turned to the Forest Fae beside me, who'd gone very still. After a minute, he shook his head. "No, you don't want to know."

However much I wanted to dig for more details, I let it be. The subject was clearly painful for him, and considering he lost his Queen and mentor that day, I didn't want to bring back those memories.

"They'd have to be working with someone here though, right?" I said, pivoting the subject minutely. "They're pulling magic away from the area, so someone around here must be helping them. There *were* two human-like shapes in that initial photo I took. Maybe someone around here was working with one of those descendants from the south?"

"It could be anyone," Espen said with a nod, and a solemn mood settled over us.

31

ESPEN

A week after my initial tryst with Lennie and Øyvin—and a few more sessions in between—we still hadn't found any new leads for our investigation, but that hadn't stopped the problems from spreading in the region. Early this morning an entire school of fish had been found floating along the banks of the fjord by the marina—too many for this to have been just an ecological problem. Øyvin and his men were dealing with it, as were some of the more weathered fishermen in town.

Meanwhile, my job for the day was assisting with the final roadside clean up from the first landslide. The terrain needed clearing of some of the smaller debris and detritus that could incapacitate regrowth or become a potential hazard should it end up in the road.

When I'd told Lennie about the group of volunteers and what we'd planned to do, she'd jumped at the opportunity to help—not even bringing her camera along. Lennie and I worked alongside Solveig and two of her knitting club friends—Jorunn and Dagny. We were all in our rain gear, the Norwegian autumn in full swing with its vacillating downpours and drizzle. We'd also brought with us brooms, gloves, and bins that we could store branches in that could either be returned to the woods to decompose or thrown into a machine and turned into mulch for the village gardeners.

While Lennie helped the ladies clear broken branches and rocks out of the drainage areas, I swept the ground for any signs of fae magic—any scars, any marks that could be a clue or needed healing—making sure I removed debris as I went so I didn't look too suspicious.

"Lennie here was staying with me for a while, you know," Solveig said to her friends in English, brushing some smaller rocks off the road with a thick-bristled broom she'd brought from home.

The white-haired duo nodded, and Lennie glanced at me, flicking her eyebrows in a flirtatious manner. She knew what was coming next. So did I but I did nothing to stop it. I didn't want to.

Solveig continued, "And, instead of heading back to America, she decided to stay for a while longer."

"So, where is she staying now?" Jorunn asked.

"With Espen," Lennie replied, joining their morning gossip session.

All three let out an "oooooh" and I felt their gazes on my back. Leaving my search, I wandered over to them before things could get really out of hand.

"It's nothing to get all excited about," Lennie said, sounding a little snarky, and I had to bite my lip to keep from smiling even as I wanted to reach out and pull her into my side. Lennie had mentioned more than once whatever was going on between us was casual—no-strings-attached fun while she was here—but that didn't stop the way my heart beat faster in her presence.

"Lennie, dear, we live in a small village. Either everything is exciting or nothing is." Solveig set her hands on her hips, and her friends giggled and nodded.

"If it's excitement you've been looking for all these years, you should've said something," I said, sauntering up beside the women as I grabbed the pile of gathered material Solvieg had swept up, dumping it into the closest bin.

"Oh, you're *much* too young for the three of us," Solveig chuckled.

Lennie coughed and stifled a laugh into the crook of her elbow, then waved them off when the ladies cast concerned looks at her.

"Age is but a number, ladies." I grinned, knowing full well the effect it had on them.

I caught Lennie rolling her eyes before turning back to some rocks that were blocking one of the drain pipes where water ran down the hill and back into the fjord.

"How long are you staying, then?" Solveig asked Lennie.

She shrugged, lifting the rocks one at a time and moving them to the side. "Until I get kicked out."

Solveig smiled knowingly, turning to me with a wink.

I returned her grin with one of my own as a pang of concern skirted up my back. She likely was only alluding to Lennie staying with me and that something was clearly going on between us, but I'd always wondered if Solveig knew, if someone had told her about the fae. She was a wise woman, always in the know about the town's happenings—good friends with all, and always kind to tourists like Lennie. It made her dangerous in regards to our secret, my people's wellbeing.

For those of us who intermingled with humans, it was common to move regularly so as to not raise wariness or doubt. When you don't age as quickly as humans, they started to get suspicious. I'd been born in the north, but had spent a lot of time in Skolvik when I joined Queen Ragnhild's Guard and always returned when I could. However, every thirty years or so, I needed to move. The way Solveig eyed me made me wonder if it was time to move again soon. As they got back to work, the ladies switched to Norwegian, probably so Lennie couldn't understand them. The only problem was, Nora had tinkered with Lennie's hearing, so she could understand everything the women were saying.

"I saw her bickering with Øyvin. Thought there was something going on there," Dagny said.

"I remember you telling me that. Who stands outside Oddvar's and argues like lovers?" Jorunn added.

"Now, now, be nice," Solveig tutted, leaning on her broom. "If you were her age, you'd both be climbing that man like you were being chased by a bear."

The women chuckled and nodded, Dagny even adding, "I still might. Think he's into older women?"

I bit my lip and got back to work, carefully watching Lennie as she listened in on the conversation happening nearby fighting back a smirk of her own. I wasn't sure what Øyvin's stance was on older women but I knew first-hand that Lennie didn't require a bear to be chasing her to climb Øyvin *or* myself.

Having finished our work and parted ways with the trio of ladies, Lennie and I wandered back into the main part of town, heading toward Oddvar's for lunch. As we reached the waterfront by the public docks, I pinched my nose and Lennie gagged, then started spluttering.

"I thought Øyvin and the fishermen were cleaning up the fish?" she asked, cupping her hands over her nose and mouth to block out the rancid stench of rotting fish permeating the chilly air. "The smell wasn't this bad down the road."

It was admittedly less than what we'd been met with this morning but, likely thanks to the way the wind and air circulated around the end of the fjord, the fishy smell lingered in the village instead of moving out quickly. I shrugged and opened the door to the café, holding it open for her. She practically bolted past me and took a deep breath once inside—tilting her face upward and looking relieved.

Oddvar gazed across the counter, far less amused by Lennie than I was, then he quickly grumbled, "Close the door!" I swiftly obliged, making sure it was secure.

Lennie motioned to an open table and yanked off her jacket, hanging it over the back of the chair before sitting down. I joined her, removing my own coat and doing the same.

"What do you want for lunch?" I asked, peering at the little plastic menu that stood atop our table. "My treat as a thank you for helping us this morning."

Lennie smiled. "I don't need a thank you for volunteering but I do like carbs, so I'm not going to say no."

I let out a chuckle and ran my hand through my hair, pushing it off my forehead. Lennie watched the movement, then quickly looked away, a blush rising in her cheeks when she realized she'd been spotted.

"How about a ham and cheese sandwich with cucumber, lettuce, and mustard?" I asked with a smirk, feeling slightly giddy at the effect I had on her.

She nodded. "Sounds good. Thank you."

"No, thank *you*," I replied, placing my hands on the table, shamelessly letting the muscles in my arms flex as I leaned down and toward her. "You didn't have to join us this morning, but I'm glad you did. It was nice to have you there."

She snorted, crossing her arms and leaning back in her chair, but her eyes raked over my body just as I'd intended before meeting my own, full of her signature sass. "You mean as a buffer between you and the ladies?"

I shrugged, challenging the look she was giving me. "Someone needs to keep them at bay. You heard how they talked about Øyvin—if I hadn't been standing there, they would have said the same about me."

"And you think I'm the woman for the job?"

"Based on how quick you are to sass everyone and desire to be *on top* of things, I think you'd do perfectly."

"Oh, really?" She rolled her lip between her teeth, her gaze dropping down my body again, and I had to steady my breathing. "Tempting."

I let out a slow shuddered breath, ready to launch across the table and carry her back to my cabin. "Choose your next words wisely, or I'll punish that mouth of yours later."

"You know what my mouth *really* wants?" she whispered, leaning forward. I angled toward her across the table, giving her a nod to continue that sentence. "Food."

I hung my head and rubbed my hand across my jaw as I straightened up. Just then a chair scraped across the floor, the air grew rather pungent, and someone sat down at the end of our table. "I'll have what she's having," Øyvin said.

"I don't think you want what we were just discussing," Lennie said, raising her brows and giving him a knowing look. "By the way, you stink. Consider showering."

Øyvin rolled his eyes. "I will have whatever *sandwich* she is having."

I smiled and stood from my chair. "Three sandwiches, coming right up," I said, then strode across the room to the counter, giving Oddvar our order.

As per usual, the sandwiches at Oddvar's were delicious—simple local ingredients paired with freshly made bread would always be a win in my book, and the same appeared to be true for Lennie considering how quickly she devoured it. Øyvin ate quickly too but was frequently interrupted by glares from other customers who were unamused by the smell still clinging to his clothes. I did my best to ignore it but Lennie had been right—he should've gone home first to shower or, at the very least, changed out of his cream-knit sweater and jeans.

"So, all the dead fishies are gone?" Lennie asked, wiping her fingers on a napkin.

Øyvin nodded, chewing on his last bit of sandwich. "All of them have been removed from the marina, taken to the local landfill to be dealt with."

"Gross," Lennie said, her lips turning into a grimace. "Any idea what caused it?"

I leaned back in my chair, equally interested in what might have caused the large school of fish to die so suddenly. This type of thing wasn't entirely unheard of, but it was usually as a result of a pollutant and I hadn't heard of any recent spills.

"Oxygen starvation," Øyvin replied, and I furrowed my brow. "As the water gets hotter, the less oxygen there is available for the fish to absorb.

It's usually a sign of pollution and global warming, but..." He cast his gaze around the table, his blue eyes speaking volumes.

I grimaced. "But it could also be related to other *things*?"

He nodded.

"You think the culprit is mimicking global warming problems to throw us off their trail?" Lennie asked, her voice barely above a whisper.

Øyvin and I both nodded. Honestly, it was a smart—albeit, awful tactic to hide the trace of magic in the fjord. Like so many other places around the world, pollution was a problem here—if we hadn't already been looking for magical problems, we might not have dug deeper into the issue to discover the root cause. This entire situation grew more frustrating by the day. All I wanted to do was protect the Forest Fae, the inhabitants of our region, but I constantly felt like I was behind or being caught off guard.

"I think it's safe to say," Øyvin piped up, checking over his shoulder to make sure none of the other customers were listening, "that whoever is behind this *definitely* lives here."

"What makes you say that? They could be visiting from the south?" Lennie tilted her head and widened her eyes.

I was curious what he had to say to that too, because my guess still remained on retaliation from the south for what had happened twenty years ago... that day that would haunt me for the rest of my life.

"First, the damage to the forest, then the mountain with the landslide, and now this. All three are regular occurrences here naturally. Whoever is behind this knows exactly how to hide their tracks, making these seem like unfortunate events. They must live here—or have been here for a long time—and know the area well. They're too consistent, too good at going undetected."

"Save for my photographic brilliance," Lennie said, wiggling her eyebrows.

Øyvin sighed and crossed his arms. "Yes, except for that hiccup. But you still didn't capture their faces."

Lennie huffed and mumbled "Asshole." I did my best not to chuckle at her reaction. Øyvin had a point though. From the rock slides to the dead fish, whoever was behind this mess was always one step ahead—they must know the area and understand its natural weaknesses.

"Any changes *elsewhere*?" I asked, making sure not to mention the fjord and inhabitants therein as we were within earshot of humans.

"None that I am aware of at this time," Øyvin replied with a long sigh. "But, I am going to do my usual rounds tomorrow morning, which includes checking on the wall."

32

ØYVIN

I pressed the button and opened the boat-garage door until it was a quarter of the way up. The wind from the morning storm rushed in, whipping around me and brushing against my navy wool-knit sweater. Taking a deep breath, I stepped toward the edge of the internal dock and dove into the water, creating an air pocket around myself as the water enveloped me.

Beneath the choppy surface, the fjord was a blissful silence that comforted me as I propelled myself east toward the frontlines. I needed to check in on my soldiers and spend some time bolstering our protections against the oil refinery and bustling waterway.

Several of my fellow Fjord Fae inhabitants nodded as I zipped past and a couple schools of fish wholly ignored me as I dodged them, doing my best not to disturb the creatures. With the great deal of strength from my power-stores, my journey wasn't long. After about fifteen minutes underwater, the wall my men held against the pollution a third of the way down the fjord came into view.

Stretching from the fjordbed to the surface, the immense shimmering shield stretched two kilometers across. The thick wall of water and power was see-through, but buffeted anything deemed a pollutant. Marine life could easily swim through it, but should a trail of oil or pieces of human debris drift up against the wall, the object would be disintegrated by our magic.

Standing at regular intervals along the base of the sheer barrier were Fjord Fae soldiers in their uniforms, albeit without the capes as this wasn't a formal occasion.

I landed against the ground with a dull thump, sediment billowing up around my feet, and was greeted with a nod from the closest fae. The water down here on the fjordbed was murky, but with our specially attuned eyesight, the haze was easy to see through. As a Fjord Fae, I had the ability to not only swim at high speeds through the water, but also walk on the waterbed. Where other beings, like humans, would float without proper SCUBA equipment or weights, we could traverse down here by adjusting our buoyancy at will—unencumbered by the pressure. Talking beneath the water was a trait Fjord Fae were born with, too. While we could have air pockets around ourselves, our ability to communicate wasn't hindered by the water between us. We could translate the reverberations, so no words were lost. It was similar in some ways to what Nora had done with Lennie's hearing—the Fjell Fae Princess had royal powers that could help with translations, whereas ours were granted to all Fjord Fae and specifically targeted toward underwater communication. Without it, we wouldn't be able to live down here, nor protect the fjord as well.

"Report?" I asked the fae next to me, Sigurd, as I scanned the wall for breaches and leaks.

"All clear this morning," the black-haired fae said as he held his hands against the wall, holding it up with his magic, the same as each soldier did down the entire stretch. "But there was a disturbance in the middle of the night."

"What happened?" I crossed my arms as a wave of anger swept through me. "And why didn't anyone inform me?"

The fae swallowed, but didn't falter. "It was a minor situation. Two of the young soldiers got into a fight—"

"About what?"

"A bad joke." Sigurd shook his head. "They're kids."

"They are soldiers in the Royal Fjord Guard that should act like it. Do I even want to know what the joke was about?"

"It's a waste of time and energy to even utter the words, sir."

My lips quirked into a minuscule grin. This was why I liked Sigurd. He was always honest and knew the importance of his job. "Thank you, Sigurd. Where are they?"

"Back on the wall." He nodded to the north. "Half a mile down. One with red hair, the other blond. Scrappy things."

Yeah, I appreciated Sigurd. At a hundred years old, with fifty of those defending the fjord, Sigurd was well versed in the activities of the Royal Guard. He even knew that I didn't ever bother with names. It was a rarity for me to remember the names of Guard members, and with a force of over three hundred fae, it was easier to just keep track of who the captains were.

"Thank you," I said with a bow of my head and left him to continue his work fortifying the wall with his power.

While swimming over to the miscreants would be faster, I decided to walk along the barrier instead. With my long strides, it took me merely five minutes to reach the two troublesome soldiers. Sigurd had been correct; based on their stature and lean limbs, these two fae were extremely young—probably part of the recent cohort of graduates from our training programs.

The blond one spotted me first and flinched. A split second later the red-haired fae grew a sickly shade of green.

"Gentlemen." It wasn't the words I wanted to use for them at that moment, but from experience, calling my troops *pieces of shit* by way of greeting wasn't always effective. At least not in times of peace.

Both bowed their heads as I came to a halt between them. The idiots were standing too close, out of position, and it took every gram of patience I had left to not immediately reposition them.

"Would either of you care to tell me what happened last night?" I asked, spreading my feet wide and crossing my arms.

Neither spoke nor made a move.

"Nothing?"

Silence.

"Well, if neither talks then both will be punished."

"He insulted my mother!" The blond one piped up, pointing at his colleague.

The red-head glared past me. "You joked about my sister!"

I rubbed my hand over my face. *Ancestors give me the strength not to kill them both right now.*

"—she came to me!"

"She'd visit Satan before she ever bothered with you!"

They continued yelling at each other while I contemplated my next course of action. As was usually the case with rookie soldiers, they needed fear shot through their veins a few times before they could show the respect I needed from them. These two were no exception. So, before they decided to start punching each other, I grabbed both of them by the collar, spun us to the other side of the barrier, and shucked them away from me. Propping my back against the magic wall, I pushed my power into it, not letting it falter now that the two imbeciles weren't supplying it with their energy.

"If either of you step out of line again, insults will be the least of your worries," I said, crossing me arms again. "Do I make myself clear?"

They both nodded and cast their gazes down.

"I said... Do I make myself clear?"

Both instantly straightened up, eyes wide, and their hands behind their backs. "Yes, sir."

"Good. Now you"—I pointed at the red-haired fae—"take up position down that way beside the boulder."

He glanced at the large rock about thirty meters from where we currently stood and nodded.

"And you stand here silently until your shift is over," I said to the blond one, who nodded continuously like the troll bobblehead toys I'd seen in the tourist center gift shop.

"If either of you steps out of line again, you'll be out of the Guard."

Once they were in position, I leaned off the wall and then left, not wasting my time with any other statements or pleasantries that had no place down here.

The rest of my inspection was calm, the soldiers manning the wall contributing enough magic to sustain the barrier that was primarily fed by the King's well of power. Without King Balder's power and immense strength, the whole thing would crumble or be weakened to a point that would render it almost useless in protecting the waters of the inner fjord.

Thankfully, the serene state continued along the length of the wall... until I reached the very northern end.

The fae manning the part of the wall that brushed against the mountain was visibly struggling. He'd created a bubble around him to keep himself dry, but his feet were left out and beads of sweat marred his wrinkled forehead.

I stepped up beside him and pressed my hands against the vacillating barrier, shocked by what I found. Something pushed back—some energy that felt like hail buffeting against my palms. Taking a deep breath, I focused on my well of power, the pool of magic that churned away within my chest, granting me the ability to manipulate the aqueous element. I gathered up an extra cup of energy and poured it down my veins, sending it into the wall. The fae beside me grunted and I tightened my jaw as my power shot upward through the barrier like a reverse waterfall.

But even with my magical boost, my gut told me we had a weak spot. The power that now stabilized the wall at this point was merely gauze over a wound.

Did this have anything to do with the illegal transfer of magic? Or the recent landslides?

"How long has the wall been shifting like that?"

"Half an hour at most, sir," the fae said, his voice strained from exertion.

"Anyone else know about it?"

He shook his head. "The next watch guard isn't due for another ten minutes. I haven't had a chance to inform anyone yet."

I nodded. Watch guards walked up and down the frontline constantly, monitoring the soldiers and communicating problems back to the captains, so I must've arrived at the right time if I was the first on the scene.

"Good job holding it for as long as you did," I said to the soldier who looked ready to collapse. "I can take it from here. You head back to base and send me two more fae as soon as you get there."

He nodded and I felt his magic ease out of the wall.

"Thank you, sir."

"Thank you for your work. Please take tomorrow off and rest. I'll make sure your shift is filled."

He took a weary step back and gave me a gentle smile. "I appreciate it." With a nod, he lightly kicked off from the ground and swam down the fjord, heading toward the outpost office I'd set up a few decades ago.

After two fae and a watch guard had taken up position on the problematic part of the wall, I'd headed back to the Royal household to report to King Balder. Some of his magic flowed within our barrier, so he'd likely already felt a shift, but it was best to inform him about what was happening. Especially in light of what had occurred above the surface recently.

I knocked on the door to Balder's office and shifted into my Fjord Fae uniform. Balder wasn't usually a stickler for formalities—at least not from me—but considering the situation, it felt necessary.

"Come in," a low voice bellowed from inside, and I entered.

Balder was sitting behind his desk poring over a pile of documents with an antique green reading light casting a warm glow across the pages in his hands.

"King Balder."

"Øyvin. Do you have a report for me?" he asked, setting aside his work, his bright green eyes lifting to mine as he sat back in his chair.

"I do, sir."

With a wave of his hand, he said, "Proceed."

"As you may have felt, there was a problem with the wall."

His brow furrowed as he nodded. "I did feel a minor disturbance, but nothing more than what I feel if there is a small leak."

I sighed and prepared my words, knowing the news I carried was more concerning than that. "It wasn't a leak. I'm not even sure what it was, but it felt like something invisible was scratching away at the wall at the northern edge by the mountain. I was able to use some of my powers to patch the spot, but I don't know how long that will hold. The soldier manning the location..." I paused, remembering how exhausted the fae had been. "Sir, he looked depleted."

"Depleted?" Balder said, straightening in his seat and leaning forward over his desk.

I nodded and thought back on the fae's appearance. He was an older, stronger fae, but he was losing control of his magic, his abilities markedly frail compared to what was required of a soldier at the wall.

I handpicked soldiers for wall-duty. If a soldier didn't have the strength to help, they were assigned elsewhere. So, this soldier should've been able to handle his job—he'd certainly done so in the past—but it was as if the wall had been draining the man of his powers.

Balder clasped his hands, and the sound of him moving brought me back to the present moment. "I've never heard of anything like this but I'll alert the Fjord Fae Council and see if anyone else has."

"When is the next meeting?" I asked, wondering if I should attend this one and see what the King's advisors had to say.

"It starts shortly, actually," Balder replied as he glanced at the clock on his bookshelf. "I'd like you to be there and share your report."

"Of course, sir."

"Who did you leave guarding the problem spot?"

I straightened up and clasped my hands behind my back. "Two soldiers are powering the wall at the weakened spot, and I have a watch guard holding a permanent position there with orders to report directly to me with any issues."

"Good—"

A knock sounded at the door.

"Come in," Balder said, and I turned to see who would interrupt my meeting with the King.

In stepped Kjetil, Chief Advisor to the King, with his copper hair cut closely to his head, piercing crystal eyes, and his jacket collar popped so tall that it ensconced his entire neck like a scarf.

"Kjetil," I nodded in greeting.

"Øyvin," he replied with a brief smile before turning to the King. "King Balder, the council is assembled in the chamber next door. We are ready for you."

"Good." Balder rose from his seat, his frame almost too large for the room. "Øyvin will be joining us today, too. He has an interesting report from the wall."

I strolled into the council chambers behind Balder with Kjetil by my side. The rest of the council—eight other Fjord Fae—took their seats around the long wooden table as Balder sat at the head, his chair larger than the rest to accommodate his position and stature. I sidled into my seat at his right, while Kjetil took up position to the King's left, still standing as he called the meeting to order.

"We have several pieces of information to discuss today, including the recent request for more housing closer to Skolvik Harbor, but first"—he glanced at me before turning to the King—"should we discuss the security matter brought forth by General Håland?"

I refrained from wincing at my rarely-used but official title. Head Guard was the more common term, and people rarely used my last name, but Kjetil had a flair for the formalities of our world.

Balder nodded once, at which the entire room focused their attention on me, and Kjetil finally sat down.

I cleared my throat and rested my hands on the table. "A disturbance was found along the wall today at the far northern end where it meets the mountain. An energy was pressing, scratching against it. The soldier manning it prior to my arrival was under significant strain and has since been replaced by two rested fae and a permanent Watch Guard who is reporting back to me on any changes."

I scanned the room, the looks on the council's faces were grave and concerned—even Kjetil had furrowed his brow. "Has anyone here heard of a power or fae that would attack the energy in the wall? Deplete the power of our soldiers as they fight against it?" I asked, hoping one of the elder council members might have any information.

Several shook their heads, and a few more shrugged as my eyes passed over them. Out of the corner of my eye I could see Balder doing the same, his chin resting on his fist as he leaned back in his chair.

"There was one instance that comes to mind," Valdemar, one of the older council members, started and my attention whipped to him as he continued. "But that was about twenty years ago and not here, not in our fjord."

Balder let out a low cough before requesting more information with a wave of his hand.

"It was a rumor, really. Chatter from some cousins of mine in the southern fjord. Their protections were quietly attacked a few weeks prior to the battle breaking out above the water."

The battle that had killed Queen Ragnhild and her Head Guard—Espen's mentor. The battle that I didn't ever like to think about, not after what happened to—

"Did their barricades fall?" the King asked, drawing me out of my thoughts and back to the present.

"Briefly," Valdemar replied with a solemn look across his weathered features. "But no one ever found out exactly what caused it and no official report was rendered." Which would explain why we'd never heard about it. I sighed as he turned to me and added, "My cousins described it in the same way, like something scratching at the wall, trying to break through."

My stomach curled into a bigger knot but I kept my features guarded. This was bad, really bad. Far worse than I'd initially imagined—a threat to us, the rest of the fae factions, and even the humans.

The room quieted as we all pondered the new information and waited for Balder to say something. After a few moments of silence, the king straightened up and clasped his hands together, resting them on the table.

"We continue Øyvin's current plan, doubling up guards at this location, but I want a continuous rotation of fae on the wall so no two fae are significantly depleted after a shift. Should we activate the reserves, too?" he asked, turning to me.

"Yes," I replied immediately, relief coursing through my veins that he took this threat as seriously as I did. "I don't want any soldiers running low."

"Not if another battle is heading our way."

The room collectively stilled at Balder's words but I responded to his warning. "Yes, sir."

Balder's gaze darkened slightly as he tilted his head toward me. "Good. But promise me this: word of these events shall not be reported to the Fjell Queen, nor our friend in the woods."

I straightened and took a deep breath. Refraining from telling them would be difficult, especially when trying to be diplomatic about the ongoing investigation, but orders were orders, and I had a duty to the fjord.

"Yes, sir."

33

LENNIE

"So, any last things I need to know before you throw me to the wolves in there?" I asked Espen as we walked into the mountain for Queen Freija's birthday ball, the magical barrier granting us passage into the behemoth.

Espen chuckled and glanced around at the other fae who were arriving for the party and shifting their attire within the tunnels. "Pretty sure you're prepared but maybe brace yourself for lots of questions and stares."

"Depends on what you're planning on dressing me in," I retorted.

He flicked his eyebrows, and a wicked look crossed his features. "What if I just removed your clothes?" He leaned in and whispered, "Naked looks good on you."

"I'd rock it," I said, giving him a daring look in return. "But can you actually do that?"

He stepped closer and I backed up against the rocky wall as other revelers sauntered past, shifting into their finery. My body hummed as he raked his gaze over me and grinned. "Haven't tried in a while, but I've seen you naked several times now, so it shouldn't be that hard..."

"Go ahead, buddy," I replied, my voice sounding breathy and seductive as I leaned in to whisper back, "And we'll see who ends up *hard*."

He brushed his tongue across his bottom lip and then shook his head as he pulled away from me. "You'll be the death of me, Lennie."

"You had a good run." I smirked.

With another shake of his head he placed his palm against my left shoulder and a wave of warmth swept over me. Glancing down, I watched as my leggings and black long-sleeve sweater disappeared and were replaced by a spectacular emerald green dress made of floaty material and embroidered with delicate silver threads in an almost branch-like pattern. The sleeves were a sheer fabric with the same silvery motif continuing across my shoulders and encircling my wrists.

I looked up at Espen, who'd shifted into his Forest Fae uniform—cape and all—and he smiled. "Green okay? Or would you prefer black?"

"Like my heart?"

He chuckled. "Your choice."

I shook my head and surveyed the finery once more, noticing the way I matched Espen. "It's perfect. Thank you."

With a wink, he proffered his arm, and I looped my hand through it before he guided me toward the ethereal music floating down the tunnels.

I was expecting the party to be held in the throne room I'd visited before, but boy was I wrong. Espen led me deeper and deeper into the mountain until the revelry noises grew louder and we stepped into what could only be classified as an enormous cavern. The space was made of the same sky-blue stone as the throne room but was probably twenty times the size, big enough to contain the hundreds of people already in attendance and the large tables of food and drink that had been laid out. Like in the throne room, there was a dias at the end of the large hall with Queen Freija's throne—or another rendition of the one I'd previously seen her in. To the left sat a band of twenty fae playing some instruments that I recognized—violins and a piano—plus a few others I'd never seen before that looked reminiscent of banjos.

"Come on, let's make our rounds," Espen said, and gently pulled me into the melee.

We wandered around the immense room and Espen greeted just about everyone. I glanced around the hall, taking in all the fae in their finery—some in sparkling dresses, others in bespoke suits, and guards in their uniforms, each one matching the faction they belonged to. The entire scene was a jewel-toned vista that I wished I could photograph, but knew better than to expose these fae to the world.

Almost every fae we passed looked at me with narrowed eyes before swiftly pasting a pleasant smile on their face when they glanced at Espen. A smirk full of challenge and mock nicety settled on my face, and I chose to ignore the stares of the party-goers, instead focusing on the feeling of having my arm looped through Espen's. The warm and pleasant sensation that filled my chest from being on his arm swelled within me, giving me the extra boost of confidence I needed to keep my head up and move through the room with as much grace as I could muster.

"Where's Øyvin?" I asked, looking around for the brute.

"Queen Freija and King Balder don't have the best relationship," Espen explained, squeezing my hand where it rested in the crook of his arm. "There was uncertainty of whether the Fjord Fae would make an appearance. Some will probably sneak in but as for an official group of visitors from the royal in question?" He shrugged. "I'm not entirely sure."

"That's a shame. I was hoping to see Øyvin in his uniform again." What could I say? That thing hugged his ass and shoulders nicely, and Øyvin's shoulders and ass were a thing of beauty. While I hadn't been his biggest fan to start, I'd never turn down an opportunity to sneak a peek at that outfit when given the chance.

Espen scoffed and chuckled. "He's never been one for parties. As you know, he likes to stay home and play his piano on a Friday night."

That, I did know. Intimately.

Some sort of look must've crossed my face because before I could continue revisiting my memory of what I'd done to those ivories the last time he'd played for me, Espen pulled me onto the dance floor. "Care to dance?"

His knowing smirk and dilating pupils spoke volumes. He knew exactly where my head had been, and I knew he'd enjoyed *that* show.

I nodded. "Lead the way, yogi-cop."

He swept us into the middle of the elegant crowd, their attire casting shimmering light across one another and the blue stone walls. Releasing my hand from the crook of his arm, he spun me around and then gently pressed me against him. With one hand at my lower back and the other grasping my palm, he guided me to the waltz-like music of string instruments. My dress swished around my ankles, and I felt very princess-y but didn't wholly despise it. The gentle turns, the festive ambiance, the handsome uniformed fae leading me—it was all mesmerizing and, before I knew it, the band moved on to a new tune. I glanced around, taking in the couples around us, and my eyes landed on a handsome pairing in crisp suits.

"Who's that?" I asked, nodding toward the stout man with his sandy hair tied into a perfect man-bun. He kept monitoring the lamps and candles, and if one went out, he quickly reignited it with a silvery ball of light from his hand.

"That is Torsten, Leif's husband, one of my men."

"Is Torsten a Fjell Fae?"

Espen nodded and spun me around again, before we continued swaying gently to the violin music. "Married to a Forest Fae. Both are great men. Very kind."

I smiled as the couple continued dancing, only stopping now and then to pilfer a sweet treat off a passing platter. "But if he's a Fjell Fae, how does he have powers to help with lighting?"

"He has a rare ability that the ancestors only bestow upon one Fjell Fae at a time. No one quite knows how or why any one specific fae is granted that blessing, but not long after one such-gifted Fjell Fae dies, another is chosen."

Oh, so that was who Nora referred to when we visited the story cave. "So, he's special?"

"We're *all* special," Espen said with a salacious wink.

I rolled my eyes but couldn't entirely disagree. Not that I would tell him that. His ego was big enough already.

"I mean, his powers differ from those rocky, earthy ones of the other Fjell Fae?"

Espen dipped me slowly before pulling me back up to face him, his eyes ablaze as my chest slowly rubbed against his. "Yes and no. He's more similar to the royal Fjell Fae—their powers are more closely aligned with the ancestors. It's said that the ancestors—those who have passed on—relinquish their powers back to earth and gain control of the air element. But somehow, parts of that power seep into the strongest of fae or appear in the form of skill sets like Torsten's as gifts."

Fascinating.

My mind wandered over the many fae I'd met, all far more powerful and unique than the rest of the humans I'd ever known, while the music slowed and then shifted to something upbeat, more like a jig than a waltz.

Espen stepped back and smiled, releasing his hold on me. "Would you like a drink?"

"I'd love one," I replied as we moved off the dance floor.

"Great. I'll be right back," he said and disappeared into the crowd, heading for the drinks station.

I was about to partake in some sort of fluffy, white meringue dessert that was carried past on a tray when a commotion at the hall's entrance had me freezing on the spot.

The chatter in the room died down and the music petered out as the crowd parted, revealing new arrivals. Whispers of the name Balder echoed around the cavernous chamber.

A group appeared between the parted masses. At the head of the spear of fae was a man as big as Halvar, with a warrior-like presence but that's where the similarities ended. Unlike Halvar, this man looked like a Viking just returned from battle—long scruffy blond-and-silver beard, small scars across his face, and piercing green eyes that looked like they'd seen centuries of war. This was not a guy to be messed with. If I punched this guy like I did the first time I met Espen, I wouldn't end up at the police station. No, I'd be chained to the bottom of the fjord.

Yeah, I was an idiot for ever thinking Øyvin was King of the Fjord, because this man sure as fuck was the keeper of that title.

To Balder's right was Øyvin, and to his left was another man with light-red hair. The entire contingent, ten large fae, wore the Fjord Fae uniform—gray and navy materials, gray boots, and short capes that clung to one shoulder. The King's cape fastened to both his shoulders and the entire underside of the thick material was covered in silver embroidery of marine life and reeds.

I glanced to the other end of the chamber and, sure enough, Freija had appeared on her throne. A regal smile graced her face, her hands neatly clasped in her lap. To her right stood her ever-loyal guard, Halvar, his stoic gaze and stance not yielding any tells on how he felt about the sudden arrival of the Fjord Fae. An arrival that had the room collectively holding their breath.

"King Balder," Freija said with a nod, never taking her eyes off the new guests.

Balder swept his arms wide and gave her a toothy grin. "Happy Birthday, Queen Freija. Apologies for our late arrival."

He didn't look sorry at all. He and his guards swaggered further into the room, stopped, and then his men bowed their heads deeply while he didn't budge further.

As the party straightened, Øyvin's eyes flicked to mine and he quirked a brow.

I gave him a small smile as Torsten and Leif appeared on either side of me, their earlier grins faltering slightly as Balder bestowed more pleasantries.

"So, you're the American," the one with the man-bun said.

I puffed out my chest before replying quietly. "That, I am."

"I'm Torsten," he added before tilting his head to his husband, but never taking his eyes off the throne. "This is Leif."

I glanced up at Leif, the tall, slender Forest Fae. His dark hair was cut short and his bright green eyes were in stark contrast to his thick brows, slightly tan skin, and black suit. It looked like he'd stepped right out of the forest and into a men's tailor shop. Leif turned and the corner of his mouth twitched when he caught me gawking.

"You two know who the red-head is?" I whispered, turning my attention back to the group of Fjord Fae in the middle of the dance floor.

"Kjetil, King Balder's chief advisor."

"So, he's like second in command?" I asked, keeping my voice as low as humanly possible.

Leif shook his head. "Kjetil is the head of Balder's advisory council. Those other Fjord Fae with them are councilors and soldiers. Øyvin is in charge of security and soldiers, whereas Kjetil and the council bestow advice."

Glancing back at the group, I refocused just in time to catch Freija rising from her light-blue throne, her eyes twinkling even from this distance. "I'm glad you could attend, old friend. Please, do enjoy yourselves." She gave a graceful nod to the band, and they swiftly started playing again—a joyful tune to combat the crazy energy that had swept through the party at the King's sudden arrival.

Balder grinned and stepped off the dance floor, most of his men following after him but a few defected, including Øyvin. He strode toward me with assured strides and a playful smirk on his lips.

"Trouble," he said, coming to a stop before me.

"Asshole." I gave him a wink which he returned with a flick of his eyebrows.

"Torsten, Leif." He nodded to each of the fae beside me with a respectful manner that was curt but enough to be considered somewhat kind.

"Come with me?" Øyvin asked, proffering his hand. "You don't mind me stealing her, do you?" He glanced at my new compatriots who grinned like they had a secret burning on their lips.

"Not at all," Torsten replied.

"It was nice to meet you, Lennie," Leif added with a genteel nod.

I returned the gesture. "It's been a pleasure gentlemen."

With that, Øyvin pulled me away and back onto the dance floor where the earlier crowd had returned after Balder's council dispersed. Øyvin guided me into the same position Espen had held me in and started moving us gracefully about the space, carefully dodging other revelers like it was second nature. His timing was impeccable and with each flourish within the tune, he executed perfect movements—from spins, to dips, to swift footwork that I almost stumbled over—it was as if he could feel the music, the vibrations.

"That dress looks good on you," he said, his voice barely a whisper. "Espen did well."

"Can't say I disagree with you. It might actually be the most elegant thing I've ever worn." Which was likely, considering the last fancy event I'd been to was my brother Jared's wedding and I'd worn a satin burnt-orange travesty of a bridesmaid dress I had yet to forgive my sister-in-law for. The clingy fabric in the Midwest summer heat and humidity had been *far* from elegant.

"Well, I like it too, although it might look better in blue," Øyvin said, pulling my focus back to the present.

I rolled my eyes but couldn't keep the small chuckle that escaped me contained. "Don't start an incident, Øyvin. Sharing is caring, remember?"

His lips quirked up at one corner. "Oh, I remember." He pressed me more firmly against him, letting his hand dip a little lower on my back. "Speaking of, where is Espen?"

"Gone to get some drinks," I replied, glancing around the room. Nora stood to our right in a sleek silvery dress with long sleeves talking to a group of women who appeared to be doting on her. The forced smile on her face told me she wasn't pleased with the attention but I didn't know how to help my new friend out of that situation. I continued my search, but couldn't find Espen.

My footsteps slowed as I kept coming up empty and Øyvin brought us to a stop before guiding me off the dance floor.

"I'll go see what is taking him so long," he said, noticing my concerned frown. "I'm sure he's just got caught up talking to people. You know what he's like—"

"Honorary mayor," I interjected.

Øyvin chuckled. "Exactly. Far too friendly. I'll be right back." With that, he sauntered into the crowd toward the drinks table. With how tall he was, he towered over a lot of the other fae, so hopefully he could spot Espen more easily than I could.

I gazed across the dazzling room, watching the Forest and Fjell fae dance away. Many had openly stared at me while I'd danced with both Espen and then Øyvin—a few straight up gawked—but I ignored them, enjoying the experience.

"You'll forgive my people for staring at you," a serene voice said, and the Queen herself stepped up beside me. "It's been almost two centuries since we've had a human in our midst." Her long navy dress made of velvet with gold motifs threaded into the bottom was spectacular, and made even more regal with the matching cape that was cinched at her shoulders and fell to the floor, pooling behind her.

My eyes widened at the timespan she mentioned, realizing how rare my acceptance here was. "That's quite a long time. Who was the last human allowed inside the mountain?"

She smiled, her lips parting gently. "He was a young man, not much older than yourself. One of my people fell in love, and, although it was quite the scandal and to-do at the time, the human man and fae woman were permitted to marry and remain part of the Fjell Fae."

"And they were happy together?" I asked, glancing around the room for no one in particular.

Freija sighed. "Until he passed. Unfortunately, he had no magic, and thus lived for only forty years after the union."

"How sad," I said, unsure of what else to say.

Queen Freija hummed in agreement. "It was inevitable, but they were happy together."

"That's the important thing in the end."

"It most certainly is," she replied, tilting her head slightly toward Halvar at her side. "I'm glad you're here," she added with a gentle nod toward me, pivoting the subject. "I wished to thank you again for your assistance. The photograph you captured was invaluable, and I dare say we'd be in a great deal of trouble without it. Because of you, we knew about the problems in the area much sooner than we might have otherwise."

I looked over to her, finally taking the opportunity to face her. She was slimmer than the last time I'd seen her, back when we'd first been summoned to the throne room. Now her cheeks were less full, her already high cheekbones much more pronounced.

"I'm glad I was able to help. If there's anything else I can—"

She shook her head and raised her hand, giving me another soft smile. "By all means, Lennie, please just enjoy yourself."

"Happy Birthday, Queen Freija," I said with a gentle nod that felt appropriate in the royal's presence. She gave one in return before her and Halvar moved on into the crowds of fae.

I glanced around the room again, noting the faces that turned away quickly as if they'd been watching my interaction with the Queen. Which, considering the guilty blushes on more than two of the fae, I'd bet money—that I didn't have—was true. With a sigh, I straightened up and headed toward the drink table. I made it all of two steps before screams pierced the air.

The band stuttered to a stop.

A commotion built within the crowd before the refreshments.

My stomach sank.

Before I knew what I was doing, I was sprinting forward, pushing my way through the throngs of chaos. When the fae finally parted, I found my yogi-fae-cop convulsing on the ground. I fell to my knees in front of him, avoiding the shattered glass and liquid beside us. Espen's skin was pale, he was gasping for air, and I didn't know what the fuck I could do.

Øyvin, or someone else with a deep baritone voice like his, barked orders. Others were yelling. The crowd shifted and moved, but Espen closed his eyes and stilled.

"No, no, no," I whispered, reaching for him—

"We need to move him, now," a female voice said, and someone hooked their hands under my arms, lifting me back to my feet.

I spun around, dazed and bewildered, my heart hammering in my chest and my hands shaking.

This can't be happening.

34

LENNIE

Øyvin stormed past with King Balder and the contingent of Fjord Fae. The grumpy fae gave me a stern look and pointed at Espen. "Stay with him," Øyvin mouthed before he disappeared into the crowds. While I'd never been one for commands, that was one I'd definitely be following.

A group of Forest Fae lifted Espen up on a stretcher of birch trees and linen and were swiftly followed by a slim fae with long tawny hair wearing a green and brown uniform. I rushed after Ylva, who was giving orders to Forest Fae left and right, her petite stature draped in authority. Keeping up with the brigade carrying Espen out of the mountain, crowds parting to give the group speedy passage, I asked, "Where are you taking him?"

She spun around, not stopping her brisk pace toward the exit, her stern eyes narrowing slightly before she sighed. "The healers hut east of the village."

"I'm coming with you."

She took a deep breath, screeched to a halt, and then placed her palm on my left shoulder. A soft wave of heat washed over me and my beautiful dress disappeared, giving way to my leggings, sweater, and boots from before. "That should make things easier. Just keep moving."

I nodded and followed her, my movement unencumbered now that I was out of the evening wear.

The fae carrying Espen ducked and dodged through the forest with ease and preternatural speed. It was difficult to keep up with them, but I somehow managed, spurred on by my own erratic pulse and anxiety every time I caught a glimpse of Espen's still form.

The healer hut was indeed just east of the village, not far from the farm Espen and I had hiked past a few weeks ago. The hut blended seamlessly into the surrounding terrain. With a grassy rooftop and short stone walls, the entire thing looked like an overturned Viking-ship, and I wondered if it was old enough to have actually housed Vikings at some point. It must have, if Espen and Øyvin were as old as they said they were. Their grandparents, or great-grandparents, may have even taken up the raiding profession to blend in with the humans of their time. I shuddered at the thought of magical Vikings and the destruction they could've caused.

Ylva pushed through the door to the hut and our group followed her inside. The long-ship building was open, formed around a central hearth, and I was instantly assaulted by the musty scent of herbs and earth, while feeling like I'd stepped back in time.

The soldiers set Espen atop a workbench on the far side of the room. Two fae women, their slightly pointy ears visible, jumped into action, their long skirts swishing around them the only noise beside the crackle of the fire in the middle of the space. The wooden plank wall beyond Espen was bedecked with vials, bottles, and roots of all shapes and sizes. There were also stacks of wood, some with the papery bark that I recognized from the birch trees that littered the landscape of this country beside their kindred pines, others looking like pieces that had fallen off charred logs.

Ylva and her team of fae left after a brief chat with one of the healers. I settled on a bench in the corner of the hot room, carefully watching as the two healers started stripping Espen of his clothes save for his pants and giving him all manner of concoctions. One was as clear as water, another was the color of dark cherries.

"What are those?"

One of the women looked up, her dark eyes sweeping over me before she shook her head. I didn't realize I'd spoken aloud, but the question still stood. The last thing they poured down his throat looked more like tar than water.

They flipped Espen over on his side, using pillows to stop him rolling over onto his back.

I watched as he retched, his dinner and drinks returning into the bucket they'd prepared at his bedside. Even as the sight and scent made my eyes water, I didn't look away. I couldn't tear my eyes away from the happy, bubbly yogi-fae-cop thing that had brought so many smiles to my face, now devoid of any emotion as he fought for his life.

Even with the elixirs the women had given him, he didn't wake up. It was as if his body was doing what it needed to, ridding itself of the poison while he slept. His eyes remained shut, not even a flutter of an eyelash, no twinkling in his amber eyes. *Why is it always the good ones?*

"What was it?" I asked aloud as he stopped, and the women began cleaning both Espen and the surrounding area.

"There are a plethora of poisons across Norway—berries, algae, mushrooms, the list is endless," the elder healer said, washing and drying her hands before coming over to me. "My name is Heidi," she added, her dark gaze scanning me from head to toe. "I take it you are the human we've heard whispers about. The one who missed two boats?"

I chuckled at the description but couldn't seem to make myself react more than that. "That's me."

The younger healer washed up and then bid us goodnight before swiftly departing. The silence in the space began to consume me, and when I didn't say anything else, Heidi nudged me with her elbow. "He's going to be all right."

"How can you be sure of that, Heidi?" I snapped.

She scoffed, and I glanced over at her to find her eyebrows meeting her hairline like I'd said some sort of joke.

"Well?"

She rolled her eyes and leaned against the post beside me. "I heard you had a sharp tongue."

Now it was my turn to scoff. I mean, she wasn't wrong, but damn did they gossip in this town.

I crossed my arms and looked her in the eyes. "Will he recover?"

She nodded gently. "We got to it quickly, but I can't be sure how much damage was done by the poison until he wakes."

"How long will he be out?"

She sighed and looked over at Espen. "Until his body is ready."

"That's not really a time frame," I quipped.

"It could be hours or days—"

"*Days?*"

"—or weeks." She raised her palms in a motion that said it was out of her hands. "We can only keep him comfortable and watch for fever spikes until he wakes."

I let out a deep breath, trying to still my racing heart. In an effort to pivot my thoughts from the unpleasant ones that were trying to make themselves at home in my head, I said, "You're English is really good, by the way."

Heidi let out a rolling laugh that bounced joyously around the room. "I've been speaking Norwegian this entire time, young lady."

My brain short circuited. "What?" I must've been too worried about Espen to notice the way her lips moved hadn't matched up with the words I heard.

She smiled, her full cheeks flush with color, her silvery up-do shimmering in the firelight.

"But I've been speaking English—"

"Oh, I fully understand English, but I don't like speaking it," Heidi interjected. "*Your* English is really good, too."

"Now who has the sharp tongue?" I retorted, quirking a single eyebrow.

Her smile didn't falter as she pushed off the pole and sauntered across the room. "Sit down over here, I'll make you some tea to calm your nerves."

"Oh, I'm—"

"You will sit or you will leave."

"Yes, Ma'am." For whatever reason, I did as I was told. Heidi had a motherly aura around her that permeated the space with a warmth that had nothing to do with the roaring hearth. It was endearing and, for some reason, I didn't want to aggravate her any more than I already had—Espen *was* under her care, after all. So, I took a seat at the sturdy wooden table near the kitchen area, sneaking looks at Espen every time a log popped in the fire.

I watched as she prepared the tea, using a whole bunch of leafy bits I couldn't name. As she set the drink down in front of me, a question formed in amongst the chaos of my brain. "What do we do about his work? Won't the police grow suspicious when he doesn't show up?"

Heidi nodded and sat down across from me, bringing her tea cup to her lips and lightly blowing across its steaming surface. "Ylva is handling that problem for us."

"How?" I asked, and took a sip. The tea was earthy, slightly herbaceous, and had a hint of sweetness to it that reminded me of honey. It was good. Not as delicious as coffee, but I needed something in my system after the shock I'd just endured.

"Ylva will mention to the Chief of Police, Bente, that Espen had a family emergency and needed to visit his sisters in the north."

"And this Bente will believe that?" I wrapped my hands around the teacup, letting it warm my fingers.

Heidi nodded. "Ylva is acquainted with Bente, and Bente knows that Ylva and Espen are good friends."

"Does Bente know...?" I waved my hands at my ears, and then around the room, referencing the fae as best I could.

"No. Definitely not," she replied before narrowing her gaze at me. "And it must stay that way. We cannot have humans finding out about us or we'll be hunted to extinction. All creatures crave power to survive and eventually rally against those perceived as more powerful than themselves. If humans found out about us, they'd ignore our true purpose to protect nature, and, instead, do their best to use us to their own advantage—be that in capitalism, politics, or war."

I raised my hands. "Hey, you won't have any trouble from me." Which was saying something considering my penchant for trouble.

She chuckled like she didn't quite believe that, but took another sip instead of challenging me on my sincerity.

The rest of my time there was met with companionable discussion, mostly me asking Heidi what the different things on her shelves were, punctuated with furtive glances at Espen and hoping he would stir. After what must've been a solid hour and the tea in my cup vanishing, I let out a long yawn and rubbed at my eyes.

A gentle smile graced Heidi's lips. "Let me send for someone to escort you back."

I yawned again and nodded, grateful for whatever she was saying as my eyes threatened to seal themselves shut for the rest of the night. It probably was time to get some sleep.

35

LENNIE

I entered Espen's little cabin and vigorously brushed my hands over my arms. With only the gentle glow from the moon to light the cabin, and me the only inhabitant, the space felt too empty and quiet. It was as if the cozy cabin was mourning.

Kicking off my shoes, I stumbled through the living room and into the bedroom where I flopped onto the bed. With my clothes still on, I curled up into the sheets and inhaled the smell of moss and leather. My muscles screamed at me from all the exertion today, but as I let the warmth beneath the covers grow, I settled into a peaceful calm. It was the same feeling I felt after I'd been on long hikes, a feeling of satisfied exhaustion. However, the satisfaction was missing tonight. Instead, it was replaced by a knot in my stomach and an ache in my chest.

Why did shitty things always happen to good people? The Espen I knew hadn't deserved this, hadn't deserved to be poisoned. Anger and sadness swelled inside my chest, exasperating the pain there, and I rubbed my palm against my sternum. It dawned on me how much I truly cared about Espen. It had been a long time since I'd cared about anyone in such a way—in fact, I wasn't quite sure my feelings for Espen, or Øyvin for that matter, could even compare to any of my prior mediocre relationships. Not that I was officially in a relationship with either of the fae, but...

Images of the two fae men flitted through my mind: Espen and his beaming smile and positivity, that mop of hair constantly falling across his brow, and Øyvin with his stoic no-nonsense attitude that was fortified by his sense of duty to the fjord. Both of them tugged on something deep inside me.

I didn't think I'd ever felt this way about anyone before, let alone for *two* men—a sense of happiness and belonging that made me excited to see them. It was a sensation that oozed comfort like a warm hug on a cold winter's morning. Espen was certainly that reassuring warmth, while Øyvin was the chilled breeze that swept across my cheeks making me so attuned to his presence.

With another yawn, I let the thought of those sensations drag me under into a fitless sleep.

Later that morning, I was back at Heidi's, having decided that my time was better spent here than sitting in the quiet shell of a house by myself. After a quick coffee pit stop at Oddvar's, I'd miraculously found my way back to the healing hut deep within the forest. And by miraculous, I meant I'd asked Øyvin for directions when we briefly crossed paths that morning outside the café.

Now safely ensconced in the secluded building, I removed the lid from the paper cup and wafted my hand over the steaming coffee, aiming the scent under Espen's nostrils. Maybe this would help wake him up? It sure as hell would work if I were the one laying unconscious instead.

"That better not be what I think it is," Heidi muttered from across the room where she was busy tending to some herbal concoction.

"Not at all," I replied, quickly replacing the lid and trying to hide the cup behind my back.

"That stuff is not allowed in here."

I frowned, my shoulders sagging. "But, coffee is human magic."

She scoffed and threw a sprig of something into the mixture. "It leads to high heart rates and headaches. It does not heal."

"It heals the *soul*, Heidi."

"Well it can *heal your soul* outside until you have drunk the entire thing." She waved her hand toward the entry.

"What?" I looked at the door and shivered. It was freezing outside, the sun completely hidden by cloud cover on the gloomy day.

"Now, out you go," she said, shooing me out the door, but leaving it open.

"You're throwing me out into the cold?"

"You may come back inside once you've finished your drink, young lady," she said with her hands on her hips like she was ready to corral me.

With a shudder, I exited and then leaned against the side of the building. Peering between the dense forest, I watched the morning fog slowly ascend from the valley. Mixed feelings washed through me as I took in the majestic scenery—part of me wished I'd brought my camera, the other part knew I couldn't risk exposing Heidi's home. I'd just have to commit this picture to my internal memory: the gray sky, the tall pines, and the chilly air. I took a deep breath before taking a sip of my coffee. It was delicious, as always, with a splash of milk and sugar in it.

"What are you doing in there?" I asked, breaking the sounds of the breeze and the creaking forest.

"Preparing concoctions for the winter," Heidi replied, her voice slightly muffled by the rocky wall between us.

"What are they for?" I took another gulp of my drink, relishing in its warmth.

"Burns and infections."

"Fae can't magically heal themselves?" I asked and furrowed my brow. All the magical creatures I'd seen in movies and read about in books had the miraculous ability to heal themselves quickly. Perhaps the fae were different though?

"Depends on the injury or malady. Broken bones will heal more quickly in fae than humans, and infections clear up swiftly, but poisons like the one Espen ingested are dangerous."

"How dangerous?" My voice wavered slightly and I swallowed a lump in my throat.

"I ran some tests overnight. He had water hemlock in his system," she said with a grave tone. "If he wasn't as strong a fae, he would have died at Queen Freija's celebration."

I shook involuntarily at the thought and tried to peer inside to where Espen lay bundled up in a comatose state but I couldn't quite see him from this angle.

Turning my gaze back to the forest, I was about to take another sip of my coffee when movement between two pines caught my eye. A moment later two fae appeared carrying another between them. The middle fae had his arms slung over the others' shoulders, and all three were wearing Forest Fae uniforms. They hobbled toward the hut and I spun toward the door.

"Uh, Heidi..."

"Wait a minute."

"Heidi!"

The elder fae woman appeared in the doorway but swallowed her retort and swore as she spotted the arrival. The middle fae's pant leg was ripped open, deep gouges in his calf covered in blood and matter I couldn't stomach to look too closely at.

The trio stormed past me and followed Heidi inside.

Not wanting to miss what was going on—and curious if this was related to our investigation or Espen's poisoning—I downed my coffee. After setting the empty cup aside next to the wall to take home and throw away later, I straightened up and walked inside.

Back within the warm healing hut, Heidi was already tending to her new patient set up on another exam table near Espen. He was grumbling and exclaiming in agony as she prodded, and honest to hell, I couldn't blame him. Something had carved open his leg.

"Hold him down," Heidi ordered, and the two healthy forest fae soldiers jumped into action. Meanwhile I settled by the entrance, keeping my distance and staying out of the way, but still close enough to hear any chatter between the fae.

The soldiers shackled the injured one to the table, one restraining his feet, the other restraining his hands. He was by no means a large fae—definitely more svelte compared to Espen and Øyvin—but from the way he shifted and the muscles in his forearms contracted, I could tell he was strong. His eyes almost bugged out of their sockets when he spotted Heidi with a dark-brown salve. She shook her head gently before resting the little glass jar on a work bench beside the table. The bench was small, holding a variety of medicinal objects as well as a small bowl that she'd filled with water. She grabbed a cloth and dabbed it in the basin. While wringing it out, she muttered something and the fae heaved a breath.

As she set to cleaning the wound of debris, the injured fae hissed but said no more, like he was trying to contain his pain. He breathed hard through every swipe and it wasn't long before Heidi was dropping a red-soaked cloth back into the bowl.

"Brace yourself, young man," Heidi said with a voice that conveyed her next actions would hurt like a bitch, and I grimaced on the fae's behalf.

She lifted her palms and set one on his knee and the other by his ankle. Taking a deep breath she closed her eyes, and, a split second later, a light glow emanated from her hands.

I watched in awe as she used the same magic I'd seen Espen use on the scarred tree weeks ago. The light slowly swept down the fae's calf and started knitting together his wound until two puckered red lines started to form.

"Wolf," Heidi muttered as she watched her magic stitch the leg back together.

The fae on the table nodded weakly, his face having gone severely pale as his whole body flexed under her touch, damn near convulsing in pain.

My stomach knotted and my throat constricted. I knew dog bites could be bad, but fucking hell.

"What are they doing this far south?" Heidi asked, turning her head from one of the soldiers to the other.

"Espen had us keeping watch, and Ylva doubled our shifts recently." The fae at the head of the table glanced at the sleeping leader in the room. "But one of the wolves attacked randomly this morning before retreating back to the small pack that has been prowling around the farm on the hill."

Heidi shook her head and a look of disgust settled across her features. "Lennie, can you pass me the bottle with the red liquid?"

I glanced over at the counter space she'd been working at this morning and panicked. There were so many bottles in different shades of red, reddish-brown, and reddish-pink, let alone the blacks and greens. How the fuck was I supposed to know which one she was—

"The one closest to the sink," she supplied.

I nodded and did as I was told. Passing her the small vessel, I stepped back and watched as she administered the tonic. Lifting the fae's head, she tilted a few drops of the liquid between his chapped lips. He stared up at her, his eyes growing heavy with thanks and the power of the concoction. She stoppered the bottle and put it aside on the work table before gently setting his head back down and patting him on the shoulder. "Get some rest."

He closed his eyes and his breathing quickly evened out until he was indeed fast asleep.

Just as swiftly as they'd arrived, the other two soldiers thanked Heidi and then made their way to the door that still stood propped open, the sound of rain now drifting in.

"I'll send word to Ylva about his recovery," Heidi said softly, a firm and genuine kindness seeping into her words. "You two be careful."

They nodded and took their leave.

I skirted around the newest patient and wandered over to Espen. Even with all the commotion, he was still fast asleep. I glanced between the two injured fae, resting my hand on Espen's bed. There was no way these two instances could be related, not unless some fae was poisoning other fae and controlling the wolves. Was that even a thing fae could do—control animals? The former seemed more realistic, and the latter sounded outlandish in my mind. No, they couldn't possibly be related. Could they?

"Do you think—"

"That these are related?" Heidi interjected as she washed up.

"Yeah."

She took a deep breath and shook her head. "Highly unlikely. Someone clearly had a grudge against Espen, or someone else at that party, and Espen was an unfortunate accident. As for the wolves, they aren't unheard of around here, just rare. I wouldn't go wandering around the forest alone anymore. If there are wolves attacking other beings, it won't be long before the humans notice something is amiss and more of them start scouring these woods with rifles in an effort to eradicate the beasts. The humans have done so before and they will do so again if the need is there. There is a massive debate in this country around wolves and hunting them, I'd advise you don't get caught up in it."

"Duly noted," I mumbled, brushing my hand across my forehead.

Heidi finished cleaning up and pulled a small flip-phone out of the pocket in her long wool dress.

"*You* have a cellphone?" I exclaimed.

She rolled her eyes. "I don't live in the 1800s anymore."

I swallowed my laugh but couldn't hide the smile. "You know, if I didn't know about all of this"—I waved my hand around—"then I'd think you were being real funny, Heidi."

"Oh, I am very funny, Lennie. But getting eaten by wolves is no laughing matter. So, I'll call for an escort."

I gave Espen's hand a gentle squeeze before crossing the room to her. "I don't need a babysitter, Heidi."

"I insist."

I shook my head. "No, Heidi. I'll be fine. I'll leave now, though, so I'm at least out in the daylight."

She returned her phone to her pocket. "Fine."

"Thank you for helping him." I glanced over my shoulder at Espen, wanting nothing more than for him to wake up and make a joke about yoga positions.

"Give him time," Heidi replied with a sigh. "He'll be back on his feet soon."

I certainly hoped so. I kinda missed the bundle of sunshine.

36

ESPEN

My head pounded and my body felt like it was on fire, as if I was burning from the inside out. I could smell coffee, though... and something that reminded me of a fruity cocktail.

Light flickered on the other side of my eyelids, but they were so heavy that I couldn't open them.

Someone was talking in English, while another person responded in Norwegian—the two carrying on a conversation I couldn't quite grasp.

So sleepy.

Sleep sounded good... really good... maybe the fire would go out if I just slept it off?

Yes, that sounded right...

37

LENNIE

Frustrated by the lack of movement from Espen as he lay unconscious and sitting around for so long, the next afternoon I decided to blatantly ignore Heidi's advice to avoid the woods and the wolf threat. Wolves were generally crepuscular or nocturnal animals, and I had no intention of provoking them like the fae soldiers probably had. What Heidi didn't know wouldn't hurt her. I needed to get outdoors, to take some photos, and to do something of value to distract myself from the endless waiting. So, I grabbed my camera, pulled on my boots, and set off on a hike.

The drizzle-filled air clung to my rain jacket and hair as I trekked up the trail by the mountain, away from town. With the need to be productive coursing through my veins spurring me on, I made my way back toward the clearing where Espen, and I had found the illegal magic transfer scars, feeling like an eternity had passed since then.

I took my time retracing my steps, capturing photos of the fjord and all manner of flora. From the white-and-black birch trees, to the little mushrooms pushing through the moss at the base of a fallen pine, nothing was left undocumented. My hands were steady, but my pulse beat to a happy rhythm. It felt good to be behind the camera again—as easy as breathing. I couldn't remember the last time I'd gone more than a week without snapping a few shots, but here I was having picked it back up.

I continued my trudge toward the clearing and when I finally reached it, I sat on one of the boulders, taking a swig of water from the bottle I'd stashed in my backpack.

The area was devoid of any other creatures, but creaks and skitters between the trees told me I wasn't entirely alone. For some, hiking by themselves was scary and too dangerous. For me, it was a chance to clear my head, an escape from reality so far removed from the frustrating and mundane parts of life. And, it wasn't like I was ever a complete moron when hiking alone—I had a first aid kit in my bag, provisions, and proper footwear. Honestly, the number of people I'd seen hiking in flip-flops in the US was ridiculous.

Hydrated and ready to keep moving, I returned my bottle to my bag and wandered over to the scarred tree. The bark was still marred with small slashes as it was the first time we'd seen it, time having done nothing to heal them. I brushed my hand across one, the tough layer scraping against my palm. A pang of annoyance and anger rippled through me. *Why would anyone want to harm this area and the fae who live here?*

With a hefty sigh and no answers, I straightened and decided to keep moving. The days were growing shorter, darkness encroaching quickly, and I wanted to be back in the village before nightfall but had time to explore a little more. I continued further into the forest that blanketed the steep mountainside next to the fjord, following a trail that wove into more dense wood, and I got distracted by the scenery once again, snapping picture after picture. Water droplets hanging off the edge of a light-green fern, a thick layer of moss draped across a slate-colored rock, and the trickle of a tiny stream that crept down the mountainside—I captured it all. Framing my shot, adjusting the focus, and clicking away, it was blissful. At the rate I was going, I would run out of space on the memory card I'd put in the camera this morning. But, I continued anyway, until a snapping noise caught my ear and I looked up...

Shit.

The sun was almost gone.

How did I miss the shift in the light?

Another cracking noise rent the air, and a shiver ran down my spine. In classic Lennie Martin fashion, I'd been distracted by my camera again. My brother Ryan would laugh in my face when he heard about this.

I carefully put the lens cap back on my camera, making sure it clicked securely into place—I didn't want to lose that again. Something shifted between the trees to my right, and I swallowed the brief lump of panic in my throat. I spun around to retrace my steps and halted.

Blocking the trail back down to Skolvik was a man right out of a Viking movie. With short hair, furs and leathers draped across his body, and a wicked grin, he looked like an animal ready to pounce.

"Going somewhere?" he asked, his voice rumbling with a threat that had me clenching my fists and shifting my feet into a tackle-ready stance.

"I was thinking home, but if you wanna play, big guy...?"

He flinched, blinking as if I'd startled him.

"You're not Norwegian."

"Nope."

A crunch escaped from the forest and another man emerged, equally clad in a weird-ass outfit. In the remnants of light, I spotted the shape of the newcomer's ears—pointed, a fae. *But what faction?* Whichever group they belonged to, my fight or flight senses were screaming foe.

"How do you understand me?" the first one asked, his brow furrowing into deep lines. "I'm not speaking English."

I grinned and flicked my eyebrows. "Magic."

They both narrowed their eyes at that and then snarled.

Bracing for a fight and incapable of keeping my mouth shut, I asked, "So, you two from around here or is this your fave vacay spot? Let me guess, it's the smell of the pine and the fresh air that *really* gets you going? Was I interrupting a tryst? Don't stop on my behalf."

My opponents smirked and tilted their heads in unison, the small motion raising every hackle I had. My skin pebbled at the sight, and my heart thundered against my ribs. Then, in the same way Espen would change the appearance of our clothes, the two fae touched their left shoulders. However, instead of shifting into new attire, they morphed into another form. I watched with my stomach in my throat as joints cracked, snouts pushed out from their faces, and fur sprouted across their bodies. Wolves.

Shit.

"What big teeth you have," I muttered, and then bolted away from their jaws.

My legs pistoned and my breaths came in jagged puffs as I careened through the dense forest, adrenaline pushing me faster than I'd ever moved. Branches whacked me in the face and thighs, and I narrowly avoided tripping over numerous rocks and slipping on the damp moss. Unfortunately, my split-second lead was disappearing as the two wolves bounded after me and howled with what I could only assume was delight.

Trust me to land myself in a shitty situation... again. First the boat, now this? I really should start to listen to authority figures. Heidi had *just* mentioned not to walk alone in the woods, especially at night, and I'd ignored her, just like I always did.

Tripping on a damn twig, I tumbled to the ground—tucking and rolling to protect my precious camera. I landed with a thud, my back taking the brunt of the blow as the air whooshed out of me. The sound of footfalls slowed and, before I could get back up, two sets of snarling teeth were a mere inch from my face.

What a way to go. I took a shallow breath, gulping down the lump in my throat as I stared up at the razor-sharp teeth. *Mom's gonna be pissed.*

One of the wolves reared back and opened its jaw, the rancid smell from its mouth turning my stomach. I squeezed my eyes shut as he lunged for my head, nicked my chin, and then yelped... never fully making contact. I blinked rapidly, hands rising to protect my face as I watched as the beast and its friend were tossed aside.

My heart hammered in my chest, and a wave of relief washed over me as a behemoth fae grumbled at the wolves. Halvar was practically cloaked in darkness, as if the shock of silver hair on his head and face were the only parts of him the moonlight was allowed to touch.

I scrambled to my feet as the wolves circled back, glaring at my savior.

"Be gone!" Halvar bellowed, his voice like rolling thunder.

The wolves sneered in reply as I stepped closer to the Fjell Fae, keeping him between me and them.

"Leave this mountain, and never return, or it will be the last one you climb."

At that, the wolf closest to Halvar lunged... but never made contact. Halvar caught the beast, wrapping his large hands around its neck. The wolf whimpered, but swatted at him with its paws, trying to use its back legs to scratch Halvar's chest.

I took a step back to avoid being trampled as Halvar growled, "Leave."

The wolf snapped back, its eyes full of a deathly ferocity.

That was apparently the wrong answer because, before I could take my next breath, Halvar grabbed the wolf's snout with one hand, the other locked on its neck, and twisted. A sickening crack echoed around us, and the wolf went limp. Halvar chucked the beast toward its accomplice who'd stilled. "May that be a warning to you. Take him, head north, and do not return."

The wolf that remained alive slowly shifted back to his fae form. Cracks and snaps were the only noises that emanated from the forest as the fae morphed from four legs to two. His furs and leathers returned to his shoulders, and his ears formed small points at the tops. With an ashen face, he carefully stepped forward and hoisted the body of his friend into his arms. Without another word, look, or nod, he turned and retreated into the forest.

After a moment of silence, and once I was certain the wolf-fae-thing had left, I muttered. "Well, fuck me sideways. That was close."

Halvar glanced over his shoulder with an unamused look and something inside me panicked a little.

"Uh... thanks, by the way." I smiled briefly, swiping the back of my hand across my chin and coming away with a smear of blood.

"It's just a scratch," he said matter-of-factly. "You're okay."

"Well, that's usually debatable." I shrugged and scoffed. "Physically? Yes. Mentally? Probably not. I *did* just witness two humanoid-like creatures snap, crack, and pop into big doggos. That shit is prime material for some gnarly nightmares, my friend." And therapy. A fuck-ton of therapy. *I wonder if the fae have therapists that I could talk to about all of this?* If I tried to tell a human therapist, they'd probably ask me to lay off the Twilight marathons while they prescribed a nice fitted straight jacket.

Halvar crossed his arms, clearly in no mood for my jokes.

I swallowed hard and took a deep breath.

"Come with me," Halvar said—an order, not an option—and started walking back toward Skolvik.

"If you could just escort me to Espen's, that would be greatly appreciated. You know, just in case that wolf decides to test their luck."

"It won't." Halvar pushed aside some branches for us to pass through without being swatted in the face.

"Well, either way—"

"We will go to Espen's to get your things. Then you'll come to the mountain with me."

I frowned, glaring daggers at the big scary fae's back. "I'll be fine at the cabin."

"Queen's orders," he grunted.

"Don't get me wrong, I really like Freija, very nice fae. But, she can't exactly order—" The glare Halvar shot at me had my mouth zipping shut faster than a farmer shucking a corncob, and I silently followed Halvar all the way back to Espen's cabin.

38

LENNIE

Halvar loomed in the kitchen as I packed my shit once more. It was weird to see the Fjell Fae outside of the mountain, and especially in Espen's cabin. His frame felt too big for the space, like he was built differently, of rocks and boulders that had no place indoors.

After putting a lackluster Band-Aid over the gash on my chin, I found a rumpled old duffel bag under Espen's bed and unceremoniously shoved my stuff inside it. Feeling the pressure from the brooding fae in the other room, I moved as quickly as possible. I couldn't be sure what living conditions I would be in thanks to Queen Freija's orders, so I borrowed some of Espen's clothes. I grabbed a green knit sweater with a Nordic pattern across the top, a fleece jacket that kind of fit me, and a pair of woolly socks. Worst case scenario, these would keep me warm, especially with the temperatures dipping every day since I'd arrived.

I threw the duffel through the doorway into the kitchen and living area, then set my sights on grabbing the last minute things I would normally forget—my toothbrush, my backpack, and my phone charger. Although, I wasn't entirely sure if where I was going would have outlets.

"Okay, we're good," I said, stepping out into the kitchen area with the last of my things.

Halvar leaned against the counter and glared at my stuff. With a silent nod, he pushed off and strode over to the front door.

I shook my head at his verbosity, slung my backpack across my shoulders, grabbed the duffel, and locked up behind us.

Halvar led me into the mountain through the same entrance I'd used previously. Instead of shifting my attire, he waved for me to follow him through the tunnels in my very distinct human hiking gear. I didn't stand out too much but a lot of the residents threw inquisitive glances in my direction as we marched deeper into the mountain.

The side of my neck tickled and I instinctively wiped at it, feeling something slick. Pulling my hand away, I found a scarlet smear of blood across my fingers. *So much for my little Band-Aid.*

"Ummm, when you said scratch," I muttered to Halvar three large strides ahead of me, "you didn't say bleeding significantly." I swept my fingers across my chin only to find more blood. "Any chance you've got a Heidi where you're taking me?"

Halvar glanced over his shoulder, but barely slowed. His eyes narrowed, assessing me, before he nodded and turned back. "Bad scratch. It will heal."

"So, you don't have a healer or some medical stuff?" The first-aid kit in my backpack was substantial, but if I needed stitches... I shuddered at the thought. There wasn't much that scared me, but needles? No thanks. Hard pass.

"We do," Halvar said, never breaking his brisk pace. "I'll send for them to clean you up."

Sensing this was as friendly as Halvar got, I said a quick, "Thank you."

We turned down another narrower corridor lined with little sconces of flickering light—magic light considering the lack of flame within the glow. The air around us grew slightly warmer somehow, as if the mountain was insulated. After another minute of walking, Halvar turned to his left and opened a large wooden door that looked straight out of a medieval castle.

Inside the room was a small bed with blankets and a single pillow, a table and chair beneath a light-orb lantern, and a worn out armchair in the corner. It couldn't be more basic, but I wasn't sure what I'd expected from a glorified cave dwelling. How should I know, I hadn't exactly spent a lot of time living within a mountain.

"Thank you," I said again, scanning the room and Halvar.

"There's a bathroom three doors down on the left," he said, making to leave. "I shall find the healer for your scratch. Stay here." With that order, he departed, closing the door behind him.

Deciding I'd neglected to follow the wise words of authority figures once already today—and learning the consequences—I did as I was told. Plus, I got the feeling upsetting Halvar might be worse than getting cornered by crazy wolves. I carefully shucked off my backpack and sat it and the duffel bag down by the table before plopping down on the bed. The mattress sank heavily beneath me, but wasn't wholly uncomfortable.

I waited only a few minutes before a knock sounded at my door and Halvar entered, followed by a young male fae with dark hair who wore a slate apron and carried an old-fashioned doctor's bag like the Mary Poppins of the mountain.

"Hi, I'm Lennie," I said with a gentle smile.

The newcomer smiled in return before turning to Halvar. "Can you translate for me?"

Halvar shrugged and crossed his arms, leaning against the wall by the door. "She understands Norwegian. Nora tinkered with her hearing."

The fae's dark eyebrows flicked upward before his lips curved again. "I'm Trygve. It's nice to meet you, Miss Lennie. You appear to have a big scratch on your chin. May I examine it?" He approached me carefully, like I was a bull that might charge him at any second. And I guessed, to him, I *was* a foreign entity that was worth being wary of. How often had he treated humans?

"Have at it." I waved at the wound.

He nodded, then gently tipped my chin, tilting it to have a closer look at the underside. With a tut, he pulled away my Band-Aid and said, "Good thing Halvar found you and stopped those wolves."

"Mm-hmm," I mumbled, his fingers still holding my head at an angle.

"The cut is small, but not too deep. I shall clean it up with alcohol, then apply a glue and bandage to hold it shut. It might leave a small scar though."

"Meh, I'm alive, so thank you and do what you need to do." While a scar could be bothersome, it honestly didn't agitate me. Would my mom have an absolute meltdown about it? One thousand percent yes, which I was kind of excited to see. It would certainly make the holidays fun if I went back to Ohio in time.

Trygve nodded again and got to work, disinfecting the cut and patching me up.

"Aside from the one on your wrist, is this your first scar?" Trygve asked, making small talk while Halvar loomed on the other side of the room.

"What do you mean 'the one on my wrist?'"

"The magic one," he said, pressing a small gauzy bandage across my wound.

"I don't have any other scars, Trygve," I replied, probably butchering his name.

He tapped my wrist and stepped back just as Halvar piped up, "Nora's magic would have left a mark when she tinkered with your linguistic hearing."

I glanced at my wrist. *It can't have.* I'd felt a slight sting when she'd done it, but hadn't seen a damn thing... And yet... Sure enough, there on my wrist, almost as small as a freckle was a tiny white dot. "Well, fuck me sideways," I muttered.

"Magic leaves scars, not unlike the one you're going to have on your chin. But these," Trygve waved his hand at my wrist, "are slightly more silver in the light."

I twisted my forearm, tilting it toward the lanterns on the wall. The little mark shimmered, barely noticeable—you'd have to know exactly where to look in order to see it.

"Is that normal?" I asked, looking between the two fae and the mark on my wrist.

Trygve turned to Halvar, as if asking for permission to speak, and Halvar gave him a gentle nod to proceed. "Again, magic can leave scars. The stronger the magic, or the greater the amount, the bigger or deeper the scar. Take your altered hearing. That is generally a power only the Royal Fae can do, and for them, is considered more of a party trick compared to their other abilities."

"If magic is given or taken by force," Halvar piped in, his voice low and serious, "then deep scars are left behind, like slashes through whatever material is acted upon. No one has ever quite understood exactly why, but it's commonly agreed upon that the scars are a repercussion from the ancestors for not using our magic for good, nor its intended purpose—to protect the natural resources of our world."

"So, what about the trees in the clearing where the illegal magic trans-fer happened?" I asked, tilting my head, the image of the damaged trees still fresh in my mind from earlier in the day.

Halvar nodded, following my line of thought. "Those were a side effect from the explosion of a large amount of magic transferred from one entity to another. It's a heinous act that would've left similar scars on the perpetrators, too."

"It's not natural," Trygve added quietly, pursing his lips and shaking his head. Then, with a sigh he glanced up at me. "Is that all your injuries, or do you have more that I need to look at?"

I shook my head, feeling a little overwhelmed by the amount of infor-mation they'd just shared, and then shouting sounded from the other side of the door—muffled, but growing louder by the second.

Halvar shifted just as the door burst open and two soldiers barreled after a seething intruder. Øyvin shadowed the threshold, his chest heav-ing, nostrils flared, his eyes as dark as the bottom of the fjord. He took one step forward and Halvar blocked his path. Then the idiot actually growled at the Fjell Fae. In response, Halvar grabbed Øyvin by the front of his wool sweater and spun, slamming him against the rocky wall. The soldiers and Trygve wisely cleared the room. I, on the other hand, sat back and watched the show—a warmth growing within my chest.

Øyvin held up a ball of water in his palm before smashing it into Hal-var's face. The Fjell Fae grumbled and then started spouting water like a cherub fountain—a very large, angry cherub fountain. Water spewed from between his lips, falling in a graceful arc to the rocky floor where it began to pool around their boots. His eyes widened, and he slipped his hands around Øyvin's throat, starting to squeeze. I pressed my lips together, stifling a laugh that threatened to bubble out, and then winced when the movement pulled at the skin on my chin.

Øyvin's gaze flicked to mine, concern etched across his features.

That split second was enough time for his magic to subside, and the water spewing from between Halvar's lips slowed to a trickle. Øyvin's face was turning red from strain and lack of oxygen where Halvar now held him by the throat. When the fountain dried up, Halvar snarled, "Don't use your tricks on me, boy."

Øyvin was released with a small shove, and he brushed off his shoulders like nothing had happened. He squared up to the older fae, glaring at him. "Don't get between me and her again."

My heart skipped a beat at Øyvin's statement, and Halvar bit back, "Don't come storming into my mountain—"

"This is *Freija's* mountain," Øyvin said, cutting him off, and I let out a hiss. Wrong words to say, buddy. I'd only known Halvar for a hot second, but even *I* knew that shit wouldn't sit well with the big guy.

"She will be staying in the mountain until Espen wakes up," Halvar said with the authority of a Viking who was obeyed and never questioned.

"She'll come back to the boat house with me—"

"Where you'll have time to watch her and keep her from wandering through the forests where she could be attacked?"

Øyvin crossed his arms and took a deep breath, but didn't reply.

"Exactly. You serve the King; you have enough responsibilities."

"And you don't?"

"I have a fortress to protect our inhabitants—"

"You know," I interrupted, "I can take care of myself. So, when you two decide to stop bickering like two little old ladies fighting for the best pew at church, let me know." I leaned back on the bed and kicked up my feet, resting my arms behind my head.

Deep sighs filled the room and the two fae backed off their dick-measuring session.

I glanced over at Øyvin, who looked wracked with anger and something I couldn't quite place. "I already agreed to stay here until Espen wakes up. I'll be fine. Perhaps you could even come visit when you get off work," I suggested, wiggling my eyebrows and hoping he got the hint.

Øyvin tilted his head and furrowed his brow, but Halvar clearly understood. He scowled, grumbled something I couldn't quite hear, and with one final glance at Øyvin, left the room, slamming the door as he went.

"I was talking about sex," I stage-whispered.

Øyvin snorted and shoved his hands in his pockets, giving me a pointed look.

At the sight, I realized it hadn't just been about sex. While the Asshole was an annoying grouch, I'd also come to enjoy our sparring matches. And, if I thought really hard about it, he wasn't the worst company on the planet, which was a revelation indeed. Perhaps there had been some sort of hallucinogenic in the wolf scratch? Or maybe the sight of him storming in here had done more to my heart than just ignite a spark of warmth within my chest.

I shifted and turned my head, starting to feel drained after the day's events.

Øyvin's gaze landed on my chin and he stilled. "Are you okay?"

"I'll be fine," I replied with a resigned sigh, and sat up again, setting my feet on the floor.

"I don't like seeing people hurt," he muttered, stepping up beside the bed, his signature scent of fresh linen joining him. He sank onto the mattress next to me, our thighs lightly brushing against each other, the sensation sending a bubble of warmth through my veins. "It's my job to protect the fae of the fjord. It's been my family's responsibility for centuries and something we take great pride in. So, when I heard..." he nodded toward me, then shook his head and shoulders, as if trying to rid himself of the emotions that were seeping out of him.

"You can talk to me."

He raised a single brow and tilted his head in such a way that I knew what his internal monologue was.

"You *can* trust me."

"Somewhat, but you don't always take things seriously."

"I know, but when it comes to family and protecting those I care about, I will be the most serious woman on the planet. You can trust in that. Scout's honor."

"I have a hard time believing you were ever a Scout."

"That's beside the point."

An exasperated sigh left him as he shook his head, but he couldn't hide the way his lips tipped up in a grin, and I loved that I made him smile. Those grins were so rare that it felt like I'd won a little piece of treasure anytime I could get one out of him. He clasped his hands together and leaned forward, resting his elbows on his knees. With a deep sigh, my grumpy fae started opening up. "My father was in this role before me. He and my mother were so proud when I took up the mantle. They passed not long after, which was tough but also a blessing in disguise, as twenty years ago my only sibling, my brother, who'd moved to the south, died, too."

A lump settled in my throat hearing of his losses and that twenty year marker—the one that kept popping up again and again.

"We weren't sure if he was part of the rebel uprising," Øyvin continued, "or if he was merely a bystander, but he died in the battle that killed Queen Ragnhild. There was nothing my forces could do for him. He was gone when they arrived." He stared at the wall across the room, dazed and lost in memories. I felt a pang of sadness at his story, and the realization that he was probably the only member left of his family had a tear welling at the corner of my eye.

"So, that's why you're so protective of the fjord," I said, voicing my thoughts and brushing away the tear before it could fall.

"I'm protective of family and the resources that my people were created to protect."

"That's fair." I gently placed my hand on his thigh, and he gazed down at it before biting his lower lip.

He brushed his fingers across the top of my hand, lightly trailing small patterns around my knuckles. Tiny sparks shot up my arm at the soothing sensation, and I pressed closer to his side. "I'm glad you're safe," he said, his voice barely above a whisper. My heart stuttered at the sentiment, the care laced through every note, every word.

He swept a strand of my hair off my shoulder and let his hand settle between my shoulder blades. The warmth from his palm sent a shiver down my spine.

"Øyvin," I whispered his name, and his eyes flicked to mine.

"You're a stubborn, troublesome woman," he uttered, gently turning my face to his and pressing his forehead against mine, our shallow breaths intermingling. "But..." he sighed like he was struggling to find the words. "I'm glad you're here."

The next thing I knew his lips were pressing against mine, and I was lifting my arms, wrapping them around his neck and pulling him into me. The kiss stole my breath, and he swept his tongue against the seam of my lips, asking for entry, which I slowly granted him, savoring the moment. My heart beat wildly in my chest, my brain losing all sense of focus on my surroundings, zoning in on the feel of the man pressed against me instead.

When I finally thought I might succumb to the feverish kisses, Øyvin pulled back, his lips now puffy and his eyes full of lust.

I ran my hands down his chest, the brush of his jacket smooth beneath my palms. *What was that?* And why did it feel so good?

Taking a deep breath in through his nose, Øyvin straightened up and rose to his feet. I scooted back but didn't feel offended by the loss of his warmth or touch. The fact that Øyvin had shared as much as he had seemed like a damn miracle. And the kiss was full of passion and acceptance—something I didn't realize I wanted from him, but was happy to have received.

He strode to the door, his face blank and his lips pursed into a fine line. "I'm glad you're all right."

"You're such a grouch," I said with a chuckle and a wink as he opened the door.

He spun in the doorway, a hint of a smile on his lips. "No, I'm a fae of the fjord."

And with that he walked out, wholly unaware of the flame within me that started to burn a little brighter. It was an unfamiliar feeling that had me wondering what the hell kind of turn my life had taken and where we would go next.

39

ØYVIN

I swallowed the lump in my throat—the annoying thing had lodged itself there while I told Lennie about my family, but finally disappeared as I left the fjell. Taking one deep breath after another, I began to rein in my breathing—in through my nose, hold for a few seconds, and then out through my mouth. This continued as I traipsed down the mountain trail toward town, the dark of night enveloping me in her shadows.

Hearing of the wolf attack on the Forest Fae soldier the other day had surprised me. Receiving word that Lennie had been attacked rattled me to my core. It was a vulnerable feeling I didn't like the taste of. She may have been a pain in the ass and could handle herself in the woods, but she was still human. A bite from one of those Forest-Fae-shifting-shits from the North wouldn't just scar her, it could flay her to pieces.

The amount of problems going on in the fjord right now wasn't just concerning, it was like a pot of water about to bubble over. I could sense it in the air and I was sure the humans could, too. But they could at least brush it off as an impending bad winter or a storm on the horizon that set all the creatures of the fjord and the forest on edge. They didn't know what truly lurked beneath the surface and skulked between the trees. Their legends and folktales were never too far from the truth, but

I hoped, for everyone's sake, that they never found out the reality they really lived in.

I sauntered past Oddvar's, locked up and closed for the night, and aimed toward my home. As I approached the line of red boathouses, I spotted someone leaning next to my front door.

"Sir," the man said, tilting his head toward the porch light so I could see his face.

Sigurd. The captain from the wall.

"What are you doing here?" I asked as I approached and began to unlock the door. I refrained from opening it though. This was my sanctuary, and I didn't like inviting work across the threshold.

"There's been a change. Kjetil sent me—"

I jerked upright, turning toward him. "Kjetil?"

"Yes, sir. When you didn't answer your phone"—*damn the mountain and its thick rock walls*—"the King's Chief Advisor was notified. He's down at the site already."

"Tell me what happened," I said sternly, crossing my arms in preparation for more bad news.

"The wall, sir, it keeps falling. The pressure is becoming too much for merely two fae to control."

"Let's go." I spun quickly, re-locked the door, and strode toward the waterline beside my house that was hidden from view of the street.

Sigurd was right. The northern part of the wall was flickering like a faulty light bulb and disappearing sporadically, letting through detritus. A collection of Fjord Fae, including Kjetil, were gathered around the opening, re-erecting it continuously. People were yelling, power straining to hold the line, chaos and panic flooding from the group.

"Press harder!"

"Steady men!"

"Where are the others?"

I landed on the fjord-bed with a dull thump, and immediately pressed my hands and shoulders into the wall, adding my power and strength to our barricade. The magic of the wall pulsed beneath my palms, pressing back with equal measure, like the whole thing was about to come down. I closed my eyes and focused on the well of energy within me. Calling forth some extra strength, I pushed the added power into the wall and opened my eyes. The flickering slowed, and the fae at my side relaxed their shoulders slightly while Kjetil stood back and nodded—not contributing his power to the effort. *And Lennie thought I was an asshole.*

"We've already sent for more reinforcements," he muttered.

I nodded. "Thank you. You all right, soldiers?" I asked, glancing down the line of fae who were aiding in keeping the wall stable.

They looked worse for wear, but all nodded—sweat staining their brows within their pockets of air as they leaned on the wall, giving it their energy, same as I did. My own brow was starting to bead with sweat but I pushed through the strain and focused on the problem before me.

"Has the King issued any new orders?" I yelled over my shoulder to Kjetil.

"None," he replied. "Only to keep the wall up."

Right, well, that was starting to become more and more difficult. With six of us channeling power into this part of the wall, and it still threatening to collapse, I needed to make a decision and fast.

"Break the wall. Reroute it south of the disturbance—"

"That would encroach on protected territory," Sigurd said, coming up to my side.

"It would, but we can't have that disturbance siphoning all the power out of our soldiers. This much energy could kill them, and I won't have that during peacetime."

"Yes, sir." Sigurd stepped back again, as if giving me leave to make the next steps.

My breaths deepened and my muscles spasmed as I thought through the steps that would do the least amount of damage and risk the fewest injuries or threats to my men. It wasn't going to be easy but, with this number of fae, we should be able to do it.

"All right," I yelled, my voice carrying through the water. "Sigurd and you two." I nodded to the two fae closest to me, "You press your energy into the edge of the wall to my left."

They nodded and shifted swiftly to my other side. As they moved, I felt that same scratching sensation against my power—what I'd felt during the previous inspection—and was relieved when it subsided as they repositioned themselves, refueling the wall.

"You three," I said to the remaining fae, "on the count of three, I want you to shift twenty paces back with me. Keep your line, but move as swiftly as you can without swimming—we can't allow whatever this invisible threat is to get beneath our feet."

They nodded and responded with a unified, "Yes, sir!"

I leaned away slightly from the wall and rolled my neck before glancing over my shoulder.

"You'd better move out of the way, Kjetil," I grunted, and the fae shifted back and to the side, where he could watch without getting trampled by us.

"One..."

"Two..."

I took a deep breath.

Please work.

"Three!"

The wall shimmered beneath my palms as we started to drag it backward. My fellow soldiers grunted and strained, but it was working, the wall was moving and not breaking—

One of the fae stumbled and fell, but jumped back to his feet quickly. However, the brief loss of power was enough to see his part of the wall collapse entirely. The pressure around us mounted, and I felt the air pocket I'd created around myself strain. I pressed more power into the barrier as we continued sliding it backward and the gap refilled where it had just fallen.

"Almost there!" I yelled, glad it was nearly over, starting to feel depleted and exhausted, my muscles aching like they hadn't been used in a decade.

"Three more steps."

Three.

Two.

One.

"And stop!" I yelled.

We'd done it. *Thank the ancestors.*

"All right, you three step back one step, let's see if this will hold, but be prepared to step in on my orders."

The three fae to my right nodded and then, in unison, they stepped away from the wall.

The pressure against my palms mounted and I pressed my shoulder against it, but there was no scratching sensation—no hail-like pelting that had besieged the wall previously. At that moment, a corps of reinforcements arrived and reported to Sigurd who pointed them in my direction. Five fae split from the contingent and joined me, pressing their hands against the wall and taking the strain.

I pushed off the wall that was now more heavily guarded and powered than it had ever been, hoping it would hold and that our monarch was all right. Without a doubt, Balder would've felt that strain on his own power.

A gentle clap sounded from my left. "Well done, General," Kjetil said, not a drop of perspiration or anxiety marring his brow. "Shall we report to the King?"

The only answer was yes, and however tired I now felt, I had a duty to uphold, one I'd sworn an oath to. With a deep breath, I nodded and we started to swim toward the King's quarters.

40

ESPEN

My head stung but the memories of piña coladas and blonde hair had me internally humming a happy tune. I liked the smell of the drink... and the blonde... both were nice and fruity but could seriously punch you in the gut... or ribs.

The fire in my veins had subsided, but I was so sleepy, my eyes remaining firmly shut.

Five more minutes wouldn't do any harm...

41

LENNIE

I wandered down the mountain tunnels toward the exit, my camera hanging around my neck. After a long rest this morning, I'd decided to spend my afternoon doing some photography around town and pay a quick visit to see if Espen was improving. I'd thrown on my jacket and boots, prepared for the cold and gray day outside, but when I stepped up toward the entrance, someone blocked my path.

"You can't go that way, young lady," the male in a gray Fjell Fae uniform said.

I pulled to an abrupt stop in front of him, a scowl settling across my features. "And why is that?"

"Orders," he replied and settled into a wider stance, like his body could ultimately stop me from leaving—which was likely true, it wasn't like I'd been working out lately or could take on any of Freija's soldiers, but still... The simple shift of his feet was annoying.

"From who?" I challenged, matching his irritating stance.

"From me," a gravelly voice said from the tunnel behind me.

I turned and found Halvar striding toward us, his silvery hair shining in the intermittent magical lighting. He was in gray fatigues and a thick knit sweater, but somehow still looked intimidating.

"Why am I being treated as a prisoner? I agreed to stay here, sure, but I didn't agree to being kept in a cage." I crossed my arms as he stopped in front of me.

"We'd need to escort you everywhere and, with the threats as they are, I cannot afford to send soldiers to babysit you out there for extended periods of time."

He had a point. I certainly didn't want to cause too many problems for Freija—it was clear she had a lot going on—but I hated being cooped up. I wanted to be outdoors, taking photos of the way the rainclouds settled over the fjord like a blanket. "Will I be able to see the light of day at some point during my stay at least? Humans need fresh air and a chance to stretch our legs or we go stir crazy."

Halvar pinched the bridge of his nose, his brow furrowing. "I can take you to see the sunset this evening. That will be worth photographing." He waved his hand toward my camera. "Just wait a few hours and refrain from taking any photos inside the fjell while you wait."

"Fine." I nodded, acquiescing to his *orders*.

The soldier at my back seemed to relax a little at that, and Halvar almost smiled. Almost. Okay maybe it was a figment of my imagination, but there was movement at the corner of his lips.

"Pick me up at four then," I said before wandering back down the maze of tunnels, toward where I hoped my room was. It was kind of difficult to remember.

"Where exactly are you taking me?" I asked as Halvar led us through the dense forest and up the switchbacks of the mountain's steep cliff side. The skies were clear, but the cold breeze stung my cheeks as it swept by.

"Only twice a year does the sun set perfectly between the two sides of the fjord. Today is one of those days," he replied.

All I could do was shrug, because, yeah, that did sound pretty epic and something I'd want to catch on camera. I'd just have appreciated a heads-up that we were hiking to the top of the mountain... at least the weather had cleared up and the clouds had dissipated.

We climbed further and further up the side of the fjell, Halvar expertly navigating us across boulders and through thickets, until we eventually reached the top. My chest heaved and my lungs ached but in a good way, like they'd needed the exercise as we traversed an open field, the terrain rocky and uneven.

"Is this really the easiest way to get wherever we're going?" I asked, narrowly avoiding twisting my ankle in a deep divot. Halvar glanced back at me and nodded.

"The other way would be a lot... steeper," he replied.

"Could it really get steeper than that?" I pointed over my shoulder with my thumb.

He nodded, and then motioned with his hand, directing it straight upward. My eyes widened, and I swallowed hard. "Well, thanks for taking me the easy route."

Halvar snorted and returned his focus to our path ahead. Or, at least, whatever path he knew, because there wasn't a visibly marked walking trail anywhere across this field. In fact, I doubted people ever came up here based on the rugged terrain and the steep drop down to the fjord on my left.

I followed Halvar as he stepped through a copse of trees at the far end of the field and onto what looked like a version of pride rock from the *Lion King* movie I'd grown up watching.

Halvar stepped aside and nodded toward the spit of rock.

"You gonna push me off?"

That earned me an eye roll.

Deciding he was unlikely to end my life here, I gingerly walked forward and then stopped in my tracks at the view before me, awe settling into my limbs.

The setting sun cleaved the sky in two, rendering the fjord gold in its waning light. It was a majestic sight to behold. I was blown away by the absolute majesty of the view, the spectacle Mother Nature was performing for us—a composition for this sliver of the world to witness and applaud. This right here—the sparkling rays, the blanket of fiery color—this was as close to a religious experience as I would ever have.

I pulled the lens cap off my camera, carefully stashing it in my jacket pocket, turned on the device, and set up my shot.

Photographing the galaxy's biggest light source was always a complicated endeavor. Capturing the sun itself and the surrounding landscape while trying to get the focus and depth of the composition right was a challenge because you always lost the detail surrounding your subject. But I did my best, making necessary adjustments and trying different things to get a decent photograph, wanting to remember this sight forever.

The mountains rolled into the fjord, the trees brushing the shoreline set alight by the fiery rays of the waning glow. The water glistened, tiny ripples forming where the wind swept down the passage and up toward me, sending tendrils of hair across my cheeks.

I snapped photo after photo, the rush of getting behind the camera filling my veins with a giddiness that brought a smile to my face.

When I felt somewhat satisfied with the shots I'd got, I turned back to Halvar and the forest where he waited, leaning against a tree like being exposed and out in the open was a threat.

"You got fresh air," he grunted as I joined him at the treeline. "We can go home now."

I took another look at the fjord below, inhaling deeply, the smell of pine and dew settling on the breeze around me. "Thank you."

I wished I'd been able to share this moment with Espen and Øyvin. I wished Øyvin could see how majestic his fjord looked in the setting light, and for Espen to see the peace that cloaked the entire scenery, the forests all along the water reaching toward the golden sky. The desire to have them here swept through me and somehow comforted me. It wasn't a surprising revelation—they'd become such prevalent figures in my life over the past weeks—but certainly a pleasant and welcomed feeling. One that warmed me from my head to my toes and found me smiling one last time toward the horizon.

Our trek back down the mountain was silent but punctuated by my grunts whenever I stubbed a toe on a rock or almost lost my balance. With the sun now fully set below the horizon, the only remaining light guiding us home was the silver glow of the moon and the weak-ass headlight I'd found in my backpack and strapped to my forehead. I was pretty sure only one battery inside it was still working based on the fragile and flickering beam.

"Don't worry your pretty, big head, I'm totally fine," I said after taking a tree branch to the face that Halvar had expertly dodged up ahead.

A low rumble emanated from the Fjell Fae, and I couldn't quite tell if it was a sigh, growl, or combo of the two. Either way, an unusual longing had settled in my limbs, and I kind of missed my bubbly Forest Fae. Espen had been a much better hiking companion.

"Can't you just take me to see him?" I asked.

"No."

"You're a stubborn troll," I grumbled.

Halvar let out an exasperated sigh as we continued to trudge through the forest back toward the fjell entrance. "Haven't you noticed how quiet it is since he was poisoned? How little has happened to worsen our circumstances since?"

I swallowed hard and thought about it for a second. He kind of had a point... but it also didn't sit right with me.

"Espen isn't the one causing all the problems," I said before quickly adding, "He isn't the one hurting *your* Queen." I hadn't missed the way Halvar looked at Freija, those tiny glances and constantly protecting her back like he was her shadow. It was the behavior of a man who was protecting his woman, not just a Guard protecting his Queen.

Halvar stopped and cast his gaze over his shoulder, his sky-blue eyes meeting mine and narrowing at my pointed remark. "Are you so certain? How well do you really know him?"

"Well enough to trust him." Espen had saved my life when I fell through the bridge on our hike. I'd watched him care for the people of the village when the landslides occurred, and, damn it, he'd taken care of me—the abandoned tourist—when he could've just left me alone. "He was with me when the first landslide happened, so it couldn't have been him," I added, pulling up in front of the behemoth fae, standing toe-to-toe with a creature that was at least several centuries my senior, if not a millennia. "Plus, I haven't seen any scars on him, and I've seen *a lot* of Espen."

Halvar sneered, lowering his voice to a gravely whisper. "You know him so well, he even told you what he did twenty years ago?"

I flinched. There was that number again. *Twenty.*

Halvar seemed to sense my hesitation. "Queen Ragnhild wanted Espen, not for his healing skills but for his ability to destroy. Every century or two, a fae comes along with the power of royalty, of a god as you humans would say. Espen can heal almost anything but he can equally tear the earth asunder. Which is exactly what he did when Ragnhild, her Head Guard, and company of soldiers were torn apart and killed. In response, he turned that battlefield into a wasteland."

I shuddered at the imagery and struggled to picture Espen in the throes of battle. He seemed so bubbly and happy all the time, like a little ray of sunshine. I couldn't imagine him being so destructive. Not my tree-pose-loving yogi-fae-cop.

"Even if that's the case, can you really believe that he is behind all of this?" I asked, because I sure as hell couldn't. It didn't add up. If he were doing this, he'd have to be healing his own scars, which I'd already witnessed him unable to do with the scars on the trees in the clearing. I'd also seen the difference between regular healing magic—when Heidi had stitched up the Forest Fae soldier—and attempts to heal illegal magic transfer scars. The latter wasn't possible.

Halvar continued walking, as if trying to evade the question.

"Well, can you?" I challenged, following after him. There wasn't a chance in hell I was going to let him make such an accusation and run away from it.

After another moment of silence, he responded. "He's always a possible threat."

I sighed, clearly there was no reasoning with the big guy. So, instead of debating him, I shut my mouth and remained quiet for the rest of the trek to the mountain entrance.

Deep down I knew Espen wasn't behind this. And it wasn't just because I kind of cared about him. Espen *cared*. I'd seen the way he reacted when he saw the photo I'd taken that started all of this. The flash of silver in the image I'd captured had rocked him. And now knowing *why* that would concern him, there was no doubt in my mind, Espen was not illegally transferring magic. He cared so much about the Forest Fae, hell even the Fjell Fae and the villagers of Skolvik. He wouldn't ever want to cause harm to any of them. I would continue to believe that even after he eventually woke up and could tell Halvar himself.

42

LENNIE

Later that evening, I wandered through the tunnels inside the mountain aimlessly, my mind caught in the maelstrom of my own thoughts as I tried to figure out who the fuck could possibly be behind all the chaos, all the destruction of the land around Skolvik, the area which these fae called home and had sworn to protect, heal, and help. No matter what Halvar had said, there was no way Espen was behind this, and I needed to find some way to prove that to Halvar without stripping the Forest Fae in a comatose state naked to reveal his lack of scars.

I really missed the bubbly Forest Fae, too. The loss of his sunny presence was starting to sink in even more, and I chewed on my bottom lip, hoping he'd wake up soon.

As I passed another cave entrance, something flickered and caught my attention. *The story cave.* Soft beams floated out of the space like someone had left the lights on, but I couldn't immediately hear anyone within.

Curiosity pulled me to a stop, my boots grinding against the rocky floor, and I backtracked and went inside. The room was silent as I peered around the space but found no one else in sight. I hesitated slightly before walking deeper into the room. Here by myself without Nora to guide me it felt kind of like I was intruding, but the guilty sensation that ran across my skin subsided when I saw the glorious images that speckled the walls of the cavern.

Pieces of the Fjell Fae's history glowed in the rock walls, telling me their stories, one magical carving at a time. Viking ships shimmered to my right, the stick figures on-board raising their fearsome swords to the starry sky above them. To my left were reindeer being chased by other figures bearing large spears. Right beside it was yet another image but, unlike the others, this one glowed a little brighter—like it was fresh. Swirls wrapped in and around boulders, like a melody of rocks and waves playing with one another. It was almost harmonious in the way the light shifted, as if twinkling lights had been set to phase within the cavern wall itself. I stepped closer, in awe of the beautiful carving, seeing the way the two clashing forces were so intertwined as if in a lover's embrace. If I had to put a name to this particular image, it would be *love*. Love in its purest and simplest form, between two entities that wanted to be near each other at all times.

I lifted my camera on instinct, barely aware of what I was doing, when a hiss sounded behind me, and I stilled.

"What do you think you're doing?"

Busted.

I spun, letting my camera hang against my chest, and found Nora in the doorway, her brow furrowed and arms crossed over her chest.

"I, um..." My throat tightened and the back of my neck heated uncomfortably at the thought of what I'd almost done. "I..."

I had nothing. This was hallowed ground, and I shouldn't even have brought my camera in here out of respect for their history and their secret. This was like getting pulled over for speeding when you knew you shouldn't be driving that fast, but worse. Oh, so much worse. I'd broken

Nora's trust in me. The one thing all of them had said, time and time again, was to not take any photos inside the mountain. And here I stood having almost done exactly that. I deserved the hatred in Nora's eyes.

"Have you been taking photos in here?" she asked, accusatory venom lacing every syllable, the easy friendship between us gone as her arms crossed over her chest.

I shook my head, but knew she'd seen me with my camera in my hand, aiming and ready to snap.

Nora's shoulders trembled and she pursed her lips, giving me a look of utter betrayal. A look I felt deep into my core. *Yeah, I fucked up.*

I reached forward, grabbing Nora's forearm as she shifted back from me, and her shirt-sleeve rode up a bit at my touch. "I'm sorry—" I gasped, seeing the skin beneath my fingers. Her arm was riddled with scars, silvery-white that matched the color of the tiny dot she'd magically placed on my wrist all those weeks ago. The sheer volume of criss-crossing marks looked painful. It looked like... Shit. They were deep scars like the ones we'd seen on the trees in the clearing. Halvar's words regarding the illegal transfer of magic rang through my mind, *"It's a heinous act that would've left similar scars on the perpetrators too."*

I sucked in a breath, my hand trembling as it held onto hers and my stomach flip-flopping. "Nora, what happened?" Nora shucked her arm out of my grip, and quickly pressed her shirt back down with a snarl.

"What d-did you do?" I asked, my voice quivering as Nora, a Royal Fjell Fae—the woman I'd thought was becoming a friend, someone I could confide in—sneered at me, her eyes full of dismay.

"Leave it," she bit out, glancing momentarily toward the wall beside us.

I looked over at the swirling image of rocks and water that her eyes had flicked to—the image that looked so new compared to the others, outshining those around it. Drawings that she was in charge of carving into the mountain as its resident historian...

My stomach dropped as the puzzle pieces connected—the stories, the scars, the new picture. "Nora, what have you done?"

"Nothing." She stepped back, and straightened her shoulders, blocking the exit.

I shook my head as my body began to shake, not believing her words. "This... this isn't nothing."

Fucking shit, *Nora* was the one stealing magic. Nora was behind all of this chaos. But who was she... I quickly glanced at the new drawing again, before looking back at her. Water. Water and boulders.

"Have you been working with someone from the fjord?" I asked, not quite believing the words that were coming out of my mouth.

Shouts rose from further down the tunnels, and she peered toward the noise before turning back to me with a grimace. "You'd never understand. Balder cares about me."

Shit. She was working with the damn King of the Fjord.

"More than himself and his own people?" I snapped, my natural instinct to protect family welling up inside me and spurring me on against a fae that was centuries my senior. "Is he making you do this? How long has this been going on?"

She shook her head. "She'd never let us be together. She'd never join our cause."

"She, who?" I asked, not following her words. "What are you talking about, Nora?"

Nora didn't answer, glancing behind her nervously. A chill ran down my spine as the echoes from the tunnels grew louder—incoherent shouting ringing through the mountain.

Before I could react, Nora grabbed my camera and yanked it into her grasp, the straps snapping at the hinges and separating from the camera, the neck strap hanging limply around my neck.

"What the fuck!" I roared and lunged after her. That was my baby! What the hell did she think she was doing? "Give that back!"

She dodged my perfect tackle, her chest heaving, my camera clutched in her hand.

My gut tumbled upside down like a rollercoaster inverting and rose back up into my throat as she stared me straight in the eyes and threw my camera against the rock wall.

A piercing scream broke free from my lips as I watched my baby shatter, falling to pieces and scattering across the cave. I fell to my knees and scrambled across the floor, picking up shards in a frenzied attempt to put it back together. But none of the fragments would fit, not even the cracked lens cap. I tried, and tried, and tried, but the pieces wouldn't stick back together. The sharp edges scratched my fingers and palm as I tried to gather them in my hand, but it was of little use.

My camera was gone. Irreparable.

How could she?

I dropped the useless remnants and looked over my shoulder expecting to find Nora sneering at me but the entrance to the cavern was empty. With my shaking hands, I covered my mouth, trying to hold myself together. Taking a deep breath to moderate the grief that surged through my heart, I tried to calm down. I wanted to curl up and cry, mourn my loss. I'd saved my money for a long time to buy that camera, and it had been like a friend to me, going with me on countless adventures around the world, capturing not just photographs, but memories, too. Memories of freedom that I wanted to sit here and grieve. However,

I knew I couldn't hang around. I needed to warn Freija and Halvar. I needed to tell my boys. I needed to move, *now*.

With one last look at the remains of my beloved camera, I grabbed my SD card and ran.

43

LENNIE

I bounded down the tunnel that led toward the exit, my hair streaming behind me, my camera strap lost somewhere along the way. I dodged between Fjell Fae merrily going about their day and crashed against the wall as I tried to make a sharp turn. A dull pain spasmed through my shoulder as it took the brunt of the blow but I kept moving. Kept running until I crashed right into Torsten.

He grasped my shoulders, steadying me as my breaths came in sharp bursts, my chest heaving.

"Throne room... where... is it?"

A crease formed across Torsten's brow. "Is everything all right?" he asked, removing his hands from me and finishing up lighting the lantern on the wall beside us.

"The Queen... danger... warn Halvar."

Torsten's eyes widened at every word and thankfully didn't dismiss my obvious distress. "Follow me," he said, spinning and breaking out into a run.

I took a big gulp of air and bolted after him and his man-bun.

I still couldn't wrap my mind around Nora and Balder being behind the illegal magic transfers and all the problems that had faced the fjord area recently but the carving on the wall in the story cave, the marks on her arm, paired with what she'd just said, all pointed directly at them. I had to warn the Queen and Halvar, I had to make sure she was safe. She'd been so kind and Halvar had saved me—the very least I could do was return the favor by giving them a heads up.

Torsten and I barreled down endless tunnels and, after a few more minutes, the arched halls started to turn from slate to the crystalline blue that adorned the entire throne room. My heart hammered in my chest as we slowed and walked through the ornate entrance to the large room where Freija held court but my stomach plummeted when I saw the scene inside.

I was too late.

Freija's navy-clad form lay collapsed in Halvar's arms, her dress pooling around her and her fingers barely clutching at his shirt sleeve. He gently pushed her hair off her cheek, settling it behind her ear, as he whispered something to her. She nodded and a tiny smile crossed her lips.

"Sir," Torsten said hesitantly.

Halvar glanced over his shoulder and I flinched at the venom in his eyes—a promise to avenge her in the most horrific manner. "The tea was poisoned," he said. The shattered remnants of Freija's tea cup lay strewn across the floor before the throne where he knelt.

Freija took a rasping breath and her head lolled back.

Halvar shifted to hold her, pulling her into his chest. "Seal the mountain, and fetch Trygve, now!" he roared, the fae turning into the beast that always lurked beneath his controlled surface as he clutched the dying monarch.

Torsten nodded and disappeared.

I glanced at the couple, my hands shaking. "Halvar, it was Nora. She's the one behind the illegal transfers. I just caught her in the story cave. There's a new carving there of water and boulders. She said something about never being allowed to be with Balder and joining a cause, plus she has scars—marks all across her arm."

Halvar's face paled even further and Freija mumbled something before staring straight into my eyes. Her eyes crinkled at the corners, that otherworldly coloring surrounding her pupils shimmering as she lifted her face to Halvar.

"Noooo..." he mumbled, holding her delicate head in his large palm, stroking away her tears that had started to fall.

She closed her eyes and, with gargantuan effort, she raised her dainty hand to his chest. Sparks of silvery light exploded from her palm and Halvar let out a pain-filled growl. The glow grew, Halvar's jaw tightened, and all I could do was watch in fearful awe as I took a few steps closer.

A large hole opened in Halvar's shirt where her hand lay, revealing a hint of muscle beneath, and the light swelled to a blinding crescendo. I raised my hand to shield my eyes but it wasn't enough—the light too bright as it arced from Freija to Halvar. I turned away just as Halvar roared, grabbing Freija's hand and laying her down in front of her throne.

Pressing my palms against my eyes, I shielded myself from the worst of the magic. However, the rising temperature in the room and the pressure building at my back was unavoidable.

"Lennie!" Halvar yelled and I peered over my shoulder, scrunching my face against the barrage of light.

Halvar's body was practically glowing, a dense cloud of sparking silver surrounding him like a halo. Thick branches of light snaked up his neck toward his beard as he panted. He held out his free palm to me. "Hand. Now," he grit out.

I hesitated for a split second, glanced at the dying Queen, and, with a silent prayer to Hell, grabbed his hand.

Scalding pain blasted through my left hand where it connected with Halvar, shooting up my arm. A scream pierced the air and it took me several moments to realize it was my own. My breaths shallowed by the second, my arm felt like it was on fire, and my head throbbed like a rock concert on steroids. With my right hand, I yanked up my sleeve and found white lightning carving a path to my shoulder, scarring the skin.

Halvar roared in agony again, his features scrunched up and his body trembling with the overwhelming amount of power flowing through him. A moment later he let go of my hand and we both wobbled at the loss of contact. The room swirled, my vision flickering in and out of focus, and I hunched down beside Halvar and Freija's lifeless body, hoping to hell I wasn't about to pass out or die myself.

Halvar and I both panted, regaining our breath as the light around us subsided and the temperature in the room dropped back to its normal chill.

A noisy commotion drew my attention to the entrance of the throne room just before a group of Fjell soldiers in their gray-and-black uniforms ran in. Their eyes widened as they took in the sight before them: the empty throne, the grieving guard, and the human tourist. One of the soldiers stepped forward and unclasped his cape, before handing it to Halvar. He accepted the material with a nod, and, after taking a deep breath, he laid it over the fallen Queen.

A lump formed in my throat at the sight and I rose to my feet again, taking a step back out of respect.

The soldiers pressed their fist over their hearts with a thump and sank to one knee, bowing their heads in reverence.

Halvar straightened up to his full height and rolled his shoulders. "Freija, Queen of the Fjell, daughter of Erik and Astrid, has fallen," he proclaimed, his voice carrying through the large room and out into the tunnels where it echoed. "Long live the Queen."

"Long live the Queen," the soldiers replied, and I mumbled the words with them, staring in a daze at the shrouded figure on the floor.

Why would Nora do this? Why would she hurt her only family? I couldn't fathom why anyone would turn on their sibling. Sure, I hated my brothers from time to time, but I'd still do whatever I could for them if they needed me. I would move mountains for them if they asked.

I pushed my hair behind my ear—

Pointy. Why the fuck is my ear pointy?

"Nooo," I gasped, running over to the glassy wall of the throne room. Sure enough, staring back at me was my usual blonde-self but with a few new amendments. "Fuck off."

$$44$$

LENNIE

"Halvar," I half yelled, half mumbled in disbelief, my voice wavering as I turned toward where the Fjell Fae stood among his soldiers by the throne. "We have a slight problem here." I pointed to my ears with both hands.

His face didn't betray a single emotion—as if he'd locked that shit down after being vulnerable with Freija in her last moments—but I could have sworn I saw his right eye twitch.

"What the fuck happened?" I pressed my hands against my forehead, my heart rate starting to run another marathon. "I can't go back to Ohio looking like this!"

What the fuck would my parents say? My brothers would laugh until they shat themselves if they even believed me, but my parents... *Fuuuck.* How could I explain myself out of this one? I lightly tapped my fingers against the points and whimpered, wondering how on earth this was happening to me.

Halvar wandered over and examined my arm without touching it, then peered at my pointy ears. "I needed your help," he said quietly so no one else could hear us. "Her magic was too much for me to contain. I needed to transfer it into another being. You were the—"

"Bullshit."

He stilled, and his top lip quirked. "You were the only living being in the room. Trust me, I wasn't aware Freija's magic could"—he waved his hand at my newly acquired ears—"transform you into a fae."

I snort-laughed at how preposterous it sounded.

"You mean to tell me I am now some sort of Demi-Fae, a Demi-Fjell-Fae? What do you even call me? A f-uman? A hum-ae? That sounds terrible. Not that one. Help me out here, Halvar, I'm spiraling."

He bit his lower lip in a contemplative manner and crossed his arms, glancing back to where Freija lay covered in a cloak on the floor behind us. "Either her powers or mine."

"Did you..." I swallowed the shock, my body not only trembling but fully reverberating. "Did you just say I have powers, too?"

Halvar sighed, his large hand rubbing across his forehead in a very human gesture that told me he was just as overwhelmed as I was. "Fjell, or those of Fjell royalty. I can't be certain until we test your skills, see if you can create rocks, fuse cracks, and... more," he trailed off.

I stared down at my hands in disbelief, the backside of the left one lightly scarred with a silvery-white lightning pattern that, after checking under the collar of my shirt, I realized extended all the way up to my shoulder. Two scars in less than twenty-four hours... I really was doing well for myself on this trip.

"So, if I'm part Fjell Fae now, do I have to take *Fae 101* with you to understand how to use this magic?" I waved at my scarred arm, trying to dismiss the rising panic that threatened to pull me under. I needed to gain back some level of control.

Halvar shook his head, his hands dropping back to his sides. "Let's take things one day at a time."

"Yeah, okay, deal," I replied, sitting down on the cold bench that had been built into the wall on this side of the room as my legs all but gave out on me. Then quickly added, "Y'all have a welcome basket or some shit, too?"

Halvar had turned to the Queen and his men there, then looked back at me, consternation written in every line of his face. "Not unless you want a hat made for a baby? I dare say it wouldn't fit over your head."

My brows rose in shock, a hysteric bubble of laughter threatening to escape me. "Did you just crack a joke, big guy?"

"No," he replied and sauntered back to the soldiers who had now taken up position around Freija's body, guarding her. I snorted and leaned back against the crystal-like wall.

At that moment, Trygve came sprinting into the room, practically flying in his simple shirt and pants attire and apron covered with countless pockets. He let out a small whimper when he noticed the guards and the body, but Halvar distracted him by pointing at me. "Check her arm."

Trygve nodded and scampered over to where I'd settled.

He flinched when he spotted my ears.

"You think they make my ass look big?" I asked mockingly, not sure whether I was distracting him or myself.

Trygve blinked and stuttered. "U-umm... you... you have a nice bottom, Miss Lennie."

"Thanks, Trygve."

"May I ask you to remove part of your shirt so I can see your entire arm? We can go to another room, if you wish?" he said, clasping his hands together.

I waved him off, then shrugged completely out of my jacket and pulled up the side of my shirt, removing my left arm from its sleeve.

Trygve set to work examining my newly acquired scars and carefully avoided staring at my chest that was thankfully covered by a tank top and bra. The markings wound up my arm in a mesmerizing pattern that reminded me of lightning. It no longer burned but I'd be lying if I said it didn't feel a little numb. I told Trygve as much when he inquired, and he gave me a contemplative nod in response.

"So, what's the verdict, Doc?"

"Well, I dare say the marks are permanent but I can give you a cream that should cool the skin and reduce any potential swelling."

"Swelling?"

He tilted his head from one side and then to the other. "I can't say for certain as you're our first case of a human being transformed into a fae."

"You mean, this has never *ever* happened before?"

"Not in recent memory, and certainly not since I've been around these past three-hundred odd years."

I rubbed my right hand across my mouth, stifling a guffaw at his age, and wondering if I would live beyond a hundred now too... or would I age and become saggy? Because I was only half fae, would only parts of me age? Would only one boob sag while the other remained full and perky? Would I lose the wrinkles but keep the damn adult acne?

"Let me find that salve," Trygve said, drawing me out of my catastrophizing thoughts.

The healer fae dug around in his apron, pulling out random tubes from his pockets and examining them. He grabbed one, sniffed it, grimaced, then returned it, retrieving another tube instead. He unstopped this one, its dark molasses-like content dripping out onto my arm when he tipped it. My skin cooled where it landed and an instinctual shiver ran down my spine from the chill. With a gentle touch, Trygve began rubbing the cream into my arm and it started to slowly dissolve into my skin, disappearing without leaving any discoloration or residue. It was as if my new magical scar absorbed every ounce and the numbness began to subside.

"Thank you, Trygve."

"You're welcome, Miss Lennie. Let me know if there is anything else you may need or if you want more of the salve."

I nodded in thanks, and pulled my arm back through my shirt before throwing my jacket back on, too.

"Now, I must speak with Halvar," Trygve said, glancing over his shoulder where the Head Guard stood beside the fallen Queen and her throne. He scurried over to the group and I followed, hanging back a bit and staying out of the way—which was a somewhat novel concept for me, but crazy times called from crazy antics.

"Halvar, sir, I know it's not a good time, but I have an important report from the healing chambers—specifically the hospice room and morgue."

Halvar narrowed his eyes and crossed his arms. "Go on."

Trygve wrung his hands, his knuckles cracking as he began. "While preparing recently deceased bodies for their burial ceremony, I noticed that quite a few had limited magic remaining in their forms. This obviously isn't entirely unusual—we all have differing levels of magic within us—but it started to become a pattern." He hesitated for a second, unable to meet Halvar's eyes. "I want to say this is only a hunch, especially during such a *delicate* time, but most of the patients had formerly had their last stories recorded by Nora." He stopped and waited for a response from Halvar, who in turn gave none except for waving his hand to get Trygve to continue.

"You know how we all gain scars over the centuries?"

Halvar nodded and I blinked at the use of the term *centuries*. That word apparently would never not be shocking.

"Well, these Fjell Fae all seemed to have the exact same scar in the crook of their arm." He demonstrated on himself, pointing at the inside of his elbow. "A deep silver gash that appeared rather recent. I-I don't want to be presumptuous here, but I do wonder if Princess Nora perhaps was stealing magic from the dying fae?"

Ding ding ding, winner right here! Step on up and grab your prize! You want a stuffed bear or perhaps a troll doll with neon green hair?

"I don't think we need to be, as you say, presumptuous, Trygve," Halvar started. "There have been similar reports of Nora's misdeeds today, and I dare say she and King Balder are behind the death of the late Queen," Halvar said, speaking with reverence and leadership that had everyone in the room listening to him. "It isn't the first time a King of the Fjord has made attempts to unsettle the delicate balance of the region. But, this one has been successful."

A shiver of energy seemed to reverberate through the room, the soldiers and myself remaining silent as the truth settled in. Balder and Nora were behind this. *Did Øyvin know?* More importantly, where was my Fjord Fae right now?

I turned away from the gathered fae and faced the shining wall once more. Watching my reflection as I ran my fingers across my newly acquired ears, I lost myself in a trance-like state. A barrage of information and images flitted through my brain, like a highlight reel of my trip. One picture after another, snippets of facts that, when strung together, painted a gruesome portrait of a power struggle I'd wandered into with my camera, blissfully unaware of the consequences.

In typical Lennie Martin fashion, I'd landed myself squarely in the middle of the mess. A mess that went so far beyond taking photos of the gorgeous scenery and accidentally capturing magic with my lens, and instead focused on the careful balancing act of protecting those stunning natural resources.

A rumbling noise broke through my daze and the stone floor began to shake minutely.

I raised my hands up like I was being caught stealing cookies from the cookie jar, and an instinctual desire to curl into a ball and protect my head sank in.

The other fae in the room started murmuring just as a crack fissured across the wall in front of me—sharp white lines forming like broken glass—and I stepped back before turning wide-eyed to Halvar. "That wasn't me," I said, pointing my thumb over my shoulder, my body starting to visibly tremble.

Halvar's usual grimace turned even more sour as another low rumble shook the mountain. It felt like an earthquake or someone shaking a beehive.

"Earthquake?" I asked, lowering my hands and hoping I wasn't about to get squashed by an entire mountain.

"We don't have big earthquakes in Norway," Trygve replied, casting a wary glance to Halvar.

The Head Guard looked around the room as more thin fractures appeared in the sky-blue stone around us, the tiny rifts reaching toward the empty throne.

Halvar took a deep breath and then began barking orders, soldiers springing into action at his words. "Deep Unit, clear the dungeons and lower levels. Evacuate to designated areas north of the Fjord and away from the town." He pointed at two fae, who in turn nodded and ran from the room. "Central Unit, evacuate to your designated area, too." Another fae bolted, his cape fluttering as he went.

The floor shook again and Halvar grumbled while I swallowed my increasing anxiety and nerves.

"Defense Unit, take up positions and send me Torsten and a battalion to the field atop the mountain. Upper Unit"—he nodded to another fae soldier—"I want you to mobilize the strongest residents to use their powers and reinforce the top of the mountain. I don't want any cave-ins." The fae nodded and charged like the others, leaving Trygve, myself, and a couple soldiers left in the throne room.

"Trygve—"

"Yes, sir," the healer fae replied, standing to attention.

"Have the Queen removed to her rooms and prepare her body. Then set up a field hospital near the northern field atop the mountain but keep your distance. Hide within the forest if you have to."

Trygve nodded like he knew exactly what all of this meant while I stared on in bewilderment, still in shock at what had happened let alone what was currently going on.

"Lennie," Halvar yelled.

"Yup," I replied, saluting him before realizing what I'd done and quickly shoving my offending hand into my jacket pocket.

His top lip twitched as he strode past me toward the exit, his soldiers following closely on his heels. "You're coming with me."

I flinched, straightened, and then scurried after him. "And where exactly are we going?"

His voice dropped several octaves as he ground out his reply. "To war."

45

LENNIE

We strode down the tunnels, the lights along the walls flickering with every shake and rumble as more soldiers fell in behind us, and Torsten—the man behind the light magic—stepped up beside Halvar. The two fae spoke briefly in hushed tones but after a few more paces Torsten glanced over his shoulder and smiled. "Welcome to the club."

I snorted and missed a step, almost falling flat on my face. Clearly obtaining new magic and becoming some form of fae hadn't improved my grace and balance.

We left the mountain through an exit I'd never seen before, its rocky archway more dusty and jagged than the smooth and clean main entrance I was used to. Stepping out into the pitch dark, I expected to be assaulted by the autumnal chill that had settled over the region recently but was instead met by slightly warmer temperatures—still cold enough to require a jacket but something in the air held a warmth the promised trouble. It was similar to the spring storms we'd get in Ohio, where the weather would suddenly shift and you could tell based on the humidity that a storm was brewing.

The soldiers around me, about thirty in total, seemed to sense it too, as each of them shifted or readjusted their uniform, preparing for something.

Halvar spun around and they all stood at attention, watching his every move, not a single syllable slipping from anyone's lips. Counter to character, I followed suit, remaining quiet and matching their rigid stances.

"Each unit of ten," Halvar began, his voice low but commanding. "Approach the field atop the mountain from your designated direction. Northeast, East, and Southeast." With each compass designation, he pointed at another fae—the unit leader I assumed—and they each nodded once. "Torsten, you're with me. Lennie, you too."

I nodded and refrained from saluting him this time.

"Our goal here tonight is to eviscerate Balder," he ground out between his clenched teeth, "and if any of you find Nora, capture her."

More nodding passed through the group, and I swallowed the lump in my throat before shaking my arms free of the tension that was building in my muscles.

Halvar continued, "As always, keep clear of the village. If any humans are in the woods, you know your cover story—"

"Costumed bachelor party on a drunken hike seeking shelter from the impending storm?" I said half under my breath, then clapped my hand over my mouth when I spotted a few of the soldiers smirking in my direction. I cast a furtive glance at Halvar who betrayed no emotion save for a tick in his jaw. Lifting my palm from my face, I mouthed an apology in his direction before shoving my hands back into my jacket pockets.

Torsten leaned over and whispered, "You're not far off. The humans tend to stay indoors when 'major storms'—our battles—whip up around here... but best stay quiet, baby fae." He winked down at me as Halvar began barking more orders and a few moments later, soldiers split off into their groups and we pressed forward through the dark forest.

Our journey through the densest part of the woods grew sluggish as the clouds above began to drizzle on us, making the moss covered ground and rocks dangerously slick. By grasping onto tree limbs and giving my thighs a serious workout, I was able to keep up with the male and female Fjell Fae soldiers, all of whom pressed on like they were indefatigable.

The ground grew steeper as we made our way up the side of the mountain, winding through trees and brush—keeping clear of any designated paths while also not inflicting damage on the wilderness around us. I grew antsier the higher we climbed, the blood in my veins humming with both excitement and nerves. Somewhere along the line I probably should have felt fear or hesitancy about walking into battle against centuries-old fae, but the shock of recent events jumbled my thoughts.

As the terrain flattened out, a rumble from above had our crew of soldiers glancing to the sky and Halvar's brow creasing into even deeper lines. Just then a creak sounded from our left and, before I could react, Halvar raised his hand, magically created a small boulder out of thin air, and threw it toward the noise. A ball of water swatted the rock and sent it tumbling to the ground and down the steep hill.

The sound of a low laugh met my ears and a warm shiver ran across my skin as a voice I recognized said, "I'm not your enemy, Halvar." Øyvin stepped out from behind a tree with a smirk on his lips as more Fjord Fae in their navy uniforms—sans cape—appeared from behind the pines. "The wall has fallen. Our King has betrayed us."

A little spark ignited in my chest, happy to see Øyvin alive and here. But the tone in his voice hinted at a raw and emotional wound within him, something I'd only heard once before, when he was telling me about the loss of his family after I'd been attacked.

"How did you know of his betrayal?" Halvar demanded.

Øyvin's lips turned into a scowl and he clenched his fists. "It wasn't difficult to guess when the wall collapsed entirely, the floorbed of the fjord began to shake, and large fissures formed across the deepest depths. No other Fjord Fae has the strength to pull that off, plus it has been *his* magic, fortified by our soldiers' power, that has held that wall intact for decades." He stuck his hand beneath the lapel of his uniform, pulling out his cellphone and waving it. "And your troops are quick to share information within your alliance. Ylva of the Forest Fae texted me about Nora and Freija. My condolences for your loss."

Halvar grunted in reply and all the soldiers remained unmoving, their preternatural stillness somewhat unnerving. It was as if they were all hovering and readying to pounce and the energy around us matched that feeling.

"Myself and a legion of my soldiers officially request an alliance to protect the fjord as a whole and bring down the King of the Fjord," Øyvin said, his shoulders squared and his posture imparting the formality of his request even as we stood at the precipice of a battle.

I looked from one Head Guard to the other, watching for any reaction from the Fjell Fae.

Halvar's ability to reveal nothing from his facial expression was amazing. Not a twitch of a brow hair, not a quiver of his lips, he had full control of his body, and I wasn't surprised in the slightest that this being—this beast of a fae—had been made Head Guard of the Fjell Fae.

The two stood there assessing each other, locked in a silent stalemate, as the appeal was considered.

"Your steadfast loyalty to the fjord and this region is noted, and your request to form an alliance is accepted," Halvar eventually replied.

Øyvin nodded slowly. "Thank you. We defer to your leadership."

More nods and looks were shared among the different soldiers at this. Moments later, Halvar and Øyvin had their fae moving into positions side by side, shifting forward and preparing. What *exactly* they were readying for, I had no fucking clue, so I just stood there like a lemon trying not to get in the way.

The earth shook once more as a roar of noise sounded from somewhere up ahead and I braced myself against a tree, my knees wobbling with the trembling ground. Halvar glanced over his shoulder at Torsten and raised his fist. The soldiers all responded by coming to a stop, their stances a clear ready position.

Halvar then nodded to Torsten and, at this signal, Torsten clapped his hands together vertically, then swiftly pulled them apart revealing a blinding ball of light the size of a soccer ball. I leaned further against the tree and watched him, my mouth agape at the blatant show of magic. He thrust his arms forward, and the ball of light shot ahead illuminating its surroundings.

The orb wove between the pines and breached the treeline, light shining brightly as it then skittered across the grassy field that could only be described as craggy and rock laden, before it crashed against a shield of water. It exploded and exposed a blockade of water-shields—like something out of a Roman war movie. I squinted and noticed more of these groupings, little squares of water across the far side of the field where rectangular shields had been erected both around and above clusters of Balder's forces. A lump lodged in my throat—based on the number of cubes, there must've been several hundred fae on the other side. *Fuuuuuuck.*

I spun on my heel and scoffed, "Hard pass. I'm out." Now seemed like a really good time to high-tail it out of here, find a boat or steal someone's car, and head back to Ohio.

An arm whipped across my middle and hauled me back, picking me up and planting me firmly beside the tree I'd been touching earlier. "Oh, no you don't."

I wiggled out of Øyvin's hold and pressed away from him. "No, you see, I really think my time has come." He stepped back, fighting a smile as Halvar called out more orders. "I've had my fun and I honestly prefer my chances in that prison cell down at Espen's police station. Speaking of, where is Espen? Still with Heidi?" *He would be really helpful right about now.*

Øyvin shook his head and lifted his hands. "No word from Ylva." He stepped closer again, his brows briefly knitting together as he scanned me from head to toe. "You're actually going to leave now, when your friends need you? When the Fjord needs you?"

"I'm pretty sure the Fjord needs me to stay out of the fucking way and keep my hands to my damn self." I gave him my best jazz hands gesture before clasping them together.

Øyvin chuckled as someone called his name and he whipped his head in their direction. His features immediately hardened and he was back to business.

"Stay hidden, Trouble," Øyvin whispered as he passed me, then flicked my ear. "And we'll talk about these later."

"Ow, Asshole!" I whisper-yelled at him, brushing the spot he'd hit. Note to self, those pointy bits were really sensitive.

He didn't look back as he and two other Fjord Fae soldiers got into position but I heard a faint laugh from him.

Doing as I was told for the... *shit*, I'd lost count of how many times now. I shook off the shock of *that* character growth and crouched down in the shelter of a large pine, its thick trunk hiding me and acting like a shield. The smell of rain and sodden earth invaded my senses and I watched in awe as our soldiers pressed forward onto the field of battle. It was, indeed, right atop the mountain, with a sheer drop down to the fjord below on our left and the treeline that swept to the right before descending into undulating hills and jagged mountains. It was the field Halvar and I had crossed on our hike earlier this evening.

Øyvin and Halvar began to work in unison, firing rocks and balls of water at the enemy forces. As the rain transformed from a drizzle to a downpour, Torsten stepped up and started throwing bolts of lightning toward Balder's forces. All together, the fae were creating a veritable thunder storm. It was mesmerizing.

Ylva and a group of Forest Fae emerged from the woods on the right, where the trees swooped around the field. Roots shot up out of the ground where her forces moved, weaving together and shielding themselves from the watery arrows shot in their direction. They in turn shot wooden arrows, branches fashioned from those around us, at the liquid blockades. Some of the shots penetrated the water shields and they flickered and fell, but were quickly replaced by another. The Forest Fae kept up their barrage though as rocks were also pelted at the opposing forces from the Fjell Fae, and water lashed across the field in waves from our Fjord Fae.

Snap.

I flinched at the noise behind me and grit my teeth together. The hairs on the back of my neck flickered up and an instinctual shiver ran down my spine.

Still crouched, I slowly turned around and found two leather boots, black pants, brown leathers criss-crossing a chest... I choked down a breath as I finally glanced up into a pair of sharp brown-and-gray eyes that shimmered with an eerie malice.

46

LENNIE

I scrambled away from Nora, almost tripping as I took in her disheveled appearance. Her hair was a mess, twigs and leaves sticking out of it, but the look in her gaze was pure anguish, like she was simultaneously angry and in agony.

Pushing up from the ground, my hands slicked with water and pine needles, I rose to my feet, making sure the big tree was still at my back and shielding me from the battlefield.

"What happened to you?" Nora asked, narrowing her eyes at me.

I snorted and brushed my palms against my jeans, ridding myself of the debris on them. "I'm not even sure I have a proper answer for that one myself." I looked at her again, my eyes landing on hers, the ones that had matched her sister's. The marbled effect within them that seemed so unusual and yet was clearly a family trait... My heart hammered in my chest as I thought of what she'd done to said sister, and a warmth within me started to build as my lips turned into a snarl. "Why'd you do it?"

"You don't understand," Nora said, shaking her head and her hands as if she could dispel what she'd done.

"Oh, I sure as hell don't understand how you could kill your sister, your family."

She began burbling. "S-she wasn't supposed to get hurt. H-he promised it wouldn't kill her."

I scoffed at the absolute lunacy of the fae in front of me as she cornered me between the trees and boulders. "You really believed him? You never for a second asked yourself: hey, does this mo-fo have some sort of ill will toward the Fjell Fae?"

"He loves me. He didn't want anyone hurt," Nora continued, opening and closing her fists—fists I knew could likely create a boulder in a split second and then catapult it at my face the next.

But still, I snickered at her response.

"He didn't," she insisted, clenching her hands and holding them shut as she turned sideways and leaned forward. She was shifting into a ready position, and yet, I couldn't keep my damn mouth shut.

"Bitch, please."

"Fuck you!"

A loud roar erupted on the battlefield and Nora cast her gaze in that direction while I maintained a vigilant watch on her every move.

"How is he still alive?" she muttered, then turned back to me and added, "The sheer volume of power remaining in Freija should have felled Halvar if he tried to take it on."

"Yeah... about that." I stepped away from the tree, shifting a few paces to the right, and hoping to hell I could pull off the crazy stunt that had just crossed my mind.

She narrowed her eyes at me. "What?"

"I got a really cool thing from the tourist gift shop."

I slapped my hands together like I'd just seen Torsten do... but nothing happened.

Nora threw her head back and laughed. "First you're calling me a bitch, now you're giving me a round of applause—"

"Oh for fuck's sake, give me a damn second."

She sneered and backed up two steps before falling into a launch position. I stopped what I was doing and instinctively brought my arms down, bent at the elbows, shifting into a tackle-ready stance I'd been trained to do by my brothers.

Nora launched and I returned fire, dropping my shoulder and barreling into her. Our bodies met with a powerful thump, and my legs scrambled to push her backwards and down to the ground. She countered by twisting her upper body and grabbing my jacket. I hooked my hands into her leathers and used our falling momentum to throw her away from me. We landed on the ground with a thud, but my last-minute movement to push her away had worked, and I scrambled to my knees and then my feet, putting as much space between us as possible. Moss and pine needles clung to my hair and clothes, the damp air within the woods acting like glue for the detritus.

Nora rose to her feet and shook her arms. Brushing her equally disheveled hair from her face, she began to pace in a semi-circle, assessing the situation. She probably hadn't been expecting me to fight back, but alas, I'd grown up playing tackle football with my brothers. Emphasis on the tackle.

Straightening my shoulders, I refocused on drawing from that weird well of energy within my chest. Holding my hands out in front of me, I took a deep breath, focused on that new sensation, and clapped.

A large ball of light formed between my palms and my lips broke into a smirk.

Nora's eyes blew wide and her skin ashened in the glow of my new light source.

"Isn't it pretty?" I asked, my tone full of mocking and bitchiness. When the dumbfounded Nora didn't reply, I added, "Want some?"

She spun on her heels and darted into the trees, heading deeper into the forest.

I lifted the orb higher before thrusting it in Nora's direction like a dodgeball. The white sphere flew after her but she dodged and it crashed into a pine tree, disintegrating.

I let out a tiny whoop before I spotted the scar I'd left on the tree trunk. *Shit.* I clambered over to it and brushed my hand across the jagged indent. "I'm sorry," I said to the tree, wishing I knew how to heal the damage I'd caused and wondering why the hell I was talking to a tree. Was this what it was like when power went to your head? No, it couldn't be.

A weathered palm settled over mine and I screeched as someone pressed against my back.

"That was brave," Espen whispered into my ear. I let out a sigh of relief and glanced over my shoulder as he gave an order and a Forest Fae darted past me after Nora.

Espen stood behind me in all his yogi-fae-cop glory, wearing his Forest Fae uniform sans cape. He looked healthy, alive, and like he hadn't been comatose for the past week. There was a slight rosiness to his cheeks, and a warmth in his chest as he gave me a gentle smile and nodded to the tree. "Stand still."

I didn't move, not even an inch. Somehow, in the middle of a battle, ensconced in his arms, with his palm atop mine against a tree, I felt safe. I felt like I belonged.

Espen spread our fingers wide over the injured part of the tree and, before I could blink, a flaring sensation grew beneath my hand, the tree bark around it glowing with a soft white light. It lasted mere seconds and when the magic subsided—withdrawing back inside Espen... or me—I lifted my hand to see what remained underneath. The bark that

I'd damaged with my beginner's light bubble had healed, stitching itself back together with barely a puckering where the mark had originally been.

I turned in Espen's hold as he wrapped his arms around me, settling his hands against my lower back.

"Glad to see you alive," I muttered, staring up at him.

His lips quirked into a gentle smile. "Me too. Although, I appear to have missed a lot."

"If you'd woken up about twenty-four hours ago, there wouldn't have been as much to catch you up on."

"Oh, don't you worry. Heidi had enough stories to tell me before Ylva called about this." He nodded toward the battlefield where more skirmishes had broken out. "The healer even mentioned a few anecdotes about a recurring visitor. Any guesses who that might've been?" He tilted his head and gave me a knowing look.

I shrugged and shook my head. "Fuck if I know."

"Mm-hmm," he mumbled, pushing me against his chest.

The moment was broken when another loud roar and a clattering of lightning sounded, snapping the increasing tension between me and Espen. He let out a long breath, the muscles in his jaw tightening as he glanced toward the battle.

"Stay here and, whatever you do, don't run out onto the field," Espen said, planting a chaste kiss on my lips. "Can you do that?"

I slowly licked my bottom lip, feeling the need to challenge him but choosing not to. "Yes."

"You sure?" He quirked his brow and his lips tilted at one corner.

"I'm trying something new," I replied, pointing to my ears. "Thought obedience would go well with my newly acquired features."

A low chuckle escaped from Espen and he leaned in, pressing a gentle kiss against my cheek. "Oh, I look forward to discussing *that* news and showing you more of our world... just need to save it from a crazy man first." He stepped back and glanced toward the battle field, which we could just see the fringes of. "I'll be right back."

47

LENNIE

Standing in the shadows of the pines, I watched as Espen stalked onto the battlefield, Balder's men monitoring him wearily but with sly grins on their faces.

"No one needs to be hurt, Balder," Espen roared across the rocky field, his voice an authoritative thunder I'd never heard from him before. "Stand down."

Yeah, that was fucking hot.

Balder tilted his head with a smirk, his eyes glowing beneath his brow as he glared at our forces. "You'll be hard pressed to challenge me now, young man."

Øyvin shook his head minutely and Espen rolled his shoulders, anger rippling off him in waves as he started to press forward. He moved with a preternatural gate, slowly lifting his hands at his sides, and my stomach flipped when I noticed what he was doing. The earth rose around him, like a blanket being carefully peeled off the face of the world. Thick portions of soil, grass, and rocks rose up like an impending wave, matching the movement of Espen's hands. As he brought his palms to chest height, he quickly drew them together and clapped. Earth and debris crashed together like a tsunami on land and hurtled toward the line of Fjord Fae protecting Balder.

They lifted watery shields in response, using the barrier to protect themselves from the onslaught, but it was useless. The line fell and arrows quickly shot from the forest to our right, Ylva screaming orders over the rumble of thunder and the torrential rain.

I fist bumped the air at their momentary victory, but never got the chance to retract my hand as it was grasped tightly and I was spun into a choke hold. I took a large gulp of air and scratched at the thick band of muscle tightening around my neck. My captor shifted me back, gaining control of my footfalls and movement as I scrambled for freedom that was unlikely to come.

I glanced over my shoulder and caught sight of the sharp jaw and red hair of my assailant. *Kjetil, the King's Chief Advisor.*

"Nowhere to run to now, tourist," he said, the sly tone to his voice sending goosebumps across my skin. While I would've loved to inform him that I wasn't a fan of running, I couldn't exactly voice that right now. He grinned like he could tell what I was thinking though—that I wanted to challenge him but couldn't. Which was the most manly dickish thing, and set the blood in my veins to boiling.

I tried to stomp on his foot but he shifted out of the way at the last second. So, I attempted to reach his eye balls, which didn't work either. He banded his other arm around my middle and half-lifted, half-moved me forward under my own steam—my feet automatically moving forward in an effort to stay upright. I could barely breathe, my lungs heaving in protest as my vision began to blur.

He pushed us through the treeline and onto the battlefield. Before I had a chance to scream for help, he let out a sharp whistle that carried across the expanse. The soldiers closest to us turned and I watched my boys look back, their eyes wide in horror.

Kjetil tightened his hold around my neck, squeezing the last remains of air within me. I scratched at his arm and bucked in a last ditch effort to ease the pressure and escape. A blubbering whimper escaped my lips—

Something whizzed past my head and the stranglehold loosened. I desperately sucked in air before wobbling, taking a shaky step back, and then falling, spinning and crashing to the ground on my stomach. My entire body trembled with adrenaline and I cast my eyes over to my captor.

A branch-shaped arrow, knots and all, was embedded in Kjetil's forehead, his bright eyes staring into the dark rainy skies.

I bit down the bile that rose in my throat and looked away just as two pairs of hands scooped up my arms and yanked me to my feet. I barely registered Torsten and Leif on either side of me as we ran back to the treeline—water bombs dropping all around us, targeting us. One of them caught Torsten's leg with a hiss and he grumbled in pain.

We reached the edge of the battlefield and bolted behind the thick pines, shielding ourselves from the chaos. I took the moment of calm to assess Torsten's calf and found the fabric on his leg singed, the skin beneath quickly turning to red welts.

"Poison?" I asked, wiping my dirty hands across my pants with little success at rendering them wholly clean.

Leif knelt down beside his love's wound, examining it with delicate fingers. He shook his head. "Looks more like a burn."

"Feels like it's burned," Torsten grit out, the usually kind fae looking ready to shred someone to pieces instead. "I could—" He snapped his head to the right, looking past the trees and out onto the field again.

Leif and I followed his gaze and found the Forest Fae forces away from the main battle, circling around Nora. Ylva was in the mix, a large wooden sword in her hand that I imagined had one of Heidi's little potions on it. The other Forest Fae in the group had whip-like weapons and bats and Nora lunged at one after the other, physically fighting them and launching balls of light at their faces. She hit several of them, but wasn't paying attention to the fury-filled fae at her back. In one swift move, Ylva swung her sword across the back of Nora's thighs and the Fjell Fae let out an agonized scream. She fell forward and shuddered before all movement stopped and the other Forest Fae soldiers stepped back, save for one. Ylva hovered over Nora, blade at the ready again, her gaze continuously snapping from the captive at her feet and the rest of the battlefield.

I couldn't tell if our other soldiers had noticed the skirmish we'd just witnessed on the far side of the clearing, but neither Øyvin nor Espen looked in that direction. They were too focused on the shifting Fjord Fae forces working for the King, many of whom had now stepped out from behind their shields and launched physical attacks—some even fighting the Fjord Fae that had allied with Øyvin. Meanwhile, Balder's attention was solely on himself and those in front of him as he stalked back and forth behind his lines with a smarmy sneer on his face.

"I am the beast within the waters," he yelled, spreading his arms wide, his long cape flapping behind him in the wind. "I am the troll beneath the mountain. I am the dawn of Ragnarok, come to create anew." Balder's chest heaved as he spoke, his voice echoing in chorus with the thunder rumbling above us. "Join me and we shall form a greater, more prosperous union without the threat of the human race!"

Honestly, if anyone was the troll from the mountain it was Halvar, but now didn't seem like the time to point that out. Right now we had bigger fish to fry, like this over-sized trout with a misguided hero complex.

The two sides closed in on each other and chaos broke out as the ground rumbled again. Øyvin roared and volleyed attacks, aiming for the King behind his soldiers, while Espen unleashed more of his destructive powers, lifting the soil and roots beneath the opposing soldiers, then pulling them down and burying them alive. A shiver ran down my spine at the sight. Halvar had said Espen was powerful, I just never expected *this*. Hell only knew where Halvar had disappeared to and part of me sincerely hoped he hadn't met his demise.

Just then, a ripple of energy shot across the field from behind Balder's forces, sending them to their knees. The line of power fizzled out as it reached our soldiers, and I watched in shock as the water shields of the Fjord Fae came crashing down. Balder shuddered and spun before a large fist shot out, smashing his jaw and sending him to the ground, too.

The entire field stilled and watched as Halvar loomed over the King, his eyes a shimmering silver that was so bright it was visible even at this distance. A split second later, Halvar was wrapped within a vortex of water, pebbles and debris buffeting him as he snarled. Thrashing against the whorl with more silvery power, Halvar brought it crashing down and raised his hands with a roar. Rocky shackles wrapped around Balder's neck and wrists, forcing him down on his knees, anchored by monstrous boulders that hadn't been there seconds ago.

Everyone came to a stop, no one shifted, no one dared launch another attack—it was as if everyone was holding their breath, waiting for Halvar's next move. My stomach roiled and the weird warmth that lingered in my chest since the magic transfer a few hours ago simmered in anticipation. It didn't have to wait long.

A moment later, Halvar began moving his hands in an infinity pattern, his silver and gray powers swirling between his palms. Slowly, and with an almost ceremonial calm, a stone axe began to form. From the sharp double-sided head all the way down to the end of the shaft, the weapon looked extremely heavy and capable of cleaving the world in two. Halvar gripped the handle and raised the blade. Balder squirmed and yelled, unable to break his rocky chains. Halvar said something and began—

Leif grabbed my shoulder and spun me around, facing us away from the scene.

The earth shuddered, a guttural scream rent the air, and murmurs drifted across the dark field and through the woods.

"Did he just..." I asked, covering my mouth with my palm in hopes that would help me not up-chuck.

"Yes," Leif replied, wrapping his arm over my shoulders, stopping me from turning around. "No need to see that on repeat every night."

"I'm surprised he didn't go for his head," Torsten chimed in, still watching the field. "But I'm sure it will be useful to have it attached to his neck while being questioned. Oh look, here comes Trygve to stop the bleeding and grab the arm—"

"Spare us the gory details, my love," Leif said with a light chuckle. "The baby fae is turning green."

He wasn't wrong. The adrenaline was starting to wash out of my system, rapidly being replaced with exhaustion and the reminder that it was well past my bedtime. The thought of what was happening behind me had my stomach flip-flopping.

Torsten hobbled over and stepped in front of me, tilting his head to one side, giving me a gentle smile. "War not to your liking?"

I shook my head, my hair sticking to my cheeks but didn't dare open my mouth as bile rose in my throat.

Torsten nodded, then cast his eyes over my shoulder.

"Thank you, gentlemen. We can take her from here," Espen said behind me.

Leif's arm slipped from my shoulders and looped it with Torsten's as the two fae headed back onto the field. Their presence was replaced by two bruised fae, their uniforms torn in places, but their gazes locked firmly on me.

"You are exceptionally good at getting yourself into sticky situations," Espen said with a chuckle as Øyvin crossed his arms.

"Shit finds me," I replied, my lips quirking into a smile as the rain started to ease and relief washed through me. I looked between the two of them, all three of us weary and tired, but still breathing. Their show of strength had been mesmerizing, but also alarming, especially Espen's.

"Espen, did you really bury those soldiers alive?" I asked, brushing my hair behind my ear.

He nodded slowly. "Yes, I did."

Damn. I swallowed hard, pushing down the lump that had formed in my throat. It was at that moment I realized Espen probably didn't just do yoga for flexibility and mad *yoga* skills. No, he likely used it to calm his mind and keep his powers in check. I shuddered at the revelation.

"But, you should know, I left them a gap to breathe. They can claw their way out and answer to Øyvin's men."

Visions of fae rising like zombies out of the soil crossed my mind and I shook my shoulders and arms, trying to rid myself of that nightmare. Fuck, that was cold and brutal.

"My captains will handle the young defectors. Most appear to have been from our recent class of graduates, likely groomed by Balder," Øyvin said, the muscles in his jaw ticking.

I let out a long sigh, and Espen opened his arms for a hug. I stumbled into them.

"Let's go," Espen murmured, placing a gentle kiss on the top of my head. "We've been invited to the interrogation, but I want to stop by Heidi's before we head over."

"Sounds good," I said, momentarily raising my arm and giving them a thumbs up. "Any chance you can carry me down the mountain?"

Øyvin snorted and started walking away, mumbling something about going to inform the fjord residents, as Espen chuckled. "You're at least part fae now," he said lightly smacking my butt. "You'll find the energy to keep moving for a little while longer." He slipped his hand into mine, the warmth there somehow soothing, and started pulling me alongside him. "Come on, you can do your favorite corpse pose later."

"Deal."

48

LENNIE

Espen and I stood vigil outside Heidi's place, the motherly healer working her magic on the assortment of injured fae within as the sun began its ascent. There had only been a handful of deaths, mostly on Balder's side, but a lot of Forest Fae had been burned by boiling water bombs like the one that had caught Torsten. Ylva had evacuated most of her forces down here to the healer hut and then, with the assistance of some Fjell Fae, she'd escorted Nora back to the mountain. The Fjell Princess had been knocked out and still hadn't roused when they'd come past here. When I asked Ylva why, she gladly informed me that her blade had been laced with some water hemlock. And I honestly felt a pop of glee at that. Payback was a bitch.

Espen stood to my right, still covered in dirt and debris, specks of mud stuck in his wet hair. I'm sure I didn't look much better.

"You feeling all right?" I asked as we leaned against the grass-covered building.

"A little depleted but I'll be okay," he replied with a gentle smile, brushing his thumb over the back of my hand.

"Uh, yeah. Those stunts you pulled were scary. Why'd you never mention you could do that whole ground tidal-wave shit?"

His shoulders sagged and he pushed his hair off his forehead. "I don't like it," he admitted with a grimace. "I don't like that destruction. I was always meant to be a healer, a helper, but for some reason the ancestors thought I should also be gifted the power to destroy."

"That's why Queen Ragnhild recruited you to join her forces?" I asked, now knowing that what Halvar had told me on our way back from the sunset photo shoot was true.

Espen nodded solemnly, like the weight of that still hung around his shoulders. "I may be able to tear the earth apart, but I choose to heal and help. She requested my help and I gave it." He let out a long sigh, gazing across the clearing toward the trees. "I can't take back the actions of my past, but I can continue to help and protect the Forest Fae and those we are in alliance with."

"That's very noble of you."

He chuckled, shaking his head. "I don't wish to be anyone's king nor pawn, but I will lead where I can and answer to the Forest Fae and our council of elders."

That sounded fucking noble to me. Before I could think about what I was doing, I pressed a quick peck to Espen's cheek and pulled back.

He looked over, his eyes warming as his lips twisted into a sneaky grin.

Heidi interrupted the moment when she stepped out of the hut, searching for something or someone. Her eyes landed on me as she finished wiping her hands on her apron. "I heard you'd undergone some changes, young lady."

Before I could respond she stormed over, grabbed my left hand, and yanked up my jacket and shirt sleeve, revealing the crisscross of silvery-white scars there. She tutted thrice, turning my arm over and then back before dropping my hand and pushing my hair out of the way, glancing at my ear. "Well, shit, it is true."

Espen chuckled, ducking his head while I refrained from moving, still kind of in shock from Heidi's attention.

"I'd say demi, not full," she said, taking a step back and setting her hands on her hips. "Until you do any training, we won't know for certain how much magic you have within you."

I raised my brows and pulled my sleeves back down. "Can you tell who's magic I have?"

Espen shifted, and I could sense his interest in the topic from where he stood beside me. He was just as curious as I was. Was this only Freija's magic or had some of Halvar's seeped in, too? And what was the difference?

"It's definitely Fjell," she said, crossing her arms and nodding to my scars. "I'd wager more royal than Halvar's based on those markings."

"So, someone told you about what happened in the throne room?"

She nodded. "Leif and Torsten are inside getting that burn tended to. Torsten told me when I asked about you."

"You asked about me?" My voice pitched higher and I brought my hand to my heart, a sarcastic smirk forming on my lips.

She waved and set her hands on her hips again. "Only curious in case we had a dead human to attend to. You wouldn't believe the amount of paperwork and tomfoolery we must manage to make it look like an *accident.*"

Espen snort-laughed and doubled over.

My jaw fell open. "Heidi! Really? Here I was thinking you cared for me."

She brushed her hands together and turned back to the door. "Glad to see we don't have that mess and that the cut on your chin is healing. Stop by for a visit some time but leave the coffee at home." Without waiting for an answer, she breezed back inside.

Espen straightened up beside me and his laughter subsided as his eyes narrowed in on my face. "How *did* you get that scar?"

I reached up to my chin, brushing across the site and grimacing when I realized my little bandage had fallen off. Must've happened during one of the many scuffles I'd had in the past twenty-four hours. Espen shifted closer and stepped in front of me, our eyes locking on each other. "It's just a scratch," I found myself mumbling, mimicking the words Halvar had used, and dropped my hand back to my side.

Espen tilted his head and gently lifted my chin with his thumb and finger, his touch warm and gentle against my cold skin. His jaw tightened as he examined the little cut. "Please tell me who did this to you." His breaths came in long exhales, like he was trying to control himself through yogic breathing.

I licked my lips, eyes still glued to his. "Some fae shifted into wolves and attacked me while I was hiking. Compared to those inside, I'm fine."

His nostrils flared and his eyes went as wide as tractor wheels. "Wolves?" he bit out.

I nodded and brought my palm to rest on his chest. His heart beat wildly beneath my hand, and he shifted his fingers from my chin to the back of my head, pulling me closer to him.

"I'm fine. Halvar came to the rescue."

That still didn't seem to satisfy Espen as his grip in my hair tightened. "They shouldn't be down this far. I should—"

"You don't *need* to do anything, Espen." I stepped into him, allowing him to wrap his arms around me, which he did. That smell of moss and leather that was so intrinsically him invaded my senses. "I'm okay, and the fae that jumped me was killed by Halvar."

"Good," he said between clenched teeth as the tension in his shoulders slowly eased out. "I'll talk to the Council of Elders and handle that."

"Problem for another time," Øyvin said from our left, and I turned to find him striding out of the woods toward us. He'd cleaned up slightly, removing the muck and debris from his face, but missing the bits of forest and mud that still clung to his uniform.

"Oh, and don't worry," I remarked to Espen. "Øyvin lost his shit enough for both of you when he found out."

Espen quirked a brow and looked over at the Fjord Fae. "Did he now?"

"Oh yeah," I replied. "He tried to fight Halvar and turned him into a little fountain."

Espen chuckled, his eyebrows climbing as he looked at Øyvin. "I'm surprised you still have teeth left after doing that."

Øyvin grunted and shrugged once, crossing his arms. "Speaking of the Fjell, we should head over there before we miss the interrogation. You ready to leave?" he asked, nodding toward the healing hut behind us, clearly aiming his question at Espen.

"Yeah, let me just do a final check on the injured and we can head over," Espen replied and released me from his hug. "Everything okay down in the fjord?"

Øyvin rubbed his palm across his chin. "It will be. The King's Council appears to have had no idea. For now, it sounds like Kjetil may have been the only one Balder confided in. The Council is assessing the situation and informing the Fjord Fae of what has happened. I've tasked one of my guards, Sigurd, with erecting the wall again with whatever power we can amass between us all without the King, and I'll do a greater assessment on our forces in the next couple of days. But first, the Council want me in attendance for Balder's interrogation."

"And they'll just let Halvar and the Fjell Fae march off with the King like that?" I asked, shoving my hands into my jacket pockets to keep them warm.

Øyvin nodded and flicked some errant moss off his sleeve. "He was captured in a battle for actions that threatened the safety of the entire fjord. While the Council and Fjord Fae tend to put themselves first—"

"You don't say," I interrupted with a smirk.

Øyvin glared in response before continuing, "—they see the tremendous value in having all factions working in harmony, with no single unit exerting hegemonic rule."

"Which is part of the reason why the Forest Fae opted to retain only a Council of Elders when Queen Ragnhild died," Espen chimed in. "Glad to hear things are okay down there."

Øyvin bowed his head gently in thanks and I nodded in agreement.

"I'm going to check on Heidi and the injured again. I'll be right back," Espen said, stepping away from me and heading inside.

Øyvin moved after him. "I'll come with you. We have a few people in here, too."

Together they moved inside, then Espen popped his head out of the doorway when I didn't follow. "You coming?"

I shook my head and stepped back against the side of the building again. "I think I've seen enough for today."

We walked back down the hillside, the guys magically shifting out of their uniforms and into human clothes as we got closer to the village just starting to stir under the low light of the rising sun.

"Where's Nora, by the way?" I'd seen her captured by Ylva and escorted back to the Fjell but I had no idea what they intended to do with her.

"She's been sent to the dungeons where she will remain," Øyvin answered.

"*Those* are prison cells you really don't want to see the inside of. Waaay worse than the ones down at the station," Espen supplied, leaning over and nudging my shoulder.

"That bad?" I asked, then yawned, the exhaustion of the past twenty-four hours and staying up all night starting to weigh on me more heavily.

Espen nodded, his eyes wide. "Let's just say, Nora will never see the sun ever again."

Shit. Yeah, hard pass. No thanks. I needed the fresh air and outdoors to thrive, always had growing up, too. The thought of being banished to a lightless cave sounded awful.

"And word has it," Øyvin added, "Halvar himself ordered her to be given a solution that will inhibit her powers and stop her from escaping."

"A solution? Like one of Heidi's potions?" I asked, looking up at him.

Øyvin nodded. "I've heard it might be diluted water hemlock."

Espen and I both sucked in air at the mention of the poison that had almost felled him and what killed her sister, and a shiver ran down my spine. While it didn't really come as a surprise, Halvar was fucking cold and brutal.

We strolled past Oddvar's where the man himself stood on the stoop, unlocking the shop for the day. He glanced over at us as we walked in his direction, his eyes narrowing at us. "You three are up early," he remarked, taking us in, and I was glad the guys had shifted their attire... *Shit.* I frantically pulled my hair forward, shielding my ears, hoping Oddvar hadn't noticed. "It'll take me some time to get the coffee machines running."

Espen glanced over at me and his eyes widened when he realized what I had just remembered. We hadn't used any magic to hide my new ears.

He quickly turned back to Oddvar as we continued walking, picking up our pace a bit. "I'm afraid we're on police business this morning, Oddvar. Øyvin and Lennie agreed to assist me with a matter but we'll certainly stop by later for some coffee," he said, giving the man a genuine smile.

"Very well," Oddvar opened the door to the café and mumbled a 'good day' as he stepped inside.

As soon as he was out of sight, Øyvin grumbled and placed his hand to my left shoulder. A light wave of warmth brushed against my ears and I breathed a sigh of relief. "That was too fucking close."

Both guys let out a "mm-hmm," their chests rising and falling a little quicker than they were a few minutes ago.

"That is going to take some getting used to," Espen said, nudging his shoulder against mine as we strode through the rest of the village.

"No kidding," I replied with a swift smile, my own heart-rate dropping down to its resting level.

"We'll teach you how to hide them," Øyvin supplied, his gaze locked on the path ahead of us as we reached the edge of town and the trail that led up into the woods—the trail that would lead us directly to the main entrance of the mountain. "But first, we need to see what the King has to say for himself."

49

LENNIE

"How long?"

The angry shout echoed against the rock walls as we neared our destination. The lights in the tunnels leading to the dungeons were fewer than those above, the flickering casting an eerie glow on the place, and the air down here was much colder, damper, than other parts of the mountain. I shivered in my jacket, glad to have it on, even if it was still slightly wet from the rain on the battlefield.

A wicked laugh echoed through the hall as we approached, Espen by my side and Øyvin a few paces ahead with a Fjell Fae soldier who was guiding us down into the dungeons. Rounding a corner, we found soldiers lining the wall outside the room where Halvar interrogated Balder. Nods flitted between Espen, Øyvin, and the Fjell soldiers—all of whom looked a little worse for wear. Several had pieces of their uniform torn open, others looked like they had been nicked but spared from the boiling bombs of water. We came to a stop and the guys flanked either side of me, their gazes locked on the prison cell.

The room Balder was held in could only be described as a cave with a large boulder slid aside to reveal the entry. The fallen king knelt within, his lone arm shackled to the ceiling, blood dripping from his crooked nose. His shirt was gone and his chest—I sucked in a breath—his chest was covered in layers of deep silver scars, slashes on top of more slashes. I shook my head at the results of his misuse of the magic he'd sworn to use for good and focused on his shackles.

"Can't he just *'Open Sesame'* himself out of that?" I whispered to Øyvin, pressing up onto my toes to reach his ear.

He shook his head and then leaned down so I didn't have to stay on my tippy-toes for the answer. "There's either something within the manacles stopping him, or he is conserving his energy for his wounds, or something else."

"Hence the reinforcements," I said, looking over my shoulder at the Fjell Fae soldiers that were gathered.

Øyvin nodded, his emotions hidden behind a stoic facade that appeared impenetrable.

I glanced back at the fallen king and winced, hoping he didn't unleash a tidal wave that would drown us within the dungeon. That would be a shitty way to go.

"How long have you been stealing power from Nora? How long have you been doing this?" Halvar's voice was low, gravelly, and altogether murderous as he waved a hand toward Balder's scar-riddled chest.

"Twenty years," Balder spat.

Espen flinched beside me and Halvar narrowed his eyes at the king, blood and saliva flecking the dirty rock-floor beneath him.

"Shame Freija couldn't have been by her dear friend's side during the skirmishes in the south twenty years ago," Balder taunted Halvar, a wicked gleam in his bloodshot eyes. "Where was she anyway?"

Halvar tightened his jaw and fists but didn't respond.

"And Nora?" Halvar asked instead. "What part did she play in your grand plans?"

"A means to an end." The king smirked.

What an ass.

"She loved you," I blurted out, getting a silent glare from Halvar in response. "Sorry," I mouthed, but stared back at the one-armed king.

Balder snorted and looked directly into my eyes, those algae colored pools filled with malice and a delusional belief that he was more powerful than those who had fought against him and his ideals on that battle field. "She was a foolish young girl. Corrupting her loneliness and longing was a pleasure, believe me."

My gut tightened at his remarks. On one hand, I despised everything Nora had done, her betrayal and involvement with Freija's death. But after hearing Balder's words, I felt slightly sorry for her. Slightly.

He continued. "While I'm saddened she accidentally killed the Queen with the tea, instead of just incapacitating her like I'd planned, it saved me doing so later." His eyes shifted to Espen before glancing back at Halvar who was circling him. "And it did eliminate a player from the board, leaving me the clear ruler."

Silence hung in the chilly air, like the truth was muffling any noises as we all waited with bated breath for someone to say something.

"What part did you play in the uprising twenty years ago?" Halvar asked and I felt Espen still, bracing for the answer.

A slick grin slowly spread across Balder's face, his eyes darting quickly to the Forest Fae beside me again. "King."

Halvar grimaced, raising his right hand and slowly clenching his fist. In response, the band of rock around Balder's remaining wrist tightened, a grinding noise emanating from the handcuff. The King panted through the pain, a line forming between his brows as he clenched his jaw.

"What part did you play?" Halvar repeated and I sucked in a breath waiting for the answer.

"One cannot easily win at chess with two opposing Queens on the board," he ground out in reply. "Remove one, and your chances improve dramatically."

Espen took a step forward but I grabbed his arm, holding him back. While I wouldn't mind seeing my yogi-fae-cop deck the prick, Halvar seemed to have things covered. Meanwhile, Øyvin didn't move a muscle; he just stared at the monarch, his boss, the leader who had betrayed his people—him included.

"Why remove Queen Freija from the board, too?" Halvar asked, no hint of sadness lacing his tone.

"She would never have joined forces, knelt at my throne, deferred to me and the opportunity to make our region stronger, better, by uniting under one ruler."

We all knew that was true. Hell, I hadn't been here long, but even in that short period of time, I had seen the love and care Freija had for her people and the mountain. She would never have bowed down to him if she didn't think it was for the good of her people.

"Even if she knew," Balder continued while Halvar loomed behind him, "deep down, that gifting her power to me would be the wisest choice she could ever make, would strengthen the fae against the vile humans." Balder glanced at me, and a shiver ran down my spine at the hatred I saw in his eyes. "But then again, why go for the crown when you can steal from the princess?" His lips curved into a wry smile.

Choking sounded from behind us and I spun to find several soldiers coughing up water. The mountain shook and I stumbled, Øyvin's hand shooting out to steady me before he withdrew. A chuckle rent the air, and I looked back to the prison cell just as Balder's shackle crumbled to the ground, releasing him from his bonds.

Halvar lunged forward, gripped the King's head, one hand beneath his jaw, and ripped it sideways. Blood splattered and I spun into Øyvin's chest as a wet thump sounded behind me. Then came another bump, which I guessed was the rest of Balder's body falling to the floor.

"What in the *Game of Thrones*, big guy?" A warning would've been greatly appreciated, as my stomach now roiled and threatened to soil Øyvin's uniform.

Øyvin's chest shuddered and Espen brushed his palm across my back in small circles. I tried to take deep breaths, inhaling in through my nose and exhaling through my mouth, but it wasn't working. The air began to smell like copper and I pressed harder against Øyvin, trying to inhale his usual fresh linen scent instead.

The wet coughs in the tunnel subsided but a few other grunts sounded from the line of soldiers behind us where they stood against the wall. I was glad I wasn't the only one struggling to stomach what we'd just witnessed. I knew Halvar was brutal, had been warned as such and seen it with my own eyes when he saved me from the wolves, but this was a whole other level of cut-throat.

"I think I need to leave," I mumbled, hoping the guys could understand my muffled words as I began to feel lightheaded.

"Okay, we are no longer needed here anyway," Espen said, his tone authoritative but kind.

Espen shifted me from Øyvin's hold, the latter unmoving as we took a few steps down the tunnel. "You coming?" Espen asked and I glanced back, making sure I looked only at Øyvin and not within the bloody cave.

Øyvin stood stock still, his chest rising and falling in a steady rhythm as he stared into the room. He glanced down, nodded once, then straightened up and cast his eyes toward us. "Let's go."

He stepped back and moved over to us just as Halvar emerged, his black-and-gray clothes darkened and his hands covered in scarlet. "You three." We halted at his words, and a flicker of panic thrummed through my veins. "Meet me in the throne room."

50

LENNIE

We were escorted out of the dungeon to the throne room, the air-quality and temperature within the tunnels returning to a more comfortable level, and my stomach slowly stopped doing somersaults as we entered the sky-blue room. Freija's body had been removed along with her tea cup, and the only sign that anything was amiss were the cracks that marred the walls where Balder had shaken the mountain. The three of us hung about, not saying a word to each other as we waited. A few minutes later, the sound of footsteps approaching had us turning.

Halvar strode into the room, two soldiers fanning out at the entrance behind him, taking up their positions. Gone was the Head Guard's bloodied attire, replaced with a clean black-and-gray uniform with the cape draped across his shoulder glinting with silver threads as it floated around him. Seeing him in clean clothes made me hyper-aware of the fact that I hadn't washed or changed in well over twenty-four hours, and I was suddenly desperate for a scalding hot shower.

The guys fell in beside me, their stance matching that of the soldiers by the entry—legs in a triangle shape, hands clasped behind their backs.

I didn't bother with such a show of militant respect or precision but I did keep my mouth shut for once, which I was sure would please the big guy who took up a position before the throne.

"Thank you both for your assistance," Halvar said, his voice a little more hoarse than his usual gruff timbre. "I believe we need to discuss an alliance that would benefit us all."

"I'm certain the Council of Elders for the Forest Fae will gladly maintain our alliance with the Fjell Fae," Espen supplied, sounding like a diplomat.

Halvar nodded once, then cast his eyes to Øyvin.

The Fjord Fae rolled back his shoulders before responding, "I will have to consult with the former King's Council, but I believe they'll be amenable to a formal alliance that extends beyond the agreement we struck last night."

"And there aren't any more traitors among the Council?"

Øyvin shook his head. "I don't believe so. When I spoke to them this morning, all appeared to have been kept in the dark. The only person Ki—" he halted, taking a deep breath before continuing, "Balder only confided in Kjetil."

"And you trust them?" Halvar asked, narrowing his eyes at the Fjord Fae.

Øyvin paused for a moment, as if considering the question with detail and care. "Yes." He nodded. "But I shall inform you both if that were to ever change." He turned to Espen, who bowed his head in return before they both focused back on Halvar.

"Good," Halvar replied. "I shall meet with our Queen's Council to discuss this matter further and we'll formalize the agreement in the coming days."

"Will you be changing to a Council-run model?" Øyvin asked, which didn't seem like an out of turn question but Halvar appeared to blanch slightly at the words.

"That is another matter I must discuss with the Council as soon as possible."

"You have contingencies in case both sisters were," Espen paused as if choosing his words carefully, "incapacitated?"

The knot in Halvar's throat bobbed sharply. "Of a sort," he replied, then shook his head and focused his steely eyes on me. "Now, let's discuss you."

Ah shit, here we go.

"Take a seat, gentlemen," Halvar said, dismissing the guys and motioning to the bench carved into the side of the room. They strode away, Espen giving me a gentle nudge with his elbow before departing.

I stood there feeling like a lemon, unsure what to do or say—which was rather unusual. So, I clasped my hands together in front of me and braced for impact.

"How are you feeling?" Halvar asked, the concern in his voice taking me a bit by surprise. Nothing about this fae screamed kindness and caring, especially not what I'd witnessed in the past few hours. But, then again, I'd seen a hint of vulnerability when he'd held Freija in his arms.

I sighed. "Well, I'm *physically* fine. Mentally, disturbed. I'm also kinda hungry. Would kill for a coffee, shower, and a piss—not necessarily in that order."

Snickers rose from the side of the room, and I dared to look in that direction before Halvar spoke again, regaining my attention immediately.

"I meant your arm, the magic." He pursed his lips, crossing his arms again, wholly unamused by my honest answer.

I shrugged and rubbed my hand across my bicep. "Fine. Still slightly sore, but fine. Trygve's salve really helped."

"Good." Halvar nodded, then continued plainly, getting straight to the point. "You must make a decision. Forsake your human world and live here, or learn how to hide your gifts and ears and go home to your Ohio."

I flinched and glanced at the two fae who perched on the bench against the wall, the same bench I'd sat on yesterday after my arm had been scored and Halvar had given me parts of his or Freija's magic—likely the latter considering the light magic I'd thrown at Nora last night.

Øyvin shrugged, and Espen smiled, raising his hands in a gesture as if saying, "the choice is all yours."

"What'll it be, Lennie?" Halvar pressed, drawing my attention back to him. "Will you go back to your old life, or will you stay here and help us protect the fjord?"

I took a deep breath and considered my options. There were so many pros and cons to account for. Without a doubt, life here was more exciting than the one I led in Ohio, but there were so many new variables that would have serious consequences for the decision I made. I now had magic in my system—a warm ball of something that sat in the middle of my sternum, waiting to be used. I had the ears, which could ultimately be hidden or brushed away with a "this is how I was born" remark. The white scars up my arm could easily be described as a tattoo. Yet, there was so much more that could never be explained.

What would happen when my family aged and I didn't? There was no way my brothers wouldn't notice, especially Andrew. My eldest brother had always watched over the rest of us kids like a hawk, as if it was his duty as the first born to protect the rest of us from harm. And he had daughters, what would happen when my nieces suddenly looked older than me?

"How does the aging process work?" I asked, looking around the room.

"Slower," Espen said, capturing my attention. "We age like humans but the process is significantly slower. Female fae, for example, will have a longer fertility period and won't reach menopause until they are many hundreds of years old. Many fae won't lose their hair or start turning gray until they are five centuries old, too."

I nodded in thanks and cast my gaze to the silver-haired fae by the throne, wondering, not for the first time, just *how* old Halvar was. But, as a demi-fae, I likely wouldn't have such longevity... or perhaps I would? As Trygve had mentioned, nothing like this had occurred in a very long time, if ever.

"There's no way to know how long you will live, until you do just that... Live," Espen added, and I pressed my lower lip between my teeth. He was right. We had no data, no variables, no stories or history to take guidance from. This decision, this life, was mine to choose what to do with. And, honest to hell, that was an intimidating prospect.

On one hand, I had really enjoyed my time in Norway. I'd made some friends, met some guys whose company I *thoroughly* enjoyed, and found a location that honestly made me excited to get out of bed every morning. On the other hand, I had a life back in the US. I had a family back there. I had my photography excursions...

The thought of photography reminded me of my shattered camera and a tremor of sadness shuddered through me. I'd gained a lot on this trip and suffered some losses, which was what life was like—it ebbed and flowed, changed.

I began to pace, carving a rectangular shape with my footsteps across the throne room floor while maintaining my distance from any of the fae in the room.

I had a good life at home: a family that loved me dearly, an albeit small group of friends that I saw on occasion, and a job that, while not ideal, put food on the table and helped me afford my travel obsession. Ohio was great, but over the past few years I'd admittedly grown bored of the scenery. I'd found myself yearning for freedom, abroad more and more, spending less time in the state I'd called home for so long, the place where I'd grown up. But... a home should be where *I* was, it should be what I created for myself, and, most importantly, it should make me happy.

I'd certainly been happy here in Skolvik. And not just because of the two fae who were perpetually on my mind. There was the village that urged me to wake up earlier to witness every facet of its beauty. There were the people—the majority of whom were grumpy and set in their ways, but quite pleasant if you didn't take their attitude personally. And there was the fjord itself, with waters so teeming with magic and life that it brought a smile to my face just looking at it.

Yes, I had definitely been happy here.

With all that in mind, the decision before me felt easier to make than I'd first anticipated...

I stopped my pacing, and stared up at the Fjell Fae by the throne.

"I'll stay," I announced with a firm nod. "On one condition."

A little whoop came from my right, and I quirked my lips into a smile as Halvar waved his hand for me to proceed.

"I want that baby fae hat you mentioned. I want to know if it'll actually fit on my head."

Halvar brushed his hand across his temple and sighed. "Handle whatever affairs you need to get in order and we'll start your training as soon as I am done with the Fjell Council." He faced Espen and Øyvin, adding, "You two make sure she doesn't reveal herself to the humans."

"Halvar, really! I'm not gonna start mooning the village." Okay, so it wasn't an entirely inconceivable act but certainly not something I was planning on doing in the foreseeable future.

Halvar's deadpanned gaze met mine briefly before he turned back to the guys. "Make sure she knows how to hide her ears," he said without inflection, waving at his own pointy ears, and then left the room, his two soldiers following closely behind him as he headed through the back door to the Queen's chambers.

I turned to the guys sitting against the wall, one of whom was trying his hardest to hide a smile, the other beaming from ear to ear. I hadn't made my decision based on the way I felt about them—happy, intrigued, attracted—but, however much I'd always said I'd never make a life-changing decisions based on a man, these two had factored into my process today.

"Don't think I made my decision because of you two," I said as my heart pattered in an excited rhythm.

"Wouldn't dream of it," Øyvin said, a sly smirk on his lips, while Espen mouthed "bullshit" and winked.

A bubble of laughter escaped from me and I stepped up in front of them, an idea forming in my head that would probably cause trouble.

"Before I officially move here," I said, the thought of immigration paperwork, job hunting, and cardboard boxes briefly crossing my mind. "I'm gonna need to take care of some things back in the US." I set my hands on my hips and widened my stance, unable to stop the sneaky grin spreading across my face. "Either of you ever been to Ohio?"

EPILOGUE

LENNIE

Winter had officially arrived in Ohio. Blistering cold wind whipped down the streets and the threat of ice and snow lingered in the air when we stepped out of the airport and hopped into a ride-share that would take us back to my apartment.

Thankfully, we'd caught a ride with the supply ship and found transportation back to the port city of Stavanger on the southwest coast of Norway. Once there, and before we caught our flight, I'd been able to retrieve my luggage from the cruise ship, which I unceremoniously dumped onto my bed once we got inside my dusty home. While I desperately needed to clean my apartment, there was a whole slew of other stuff that needed to be dealt with.

I needed to pick up my things from the office and clean up my desk at the job that had fired my ass for being gone for so long. Once that was taken care of, I would have to pack up all the shit in my apartment and shove what I could in some extra suitcases to take back to Norway. There was no way in hell I was shipping stuff out there—I'd almost had a heart attack when I saw the cost to mail a single box. So I settled on buying two more obnoxiously large suitcases and calling it good. I could always buy new things in Skolvik.

Before I could move out though, or even take action on my next step, there was a pressing issue that needed attending to: meeting the parents.

We pulled up to my parents' house covered in twinkly lights, my dad having gone all out for the holidays. It was one of his favorite hobbies—some years he even set the lights to music. While it was fun and festive, it was also obnoxiously bright.

We got out of my car, Espen and Øyvin silent behind me, taking it all in as we reached the front door of my picture-perfect suburban, childhood home. I knocked twice, then let myself in. "Hello! Anyone have a pair of sunglasses? I think I need them if I go outside again."

Peels of laughter met my ears, my nieces in full-energy mode, barely visible as they ran past the entrance to the kitchen at the other end of the hallway. I kicked off my shoes—motioning for the guys to do the same—lest we get salt and ice-melt on my Mom's hardwood floors.

"The prodigal daughter returns," a male voice said, and I looked up to find my brother Ryan sauntering down the hallway, his arms open wide and wearing a button-down shirt and jeans. "Glad to see you're alive, Sis." I stepped into his hug and gave him a quick squeeze.

"One of us has to give mom and dad something to worry about. Better it be me than you, right?" I raised my brows at Ryan.

He snorted a laugh. "Most definitely." He glanced behind me and gave the guys a bro-nod, tilting his head up quickly in their direction. "What's up, I'm Ryan."

"Espen."

"Øyvin."

"And you two are...?" Ryan prodded, crossing his arms with a con-spiratorial grin that had my heart fluttering in panic.

"Friends," I chimed in quickly. "These are my friends from Norway."

"Uh huh." He smiled. "Do you speak English?"

I smacked my brother in the stomach with my hand. "Shut up, yes they do."

"It's nice to meet you, Ryan," Espen piped up. "Thank you for having us over."

"Well, don't thank me. Thank Mom."

Espen smiled in response, while Øyvin was giving us all his usual silent treatment.

I pulled off my jacket and grabbed the guys' coats too, hanging them up in the already stuffed hallway closet.

"Nice tattoo," Ryan said, nodding toward my left arm. I glanced down and found my sleeve had rolled up when I'd removed my jacket.

"Don't tell Mom," I replied, quickly pushing the material back into place and hiding the lightning-shaped scars.

"Sure. How big is it?"

I shrugged, hoping he'd let it go.

"Go on, Sis, you can tell me." I fucking doubted that would be wise but he'd already seen it, so I was shit out of luck.

"Sleeve-ish," I mumbled, and Espen chuckled before trying to hide the noise with a not-so-subtle cough.

"Seriously? Damn that must've taken hours, and a lot of money that you don't have." Ryan glanced at Øyvin and Espen before continuing. "But I've heard white tattoos are the in thing nowadays in Europe. I also heard the white ink tends to change color pretty quickly though. Some even turn gray or yellow with time."

I stilled. He was rambling. Ryan only ever rambled when he was trying to deflect.

"You know a lot about tattoos all of a sudden. Do *you* have something to share, brother dearest?" I crossed my arms and started tapping my foot, giving him a challenging glare.

He paled and swallowed hard. "No."

Gotcha.

"I'll show you mine if you show me yours."

"Nothing to share." He shook his head and pushed his hand through his dark brown hair.

"On the count of three. One..." I held up a single finger, starting my visual countdown.

"Honestly, Lennie, this is how you behave in front of your boyfriends?"

"Yes. Two..."

"No, I can't."

"Why not?" I dropped my hand down, a little annoyed that he wouldn't let me finish. "I'll tell Mom about that time in college when you were supposed to—"

"Because it's on my ass," he hissed before glancing over his shoulder to make sure my parents hadn't heard him from the other room.

"What?" My eyes widened in shock.

Espen and Øyvin both stifled coughs behind me.

"I put PhD on my butt, so I could forever be a smart ass."

"You don't even have a PhD!" I yelled, raising my arms. "Were you drunk?"

He flipped me off and waltzed away, shouting toward the kitchen, "Mom, Lennie got a tattoo and brought home two Vikings."

Wonderful. Happy Holidays to me!

"Lennie, what's this about a tattoo and—" my mom rounded the corner, wiping her hands with a kitchen towel, then stilled, staring at the two fae behind me, taking in their broad stature "—oh my."

"Hi, Mom. I'm back. Kind of."

WANT MORE FROM SKOLVIK?

Lennie's story continues in ***Christmas on the Fjord***! Which can be **<u>found here!</u>**

REVIEW

Thank you for reading! I hope you enjoyed Lennie's story and all of her unhinged chaos. If you did, please consider leaving a review on Amazon, Goodreads, or Social Media!

Reviews are extremely helpful for indie authors, and I'd greatly appreciate your support!

Best wishes,
Elle

THANK YOU

Thank you so much for reading this book! I hope you enjoyed Lennie's journey and laughed as much as I did while writing this story.

To Aimee: Goddess of Punctuation and Chaos, thank you for all your support and work editing this. Your critical eye, attention to details, and understanding of my humor made this whole editing experience a blast. We freed the tatas!

To Brit: Thank you for catching all of my misplaced commas and those tiny little details. You da best!

To B., Riley, and Krystal: Thank you for your feedback and for cheering me on when I needed it the most. Your support means so much to me.

To Heidi: Thank you so much for double checking my Norwegian. Who would have guessed all those years ago when we were borrowing each other's books in elementary school that we'd one day be writing stories. Tusen tusen takk.

To all the readers and supporters on bookstagram and booktok. Thank you for all the unhinged book chats, theorizing, and support for my own work. I love hanging out with all of you and making you laugh. I quite frankly wouldn't be able to do this without your support. Thank you.

To my husband, Carl: Thank you for everything. For holding me together when I was falling apart, for listening to me plot and plan, and for feeding me when I inevitably forgot to eat lunch. I love you soooooooooo much!

Finally, to River: thank you for being by my side or joining me for a reading break in the rocking chairs. You are the best snuggle pup.

About the Author

Hey! I'm Elle Thrasher, an author of romantic fantasy books.

My books are filled with relatable heroines, swoon-worthy heroes, lots of laughs, and locations that will give you wanderlust.

While I'm originally from the UK, and lived in Norway for seven years too, I now live in the US with my husband and one very fluffy dog. When I'm not writing, I can usually be found drinking a cup of tea, staring at my never-ending tbr, or taking a joke waaaaay too far.

Follow me on <u>Instagram</u> for updates and don't forget to sign up for my <u>newsletter</u> to receive behind-the-scenes info, bonus material, and details about upcoming books!

www.ellethrasher.com

ALSO BY ELLE THRASHER

The Cerulean Lazulum Series

(Urban Fantasy)

Cavendish

Hawke

The Nordic Fae Series

(Romantic Fantasy)

The Fae of the Fjord

Christmas on the Fjord

The Fae of the Forest

The Fae of the Fjell

www.ingramcontent.com/pod-product-compliance
Lightning Source LLC
Chambersburg PA
CBHW030058310726
48970CB00004B/1063